NO MERCY FROM CROWS

Mage of Merced Volume II

By Aimee L. Gross

Moon Road Press
Auburn, Kansas

First Edition
First Printing: 2021

Text Copyright © 2020 Aimee L. Gross
Cover, Illustrations and Interior Design Copyright © Aimee L. Gross
All rights reserved
ISBN: 978-0-9909681-1-5

Library of Congress Control Number: 2021909730

Moon Road Press
6501 SW Vorse Road
Auburn, KS 66402

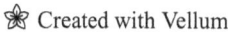 Created with Vellum

To the best of 2020, our first grandchild.
So many stories to tell you, Jack!

CHAPTER ONE

When my da sent me on a ship to Lohr Island to escape the retribution of thwarted mages, I was also to be schooled there in the practice of magic. I expected to reside with the island folk for as long as my lessons took. Then, I could return home to Merced to fight the Scytheran invaders. We would rout their pawns, the Keltanese army. Our lives could go back to what was before. I was not such a fool I thought it would all be easy, but what did happen was nothing like I reckoned when I set out.

Firstly, I found myself not well suited to sea-going life. I tossed up every scrap I had eaten in recent days and expected next to see my boot soles emerge, all before we had cleared the coast and reached what the sailors called 'open water'.

"'Tis likely better you stay in your hammock," Lichan advised when he came below deck to see how I fared. I only moaned at him and never opened my eyes. My dog Wieser, curled on the planks under my sling-bed, heaved a great sigh but made no attempt to stir. She was still recovering from a magical attack. I had no ready excuse for my puny behavior.

"When you want feeding, come up and I'll steer you to the cook's mate," Lichan said as he walked away. I could hear his footfalls fade and concentrated on that so I would not think about food of any sort. Any at all.

My guide crow, Gargle, had stood on the deck railing and watched with what looked to me to be amusement when I had started our voyage with my head hanging over the side, retching. He did not come below when Wieser and I abandoned the deck for this shadowy cabin at the waterline. I heard from Lichan that the bird could be found atop the highest mast, facing into the wind with apparent relish. I remembered he seemed always to like to travel by sled, sleigh or wagon without taking the trouble to fly. Gargle was as unfussed by seasickness as the gulls who wheeled around the masts.

I was not the only passenger to Lohr Island. Lichan told me another boy had come aboard just before we sailed. He did not have a cabin to himself like me, but slept in a crewman's hammock during the night watch. The sailor took the spot during the day and the boy was working off his passage by aiding the cook in the galley. I was thankful my da had not made similar arrangements for me—because the thought of the smells and sounds of the galley brought the surge of bile right back. I had yet to meet the boy, whose name was Cilliyon. At first, I thought Lichan spoke of 'silly Yohn' but no. The other passenger pulled his weight; I might be referred to on deck as 'silly Judian' more likely.

It was this thought that levered me from my hammock and forced one foot after the other to mount the steps that led to the deck planks. Wieser followed me, giving me her look of reproach all the while.

"I've had enough of the cabin, Wieser. I have to show I'm somewhat more useful than a crate in the hold." Her expression did not change.

We had been underway for five days, and the breeze on deck had shifted from warm to chill. It was summer in my home country of Merced. Could we have sailed so far in five days that the weather differed? My thought was interrupted by raucous cawing, followed by Gargle swooping around my ears. I did not dare swing my head about to look at him—the seasickness was too near. I waited until he settled on a rope line tied around a post on the deck.

"You look glossy and pleased with yourself," I told him. "Not that such would be a change. Have the sailors not commenced throwing shoes at you yet?"

"A land bird can be considered good luck on a ship," Lichan allowed, coming up beside me. "Though one black in color stretches the point. You will find no more superstitious man than one who sails the sea."

"Is Wieser bad luck, then, since she is black?"

Lichan looked out at the horizon with lips pursed. "Depends who you ask onboard, I reckon. It could be as well to keep her mostly below. The men look always for somewhere to place blame if any ill-luck befalls us on our way."

"They wouldn't hurt her? Or throw her off?" I stepped closer to her and wound my fingers in the curly fur at her shoulders.

"Now, no need for such talk as that," Lichan said, sounding very like Virda, his mother and our family's good neighbor for all my life.

"What sort of ill fortune do you mean?" My head was starting to spin as the motion of the deck made me shift and rock to keep my feet. I thought of retreating to my hammock. Lichan didn't seem to be giving up an answer to my question, so I said instead, "Is there some sort of work for me? I'd like to be of use. My da says the trip will last at least two months."

"Aye, every bit of that. We have livestock in the main hold. Would caring for them be something you know from life on the farm?"

"Feeding them, mucking out? I can do that well enough, yah." A particularly bitter gust drove spray before it, making me shiver. "I wasn't expecting this cold," I said, pulling my collar up over my neck.

"Nor I," he said shortly, and shouted some orders to the men in the rigging. It seemed to me the deck was lurching more and more. Lichan took his leave with furrowed brow, after directing me to go below to see the man in charge of the animals in the hold. I was happy to take myself away from the wind and endless water and told Gargle not to be a nuisance as I left. He flapped his way back up to the tallest mast in response.

In the dim reaches below decks, I found the stock by following the rich scent of barnyard. Wieser was challenged to clamber down the steep stair into the lowest hold, but I lifted her where she needed aid. A dozen black, shaggy sheep watched me from their pen, looking like a flock of Wiesers. Several fat cattle, and crates of ducks, geese and chickens were tethered or tucked about the hold. Mucking out was overdue, from the bite to the smell. A lardy man with a bristly black mustache lay sleeping on the hay pile.

"I've come to help you with the stock," I said. He kept snoring. I said it again louder. When I leaned closer, thinking to shake him by the shoulder, I smelled the drink on his breath. The sailors all seemed quite fond of their ration of spirits, so I had noted in even my scant time out of the hammock. The rest of them didn't seem to neglect their duties, though. I poked about and found the pitchfork and a barrow, so I could set to work.

I had cleaned all that needed cleaning and spread fresh bedding before the man stirred. He snorted and sat up, caught sight of Wieser, and growled, "Blasted sheep, how are ye gettin' out?"

"She isn't a sheep, she's my dog. I'm Judian Lebannen. When do these all get fed?" I swept a hand around to indicate the animals.

"You've got to clean the pens first off," he said, squinting first at Wieser, to make sure she wasn't a sheep, I imagine, and then at me.

"I've done that."

"Hoist the soiled bedding up and over the side," he continued. He stood and hitched his trousers up. "Here, I'll show ye how. My name's Cuffer. Push the barrow under the hatch."

We hoisted the barrow up to the deck with ropes and a pulley, then trouped up the stair topside to push it along to the stern and tip the soiled straw and dung over the rail. The empty barrow we let back down into the hold, while Wieser watched from below.

"Pays to be neat aboard," Cuffer said virtuously.

I looked at him sidelong.

"We feed them now?" I asked.

"Aye, lad, as soon as we eat." Cuffer led the way to the galley. I wasn't too certain about eating, but a hot drink of some kind might bring feeling back to my numb lips and fingers.

In the narrow space with a stove and a trestle table, we found a boy scraping carrots.

"Cilliyon," Cuffer hailed him. "What will you feed us this day?"

4

The fair-haired boy ducked his head and reached across the stove to lift a pot lid. "Looks like salt pork and cabbage."

Certainly, it smelled like it, too. I nearly turned tail right then, but remembered the pouch of herbs at my waist. "Could I get just hot water to steep some herbs?" I said, grateful for the remedies I carried.

Cilliyon ladled water from a barrel into a small kettle and set it on the heat. Cuffer and I sat on a bench. The man watched with interest while I sorted through the packets from my leather pouch.

"I think I heard you was one what could do magic," Cuffer said.

"My brother's wife Annora made this pouch and filled it with herbs for me when I left home," I answered. "She's the one that knows herb-lore and spells. She taught me some." I found the packet I wanted, good for stomach complaints according to Annora.

Cuffer took his bowl of greasy cabbage. I got a chipped mug from the galley boy. He offered a square of hard bread as well, and Cuffer cried, "Ship biscuit! Full of weevils yet?"

He tapped one on the table in judicious examination and pointed out the half-dozen pale grain weevils that had been shaken loose. "By the end of the voyage, they'll be more bug than flour."

I did not want to dwell on that prospect, so watched my cup of herbs stewing. "Why are we the only ones in here? Doesn't the crew get a meal?"

Cilliyon answered. "They're thinking a storm is coming up. It may get too rough to feed the men, but they can't come now because they have to get ready for the gale."

He must have been on a ship before. "Is that why the ship is rolling more?"

"It may be a little rougher," allowed Cuffer, "but this is nothing to what the sea can do in a big blow."

I sipped my mint and chamomile concoction and thought of the solid, steady rock of my mountain home. The ship's cook came through carrying a basket of eggs, steady on his feet and in no danger of dashing them all on the deck. This was because he had 'sea legs' like the rest of the crew, I'd been told. I wondered when my legs would change from land to sea.

The cook stowed his basket and growled, "Clamp the lid on that pot, boy, or we'll all be wearing the slop." Cilliyon hurried to comply, snapping on a metal strap that spanned the handles. I noted for the first time the railing around the stovetop.

A great lurch and roll came not from my stomach but from the ship itself. I slopped some of my drink on the way to my mouth. Timbers groaned.

"Finish that," the cook pointed at us. "Galley's shutting down. The fire has to be put out."

"Fine thing we ate when we had the chance," Cuffer said as we made our way back to the hold. It was dim below even at high daylight, but now with darkening clouds above us, the stairs were difficult to see. Coupled with the pitching of the passage, I had to put my arms out to the walls to steady myself.

Cuffer paused to light a lantern. "Once these beasts are fed, it'll be wise to secure everything we can. I feel a great blow building. My bones tell me."

The tilting and rolling told it plain enough to me. The stock all seemed placid enough though and put their heads into their rations with no hesitation. While they munched and scratched and pecked, I followed Cuffer's directions for strapping down any article that swung or shifted with the motion of the ship.

As we finished, one of the young sailors appeared with a lantern. He said nothing to Cuffer but lifted his light to peer at me. "Are you that one as can do magery? Judian Lebannen by name?"

"That's my name, but I don't claim to do more than low magic spell-work." I wiped my palms on my trousers. "Do you need a remedy?"

He shook his head. "I've been hunting you all over. Shipmaster Alisdar wants to see you above. Thinks you're a weather worker what can do sommat with this storm." He gestured impatiently; a summons from the shipmaster was not a slight matter, it seemed.

Cuffer, too, urgently propelled me to the stair. "Hold your hat and call him 'sir' when you answer him."

"I haven't got a hat," I protested. At once, Cuffer mashed his own rancid brown wool cap on my head. "All right, I'm going. Keep care of Wieser, will you?"

I followed the sailor up steps and through passages, bracing myself against the walls when it was do that or fly headlong. The sailor tried to hurry me, but short of hoisting me on his shoulder, he had to wait for me to catch him up as best I could. At last, he stopped before a thick oak door and rapped it smartly.

Bid to enter by a gruff voice, we came into a high cabin Lichan had called the shipmaster's ready room when he showed me about at departure. I saw Lichan, bent over a table with maps and charts spread wide. He nodded to me.

Other officers ranged about the table, but one stood with his back to me, looking out an arch of windowpanes streaming with wind-driven spray.

"Here is young Lebannen, Shipmaster," Lichan said. The man swung round.

Shipmaster Alisdar's eyes were the blue of thick mountain ice, his hair snowy. The lines on his face showed more time spent glowering than smiling. I ducked my head, and then remembered to snatch off Cuffer's oily hat and hold it.

"My first officer says you have magic."

"A little, Shipmaster. I'm sent to Lohr Island to learn more."

He looked less than pleased. "We are in peril. I need a weather mage to calm these winds."

"I have never done with weather and winds. Sir." I swallowed.

"Have you skills with currents?"

"The water paths? I have never been aboard a ship before. I have only heard of the currents from my neighbor. She is Lichan's mother, sir."

He narrowed his eyes. "I was told you had defeated two mages and helped win the battle to liberate Bale Harbour."

"I played a part in that, sir. A part, only." The planks rolled under us. "Is this a natural storm, or do you suspect magic at work in the weather already?"

This question seemed to please him better. "The currents are altered somehow and carry us into colder waters than they should do. We sail into the gap winds offshore of the Tantec Mountains." He motioned me to one of the maps and pointed to a place amid a wash of pale blue ink.

"The winds and the currents are at cross purposes here. Waves pile upon each other to create heavy seas."

"You would sail the ship away from here, if you could, I expect …" He gave a curt nod. I tilted my head to try and make sense out of his map. "Where will we be carried on this path?"

"To Scythera, if you cannot aid us with magic."

The last place I wanted to go—the mages I had fought came from that country. Mages from Scythera still sought me, my da and I feared, bent on revenge. Could they be using magic to divert all the Mercedian ships their way, in hopes of bringing me to them? My da had put me aboard *Moon Road* to hide me far away from their fury.

But how important could I be to learned mages, in truth? To me, it seemed I had won over them more by luck than skill. Though perhaps I knew what they did not on that score.

"I have a book, given me by my da when I came of age. It contains magic lore I have not yet learned, but maybe I can find something there."

"Bring it," the shipmaster said as he turned away.

The young sailor escorted me to my cabin and back to the ready room, where I undid the clasp of the tooled leather binding, and laid my book open on the map table.

"This was my mother's. She knew much, I'm told, but I cannot read all the languages within." I turned pages, seeking anything I could recognize that might pertain to the sea. Lichan came to look over my shoulder.

I saw a great deal of healing lore, renderings of plants with instructions for the preparation of draughts and extracts. I began to flip faster as the ship pitched and groaned, my desperation rising with the wind. *These men cannot all be depending on me to find some help … help that might not even be here …*

Lichan stayed my hand. The page he leaned closer to was written in a different style than the others, with curvy black script whose characters I did not know.

"Can you read it?" I asked.

He nodded and leaned closer still. "This is from the maritime provinces of the southern sea. Lohr Island lies that way." He turned another page. "Ah, and here is more sea-lore. From the far north …"

The shipmaster came closer.

"It tells how to raise a favorable wind, sir, but not how to calm a gale." Lichan grimaced.

The shipmaster's eye found me. "Can you do what it instructs?"

"If he can translate the words. Read it out to me, Lichan. I'll copy it in Mercedish and try to cast it." I pulled the leather folio of sheets Annora had made for me from its place inside my tunic. I felt my stomach twisting again and prayed not to puke in front of the officers.

With my hastily scribbled spell clutched in my fist, Lichan led me on deck into the needle-teeth of the spray. Gargle swooped to my shoulder in a flurry of wingbeats, in defiance of the storm's slashing wind. I was amazed he could fly in such a tempest.

"I need to look at the spell words without the ink running," I shouted to Lichan. He installed me in a tight corner by the steps to the wheel and blocked the wind as best he could with his cloak spread wide, his back to the maelstrom. I could not see the waves, which was for the best, but I could still feel the ship claw up each towering swell and tip forward before she bucked her way down the far side.

Gargle prodded me behind the ear with his beak. I wrapped my hand around the talisman moonstone I wore at my throat. It was for protection, not spell casting, but I reckoned we could all use some protection now. I spoke the words, hoping Mercedish carried the same meaning as the language it had been writ in. Supposing it had to be only the original sounds and rhythm for the spell to work?

A fierce torque of the ship threw me to my knees. Lichan pulled me up and tied me to the stair with a stout rope about my waist. "Again!" he yelled.

My paper grew crumpled and smeared; I struggled to make out the words. I dashed salt water out of my eyes and began again, my voice rising and falling in time with the ship's desperate scramble up each soaring wave, and her plummet downwards to bury her bow in the trough between.

Straining upward, over the crest, and down, over and over the ship battled the furies rising from the deep to savage her. I fought to form the words before the wind tore them away from my lips. I did my utmost to focus as Annora had taught me, emptying my mind of all except the spell words. Soon, I could no longer hear the howl of the wind; next time through the spell I did not feel the shudders of the deck beneath my feet. When the ink had run away, I repeated the words from memory, again and again. No longer aware of soaking clothes and the cold bite of the wind.

The last time through the words I closed my eyes. I passed from any awareness of the ship and seemed to float somewhere above her in the black clouds. *I wonder if I have died?* I thought, and then passed from any awareness at all.

CHAPTER TWO

I opened my eyes to the shipmaster's ice-blue gaze on my face. "Will he have his wits?" he rumbled.

"I'll have hell to pay if he doesn't, sir," Lichan said from somewhere nearby. I tried to sit up, but found the shipmaster's broad hand on my chest enough to keep me flat on the bunk where I rested.

I turned my head to see that I was in a cabin adjoining the shipmaster's ready room, apparently in his own bed, a mattress instead of a hammock.

My throat felt on fire. I moved my mouth to say, "The storm? How do we fare?" but managed only a strangled cough. I signed in the air as if writing and Lichan put a paper and stylus in my hand. I wrote the words instead.

"The storm died down by sunset. The current still carries us toward Scythera, but we've sailed out of the gap wind's influence. You appear to have brought us fair winds, even though we do not go where we wish."

Next, I scrawled:

How long have I been out?

Lichan leaned over me. "All night and the better part of the morning. You went insensible on deck and I brought you in here. I feared you might not wake."

I wrote what I most wanted to know:

Did the spell work?

"The gale took its time slowing, but it did seem something happened. Can you not speak, Judian? What takes your voice?"

I pointed to my throat and lifted my shoulders. No spell I had cast had ever had any effect like this. I could not dismiss the idea that the Scytheran mages had set the maelstrom upon us and waited for me to show myself by doing magic. They might then abate the provoking storm, but still draw me to them. Could they also fix me so that I could do no more spellcasting to evade them?

Is there no chance of altering our course?

"If a way can be devised to alter the prevailing wind and current— return both to their customary direction for this time of year." Shipmaster Alisdar did not sound as if he held out much hope. Reflecting his opinion of me, I gathered.

My paper was covered over with my writing. Lichan dispatched a sailor to the deck to obtain a slate and chalk from the quartermaster, so I could write and then wipe off my words. When I was handed this, I rose unsteadily and prepared to take my leave.

"Study your book, boy," said the shipmaster without turning away from the window, his hands clasped behind his back. "Go back below and study hard."

In the hold, Cuffer greeted me and asked after his hat, which I had lost somewhere above. I wrote as much on my board. He looked at me quizzically.

"Just say," he urged. "I am not a lettered man."

I gestured to my lips and shook my head.

He clapped a hand to his forehead and cried, "Oh, they have cut out your tongue? Blasted sailors! Superstitious as old fishwives, they are —" breaking off as I shook my head vehemently.

With his eyes on me at last, I opened my mouth to show my tongue in its customary place and held up my hands to sign I did not know why no sound came.

"Eh." He scratched his grizzled cheek. "Well, perhaps you will heal. Not be mute forever."

He turned away to sort through a wooden crate, seeking a tool, he said. After he drilled two holes in my slate, he threaded a length of twine through and knotted it, so I could wear it about my neck. As he lifted the twine over my head, he offered, "There's those on board as can read, officers and suchlike. Tobal the cook. Mebbe he can read me anything you write that's important."

Since the cook worked far away in the galley, I did not see how he would be good for any urgent relay of vital information, but Cuffer did pat my shoulder kindly when he hung my slate on me. I was like the mute boy I had seen in the harbour town market, begging for food and copper coins.

Wieser, to whom I talked as much as I did to any person I knew, did not seem to notice anything different in my silence and stayed by my side as she always did. I twisted my fingers in the fur of her ruff and tried to be as easy in my mind about my absent voice as she seemed to be.

Cuffer and I worked the following fortnight in a strange sort of dance. He spoke to me as before, but pointed and tugged and turned me about by my shoulders to see what he wanted done as if I had also lost hearing and sense. He made always certain I went with him to the galley to be fed up, since I was doing most all his labor. He was never impatient or harsh, however, and growled at the sailor who suggested a brisk whipping would surely cure me.

The *Moon Road* sailed inexorably on across the sea, north toward Scythera.

I snatched all the moments I could to pore over my book of magic, willing it to reveal some secret or remedy to restore my voice. Or, spellcraft to turn the current and wind to their proper directions. I chalked the runes of concealment as Annora taught me when we fled the mages in Merced, covering the floor around my cabin's hammock and the planks of the hold where I toiled. Endlessly, I formed sigils to obscure myself from any prying mage's mind. I still wore the moon-stone pendant the toothless old Traveller had given me: "for the strong magic" she had muttered. For protection and defense, Annora clarified.

When exhausted from studying the book's pages, I took to staring into the black depths of the obsidian blade the cave spirits of my home-land had given me—still uncertain if I had used it to escape the mages, or if the knife had used me. What had called the kavsprit to that battle in the darkness? Four Keltanese soldiers had died there, and the two mages might have been destroyed. No one knew how to tell if they were vanquished or had simply vanished.

Leastways, Da had sent me on this voyage both to escape the mages' potential pursuit and to learn to use magic to defend Merced from her invaders. I brooded over what could be happening to my family, my brother Wils and his bride, and to Da and little Morie, to Lichan's mother Virda … the villagers I had known all my life and the harbourtown folk I had met. The Keltanese soldier we had discovered nearly frozen in our burned barn, saved by Annora's care: Gevarr, with his smile like the flash of a knife-edge catching the sun.

I wondered whether Gevarr and Wils had yet come to blows over Annora.

Because I studied late most nights, I had to keep asking for more candles so I could see to read in my cabin. One evening, Lichan came down with a lantern. It was the curious shipboard-type that hung and swiveled as the ship moved, so that the oil would not spill.

"Shipmaster is anxious for some word from you. Or rather, some writing to say you have a solution to our problem."

I shook my head. I had nothing to offer as yet, so I wrote asking Lichan if he could take time from his duties to translate more of the passages he could read that I could not.

When I showed him my scrawled question on the slate, Lichan nodded and promised to come back at the end of his watch.

When he returned, Gargle the crow rode along, gripped tight to Lichan's shoulder. The bird fluttered to my hammock's rope to preen. In truth, I had not been on deck to see him since my loss of voice. Perhaps the bird wondered at my absence and came down to see how I fared?

I had compelling reasons for hiding below. Ever since the storm, I had been plagued with nightmares. I feared my constant dreams of mages seeking me were more than dreams and kept away from the deck, out of sight. Scytheran mages were known to possess creatures and use the animals' eyes, thus to see from far away. My runes and talisman were to deflect a different sort of perception, but a gull or cormorant in the sky would see by sun's light. I kept to the shadows.

My crow turned his sleek head to examine me closely, first with one eye, then the other. He gave no sign he found my silence unexpected, though I usually had plenty to say to him. Mostly regarding his manners. He uttered one *graaak* and, upon settling his wings, closed his eyes.

"It landed on me when I headed below," Lichan said, "as if it knew I was coming to see you. It is a curious bird."

I would have liked to tell him, 'My brother's wife told me crows always think they know best, and indeed this one acts true to that' but it would take too long to write. Instead, because my cabin had no table, I gestured for us to sit on the floor.

We spread out the book and paper on the planks. He set to copying the Mercedish translation of the passages I could not read. It was not Lohrian he labored over, for that language has a root akin to Mercedish, and is not so difficult to tease meaning from. Lichan told me he worked now to shift words written in Yeganil, the language of Yega. Which country lies far to the north, even farther north than Scythera. He had learned their talk in his travels. Where my mother had learned it, I could not begin to guess. Nor why those passages were written in such a blocky, heavy hand, compared to what must be her delicate one.

Wieser curled on the planks beside me, as we strove on scribbling and scratching our heads in puzzlement at times. It was Lichan who first began to yawn, which started me to do the same. Before long, our mouths were open more than they were shut. I finally wrote on my slate that we'd best stop for now, and closed my book with the loose sheets stuck within to mark the place we left off.

Gargle declined to leave when Lichan departed. He simply opened one eye and shrugged his wings. *Stay then*, I thought, and found I was glad to have his company. Such as it was, for he returned at once to dozing.

I again had restless dreams of pursuit; both by sea birds above and great fish below the waves, seeking and casting about to find me. A sense of malevolent interest seemed always just beyond true certainty, as if the mages drew a veil over my thought so I would not recognize their minds behind animal eyes.

Sweating and twisted up in my hammock, I snapped my eyes open at the sound of the warning bell clanging on deck. It was scarcely dawn. Feet pounded above me, and Wieser leapt up to bark. Gargle, too, took up the cry, cawing and flapping in my face.

I rushed topside, without my slate and chalk, and tried to make sense of the crew's urgent shouts. I had expected fire or suchlike catastrophe at the least, but the racing about appeared to be an attempt to put more canvas to the wind and increase speed. The faces I saw showed desperate fear, those men clambering in the rigging looked frantic, reckless. I sought someone who could tell me what spurred the panic and spotted Lichan at last, shouting orders on the bridge.

"Slavers!" he cried at the sight of me. "Pirate slavers. Get to the hold and keep hidden with the livestock!" He whirled away and resumed hollering at men above, his hands cupped around his mouth.

I stopped in my cabin only to retrieve my slate and book of magic, jamming both into my gear bag. I hurried to the hold with Wieser and Gargle, neither as breathless as I when I pulled up at the sheep pen. Wieser was mistaken once before as being one of that flock by Cuffer, though he was the worse for spirits at the time. Still, I opened the gate enough to slip her within and pressed a finger to my lips to sign for her to be still. I could be nothing but silent, myself, but Gargle grumbled and gurgled at Cuffer and the chickens before taking up a place atop a crate near the ceiling beams.

Cilliyon and the cook came next, panting to Cuffer that the slaver ship was such a fast one, it would surely catch us. I found a place between baled hay and the ox pen and slipped into it. Cilliyon squashed in next to me, uninvited. His eyes were so round with terror I had no heart to push him out.

I had seen slaves once. Desolate, hollow-eyed men with lank hair, packed into wagons bound from Bale Harbour to the mines of Keltane. This during the occupation of Merced when I toiled to defeat our invaders. My guts twisted at the thought of being bound a slave.

Cuffer and the cook stumbled about the hold looking for space to conceal their own greater bulk. Gargle gave his laughing call as they tipped the wheelbarrow on its side and crouched behind it. At once, the two of them commenced shoving each other into view beyond the opposite edges. Cilliyon met my eye and rolled his with a wan grin.

I wanted to ask what the slavers would do—take us all away with them? Take over the ship and make for another destination? Were slavers from Scythera or from some other country? I dug in my bag for my slate and chalk. Cilliyon could read, though he might not know the answers to any of my questions.

I had just begun to write when the deck above resounded with a deafening *thud*. The timbers beside me trembled. Cilliyon gripped my arm, sending my chalk into the hay, while Cuffer wailed, "Aiee! Their catapult, they're after the masts!" and gave a mighty push to the cook that sent him sprawling onto the hold planks.

Tobal the cook sprang up cursing while he sought some less contentious hidey hole. He dove in among the sheep with Wieser, who fit in much better than he did by appearance. I resolved I would not eat any food the man fixed until he had first cleaned off all the sheep flop. If any of us lived to consider eating in future.

I poked about in the hay for my chalk stick. Cilliyon proved as hard to shake off as Morie when she was scared—but Morie was a little slip of a girl. Surely Cilliyon must be approaching my age, so nearly a man. I jerked my arm free of his grip just as another boom echoed through the wood of the hull.

At last, my fingers closed on the chalk. I shoved the slate against my middle to steady it and wrote to ask if the pirates would sink us, before turning the slate smartly in front of Cilliyon's nose.

He scanned the words and shook his head. "Not sink us. They'll try to shred the sails to stop us. Cook says then they will overcome the crew and commandeer the ship. Take the cargo, and us too, where all can be sold. Slavers have their own ports where stolen goods and peoples are bought and sold."

Another bang of a different sort sounded.

"Listen, our men are fighting back," Cilliyon said. I took to looking up above our heads, also, as if I could see what was happening through the decking. Cuffer moaned and tried to pull the wheelbarrow over his back like a turtle shell.

We traded blows with our pursuers for the better part of an hour, then all was silence for some moments. I began to wonder how long we should stay hidden, as my legs were cramping folded beneath me. Had we escaped or been taken? I found my chalk stick sweaty in my fist when I made to write a question for Cilliyon and wiped my hand on my trousers.

Before I could take up my chalk again, heavy boots thudded on the hold steps. Through a gap in the bales, I could make out a man I had never seen before, with leather breeches and a flowing red shirt. He jumped to the floor of the hold from several treads up and looked about him. He held a cutlass, the curved sword that sailors carry. His hair was curly like mountain sheep wool, curlier than Wieser's coat or even the wool of the black plains sheep she was hidden among.

He appeared to be taking stock of the animals in the hold. He merely turned about in place, instead of searching behind and under things for folk gone for cover. I held my breath anyway, sure it was better not to be noticed. He showed his back to mount the steps, then said over his shoulder, "Those of you below, stay here with your charges. Don't think of anything foolish to do." He spoke in Mercedish, logical since our ship's markings showed us to hail from Merced.

And where did the pirate slaver hail from? What possible foolish action *could* be thought of that would get us out of this? I tried to formulate some question to write for Cilliyon to answer for me, when I glanced at him to find his face running with tears.

I must have looked disgusted, for he dashed at his cheeks with the back of a hand. "Please," he said. "Help me. They cannot find out I'm a girl or I'm done for sure."

My chalk fell out of my hand and was lost in the hay again.

CHAPTER THREE

My expression had to be one of astonishment and my eye went first to her shirtfront, searching for some hint of curve. She flushed red as a radish and crossed her arms over her chest. Which was as flat as my own as far as I could tell. I coughed and searched the straw for my dropped chalk.

If only I could have spoken, I had a great many questions I wanted answered prompt and true. As it was, I took my rediscovered chalk to the slate to write:

Cook knows?

I shoved the slate under her downcast eyes. She sniffled and shook her head. Not one fair hair on it was longer than my thumb. Still flummoxed, I wrote to ask who else aboard knew.

"Only you. Will you help me?"

I scrawled HOW and put three question marks after.

"With magic, of course. Use your spellcasting to disguise my womanhood better than breast-binding and cropped hair."

Womanhood was a bit far-reaching, I thought, since she had looked utterly straight up and down when I had seen her at the stove and table.

I supposed she might have a bosom, after all, bound down with wrappings … I shook my head to clear it and wrote that I could do no magic now, since I could not speak.

She fairly flung her hands over her eyes, trembling next to me. Cuffer and the cook were too far away to have heard her hushed voice between the bales. I looked at her with some exasperation as her shoulders shook, but she made no sobbing sounds.

Cursing myself for a fool, I drew the moonstone pendant from my tunic and lifted it over my head. Gargle flapped down to peck at my hand as I began to write on the slate what the pendant was for: protection. The talisman did not, however, protect me from his jabbing beak, so I shoved at him with the slate. It grew crowded amongst the bales with two people and a bossy crow.

Cilliyon raised her eyes to me when I touched her arm. I held out the leather thong and Gargle stuck his head between us, eyes glittering. I got my elbow in his front to push him back.

She sniffled and caught the pendant in her palm, then looked at the slate. "What does it protect you from?"

Me, from mages seeking me.
You from slavers?

"Is it strong magic?"

I drew another question mark and shrugged.

Gargle groused and pulled bits of hay from the bale to strew about. I could believe he had not wanted me to give up my moonstone, since he always seemed to think he knew best in all things, but I had nothing else to offer the girl. Did he suppose I should let her take her chances, as I would take my own?

She settled the leather around her neck and dropped the stone down the front of her tunic. She then dispelled any doubt I could have been having about her wits, by asking, "What will protect you now?" which was late to be thinking about it since she had already taken my talisman.

I thought for a moment before writing that the runes I knew might help me.

Cuffer and Tobal emerged from their hiding places and came to us, carefully staying out of one another's way, never mentioning fighting over the wheelbarrow. I wiped the last words from my slate.

"I wonder," the cook said morosely, "how much we might bring at auction?"

"That's all you can find to worry you, Tobal? It's not as if *you* get the coin when you're sold!" Cuffer straightened his tunic, rucked up from his stint under the barrow. "Who will buy aged fellows such as us, anyway? The young ones, that's what slavers want, with years of work left in them."

I did not find the thought of being sold into years of servitude appealing, but if thereby I avoided capture by the Scytheran mages … that was at least *some* merit to the idea. Even if the slavers turned out to be Scytheran, they did not seem to have captured *Moon Road* by magery. Why break the masts and shred the sails when spellwork would have the desired result while avoiding damage?

The oxen, sheep and fowl began making noises suggesting they expected to be fed whether pirates or customary crew steered the vessel. I wrote on my slate that we might as well be about our chores and had Cilliyon read it to Cuffer. He grunted and handed me a pitchfork.

Tobal regarded Cilliyon for a moment, then said gruffly, "I suppose men will all still have to eat, too, whatever flag they fly under." The two set off for the galley, Cilliyon waiting until Tobal was occupied climbing above before she caught my eye. Too far away to speak, she seemed to cast about for a way to convey some comment, then touched her tunic front just where the moonstone lay beneath the fabric. She gave a slight nod. I nodded back.

Wieser left her sheep flock when I entered the pen to muck it and lay by the gate to keep the sheep from milling out into the main hold. Cuffer made a show of righting the wheelbarrow and bringing it to me to receive the soiled bedding. I wished I could ask him what he knew about our chances for a lengthy future as opposed to lives cut short by pirate slavers.

～

More answers came when all hands were summoned to the deck just after full noon. Cuffer and I were shoved into ranks under a cold bright sun along with all the deckhands from either watch. A few of the men wore bloodied clothes or a bandage wound about an arm or shoulder. And the ranks seemed thinned … I saw Tobal and Cilliyon, wearing stained aprons, join the line prodded by the butt of a pirate's coiled whip.

Lichan and the other officers, bound together in chains, stood on the upper deck at the rail. Shipmaster Alisdar stood apart, his wrists looped with iron links, features stony, jaw clenched. Between the groups stood the pirate who had come below, his scarlet shirt like fresh blood in the sun's light.

The pirate stood tall, legs apart and fists on his hips. "I am Kruthe, in command of *Chikoro*," he gestured at the three-masted ship secured alongside us, "and now master of *Moon Road* as well. Repair of the sails has commenced so we will be underway shortly. Each of you will continue your work as before while we make for the port I've chosen to receive your goods and yourselves at auction. Both men and goods are worth more undamaged." He gave us a cocky smile. "None of my men will hesitate to hurt you if you choose to cause trouble. If you are damaged beyond value, the sea makes for ready disposal. I trust you will all strive to retain your current usefulness, eh?"

All the crew remained silent. Gargle cawed from the masthead. Kruthe squinted up at him and laughed. "It seems your land bird did not bring you such luck as you might have hoped."

Surely at least a few of the sailors were wishing they had pitched Gargle, Wieser and me into the wake when some opportunity presented. Though a pirate attack was hardly my fault, we would not have been in these waters at all if the Scytheran mages weren't manipulating the winds and currents to bring me to them. Or so I supposed.

Next, a pair of men, one old and bent and the other only a little older than me, stepped from behind the bound officers.

The old one wore the long robe with trailing sleeves I had seen on the mages I fought in Merced. The young one had on a similar long garment over his tunic, save for having no sleeves attached. He supported the doddering grey-beard by an elbow as they shuffled forward to stand beside Kruthe.

The pirate placed a hand on the old man's shoulder, causing him to sag sidewise though the touch did not look heavy. "Here is the reason you were brought to me—Mage Balin and his apprentice Ibbot have powers over wind and water. It is said a weather worker with strong gifts can change fortunes the world over. They have for a certainty changed yours!" Kruthe laughed again, enjoying his joke. He was alone in his mirth, neither his men nor the mages joined him. The men of *Moon Road* continued their silent audience; some shivered in the wind.

"So know this: any plotting on your part cannot be hidden. The mages will learn of it by their magic and carry the tale to me. In that instant, you will become valueless to me and over the rail you will go, able-bodied or no. Be wise."

He said more, but it all amounted to the same thing. We were doomed to be taken where he willed. But were his mages Scytheran, and is that where he would bring us? He spoke fluent Mercedish, with a lilting accent I had never heard—was that how Scytherans spoke in other tongues? The mages I had defeated in the cave had harsh, guttural voices. Kruthe's was not at all like their accents.

I did not think Cuffer could answer these questions. I despaired of speaking to Lichan. We learned the shipmaster and officers would be kept secured away from the crew as a "precaution against wrong-headedness."

Still, they would have to eat. If Cilliyon could take them their rations, she could perhaps ask my questions of Lichan and carry back his answers ... it was as I thought this that I felt eyes on me, the sensation of spiderwebs catching at my hair, yet it was truly my mind being touched: I had felt this before from mages. I raised my eyes to find the younger mage staring straight at me, unblinking. The older one looked as if he chewed his tongue, while he gazed up into the clouds.

I strove to look as blank as the men to either side of me. Cuffer perpetually had a bit of vagueness about him, to my right. The sailor on my left stood as though resigned to fate, arms hugging his loose-woven shirt to his chest.

I waited for the mage to point at me and say what I was; Kruthe had said they would know at once.

The boy never released the elder's arm, never raised his other hand to pick me out of the crew as magical, and therefore trouble. Would he keep silent if he knew? Could he be one of the Scytheran mages pursuing me, and not recognize who I was? I tried to convince myself he was only noting my slate slung around my neck. Just a mute boy who tends animals. Because otherwise, why did the apprentice not say he had spotted me?

We were dismissed back to our work, off-watch crew to their hammocks, though how they could possibly sleep was beyond my ken. I saw Kruthe direct his men to escort the shipmaster back to his cabin, but the officers were sent below to the hold with Cuffer and me.

"Be wise" echoed in my head in Kruthe's curiously pleasant lilt. The slaver's men had to unchain each man and escort him down the steeply slanted steps, then secure him to his fellows again at the bottom. Cuffer and I were waved on through irritably. I took care not to catch Lichan's eye. He, too, made no sign that would call attention to me.

The officers ended up chained like livestock to beams in the hold, in pairs with scant six feet of length to move about. I felt I would like to complain about their treatment but dared not.

"You two," barked one of the slavers.

When Cuffer and I looked his way he continued, "Give them water buckets and piss pots. We'll tell you about feeding them later."

One slaver was stationed to watch them, and us I supposed, while the others went back above. If they always kept watch, how would I speak to Lichan? Provided I chose to be unwise, for I was still undecided.

Cuffer and I finished our chores. Under the eye of the slaver guard, I did not have to do all the work. *Cuffer must want to appear valuable*, I thought with some lack of charity. I handed him feed for the geese, which were ever ill-tempered and inclined to hiss and snap.

As I moved about the hold, I made sure to kick straw over my runes chalked on the planks. The mages might not come below deck, indeed the older one looked as if the stairs would be beyond him, but I could not count on the meaning of my marks going unnoticed by all who would pass through the hold now. I would obscure my nature as long as I could. While tending the oxen, I hid my bag, containing my mother's book, deeper among the bales.

What to do about my cabin, though? Its floor covered over with runes and marking me as no usual animal tender if I claimed the accommodation by returning there. How long before Kruthe or one of his men began to question who occupied that high berth, which suggested means beyond those of a stock keeper?

I determined I must not go back to the cabin and resolved to play my role as a mute as carefully as ever I could. I had often noted how little folk seemed to expect of young children or those addled or lacking any of the senses, be it sight, hearing, voice or limb. The soldiers occupying Bale Harbour and our village at home had scarcely noticed me as I went about fighting against their aims. If only I could go undetected by these two mages, I might do the same here.

Wieser bumped her head against my palm and I scratched her ears.

First, I must find out if thwarting the pirate slavers was in my interest, or if I would end up in worse straits thereby, such as carried into the very hands of Scytheran mages bent on my destruction.

Unless I already lay in their hands.

CHAPTER FOUR

W e were forbidden to speak to the prisoners, and very nearly to each other, Cuffer and I. Which meant that I could convey nothing to him at all, since he could not read. I took to leaving my slate off my neck and just doing what I could see needed done. I watched for a chance to write questions to Lichan, but the guards never slept on duty. Like hawks, they were, scarcely blinking. I wondered if their vigilance was enspelled by the mages Kruthe had brought.

Once the damaged sails were restored, we sailed on. I never went above, and the guards said precious little to one another at change of watch. I was always alert to overhear word that we neared our destination and what it might prove to be. The brutes more grunted to each other than spoke.

None of the *Moon Road*'s sailors above seemed to have given me up as the rune-writer in the forward cabin. Surely it had been inspected by now. Perhaps someone had claimed the signs were drawn by the occupant on the last voyage. Since I had my bag of belongings below with me, it was empty enough.

Another pirate came down to count the animals and the men likewise. A tally of assets, I supposed. "Can the mute hear? Or is he deaf as well?" he sniffed to Cuffer.

"He hears well enough."

"He is the shepherd, with his stock dog?"

Cuffer looked at the black sheep. He glanced at me and I gave the merest nod. "Aye. Shepherd boy. Aids me here on the journey."

He made a tick on his parchment.

"Have him carry on. Once the animals are sold, the auction will sort out the slaves. Likely the sheep buyer will have a shepherd already. Could likely use the dog, though."

My heart froze. I had never thought I might be separated from Wieser. Since she had come to me, the night Da and Wils went away to war, she had never left my side. An herbalist well-versed in magic in Bale Harbour had told me my dog was "not a usual one." Wieser had some magic herself, or ability to understand beyond her senses. She might not speak. Now neither did I, but we had ever been able to know one another's intention and meaning. I could not face her loss.

It had nearly undone me when I thought she was killed by the mages—they, too, had recognized her as more than she appeared.

If we had been in the mountains of home, or even at the fortress in the pass where we found Da, I could have taken her and escaped some-how. Here we were trapped aboard with ocean all around us.

My fear must have shown on my face, because Cuffer looked at me with worry-creased brows as the pirate made his way over to the fowl. I gave a sharp shake of my head to put him off asking me what was wrong. I couldn't answer him, anyway.

The man gave me a surely unintended gift when he gripped the handrail to mount the stairs. "Keep them all alive for two more days. Then we'll reach port and get them off loaded."

Two days to reach land. I would find a way to get us off the ship and out of this. I had to. On land, or near enough we could swim to it, Wieser and I could get away.

I'd slept by Wieser's side in the hay each night since our capture. Gargle came below each day at dusk and went above at dawn. That night in the darkness, I worked to wrap my mother's book of magic in my oiled leather tunic, tightly binding bale twine about it. I then secured it in its wooden box and wrapped that as well, with the oiled trousers. I must preserve it from being ruined in the sea if I did have to take to the waves.

I watched the guards for signs of the weather. Other than being dressed in woolens for warmth, none were wet from rain or snow when they came below. Since we were no longer allowed to go up to the galley, we were brought food along with the officers' rations. I ate only a little of this and hid all the rest in my bag. As Cuffer had predicted, the weevils were ascendant in the ship biscuit now, but I could not be choosy. Wieser also limited herself, leaving some of her meal for me to pack away.

I wished the bag had been made of black canvas, for least visibility in the dark, but when Annora had made it, Lichan's mother had told her to use any color except that. A black seabag was considered bad luck by sailors. Mine was a mossy green. Could have been worse, pale sail canvas would have stood out more in the night. Past first sleep, following two bells, was when I aimed to slip away. The deck above was quietest then, as a rule.

If that proved impossible, I might be forced to wait until we made port and commenced off loading. Wieser worried me most. She had such difficulty climbing the steeply slanted stair and weighed too much for me to carry up while also holding my bag. I fretted over this all the following day, but could come up with no plausible way to achieve getting her on deck without calling attention to the effort.

No other slaver made any remark about nearness to port or ending the voyage. I fretted about this as well. If they didn't already know what I was, could the mages be plotting to make me reveal myself by trying to escape to protect my magical dog?

I had no choice. Whether in a Scytheran port or some other country, I had to make good my escape first and then sort the rest.

Gargle gave me an idea, by hopping on the wheelbarrow full of muck and soiled straw for a ride up to the open hatch. As we pulled the ropes to raise the barrow, I thought of doing so to haul up Wieser and my bag at the same time. I could then race up to get her and we'd go over the side. I would have to have a way of distracting the guard on deck, though. Some way …

Tomorrow would mark the second day since the pirate had said two days left to keep all the stock alive. Two days to landfall. How close to land would the vessel be the night before? Could I see the shore in the dark, or did I risk swimming out to sea by mistake? Which way would the tide be running? What phase was the moon? When I was out in the world, I always knew where on the horizon to expect moonrise, and when.

Blast the sailor's life! I did not care if I never again went to sea, once I felt solid earth under my feet. Though if this dry land I finally reached lay across the wide ocean, it would mean I could never go home ...

Cuffer cornered me by the grain bin. "I see you saving food back," he whispered hoarsely. "Do not think of jumping ship. These waters are cold, you'd be dead in minutes. Wait until we dock and I'll help ye."

I could only nod, but he was satisfied and turned away. How could I tell him what I needed in the way of help? He was smarter than he let on, and more keen of eye, too. Would he know when my opportunity came?

Menacing dreams still haunted me every night. I dreamed that night of struggling, submerged in freezing water with my lungs fair bursting, banging my fists on a shelf of ice above me, unable to find the way up to the air. Wieser writhing underwater beside me, legs kicking weaker and weaker, bubbles rising from her snout and then trailing away to nothing. In my panic, I screamed, "NO!" and startled awake. Cuffer stared at me from his place on the straw. Warm, living Wieser nosed at me. Gargle clacked his beak irritably from his perch on the bales.

"I thought he was mute," said the guard, pointing at me in accusation.

So I had cried out. I had not made a sound since the night of the storm.

"Some nights he has bad dreams," Cuffer muttered. "Then he might make some insensible noise."

"He said no." The guard lowered his brows obstinately. "That's a word, not a noise."

By his accent, the man was one of us, Mercedian. Perhaps pirates had no allegiance except to their leader, though.

I wracked my mind as in a fever. If my voice was restored, better no one knew, so that I might use it as a surprise. The risk of trying again to speak was too great if I could not do so away from anyone's hearing. Yet, I knew some spoken spells which might aid my escape, as long as I could remember how to cast correctly after so long without practice. I looked bewildered and pointed at my throat as I had when I lost the power of speech.

"You see?" Cuffer said, bless him all five gods. "In his dreams he might speak, but awake his mind is addled such that he loses the capacity. Some trauma befell him, I believe, in a gale when we set out. Mebbe lightning strike. No one saw exactly."

The guard peered at me for a further moment, while my palms grew damp. He turned away, though, and I settled onto my straw and pretended to return to sleep.

At dawn's breaking, Cuffer and I set about our customary work as soon as Gargle flapped his way out the opened hatch. Cold air flowed down from above, a patch of smooth iron grey sky was all I could see. A day guard arrived with food and the night watchman made no mention of my crying out, for I listened carefully as he took his leave.

I judged it to be noon or better when the ship sailed into port, which was evidenced by the shouted orders drifting down from above to trim sails and other tasks I did not understand. Cuffer seemed to know. He signed for me to hang my slate about my neck, so I retrieved it from my bag.

After many shouts of "make fast" and such like, great bustle commenced for hauling the animals up in the winch. I quietly led Wieser to a dark corner and bade her stay with a hand signal. I did not want her sent up with the flock. I prayed the tally-sheet pirate would not miss her above.

Word came when our hold was emptied, all to report topside. The prisoners were escorted up the ladder one by one. Cuffer and I followed.

We were crammed together on deck with the sailors and countless crates, bales and barrels. Work continued on the docks as I had observed in Bale Harbour; wagons loaded, cargo shifted like pieces on a game board. I had only a moment to look about at the wharves and try to get my bearings. The wind bit like a whip made of ice.

Cilliyon eased up beside me but did not speak. Tobal stood next to her. I dared write on my slate:

Is this Scythera?

Without looking at it. I tipped the slate toward Tobal, who shook his head just a twitch.

Somewhere else was good fortune.

I hoped.

It certainly was cold, though. Cilliyon looked pale and chilled through. I wondered if she had any heavier clothes than she wore now. *Worry about yourself and your own skin,* I berated myself. *She's already wearing your moonstone.* I wiped the words from my slate.

Kruthe strode out of the shipmaster's ready room, shrugging on a heavy cloak. At his heels, the young mage walked the ancient one out into the wind. The old one seemed to waver as if buffeted by the gusts but turned his face to it with apparent pleasure. Shipmaster Alisdar did not appear.

"Sailors will remain aboard tonight, until the ship's disposition is determined tomorrow. Officers may be ransomed, so will be held ashore. Cargo hands, all from below decks, remain aboard—" Kruthe went on but I didn't hear him. The mages had made their way down onto the deck where we stood. The pair walked among the men. The old mage was sniffing each as he passed, elbow supported by the young one. I felt deafened by stark fear. They were hunting me.

As they drew closer, I could see the old man's eyes under his wiry brows—completely white, no color at all. He was surely as blind as the miller's father back home. Each step brought them nearer. I held my breath.

I wanted to run, jump over the rail. But how could I? Wieser was still waiting below. My bag with its precious book rested there as well.

I felt Cilliyon grasp my hand and dared not shake her off. I gritted my teeth. The mage inhaled deeply, only two sailors away.

Then he stood before Cilliyon. He drew in a breath, then another.

His brows bunched and he leaned closer. A short, sharp sniff, a nod, and the young mage called up to Kruthe, "It's this one!"

Two of the pirates ran to grasp her by either arm and dragged her up to Kruthe. She cried out, "No! Why? Why?" and struggled but was no match for two men.

As he guided the old mage around to aim him toward the upper deck, the young man met my gaze. I could see in his eyes, his knowledge it was not Cilliyon they sought. He knew it was me instead.

CHAPTER FIVE

Cuffer and I had to pull Tobal along with us when Kruthe dismissed the crew from the deck. The cook kept looking over his shoulder at the stairs to the ready room, saying, "What could they want with a galley boy? Why did they take him?" Cuffer did not know and I could not say.

How long would it take her to give me up as the source of her moonstone pendant, if that was the magic the old mage had scented? Why had the young mage not tapped me as the magical one? I was certain he knew …

We deposited Tobal in the galley and went back to the hold. As we no longer had the officers there, no guard came down. That, at least, counted as a smile from the gods.

"Listen, Judian." Cuffer looked about him as if spies or pirates might yet be lurking. "You must wait until dark falls, then we'll make some disturbance so you can slip away on the dock. This is a deep-water port, with mountain country all around. I was here once, if this is the place I remember—I think it is the far north, where the gods' lights dance in the night sky. 'Tis very cold, I hope you have more woolens than I've seen." He fretted around among the animal gear and jerked free a horrid smelly half-size blanket which he pressed into my arms. I nodded thanks and tried to close my nose.

"Go inland and up into the forest. Then you can head south—"

"There are too many river cliffs nearby southwards," came another voice at the top of the stair. The student mage stepped down the treads and onto the straw-covered planks. "Better he should continue east for a time first."

Cuffer opened and closed his mouth soundlessly, then stammered, "I, I—You ... Well ..."

I waited, defeated, for my escort to Kruthe and the old mage. *Cilliyon must have—*

"She has said nothing. Yes, it's easy enough to mark her as a girl once her shirt is opened to retrieve the talisman. It is yours, is it not?"

I closed my mouth tight, remembering to play mute and thinking, *Why do you ask, anyway? You seem to already know.*

"My name is Ibbot. I want to come with you. I can make sure we get away cleanly."

My look made him chuckle. "You do not believe me? You cannot understand my desire to be shed of that toothless old boar and his keepers? I am as much a slave as they will see to it you become, if you stay to face your fate." Another thought appeared to occur to him. "Do you want to take the girl along with us? I can see to that as well. She will be quite grateful, it is safe to say. She is so very frightened."

As anyone would wager. Since he seemed to be able to know my mind's contents anyway, I decided I might as well try to speak. It came out a croak, but a voice none-the-less. "Why not go alone?"

"Greater safety in greater numbers where the wild lands are concerned. That, and Master Mage Balin will attempt to find me with magic, once he takes note of my absence. The old man can be formidable yet, if he can pull his mind out of the clouds and wind. You will help me to elude him."

"How will I?"

He grinned. "Whatever else is in you, there is high magic there, too. You do not have to trust me. Just let's help one another for the present."

I thought for a bit, until Cuffer began shuffling his feet and our visitor also became impatient.

"Or, I can take you up to Kruthe and Master Balin and tell them what a valuable treasure I have discovered." Though his expression did not change, nor his reasonable tone alter, ice came and went in his eyes. I had no doubt he was giving me the only offer of escape he would make.

"When?" I said, for my voice was still raspy and I used as few words as possible. "Do we go?"

He flashed another grin. "I will come for you just after midnight. Have your friend haul you and your gear up in the barrow. I will meet you at the hatch."

"My dog."

"By all means. And your crow will come along on his own, yes?"

I shrugged and nodded. "The girl? If she stays behind?"

"Oh, unpleasantness in her view. Could bring a good price. She is a pretty enough little thing to men who are a long time from their last woman." He had not even a tinge of concern in his voice, but went on, "Shall we rescue her? Do the proper thing?"

I nodded again, more slowly.

The thing he was most right about was that I did not trust him.

Snow squalls blew in at sunset. Heavy sleet began to coat the rigging at full dark. Sailors and pirates alike were dispatched to knock the ice away lest it snap masts and crosspieces or tear the canvas away from the rigging. Cuffer explained we could become top-heavy and capsize if the ice was not managed, especially since we were off-loaded for the most part.

I wondered if the Master Mage Balin would not realize his student was doing weather work, despite the old man being blind. For I was sure as sure it was Ibbot creating the icy diversion to cover our escape.

Tobal brought food to us himself, still shaking his head over Cilliyon. What could the matter be for his galley help to be singled out and taken away? I did not speak in front of him, waiting instead until he went off muttering before I asked Cuffer if he should be told she was disguised as a boy.

"All the ill fortune will be laid at her feet then, for it is the worst of bad luck to have a female aboard. Would spare you and your animals from blame, though."

"With luck, I'll be gone. I just wondered if Tobal or anyone would help her if I didn't take her with me." I prayed he would say her protection would be seen to, perhaps that he would try to help in some way.

But no. "What could any one of us do? They are too many." Cuffer handed me most of his food to pack away.

I packed all of mine, as I had no appetite. Wieser I called out to eat a little. She responded to my voice as placidly as she had obeyed my silent hand signals.

I had a feeling she knew what was afoot, but still I told her we were going to flee and she must be quiet and very good. As if she was ever anything else but good.

Gargle came below when the snow began and dozed on the railing of an empty pen. I wished I could ask either of my animals what they thought of Ibbot and get an answer.

I was curious, though. How much had he been taught and how much more did he have to learn? Was he bound in some way to the old mage, or were they both bound to Kruthe? He wanted me to think he was escaping from bondage of some sort, rather than just taking his leave of an old man he resented doing for. He bore watching.

The storm continued while Cuffer and I waited, evidently forgotten or we would have been called up to battle the ice as well. So, I wondered if Ibbot had made sure our absence above was overlooked. My misgivings grew and seemed to double back on one another. I chewed my lip until it bled.

At just past the midnight bell toll, Ibbot opened the hatch above. It should have been iced shut by rights; I would have to be cautious if he could so easily work many spells at once. I looked up into swirls of freezing mist and saw Ibbot beckon.

"Journey safe with the gods, friend Judian," Cuffer said gruffly. I signaled Wieser to jump into the barrow and set my bag beside her. I poked Gargle awake and he shook out his wings and surveyed the scene. He *humphed* but kept his eyes open. I pointed to the barrow. He hopped down to perch on my bag.

I helped Cuffer haul the rope to raise Wieser and the bag, which made nearly a full barrow load. When the tackle was tied off securely on the cleat, I took my leave quickly.

"Best chance, friend Cuffer," I said. "May you find your way home again."

"Acch, this is my home, in a hold full of creatures sailing the seas. I will miss you, boy." He shook my hand and I climbed away up the ladder stair.

The mist wafted thick and chopping the ice continued to occupy all of the hands I could see. No one noted me as I joined Ibbot and we extricated Wieser and my bag from the barrow. He closed the hatch and ice coated it instantly, though it had been bare wood and clasps just a breath before.

Gargle lit on my shoulder, grasping tight. Ibbot led me to the same place under the stairs to the upper deck, where I had stood to turn the tempest aside with magic and raise fair wind. I wondered if I still had the ability to do potent magic, or if my voiceless state reflected loss of more than words. Did the return of my voice mean a restoration of the spellcasting as well? I thought I might need all my skills now more than ever.

From beneath the stair treads, Cilliyon's ghost-white face looked out. Her hair coiled in damp ringlets and she shivered from cold and wet. Or terror. She wore only the tunic and trousers she had been clad in when hauled away to the ready room.

I turned on Ibbot. "Find her some warm clothes! She'll take sick wearing no more than that and then how will she travel?"

He took a step back and looked as if he had never considered the possibility of deadly chill from his lofty magical view of the world. He went up the stairs two at a time. I crouched under the planks with Cilliyon. Wieser pushed in snug against her, though how much warmth a wet dog might provide I couldn't say.

Through chattering teeth, she said, "Can we really get away?"

"Ibbot has kept us unnoticed so far. I lived in mountains, though in another part of the world. And I know how to travel without attracting attention. Just do what I tell you."

She nodded as I spoke. "He said you could talk now. Why is he helping us?"

Ibbot clattered down the steps. He must have powerful magic indeed, if he had to take no thought of keeping quiet or trying to stay out of sight. I found no comfort in that. He swung under the treads with us and thrust the self-same cloak I had seen Kruthe wear on deck into Cilliyon's shaking hands.

"Are you mad?" My voice came so strangled I might have been losing its use again.

"Put it on. He'll never miss it. Until after I'm too far away, that is." He looked over his shoulder, at last giving some sign that he might spare attention to keeping our flight unmarked.

I helped Cilliyon wrap herself in the heavy brown wool and gave silent thanks it was not bright scarlet like the pirate slaver's shirt.

"Can we leave now? I think it's best," said Ibbot, still looking behind him.

"Where will we leave the ship," I said, "by the gangway? Isn't it pulled up at night?"

"Ah, your dog. She cannot climb down the mooring lines? Well, no, I see. We'll lower the gangplank, then. That will have to do."

I shook my head, wondering at his mood. He sounded in good spirits, cheerful even. Perhaps he *was* mad. Cilliyon took the hand I offered to help her rise and clung to it still as we crossed the deck following Ibbot. Her hand felt cold as river clay.

As if we were invisible, crew passed all around us. Hoar frost from the mist rimed their beards and hair while, grim-faced, they swung sledge and cudgel at the ever-accumulating ice. Others shoveled the crusts and fragments off the deck into the bay. We might have been wraiths in their midst for all the notice we collected moving among them.

Ibbot examined with interest the apparatus for extending the plank, as if it was a curiosity encountered at a country market. "Look here, doesn't this make it go out?"

"How do I know? It's not as if I've ever done it."

"Now, do not make me sorry I've brought you along. And your girl."

"What gives you the idea she's my girl?"

He raised his eyebrows. "She was wearing your protection talisman, after all. Why would you give her that if you had no interest in her?"

Cilliyon was looking from one to the other of us, eyes guarded. With a huff of exasperation, she reached out to grasp a lever attached to the mechanism and shoved it toward the deck. The handle moved only a little. She leaned her weight on it without further effect. "It's frozen solid." She wrapped her arms around herself under the cloak.

Ibbot closed his eyes and interlaced his fingers before his downturned face. He muttered the rising, falling singsong I recognized as spellcasting, though the words were none I'd heard before. The lever and the gears became wet instead of iced-over, while we stood and watched.

He shook out his hands and reached for the lever, but I put my hand to it first and pushed it down. The gangway thrust out to the dock and slapped into place with a slushy smack.

I wasted no time heading down the slick wood, Cilliyon, Ibbot and Wieser following on. Gargle still clung to my shoulder, silent for once in his existence. My bag nearly over balanced me with its weight slung over one shoulder. Neither of my companions carried any belongings at all that I could see. I glimpsed restless black water under the gangway by the light of guttering torches ranged along the dock. I could not afford to slip and fall in. I watched where I set my feet at each step.

Once on the dock with Wieser, I did not pause while the other two made their way carefully behind me. I tried to look as if I had business pressing me which left no time for lingering on the wharf. I struck out for the stone stairs that led up to the street level.

As I gripped the freezing rope railing, strung between iron posts, I thought with dismay about Ibbot's apparently vastly superior magical skill—superior in every way to mine. Did he ask me along because he thought I could do the sorts of spells I had seen him enact? Because I had learned to stop a team of horses, send messenger crows where I wished, and once I had shot a mage-possessed hawk from the night sky during a gale. As for my confrontation with the two mages in the tunnel at Merced's sea cliffs—I still did not know if I had defeated them at all, let alone with magical prowess. I suspected I was sought because I was perceived to be some threat to Scythera's mages, but I would have given much to know exactly how I might be that.

Ibbot pulled Cilliyon along by the arm to catch me up. "Where are we going now?" he asked, as if inquiring about the next mummer or food vendor we might encounter at a festival.

"Out of sight and out of the weather. Do you know your way around this town?"

"No, not at all. Never been here."

"Then how did you know the terrain to the east and south?"

"Looked at maps, is all. Maps and charts help Mage Balin focus his weather working."

"But he's blind!" Cilliyon said.

"It's magic," Ibbot said. He flashed his teeth in a broad smile that looked to me to bear slyness behind it.

I found myself liking him less and less. I turned away and continued up the stairway. "Do you have any money?" I asked him over my shoulder.

"Not a scrap. Do we need some?"

I had coin my da had given me to use for my needs during studies on Lohr Island. I wasn't sure I should let on, though. We needed to find somewhere to hide for the night, then take off at first light if the weather broke. Heading into the mountains in the dark in this sort of storm was a sure way to court a death by falling, drowning or freezing.

We reached the top of the stairs. Glazed cobbles stretched away right and left. Gargle took wing and flew away to the left, followed by Wieser plodding with her head down. I turned to the left to keep Gargle and Wieser in my line of sight. They might have something in mind. More than what could be said for me.

There appeared to be enough greater warmth above the harbour that the streets were more wet than iced over, though the chill still made clouds of our breath. Deserted roadway stretched before us, no wagons, no folk on their way to a hearth we might share. I looked for an inn, but the area seemed mainly warehouses and shipping store-fronts. All of them shuttered and dark.

Gargle and Wieser led on. I was soon as wet as if I had fallen off the gangway into the sea, though what swirled from the sky could be called cleaner, at least. My oilskins were still wrapped around my mother's book in my bag. Gargle lit on a board scribed with heavy black lettering in a language I did not know.

"Do you know what that says?" I pointed.

Ibbot looked up with a hand over his brow to block the drizzle.

"Nagelin Stables," he said. Wieser sat beneath the weathered sign and gave me a soulful look.

"We'll try here," I said. I slid the door aside, as it was not secured in any way, and stepped into the blackness within.

CHAPTER SIX

Inside it was blessedly dry and familiar. Horses shifted their hooves, whickering in stalls along either side of a central corridor. No sour smell of ill-kept animals; whoever Nagelin might be, he took care to give fresh bedding and sweet hay. Unless Nagelin was the name of the town? Best not go calling for Master Nagelin, in that case.

Ibbot and Cilliyon followed me inside. Ibbot held up a palm sized white stone with a glimmer at its heart, spoke a word, and shone the stone about with its light delving into the corners. The view confirmed what my nose and ears had already told me.

"Come along." I went after Gargle and Wieser, both of whom were making themselves comfortable in an empty stall at the far end of the row.

Ibbot showed he was a fool by asking if we could warm ourselves with a fire. "In a barn? With hay all around?" Cilliyon sneered, before I could point out the plainly obvious risk of burning the place down.

"The animals' bodies will provide some heat. Can't you dry our clothes by magic?" I said, pulling a bale into the box so we could sit. Cilliyon fetched another. She was stronger than she looked.

He evaded my glance. "Better if I concentrate on concealing our flight, I think."

"What is it that is keeping Master Mage Balin from recognizing your weather work? Or using his own magic to dispel it?"

"A strong sleeping draught I put in his bedtime wine. He won't wake before midmorning at the earliest. More likely noon."

"We ought to move out at dawn. Will it still have to be drizzling ice?"

"By my spell work, we will not be missed until my master wakes and wonders why his attendant is not bringing his gruel and tea." He lifted a lip. "Kruthe is so worried about his prize, and his own ship, that he won't give a thought to the whereabouts of his weather worker's helper."

"Have you ensorcelled Kruthe, too? So that he isn't demanding his weather mage stop the ice from falling?"

"Someone as full of himself as Kruthe, is easiest to distract and deceive."

"What if he misses his cloak?" Cilliyon asked. She rubbed her hands together and blew on them.

"It isn't his only one. Just his favorite."

Both Cilliyon and I glared at him. He held up his hands, in mock fearfulness. "I had to take the first warm garment that came to hand, didn't I? There was not time to go rooting amongst the crew's clothes, surely you can see. Besides, is it not keeping you properly warm, as your friend insisted was necessary? It seems a nice thick cloak, to be sure."

I began to feel what I wanted most was for him to stop talking.

Still, I had to ask, "What was Balin looking for when he took Cilliyon?"

"As I may have complained, he is oblivious to most of life save his precious weather. I sensed someone with high magic. It was I who suggested Mage Balin seek out that person. I knew on deck she was not the one. Only she did bear a sign, a talisman of magical protection. Which I surmised could only have come from you. I wanted you free of Kruthe so you might help me make good my escape. Who are you, anyway?"

Could he really not know? Was he trying to trick me? "And how have I helped you?"

"Your animal guides led us here, at your direction, no? Do tell me. Who are you?"

"I am Fenn," I said, giving my father's name. "Fenn Tedesch." Lichan's surname, surely he wouldn't know that either.

"Why were you bound for Lohr Island?"

"Going home. Why was your mage altering the wind and current to bring us off course?"

"Kruthe. He bought my master years ago, and me, too. He plies his slaver trade all over these northern waters and is dreaded by all. Why hunt rich vessels when you can have them brought right to you?"

"You say he has been doing this for years?"

He grew evasive again. "Likely he did it less easily before he purchased Mage Balin. Master's weather work spurs the pirate's profits, no doubt about that." He turned to Cilliyon. "And you are not a galley boy. Who are you exactly?"

Cilliyon looked at her lap for a moment. Considering a false name, like me? "I am Cilliyon Marcate. I am a fugitive from Merced, fleeing the war there."

"Ah. And why the disguise?"

"Women are bad luck on a ship, which surely you've been told. Shouldn't we look for someone hereabouts, the owner or something?" Cilliyon peered into the shadows.

I gave her a tetchy look. "So he can throw us out into the wet? Besides, he's probably home in his bed. Better we keep quiet and leave before anyone comes looking and discovers us in a stall which is supposed to be empty."

"In that case, I need to tend to myself before I try to sleep."

I was used to oblique references like this from my little sister and my brother's bride. Ibbot looked clueless. I said, "That's what a stall full of straw is for," and turned away. I nudged Ibbot and spun my hand to get across to him that he should turn his back as well.

She snorted. "No. I hardly think so. Give me your light, Ibbot."

"It won't work for you."

"Oh, go with her and find her a corner you can shine the light on for her."

She grimaced. "Just remember to turn your back, right?"

He walked off grumbling about having to put up with girlishness.

"I expect I could have sent you along with her," I said to Wieser. "Next time we'll try that."

Moments later I heard a shrill shriek, abruptly cut off. I rushed in the direction it came from, ready to curse Ibbot if he had gotten rude with her. But I found them both whey-faced and shaken, his hand still clapped over her mouth.

A man's body lay stretched out on the straw at their feet.

He appeared dead, his color ash grey, a bloody crushed dent on his forehead. I thought he might have been kicked by one of the horses, which had fled. Yet when I looked closer, a shovel lay beside him with a bent and bloodied scoop.

I knelt to make sure he was dead. No heartbeat, no breath. Not all that cold considering the night air, so not gone long.

Which meant whoever had killed him could still be in the stable.

I rose with my obsidian knife in my hand. "We're leaving before we get blamed for this. Come on."

"Out into my storm? Have a heart. Cilliyon's cold."

"I'm not so cold that I'm staying here to get thrown in jail! I'm with you, Fenn."

She had some wits about her, because she knew my real name, and played along with my falseness to Ibbot. I was less sorry she'd come along on our escape than I had been. "Let's get our things and leave by the other end of the stable, out the back."

I actually intended to go out the way we had come in, but in case the murderer stood in a corner listening, it seemed wiser to confuse him as to our intent. If he spoke Mercedish, that is. I motioned the other two to follow me and went back to collect my bag and my crow.

Gargle showed himself the most reluctant to leave, a dead body here or there making him no never mind, evidently. That did suggest no murderer lurking in the shadows, but I insisted we were going whether he came along or no. He lit on my shoulder and pecked me on the ear.

We would have got clean away, too, slipping out the front, but that we encountered two sodden young men arriving with a lantern between them, evidently grooms at the stable. I had no manner of luck at all.

Gargle pecked me again. Suggesting, perhaps, that if I'd listened to him and not left just then, we might have missed running smack into them.

One spoke to Ibbot, the tallest of our party, in a language I did not know. He answered cheerfully and at some length, then drew his robes closer around him in the still cascading icy mist and stepped out into the street. Cilliyon and I followed, with Wieser bringing up the rear.

When we rounded the next corner, I could stand it no longer. "What did you say?"

"I said we could not raise anyone to see to our mounts and left them so we could find an inn. We would return to settle accounts after the weather cleared." He kept walking, head down.

"They'll find no wet horses or tack inside."

"Perhaps you might have done better if you spoke the language."

I had no answer to that, beyond walking faster to put more distance between the dead body and ourselves.

It was Cilliyon who asked, "What language was that? Where are we?"

Ibbot gave an airy wave of his hand. "Far north somewhere. I've not been in this particular port before, I don't believe, but the language is Yeganil, as on the stable sign."

"We're in Yega, then?" I asked, for that was the language Lichan had been translating from my book. I heartily wished we had him along, rather than Ibbot. In terms of trustworthiness, at least.

"Seems likely."

"Find the road out of town to the east," I told Wieser and Gargle. They took the lead.

"It's still hours until dawn," protested Ibbot. "I thought it was dangerous to go into the mountains in the dark."

"I'm weighing one danger against another now." I wiped water from my face, mostly pointless as the sleet continued. "When we're well clear of anyone's view, you can use your light. Not until I say, understand?"

We walked on in the night.

Cilliyon stumbled and I caught her, only because I was closest. I still received an arch look from Ibbot which made me press my lips together. I set her on her feet and told her to take more care where she stepped on the slick cobbles.

We passed shops and some dark inns as we made our way east, then a central marketplace empty of folk but with bedraggled booths both soaked and glistening with ice. I had thought we might see more workers making their way to the district we had come from, or on their way to the always bustling wharves below, but we encountered no one else up and about. The fewer who noted our presence, three travelers with a dog and a crow, the fewer who could remember having seen us when the stable grooms told about the three who emerged from the place of a killing this day.

I was just beginning to feel encouraged when we arrived at the wall that enclosed the port city, with a stout and guarded gate in its east face.

Gargle and Wieser rejoined us when I hissed for them. I ducked down a side alley with Ibbot and Cilliyon.

"What is your plan?" Ibbot asked eagerly.

"I haven't got one. Let me think."

If we hid until another party went through past the guards, perhaps we could join them and not attract so much notice ourselves. We could not count on that, I thought. Or, if we could attach ourselves to someone else somehow ... perhaps hide in the bed of a wagon? As it was a port like Bale Harbour back home, surely cargo wagons came in and out of the town? I hated to risk stealing a wagon outright. Sneaking aboard one could work, though. Gargle could fly out, Wieser might walk through unchallenged by guards ...

I peeked around the corner for a better look. The gate itself was barred, with a small window hatch that a man would open to see who was on the other side. A gatehouse stood to the right, made of stone like the wall, with the light of a fire within casting the shadows of two men through a larger window overlooking the street. More than two guards could be inside, judging by the size of the wood-shingled house.

I wished I knew more about the country of Yega.

I pulled my head back and tugged Ibbot's sleeve. "Do you think you can find a cargo wagon outbound through this gate? Since you know the language?"

"Oh, so we can hide in it?"

"First I want to see if the guards inspect what cargo goes through, but yes, I am thinking so."

"Stay here for now and I will see what I can scare up." He stepped away.

"Wait. Can you make it just a little warmer, so we are only wet instead of frozen?"

"Mmm, I fear I must keep them occupied with ice in the ships below, lest they come after us before we get far enough away. It is a bit warmer up here, can you tell? That is as much as I dare."

I nodded and waved him off.

When I looked about our alley refuge more closely, I saw a small overhang above a doorway. It was enough to keep some of the sleet off Cilliyon, and I settled her under it. I sat on my bag and hunched under my cloak, but both were so wet it was of little use. I hoped Ibbot would find a likely merchant transport sooner rather than later.

It only seemed half an age until he returned. I was occupying myself by squishing a rhythm with my boots in the alley mud when he trotted up.

"You attract less attention walking than running," I remarked, without looking up.

"Surely I give the appearance of someone wanting to stay as dry as possible."

"Is there anything in the world that is dry?" came plaintively from under the overhang.

"What did you find?" I said.

"A wagon load of turnips is heading east at dawn, drawn by a team of mules. A load of barrels, of some sort of grease, I think, is also departing. It is heavier and has a team of oxen being harnessed at the inn one street over. I found a load of lumber, but it is not covered. We want a cover, yes?"

"Yes." I considered which draft animals I might stop with magic as I had done with Annora in the mountain pass at home. The others could clamber on the back while I held up the animals at the front. But how to accomplish it without anyone observing? "Do they all plan to head out at first light?"

"I gather that is usual practice here. The drivers of the heaviest wagons were most concerned about the mountain roads, unpaved and treacherous with mud. Should we go in the turnips?"

Mules, though. Much more a mind of their own than horses. "Where is the turnip wagon now? Might we get aboard before the driver moves it out?"

He beamed. "Standing ready, unattended in the inn yard. The driver is eating meat pie and drinking ale in the common room."

"Can you perform your influence again to cause us not to be noticed when we climb on?"

"Of course! The men harnessing the team won't even glance our way."

"But will the gate guards examine the cargo that's leaving? If I don't see any rigs go out—"

He gave an airy laugh. "I heard them talking. If a load is secured under tarps, departing wagons are waved through. All will be well."

I allowed myself to be persuaded. We gathered our troop and crossed one street over to the inn Ibbot had found. Thick canvas was lashed down tight over the load of turnips, and we had to shift some roots about to make room. I tucked Wieser in with us. Gargle I directed to keep watch above and follow. He did not like it, but he was the only one with wings, after all. I retied the knots securing the canvas, working from within and poking them outside once done.

We were well settled reclining among the earthy scent of turnips, listening to the sound of sleet on the canvas over our heads, when the wagon jerked and began to roll. The driver called farewell to someone in the inn yard, and we were off.

I had again just begun to relax and appreciate being in a conveyance on dry (so to speak) land instead of on the sea, when I heard the slap of feet pounding by at a dead run. When we swung around the corner and approached the east gate, a mob of voices shouted at once.

"The stableman's been murdered. Old Hencrik's dead. Three men and a dog seen leaving the stable, hunt them down. They're killers." Ibbot translated for us in a whisper.

Truly, no manner of luck at all.

CHAPTER SEVEN

W ieser's hackles sprang up under my hand, though she made no noise at the sound of boots pacing around our wagon, splashing in the crusted puddles. Conversation continued, perhaps the driver asking questions, or the guards inquiring about his cargo and destination. Ibbot could tell us later; I did not want him to speak now, however quietly.

It was dark under the canvas, and I felt rather than saw Cilliyon cover her mouth with both hands. Lest any sound or breath betray us.

My own mouth was dry, in truth the only thing in our current circumstances that *was* dry, but I dared not swallow or try to unstick my tongue from the roof of my mouth.

A hand slapped twice on the side of the wagon bed, making me jerk in surprise. The driver clucked to his mule team and we began to roll once more. I let out my breath as we rumbled over the cobbles. Once we cleared the gate, the cobbles ended, and the wheels rolled through quieter roadbed, with little sound at all.

"What was said?" I asked Ibbot, still keeping my voice pitched low.

"Our driver is asked to carry what is actually quite a good description of us to the next town, in case we have got away from the officials at this last town. Which is Port Freyzik, in case you want to know.

They did try to make him uncover his cargo, but he showed them the ropes were still knotted securely all around and begged them not to get his turnips all wet and rotten. Robbery was the apparent motive for the killing, as funds are missing from the stable till. Unless the grooms stole it before reporting the murder. That last wasn't what they said, I put that in."

"It may be best if we leave our wagon well before the next town then. I wonder how far it is?"

"I don't recall from the maps I saw. But of course, all the departing wagons, whichever way they are going, will be given our descriptions. Best we do something to change our looks, whatever way we go."

"You can do that with a spell?"

"I could, but such spellwork requires focus and I'm still a bit preoccupied with the weather. Actually, I was thinking of stealing some other clothes. And your girl could dress as one to confound our pursuers."

"Quit calling me his girl," Cilliyon said, before I could say the same.

"Have it your own way. Why did he want to bring you along, then?"

She didn't say anything, so I felt I had to say, "It's not as if it was my idea. No one else was coming forward to help her. You said the pirates would—that it would be unpleasantness, so you could bring her with us …" I trailed off.

"Thank you in any case," Cilliyon said in a small voice. I heard a sound I recognized as Wieser administering a generous lick, then Cilliyon thanked her and sighed.

I recalled my brother setting his men on watch when he came back to our farmstead after escaping the seige, and told the other two, "I'll take first watch while you sleep. I'll wake one of you for your turn. Or wake both of you if I decide it's time to abandon the wagon."

"Bit lumpy for a bed, these roots," Ibbot said ruefully.

"Delicate, are you? My bag's too wet to be cozy, and so's my dog. Make do. In fact, I think I'll stow some of these turnips in my bag. We may want them to eat later."

"I don't really care for them over much."

"When there's nothing else to eat, you'll find you care for them very much." I remembered saying something similar to my sister Morie after the Keltanese soldiers invaded. Still, I myself continued to avoid cabbages whenever possible.

"What are you going to watch, isn't it going to be dark under here even when the sun is all the way up?" Cilliyon asked.

"Likely, yah. Mostly I'll be listening. My crow will let me know if he sees something I should know." He was just as liable to come scratching and poking at the canvas looking for a handout, but no need to worry her. "Watch is just a way to say staying awake and paying attention to what's happening. It doesn't mean watching like looking."

"Don't talk her to death. If you want her to sleep."

"Both of you go to sleep." *Be blasted before I'll say anything else.*

The driver maintained a steady pace, up and over ridges and down through low spots where the wheels splashed through rocky creek beds. I found a spot where I could prise up the edge of the canvas and peer out. It was easy to see why it remained so dark under our cover. We travelled through heavy timber, with little sunlight able to reach the roadway.

I was just thinking of waking Ibbot for his turn keeping watch when he startled me by saying, "I'm curious about that knife you had at the stable. How did you come by it?"

"It was given to me."

"It is a unique piece. Obsidian, is it not? Very rare. In fact, I have never seen its equal."

I did not rise to that and held my tongue.

"Who gave it to you?" he asked bluntly.

"They prefer not to be disclosed, my benefactors." Indeed, kavsprit of my homeland preferred no contact with folk who lived above ground. We left the spirits offerings whenever we had to be in their realm, to appease the affront our presence caused. Save for me, I had never heard of anyone else being given a gift in return for that due deference. My knife had also caught the attention of the Scytheran mages I battled and had—perhaps—defeated them with its uncanny power.

"Your knife bespeaks high magic. Is it the source of what I sense in you?"

How could I know? In any case, I made no answer.

He pressed me further. "Who has trained you, as a mage?"

"How old are you?" I countered. "You are not fully a mage, are you. When did you enter training with Mage Balin?"

He laughed without humor. "I am seventeen, only a little older than you. My gifts were noted early on, so I was indentured at twelve. What are you, now? Fifteen? Sixteen? When were you apprenticed?"

In truth I was just a man at my last birthday, when I turned thirteen. It pleased me that I seemed older. Then I chided myself—he might be only telling me what I would wish to hear. "Did you leave home at twelve, to go with your master?"

"That is the way of it. In my time I have learned much." His voice had altered, instead of curiousity it was now tinged with menace. I could not see his expression, there was not enough light. "I can call forth dark and terrible things, horrors without true names."

I hesitated. "Why would you want to?"

The air seemed to shift. Whatever he had been building drained away. "Why indeed," he said softly, voice now bleak.

"What purpose can you have in trying to frighten me now? Do you truly just desire to escape a harsh master, or are you about some other scheme?" I said this gently, as one might talk to soothe a skittish horse. I was aware of Cilliyon awake and listening, though she had not made a sound. Wieser's ears were also pricked.

Ibbot did not speak for a time. When he did, it was not to answer what I had asked. Instead, he shook out his robes about his legs and said, "I think I am finally nearly dry. Look how long it has taken!"

He said no more. I decided not to push him, but neither did I try to take my turn at sleeping.

The wagon rolled on.

～

When I judged it nearly midday, I rooted about in my bag and brought out some of the hard bread and cured meat I had saved. "We'll all be thirsty after this," I said as I shared it around. "I'll find us some water when we leave the wagon."

"Who would think I would want for water ever again?" Cilliyon said.

"How did you come to be aboard *Moon Road*?" I asked her.

"When the soldiers invaded, my father thought to send me to safety. He paid to have me smuggled out of the capital and put aboard an outbound vessel. He feared he would be a target when the Keltanese stormed the city, and I would be used to make him do what they wanted."

It was quite the longest speech I had heard from her.

"Your father is an important man, then?" Ibbot said around a mouthful of biscuit.

She seemed to realize she might have said too much, and responded off hand, "Everyone was frightened. Many families fled."

"It's still true that few of those folk left at home know it was the Scytherans who brought about the war," I said, to deflect Ibbot's interest. "I learned in fighting the Keltanese that the mages from Scythera tricked Keltane's ruler to invade. Then the mages directed the soldiers where to strike."

"Indeed? To what end?" Ibbot wanted to know.

"I have heard how they have drought and famine in Scythera, and people are desperate for relief. It was Scythera that wanted our deep-water harbour and our land's abundance, not Keltane."

"And here I thought your home was Lohr Island, didn't you say, Fenn?"

Pah! Yes, I had said as much. Keeping track of deceptions was blasted difficult. What did Ibbot suspect and what did he know?

He continued, "I seem to recall hearing something about your role in liberating the harbour in Merced."

"I was there. Others did the greater share. I was a messenger only." Mostly true. My actual confrontation with the enemy mages came later.

Our wagon slowed as we talked, and I hastened to shush everyone so we could prepare to get out. "Can you keep the driver occupied with the mules? I don't want him to notice he's had passengers. He's probably stopping to let the team rest and eat a little, if that helps."

Ibbot answered at once. "Have no concern, I will set him seeking a reason for phantom lameness."

A splendid idea, because the driver would be bent over at the front of the wagon, looking at hooves, while we slipped out the back. I busied myself with snagging my knots and pulling them inside to untie.

I put my eye to the space between canvas edge and wagon side to see where we had pulled up. A glittering black eye peered back in at me. Gargle, come to see what he could see. I shooed him away to have a decent look and found we were in a clearing with a stream; tall, thin evergreens crowded all around a patch of winter-browned grass. It was no longer sleeting, though the sunlight shone pallid through dull grey clouds.

I pulled the opening longer, so I would be able to slide one leg out and roll over the side. By the light I let in, I could see Ibbot muttering and gesturing with one hand as if he tipped a hoof up to inspect it for a possible stone bruise. "Safe to go?" I said softly.

He nodded and pointed his other hand at me and then at Cilliyon. I pulled my bag toward me and went over the side. I drew my bag out after me, set it on the ground, then put a hand back inside to aid Cilliyon over and out. Wieser came next. She had to be lifted which took both of us on the outside to accomplish. I could hear the mule driver crooning to his team at the front.

"Ibbot, come on."

A lanky leg extended through the gap, followed by his body twisted up in his robe. He more or less tumbled to the ground before I could catch him. I could not afford to laugh aloud, but he looked like a scarecrow knocked over and stirred up by a wind devil. I pushed Cilliyon toward the nearest trees and bent to help set him on his feet. Gargle did not hesitate to mock him loudly, but perhaps Ibbot did not speak crow.

Evidently neither did I, as I found out when I straightened again to face the muleteer staring at me from behind a cocked crossbow. Wieser rumbled low in her throat. I froze with my handful of Ibbot's robe front. Cilliyon cried out.

The man loosed a torrent of Yeganil. I contrived to look as if I could not understand his words, for indeed I could not. I tightened my grip on Ibbot, hoping he would take my meaning that he should not let on that he understood either.

The driver swung his weapon toward Cilliyon and pointed it to us to indicate he wanted her to come back to the wagon. She sidled closer cautiously, Wieser by her side growling low.

He did not have the look of a man who would hesitate to shoot stowaways. He was road-hardened and sunburnt, with a balding fur cape tied about him with rope akin to that which secured the canvas cover. Nothing wasted.

I held up my hand palm out toward him, a gesture imploring him to wait. Then slowly I released my grip on Ibbot and settled him fully upright. Cilliyon came to stand by my other side and hang onto my arm while cowering a bit behind me, a girlish act despite that she still wore trousers. With flushed cheeks and lips reddened from biting them, she did look more the part of a girl than a young man. If he could by the slightest chance be persuaded we were not the three male fugitives he'd been told of by the gate guard ... we might possibly be warned off instead of captured.

"Do you speak any other tongue?" I tried in Mercedish. No glimmer of comprehension in his eyes.

Nor mercy, either.

I said the same in Keltanese, though that was a long wager—a landlocked country away across the sea. Those were the only two languages I could speak fluently.

He stripped off the rope that bound his cloak, no doubt preparing to bind us with it, when Ibbot flashed out with his arms and spoke a harsh word. Blinding light erupted from his hands. I threw my arm over my eyes and turned away, shielding Cilliyon with my body. When I looked back, the driver lay splayed on the frozen grass, jaw slack, eyes open but unseeing.

CHAPTER EIGHT

"I bbot! By the gods!" I lunged toward the stricken man.

"You've killed him!" Cilliyon cried. "Oh, Ibbot, why?"

"He'd just threatened Fenn with a bolt in the heart! Have you suddenly decided you'd *like* to be trussed up and try your chances in jail? I've saved you both!" Ibbot crossed his arms. "Anyway, he may not be dead."

"He may be only stunned," I told Cilliyon as I looked him over. I waved them quiet while I laid my ear on his chest. He stank of stale pipe smoke and ale, but I felt a faint shudder from his heart. Irregular and too slow.

"Can you fix him?" I looked up at Ibbot.

"There's no taking it back," he said, aghast at my foolishness.

I closed the man's eyelids, unnerved by the vacant stare. Cilliyon knelt beside me. "Can you do anything for him?"

Wieser had taken long and long to recover from being stunned in the cliff tunnel. Annora had made potions and special food for her—which I had paid insufficient attention to, as I was recovering myself. I shook my head. I did not know how to help him.

"What are you lingering here for? We wanted to get out of the wagon, didn't we? We're out! Let's be on our way."

I didn't even look at him. To Cilliyon I said, "Lead the mules over nearer the water. Can you unharness them? I'll hobble them where they can drink and eat."

Ibbot ran a shaking hand through his hair. "Oh, gods preserve me and all my peaches! You cannot be serious. Do you think he'd do the same for you?"

"Help me pull the canvas back. We'll lay him on the turnips and give him some shelter under the canvas, best prop it up so someone could see him under there …"

Ibbot had not moved from where he stood.

"What happened, Ibbot? I thought you had him occupied at the front of the wagon?"

"I lost my concentration when I fell." He shrugged. "And you do notice my storm has abated? That means I am too far away from the sea to influence the port now, Mage Balin's probably awake and we NEED TO BE GOING!"

"Help me or don't help me, I am not leaving him for dead. I am already wanted for a murder I did not do. I will not do murder now to make that come even."

With an abundance of grumbling and grousing, he aided me in the end. The driver had not stirred at all, but he was still breathing when we left the clearing and struck off into the woods.

The muleteer had two water jugs. We left one filled at his side in the wagon bed and took the other away with us for use on the trek.

"If he lives, will he remember us?" Cilliyon asked with a last look over her shoulder.

"Let us hope not," Ibbot said sourly.

"I expect he'll recall you best of all." I let the branch I was holding aside for Cilliyon slap back as he approached.

I led us roughly east, but avoiding the road made for slow going. I knew the mountains of my home so well, I could wander for days afield and never be lost. This was all strange country. I might lead us to the edge of a cliff, or a roaring river, and have to retrace far distance to find a way around such an obstacle. How we needed a map! Failing that, we would have to skirt the road or risk discovery as wanted men. I didn't wish to trust Ibbot to alter our appearance with magic. So we had to had to travel carefully out of sight, at least until we were able to alter our appearance with stolen clothes.

"And we should steal some horses as well, since walking is wearing on me already," Ibbot said, startling me again with his apparent ability to know what I was thinking. He did not seem to be able to do so all the time, though. It was curiously intermittent.

Rather like my own magical ability, which I had complained to Annora came to me in bursts and starts, never wholly predictable. My chance of developing true skill lay in getting to Lohr Island for instruction. I was far and away from there now.

I worried for Lichan, Cuffer, Tobal and Shipmaster Alisdare. If the officers could be ransomed and brought home, would the rest of the crew be sold with the vessel? Or parceled out in the auction Kruthe spoke of?

Wieser took to walking between Ibbot and me, which usually meant she followed me and led him. Gargle flew from branch to branch, calling to his brethren as he encountered them in the canopy.

"Why don't you ask your crow how much farther it is to a settlement or farmstead?"

"I don't talk to him. Or rather, he doesn't answer me like that," I puffed as I made my way down a rock fall. I checked the sun's drop; I judged another two hours before we either had to reach a town or make our own shelter for the night. Days were shorter and nights longer in the far north, Da had taught me, particularly in these cold months of the year.

"Possess him then," Ibbot insisted. He stood fast at the top of the rocks. He was not showing himself to be over good at mountaineering. Likely he was afraid to descend. "Fly out and see where we should go from on high."

I lacked the skill to do that but saw no need to admit it. Let Ibbot read it in me if he could.

Wieser picked her way after me, and I held out a hand for Cilliyon to grab as she chose her path down. "Stay to the left," she called up to Ibbot.

"Do you think Fenn will be gallant and help me, too?"

"I dunno," she snapped. "Are you ever gallant to anybody?"

"Are you ever gallant to anybody?" he mocked in a high voice and gathered his robe about him to start down.

I cut a straight sapling and stripped off the branches. "Use this for a staff, it will help you keep your balance. Your hands will get pitch on them, but I'll scrape the bark off and make it neater tonight. Maybe wrap it in leather at the grip." Cilliyon was who I handed it to, not Ibbot. She was twice the mountaineer he was.

"You'd be wise to try to suit me better," he said when he stood beside us. "You've seen what I can do."

"Knock me flat then. Leave me for dead. You won't last one night in these mountains. It's clear as clear you've never made your way in the wilderness. Creatures are waiting to make you their next meal."

He met my eye for the space of a few breaths, then shifted his head to crack his neck and pointed past me. "Lead on, wise one."

I had to think we would have reached the next town by nightfall in the turnip wagon, but we were so much slower on foot that we came to no other sign of folks before I declared we must make shelter for the night. I chose a rock overhang, and set Ibbot to gathering tinder and small branches, while I collected small logs of downed wood. Cilliyon pulled pine boughs in to make a pallet.

When I directed Ibbot to drag rocks in place to make a fire ring, he placed them under the rock shelf.

"No," I told him when I saw. "The heat from the fire causes this kind of rock to crack. You don't want to be lying under it asleep when a goat-sized chunk pops off to fall on your head."

He looked above him skeptically.

"Move it out here," I scuffed the dirt with my boot in the proper place.

"Won't we be cold? With the fire out there?"

"Just do what I tell you."

I heard him set to shifting them once I turned my back.

We shared the food and water, Gargle and Wieser, too, though Ibbot thought they at least should forage for their own. Cilliyon rolled her eyes and combed tangles from Wieser's coat with her fingers. Annora used to do the same, I remembered.

Night fell hard and fast. It was difficult to judge how high in the mountains we were by the thinness of the air. I was out of condition after my time at sea, and as short of breath as the others. That we were far north showed evident as we gaped at the clearing sky; the dancing lights Cuffer had told me about spun and shimmered in wild profusion above the treetops. I was unable to turn my eyes away and could not help but smile. The lights must be the gods' brand of magic.

I claimed first watch, and grinned to myself hearing Ibbot try to persuade Cilliyon to share body warmth on the pine boughs. "I've no need of you, what with my cloak and Wieser."

"Who got you that cloak?" he grumped, turning his back to her.

She was facing me where I perched on a rock above as look out. She caught my eye and smiled as she pulled the cloak about her. Still smiling, she closed her eyes.

I fed the fire and puttered about to stay awake. Worked on Cilliyon's staff. Gargle came and went as was his wont in nighttime hours. Wolves called from ridge top to ridge top, claiming their territory and the prey within. Other night creatures snuffled and woofed in the darkness. I tried to think of a plan to get to Lohr Island, or at least a plan to get back to somewhere I understood the language. That would be a start of independence, as it chafed me terribly to have to stay stuck to Ibbot because he spoke Yeganil. Lichan did, too, and I would trade one for the other as a companion in the space of a heartbeat.

Cilliyon came to me after a couple of hours, ready to take her spell at watch. She yawned and tried to give me her cloak.

"You'll want it," I said. "It's a damp chill even with the fire."

She looked doubtful. "Wieser's warm but not warm enough by herself, and I can't believe you'll want to cozy up to Ibbot."

"No."

"Have it while I'm on watch, I'll be fine without it."

I took it in the end and was grateful for it. I thought her kind.

I also thought I would be unable to sleep for worrying, but soon dropped off to the soothing rumble of Ibbot's snores. I feared dreams of pursuit by the Scytheran mages might haunt me, but as I had not slept since we left *Moon Road*, I fell deep into untroubled slumber.

How long before I jerked awake to Ibbot's scream, I cannot say. I struggled to my feet from my depth of insensibility, to find him still curled on the boughs. His face was a rictus of horror, but his eyes remained shut tight. Cilliyon came running. I put my hand out to stop her from touching him.

"It is best not to wake them suddenly, from the Night Terrors," I told her.

He threw himself over onto his other side, cried out again and covered his face with an arm, warding off something that lived only in his dream. A ragged sob, a hunch of his shoulders, and he began to rock himself to and fro slightly.

Gargle came to peer at him from above, where a bit of rock projected. He shook out his feathers and called *Grock!* once. Wieser rose and walked over to stretch out beside him, along his back, and he gradually stopped his rocking as he pressed against her shaggy warmth.

I inclined my head toward our lookout perch and picked up Cilliyon's cloak. She walked there with me in silence.

I settled myself on the rock and fed the fire. When I offered her the cloak, she spread it around both our shoulders as she sat beside me. It was large enough.

"Will you wake him to keep watch?"

"No, I think it's better if he sleeps on. He won't recall in the morning. My little sister used to have Night Terrors. She could never say what it was about when she woke."

"Is it the same for mages?"

I raised my shoulders. After another stretch of silence, I asked her, "Where do you want to end up, Cilliyon? I only meant to get you away from the slavers, but I still aim to go to Lohr Island for my part."

"That is where I was supposed to go. To be hidden among the Temple Supplicates. My father arranged it."

"What are you to do once there? Stay until the war is sorted out?"

She nodded. "I don't know anywhere else to go, or anything else to plan to do. May I travel on with you?" At the last, her voice was small again, as if it cost her to ask me.

"Easier to answer if I knew how I was going to make my own way there. And I don't know where Ibbot wants to go, but he is the only one who can speak this country's tongue."

"Do you trust him?"

"No."

"Why did he attack that driver? We could have found another way."

"He was scared. For all his bluster, I think he is the most scared of us all. I don't know what his master will do to him if he's caught, or Kruthe, for that matter. But he knows and he is desperate."

She didn't say anything for a time. When she laid her head on my shoulder and fell asleep, I found I did not mind. I looked out over the valley until dawn crept over the ridge.

CHAPTER NINE

When I woke Ibbot, he made no mention of not taking his turn at watch in the night. He was drawn and irritable, quick to complain about eating the same things as the supper before.

"Can't your bird find us a nest with some eggs?"

"Birds are not nesting this time of year."

"Make some do so with magic. Or what good are you?"

"Enough good not to waste time on nonsense when we need to keep moving."

He bit into his biscuit like a snake striking. I broke the fire apart and scattered the ashes and rock ring. Light snow began to sift through the trees.

"Where do you take us now?" he asked, still sullen.

"We'll continue to skirt the road until we come to clothes or conveyance to steal. When we can do so safely, I want you to obtain some sort of map."

"I'm surprised at you, to be sure. Talking so easily of theft when you took such exception to a simple stunning. Can't we just follow roads or rivers?"

"The folk who live here know their way about, so there may not be many maps easy to hand. Be alert. And realize, roads lead to towns, which lead to officials looking for murderers. Or, I might follow a river to a lake that is miles and miles across, and then what?"

Cilliyon came back from whatever tending to themselves girls are compelled to do off in the bushes behind rocks. She seemed taken aback to find the two of us snarling at each other.

Ibbot was not through complaining. "You need to get shed of your sea bag. It marks you as a sailor. Did I mention that was part of the description the stable grooms gave?"

"You must have forgotten to tell us that particular bit." I could not abandon the bag until I had something else to substitute, because I could not lose my mother's book of magic lore. Nor did I want the others to know I carried it. Not so much Cilliyon, but Ibbot, definitely no.

"We're off," I announced, and shouldered my bag. Cilliyon took up her staff. Ibbot brought up the rear, just behind Wieser.

The snowfall thickened as we walked on. Even so, I was able to see smoke rise from a chimney through the flakes and the trees. A small stone house was tucked back from the road, snow just beginning to coat the slate roof. There was no handy line of drying clothes to choose from, it being ill weather for hanging out the wash. The dwelling was too small, it seemed, to have a separate washhouse such as we had at home. And the smoke curling skyward suggested someone tended the hearth within.

We squatted behind a rock, eyeing the place with growing frustration. I cast about for some plausible excuse we could use for knocking on the door and requesting to come in. Further, how would we get what we needed once we got in?

"I could stun someone," Ibbot offered.

"No!" Cilliyon and I said together.

"Can't you make them look the other way while we sneak in the back and make off with a blanket at least?" I suggested.

"His brand of distraction didn't work so well with the muleteer," Cilliyon said.

"It worked fine right up until I fell out of the wagon, since no one caught me. And how do you know there *is* a back door?"

"Anybody who lives in the mountains has a back door—what if a bear comes in the front door? You have to be able to get out another way."

There was only one small window. It was covered with oiled sheepskin rather than glass; some light would pass through but I couldn't look in to see how many people were inside.

"Wieser," I said. She wagged her tail. "Go and bark at the door until someone comes." She trotted off around the rock at once.

"What if they shoot her? They might think she's a mad dog, after all."

"Anybody who lives out in the country would know it's the wrong time of year for Water Fear in animals. That comes in the hot months."

He had no retort for that, because it was perfectly true. I watched Wieser set up her racket on the stoop. She could be loud as loud when I wanted her to be.

When the door opened a crack, she leapt about happily and bowed down, acting like a pup. I hoped it made her size and shaggy black coat less threatening. When she rolled over and showed her belly, the door swung wide and an old woman stepped out.

She bent over Wieser and petted her, tolerating the swipes of the pink tongue. And slick as that, my dog was invited inside.

"What now?" Cilliyon asked.

"We wait a short while and come inquiring for my lost dog. Or Ibbot will, since he can be understood. We'll sneak in while they are talking."

"I hate to steal from an old lady."

"Who may have a big son with an axe, you might think about that," Ibbot put in.

"I do not know what it would be like to have a perfect plan. Maybe either of you have one of those to tell us about?"

When I judged we had waited in the swirling snowflake eddies long enough, I sent Ibbot to the front door. Cilliyon and I slipped around the back keeping to the trees that crowded close.

There was a back door. Not so foreign a land after all. For I confess, I had begun to doubt my mountain lore applied in this country as it did at home.

Cilliyon cleared her throat. "I'm not going to knock an old woman in the head, just so you understand that."

To distract the girl, I said, "Did you notice how she wore a scarf over her hair? We need one of those for you, to hide your shorn hair. I hope the lady has more than one."

"I won't stand by for you to hit her over the head, either. Or Ibbot to curse her or stun her or whatever he does."

"None of those is my first choice. I have had to do things before now I might not have wanted to do, though. Just so *you* understand."

That at least silenced her. We slunk up to the back of the house.

The latch was a simple one, probably only barred at night if then. I hustled us inside behind a table and crouched low, while I peered around the edge looking toward Ibbot and the woman. I saw them at the hearth, Ibbot with his unbooted feet to the merry flames, smiling while the lady of the house poured him a hot drink from the steaming kettle she held over his mug. Wieser was curled at his knee.

He caught sight of me and said, "My friends will arrive soon, or—" and then he must have repeated it in Yeganil. The woman nodded and gabbled at him, very jolly. When she shifted aside to hang the kettle back on the iron arm, he waved us off furiously, turning it into a scratch of his ear when she swung round to him again.

Cilliyon and I retreated, slipped out the back the way we had come. *Off to the front, I suppose.*

"It seems he can be charming when he has to be," Cilliyon said.

"I wouldn't get used to it. We'd better play mute." I knocked on the door.

The hospitable lady opened it wide at once and ushered us in. Ibbot stood sipping from his cup. He motioned toward us and said something she understood. Probably that we lacked wits, because she then elaborately mimed taking off our cloaks and hanging them by the fire. Then she acted out holding a bowl and spooning food, while her eyes sparkled.

We nodded and clasped our hands before us to signify thanks. At least, I hoped the meaning was the same as at home.

Ibbot conferred with his newfound friend and pointed at Cilliyon. I saw him make the usual man's gesture with his hands depicting a woman's curves, then shake his head sadly. The old woman *tsk'ed* gently and came to take Cilliyon by the hand. She rubbed gnarly fingers through the short fair curls drying by the firelight. She held up a bent finger, meaning *wait* or *I have an idea* perhaps? She led the girl behind a blanket draped across a corner of the one-room home.

I looked hard at Ibbot, but he only met my gaze with raised eyebrows. After a short time Cilliyon emerged—though if I had not seen her go in, I would not have known her coming out.

She wore a plainspun skirt and bodice laced over a loose-sleeved blouse. Evidently her binding had been removed, because there was no mistaking her gender in her new clothes. She dropped her eyes and flushed prettily when Ibbot and I stared.

Our hostess clapped her hands in delight and set about dishing up beans and dark bread for us. There seemed to be a large amount of food for one old woman to fix for herself … if no one else was expected. I tried to catch Ibbot's eye, but he had them both fastened on Cilliyon.

The lady chatted to him, but he responded with few words. Snow continued. If we were not going to move in here with the old one, we needed to walk to the town, now that we were so clearly not a party of three young men and a dog. When our bowls were empty, and I had waved off another helping and glared at Ibbot until he did the same, Cilliyon rose to offer help with the clearing away. The old woman demurred, apparently, but Cilliyon followed her to the basin and stood to one side.

Once the lady set to clattering bowls and spoons, I moved close to Ibbot. "What have you told her?"

"Cilliyon and I are running away to be wed, fleeing from her father who opposes the match. You are her brother, helping her to escape with her true love. Thus, she was disguised as a boy! Brilliant, yes?"

It seemed to have appealed to the old lady, right enough. Cilliyon would be less pleased. "We need to leave, be on our way. Why did she have enough food for a harvest crew?"

"Ah, that. Her two sons are coming from town to collect her, since the storm is predicted to grow much harsher. We can ride in with them!" He beamed at me, looking as delighted as I had ever seen my little sister Morie look when she was getting her own way.

I grew restless as I watched the snow accumulate ever deeper, thinking the storm must be the start of this mountain range's true winter season. Likely soon it would be as at home, with ground completely buried, not visible until spring thaw. We had picked the worst time of all to travel.

Was it not also the worst time to pursue fugitives, as well? There was that … perhaps the pirates and the lawmen would give us up as surely lost in the bitter mountain winter.

If only we could avoid that becoming the truth of the matter.

At last, a wagon drew into the yard, driven by two broad-built men who did look as if they could handily wield axes against intruders, per Ibbot's earlier remark. They proved as jovial as their mother, however. First one and then the other clapped Ibbot on the back. Each pumped his hand until I thought his arm might part company with his shoulder. They held their hats in their hands while shyly bobbing their great wooly heads to Cilliyon.

She had not yet been advised of her imminent joining ceremony, so curtsied back, looking mystified. It was difficult to believe she had been able to pass as a boy so readily, watching her now in a skirt behaving utterly girlish with fellows buzzing around her. Despite her confusion, I could see she enjoyed their attention. I busied myself with watching the old lady put out her fire and prepare to leave the house. I knew something about such tasks, but she would not accept my help.

It seemed from all they did getting ready to vacate that she was expected to stay in town, perhaps for the entire winter season. She had packed all her clothes and sundries, leaving only enough food and fuel that a desperate traveler might escape death from freezing and starvation if he happened upon the place. She left a note on the hearth, explaining her absence. Or so I surmised, being unable to read it.

If she kept animals on the place, they had been settled in town earlier by the sons. I was put strongly in mind of my time helping our neighbor Virda, Lichan's mother, escape with me into the mountains when the Keltanese invasion threatened. I missed my home.

While the two hulking sons ate their share of beans and bread, I put

Cilliyon's galley boy clothing into my bag. Tunic and trousers I expected, but wadded within the pile was a long length of flannel about a hand span in width. This I shoved in hurriedly, once I realized it was her bindings.

The sons helped their mother down the path to the wagon, despite that she seemed plenty spry to my view. The snow came nearly knee deep, though light and airy. The wagon was roofed and cozy within, stocked with warmed rocks and heavy woolen blankets to cover us. The old lady shook her finger at Ibbot when he tried to settle next to Cilliyon and draw a blanket over the two of them. Admonishing him to behave himself, it appeared. She put me beside Ibbot and pointedly tucked Cilliyon under the same blanket with her. Cilliyon gave Ibbot a questioning look and he grinned wide.

I wanted to be present when he explained his ruse to her.

Wieser wedged herself between Ibbot and me, while the old one's sons rode on the seat out in the blowing snow. Gargle clung to the top of the wagon voicing continual opposition to the entire enterprise, or else just complaining about the weather.

CHAPTER TEN

As daylight faded, we rolled into a town built of thick logs. Men walked to and fro with pickaxes and shovels on their shoulders, their faces streaked with black grime in contrast to the stark white of the swirling snow. Pony carts trundled up and down the street. I wondered about the reason for the small size of the rigs.

We arrived at a rambling house on the main road, much larger than Guthy's rooms-to-let for old seamen where I had stayed in Bale Harbour. We were greeted by a young woman with cheeks red as apples, and the rest of her apple-round too, who embraced the old woman and helped her up the steps. We followed.

I could see no way around Ibbot translating for me at this point. Still, being helpless to glean meaning from his chatter to our hosts and theirs back to him made me feel too much at disadvantage. I told him in Mercedish to tell me what they were saying, and he began to keep up a running account in brief asides. I would not say he looked happy to be yielding his control of all the information—so I reminded myself to be alert for signs he was not telling me true.

I wondered how long it might take me to come to some fluency in Yeganil.

The old woman's name was Yuli Ingnaf, and her son Hengel was the husband of Kunitka, the young woman. The large home was a boarding house; unmarried miners rented rooms and ate at the dozen trestle tables by the hearth. The young couple ran the place and Yuli would spend the winter months with them, helping in the kitchen.

I supposed the other son, Piet, to be one of the miners. I was wrong about that, as it happened, though he did live at the boarding house. The story of the young lovers was told again with embellishments from Ibbot, judging from the length of the discourse and the starry eyes of Kunitka.

Of course, we must stay, at least to wait out the storm and keep safe. If other folk came hunting us, our hosts all would deny having seen anyone of the kind. We were given more hot drinks and some sort of sweet bread with crunchy, savory seeds in the dough. I asked Ibbot to compliment the cook, which brought yet more color to Kunitka's bright cheeks.

Yuli had customary winter rooms on the lower floor with her son and his wife. The boys had unloaded her belongings while we sat at the fire. I had wanted to be useful and help, but Ibbot said they considered it rude for guests to do household work. He might have only wanted to avoid the job himself, for I had never heard of such custom. I had never been in Yega before either, so I let it rest.

Kunitka escorted us up the stairs, to the rooms we would use while we stayed with them. Few empty rooms, she said apologetically via Ibbot, so we could not each have our own.

First, she opened a door to a tiny room tucked under the eaves. It contained a narrow bed and a small table with a candlestick and pipe rest. The windowpanes bore frost on the inside.

Ibbot apparently thought this the ideal place for the soon-to-be-bride's brother to sleep, since he pointed at me. Kunitka shook her head. I could tell from the twist of his mouth that the next remark she made told him it was his room.

She led the way down to the other end of the hall, to a more spacious room with a larger mattress. I tried hard not to smile, since Cilliyon still had not been told the rebellious lovers tale. Ibbot had not yet revealed the ruse to her, and he did not do so now, either. Instead, he engaged in a brief intense conference with our landlady. Which did not satisfy him, judging from his continued downcast features.

Kunitka took her leave after showing us the communal washroom and handing us each a rough grey towel. She waved happily as she headed below stairs.

"Just what is going on?" Cilliyon said. There was more ice in the hallway than outdoors, all from her tone.

Choking back a laugh, I told her Ibbot's fabrication about running away with her to be wed. "That seems to be why they are all so pleased to aid us."

She crossed her arms and narrowed her eyes at Ibbot. "And the room arrangements?"

"If we could not all have our own, I thought you should be alone and I should share with Fenn," he tried.

"I can see what you thought. You pointed at Fenn by the little room."

"Now, hold on. I told her when I saw the second room that it should go for Fenn and me. But evidently, it is not considered fitting in this country for an unmarried girl to lodge alone. Being with a male member of her family ensures her virtue, so Kunitka explained."

I couldn't help smiling now. "I guess you should have said you had already married her then, when you came up with your tale."

Cilliyon jabbed a finger my way. "Just you stop smirking, and right now, too! Why boys have to be so exasperating I'm sure I don't know. I hope you will like the floor with Wieser." She turned on her heel, went into our room and closed the door with a solid kick.

"Gods know I do give it my best effort," Ibbot sighed. At my look of inquiry, he added, "To be exasperating." He whistled as he sauntered to the washroom.

Left standing with my bag and my dog in the hall, I decided Cilliyon might at least let me put the bag in the room. I knocked on the door.

"Who is it?"

"Who d'you think? Could I just hand you my bag? Then I'll go away somewhere."

"Somewhere far away?"

"I was thinking maybe down to the hearth room. Where do you want me to go?"

She pulled the door open. "I'll give it some thought." She held out her hand to take the bag's strap. "It's more him I'm mad at."

She acted as if I should say something in answer to that. "He just likes to keep the pot stirred. Pay him no mind."

Not the sentiment she was hoping for, I could see from the way her lips tightened. *Well, how should I know what you wanted to hear?* When she turned away and shut the door, I clumped down the stairs with Wieser. There, I took up a bench by the fire.

I spent some time trying to eavesdrop and pick out words I could construe the meaning of by context and repetition. Such as, what Hengel called Yuli several times must mean mum or mother. Kunitka came by with firewood to add to the stack on the fireplace hearth. By the gods, it went hard with me not to offer to carry it for her. She did not seem to expect me to, though. Perhaps Ibbot was being truthful about a local custom of refusing help from guests.

Kunitka offered me a clay pipe from the mantle and I wondered if it was rude to decline. She opened a tin of sweet pipeweed for me to pack in it and even pulled out a glowing twig from the fire and lit it for me. Perhaps in Yega women waited on all men this way, or perhaps she did so because I was her guest.

I didn't actually smoke, had never tried it, but I went through the motions I had seen my da do a hundred times and more. She seemed satisfied I was enjoying it.

I pointed to her and said, "Kunitka." She nodded and smiled, repeating her name in agreement. I pointed at myself and very nearly said "Judian" before I remembered I was using Da's given name. "Fenn," I said. She repeated this as well, with a lovely lilt to her voice.

She then went around the immediate fireside laying her hand on the bench, the hearthstones, the mantle, the firewood, Wieser, a table, and tapping the floorboard with her foot while giving the word for each, until I laughed and held up my hand. I repeated the words back to her fairly well. She shook my hand and went back to the kitchen humming.

I ran through the terms several times, trying to fix them in my mind. Morie had seemed to have no difficulty picking up a rough Keltanese vocabulary last spring, but I suspected learning language to be easier when the learner was younger rather than grown. Little Yegan children probably spoke Yeganil with no trouble at all.

Piet came in beating snow from his shoulders and shaking off his fur cap. He said something I took to be about the conditions out of doors, but since none of the words had been included in my schooling at the fireside, I could only smile in vague apology and shrug. He didn't seem offended, just inclined his head to me and walked toward the kitchen calling for Hengel.

Ibbot wandered into the keeping room. He hailed Piet and asked a question to which he received a long-winded response. Several more comments were exchanged before Hengel came in from the kitchen, then he joined the two of them in the discussion.

I really had to learn to understand them if we were to be in Yega any time at all. I did not even have any idea how large a country this was from my lessons with Da, or how long it might take to traverse. He had focused instruction closer to Merced and neighboring Keltane rather than across the world altogether.

When the brothers went to the kitchen, Ibbot walked over to me.

"How angry is your sister?"

"The wedding may be in jeopardy," I said. "What news did Piet carry in?"

"He has been out checking on the surrounding farmsteads and bringing folk into town if they will come. He says the pass will close to the west by nightfall and there is a great risk of avalanche along the road east. We may be snowed in here for a lengthy time."

I had been snowed in at home many stretches of mountain winter. We prepared for it each year, as it seemed the folk here did also. Again, I reassured myself: if we were prevented from leaving here, so were pursuers prevented from reaching us. "Surely more than that was said?"

"The name of our haven is Lunenhelm. Mining continues here year-round, but they are seldom able to ship the ore to be smelted, whatever smelting entails, once the winter comes, so they pile it up at the edge of town. The piles are huge by spring."

'Why don't they just leave it under the ground in the mine until spring?" The sound of a heavy bell ringing carried in on the wind. Wieser pricked an ear where she lay at my feet.

"Some of the mines must be worked continually due to flooding. Their pumps have to be kept running. Not all of them are prone to flood, he said. Why they work the other mines all year, I have no idea." He rubbed his neck. "It sounds like brutal work to me. Did you see the miners walking around town? Filthy. Soon a hoard of them will descend on Kunitka to be fed. They will clean up and sleep and go back into the earth again tomorrow. There are others who rouse from their beds to clamber under the ground and carry on working through the night. I don't wonder any longer why all the towels are grey, having seen the miners."

"What are they mining?"

"Metal ore, copper I think, some others I am not familiar with. Somewhere there must be a coal vein, because I've seen that being burned for heat like they burn peat at home."

"Peat? Where is your home, Ibbot?"

He regarded me evenly for a moment, his features still. "It doesn't matter," he said at last. "I'm long away from there."

I knew precious little about Scythera. Did they burn this peat there for heat? I debated whether now was the time to ask him directly if he was a Scytheran mage. Perhaps many countries had master mages and young mages in training. Perhaps being bought and sold as he had claimed to be was a common thing.

The brothers piled on yet thicker furs and left again. Ibbot said they were still rounding up folk to shelter from the storm. The wind had certainly risen fierce, shrieking through the streets and rattling the windowpanes. We were lucky both in our quarters and in our new friends, I thought.

"Why are the Ingnaf brothers in charge of fetching everyone in from the weather? Or is there a group of men out there working together?"

Kunitka came in to lay a bulky dark cloth on the floor by the outer door. I expected the miners would place their dirty wet boots on it when they came in. Rank on rank of hooks had been hammered into the wall for cloaks and furs.

Ibbot went over to ask her my question about her husband and brother-in-law and the rescue effort.

As they spoke, I again heard a bell toll over the rushing wail of the wind. Not long after, men began to stamp up the porch steps and through the doorway, shedding their boots and lining them up on Kunitka's cloth. The snow-coated outerwear they hung on the hooks began to drip at once in the warmth of the hearth room. Only half the hooks were taken when the procession ended. I surmised the night workers were already in place underground. Wieser watched the miners curiously, sniffing the air.

They were not rowdy like sailors. Most trudged to the stairs and said little. Many nodded to Kunitka, some to Ibbot and me as well, but they seemed largely worn down by their day's work. It must be brutal hard, as Ibbot had said.

Ibbot himself did not look too lively when he returned to me at the fireside. He was pale and twitchy, and fidgeted with his tunic laces.

"What is it?" I asked.

"It seems Piet Ingnaf is not a miner and does not run the boarding house with his brother. He is in charge of public safety during the storm because he is the town constable. The law."

CHAPTER ELEVEN

"Now what should we do? Should we leave at once?" Cilliyon paced between the window and the bed, knuckles white across clenched fists.

I shook my head. "That would be foolish. We can't leave unnoticed. They have saved us from the storm and given us every sort of comfort. There would be more questions if we went than if we stay."

"Fenn is right about that. Not to mention, we would die in the attempt to flee." Ibbot had recovered his cocksure demeanor since the shock downstairs. He lounged on the coverlet with his hands behind his head.

"Keep your voice down," I cautioned him. I had left the door open, since I was fairly certain the groom was not supposed to be shut in a room with the prospective bride even if the brother was present. "And besides, if the town is cut off, how is Piet going to hear anything about us from the coast?"

"I'm growing to feel this is just a bit of irony we will recount to our many children," Ibbot told Cilliyon.

"You'll die unshriven if you wait for a child of ours to tell your tale to."

He bared his teeth at her, in a way that could not be counted a smile.

I felt pleased for some reason to have her reject him at every turn, probably because I still didn't trust him. "We are supposed to eat after the miners, with the family. We should just go down and act exactly as we have been. Can you do that?"

Cilliyon nodded. She hesitated, then stamped her foot and said, "I want you to think of a reason I can't be married off to Ibbot while we're stuck here. Yuli and Kunitka keep shaking their heads and clucking their tongues at me, petting me as if I was a poor mewly kitten. I think they would just love to have a wedding to break up the boredom of being snowbound." She glared at Ibbot when he grinned all the wider.

"Well," I said, "of course you cannot be married until we reach … your—I mean *our*—uncle at the temple where he is Dedicate. He will be the one to celebrate the joining, so that our father will accept it."

"Where are you going to say that is?" Ibbot wanted to know. "Plus, how are you certain anyone in these parts is of the same religion as that?"

"Don't you know?"

"I told you, I've never been here before."

"But you speak the language," Cilliyon said.

"I've been to the *country* before. Just never to this icy, forsaken part of it."

"What I heard earlier sounded like temple bells tolling." I looked out the window but could see nothing save white and more white.

He shook his head. "That is how they mark the change of shifts at the mines, I'm told."

I waved a hand. "We are going to say we are waiting to reach our uncle before the marriage can take place. You," I pointed at Ibbot, "find a way to come by a map and we'll decide where that uncle lives, besides east."

Neither of them argued, for a wonder. We went downstairs as soon as we heard miners beginning to make their way up to their rooms after their meal.

We found Yuli and Kunitka clearing bowls and cutlery. I asked Ibbot again if we might help, but he shook his head and sat by the fire. "Women's work," he said dismissively.

Where I came from, women's work was birthing. The growing, preserving of foodstuff and feeding of folk was not just for women, but something an entire family shared in, men, women and children alike. Everyone was expected to do a share.

Nevertheless, Cilliyon and I joined him at the hearth. "Won't it be dark soon? Are Piet and Hengel back yet?" she said, looking toward the kitchen doors.

"I was upstairs with you both, so I know no more than you."

"I think she was suggesting you ask the ladies, Ibbot."

He levered himself out of his chair with a put-upon air and walked over to them. He shortly returned to report they would have to be returning soon, because even with lanterns, they could not see to follow the road since all was covered over so deeply.

Before long, a great bustle erupted when the brothers arrived with a host of rescued travelers, discovered half-frozen on the road from the west. Hot blankets, hot drinks and hot food were all doled out in quantity. A family of lumbermen, a father and five sons, had been overtaken by the storm on their way deeper into the forests. A young miner with his wife, tiny babe and two small sons had been stranded when their wagon slipped off the track and snapped an axle.

To make an even dozen rescued, Piet and Hengel carried a final traveler inside to the fire. He had not spoken or moved, but breathed quite regular, reported the lumbermen. They had discovered him in a wagon bed along the way and didn't like to leave him.

It was the muleteer.

Ibbot backed toward the kitchen. I took Cilliyon's hand and followed him. If he'd thought we would find privacy there because of all the activity in the hearth room, he was disappointed.

Yuli threw up her hands at the sight of us, in apparent distress that we had not been fed yet. She chivvied us into sturdy chairs at the table near the kitchen fire. Still gabbling, she thrust bowls of thick sausage and parsnip soup with dumplings in front of us, and a loaf of bark-brown bread on a wooden board. She handed me a hard cheese along with a gleaming knife to slice it and told Ibbot we must feel free to start without the rest of them, since we were guests.

As it might be the last meal we would have, should the mule driver wake and tell who we were and what we had done, I began at once. I burned my mouth on a too-hot spoonful. Cilliyon just looked at her food, but Ibbot was like-minded to me and broke bread eagerly.

Wieser sat on the floor beside me. Kunitka gave her a generous amount of bread and gravy with a cooked egg mixed in. I was pleased she seemed to be viewed as valuable. No one had suggested I put her in a stable. Thus, she would be handy if we fled.

Where Gargle was riding out the storm, I didn't know. Should we decide to run, he would find me.

Yuli continued to race around the kitchen, while Kunitka came and went with armfuls of food or clothes. At each encounter, the women said the same words; I imagined it was some version of "My, oh my, what a night this is!" in Yeganil.

Ibbot mused quietly, "They will have to adjust the sleeping arrangements. For decency. The young mother and baby will probably be put in with you, Cilliyon. The little boys with their father somewhere else, as well as the family of woodsmen together. Being all male." He tapped his front teeth with his spoon.

"What are you thinking?" I asked.

"That you and I will be shifted out of our places and might volunteer to stay by the hearth here on the lower floor, if the injured man is to be kept by the fire for the night."

"Why?" Cilliyon said a little too loudly. Yuli turned her way.

I handed Cilliyon the bread as if that was what she had asked for and gave her a quelling look besides.

Ibbot continued, "So we know if he wakes up. And if he does wake and says he knows us, we can claim he is confused by his ordeal and talking out of his head."

"Not remembering us from before, but thinking he's seen us out there because he saw us during the night here," I said, nodding.

"It sounds plausible, don't you think?"

Perhaps. The driver had not seemed a man given to confusion before Ibbot stunned him, though. Who could say how he might act if he did wake now?

"I leave it to you to get us set for the hearth, if as you say, that is where he will be tended."

"It might be better if only one of us was there, so as not to jog his memory. By seeing the pair of us together again, you see."

Something about his tone prickled at me. "Which of us do you suggest?"

"You, Fenn," Cilliyon said at once. She kept her eyes on Ibbot's face.

For his part, he now used his spoon to trace circles in the broth at the bottom of his bowl, unconcerned. "I'm not sure it matters, really. I don't mind doing it. Unless you truly want to."

"Tell them I have a little skill as a healer." I did, though I had not learned much, and as I had said at the time Ibbot stunned the man, I did not know what to do for that.

He didn't answer, just inclined his head and rose to go back to the hearth room.

"He's up to something," Cilliyon said as she watched him slip through the door while Kunitka came in.

"Yes, but what? If he stays down here, I'll make sure I do as well."

Kunitka sorted out the changes without disturbing the now slumbering miners. They had to be fresh for the morning, it seemed. It played out as Ibbot had guessed, with Cilliyon sharing with the mother and infant, and himself booted out of the tiny room under the eaves so the miner and two young sons could sleep there. The family of lumbermen, who had brought the driver in, laid pallets next to the hearth. Ibbot and I were settled on blanket-draped chairs close by, with the muleteer between us on two benches lashed together.

Ibbot must have said something about me caring for him, because Piet opened the blankets so I could look him over. I asked questions about how and where he had been found, not betraying I knew anything about the circumstances, with Ibbot translating.

The man showed frostbite of his feet, hands, ears and nose. I had seen a lesser amount on Gevarr, the Keltanese soldier we found at our farm after the invasion. I had watched my brother's wife treat him throughout his healing and knew what to do. Slow warming was best, in tepid water. Yuli agreed, judging from the haste with which she brought me a wide bowlful.

Ibbot sat back, eyes hooded, expression unusually still. Kunitka lit him a pipe and he thanked her graciously, but mostly allowed the smoke to curl away without puffing on the stem.

It came to me to wonder what Ibbot could do to the man with magic, while sitting there appearing to do nothing.

And what could I do to stop him?

How could he be such a wood wit as to do anything to the muleteer under the very nose of the local lawman? Piet struck me as no one's fool.

The driver's injuries would not be paining him until the blood came back into the dying flesh. Then they would burn him brutally, and the pain might rouse him when slowly freezing had not done so. I should not plan to sleep tonight, lest Ibbot have concocted a plan to act at the first sign of wakening in my charge.

Cilliyon came downstairs to see how we fared. She pressed my moonstone pendant into my hand, making sure Ibbot could not see. I thought the slavers must surely have taken it from her, though I had never asked. I had not noted it around her neck in her new blouse. Not that I had been looking at her throat, or anyplace else, either.

What to do with it? Put it on myself? Put it on the driver in hopes it could protect him from Ibbot? How did the Yegans feel about magic and magical works? Such was not accepted everywhere, just as worship of the Five was not the only faith. I had heard many peoples feared the power of mages or thought them evil.

And some were evil, so I knew from experience. In the end, I slipped the pendant over my own head when Ibbot was gazing into the fire and made sure it lay obscured within my tunic.

I soaked the muleteer's feet and hands in turn. The forest axe men were talking with Piet, holding out belongings I realized must be the driver's. They had gone through his pockets and wagon, any baggage, I supposed, trying to figure out who he was and what had befallen him. A pipe, a loop of rope, smoke-weed pouch, a bag of stones for gaming in taverns, a flint for striking sparks to light a fire. A wicked-looking skinning knife, for game and whatever else he might need to slice or slash. I did not see the crossbow he had aimed at me among the items.

I noted his water flask in a woodsman's hand. We had the other one, could it be identified as being the partner of this one? The one we had borrowed was in my bag and I resolved to get rid of it at the earliest opportunity.

There was not a scrap of paper at all, no writing of any sort. I found this good—he had not been given a written description of the fugitives at the port city gate. If he came to with memory of what he had been told, words would be easier to dispute or discount than an official writing.

It also meant there was no way of knowing his name, who he was or if he had family somewhere who would want to know what had happened to him. I wondered what had been done with the hobbled mule team. One of the forester's sons drew a turnip out of his pocket and held it out. He said something to Piet that I expect described the cargo they had found him lying in. That might be one way to trace him. I had some of those same turnips in my bag as well, but I did not think turnips could be considered distinctive. Not like a waterflask might be …

Piet found a cloth sack of sufficient size to hold all the items and tied off the neck of it. He slung it over his back and went off to the rear of the house, in the direction of the family's rooms. So, he did live at the boarding house with his brother and his wife. We were truly in the headquarters of the law for the whole town. Virtually anyplace else would have been better to be weather-bound.

Yuli brought me soft cloths to dry the driver's feet and hands. Hengel came sipping a steaming cup, watched for a little time, and told something to Ibbot while pointing at me. Ibbot roused himself to translate. "He says they have no healer at present, the last being an old man who passed over a year ago. He wonders if you might look at some other folk who have been in need, while you are waylaid here."

"Tell him I will be glad to try, but be sure he understands, I am not a trained healer. I have only learned some lore from my brother's bride."

"I'd better leave off the part about your brother's lady, or you'll confuse our fleeing lovers' tale with too many relatives."

I smiled and nodded to Hengel. "As you say. Just do not make them expect too much."

"Yours is a queer sort of magic," he said, before turning to Hengel.

I did not know what he meant, since to my mind I was not using any magic on the man's frostbite. Only warmed water. Although, when I looked closer, the surface of the water seemed to move in the reflected firelight in some ... unexpected way. Coming together and parting throughout the bowl, though nothing touched it at all. Curious, almost living shapes. The bowl was rock steady on the floor.

I frowned at the sight. And raised my eyes to find Ibbot watching me with a faint smile playing about his mouth. He turned to face the crackling fire.

CHAPTER TWELVE

E ventually, the rushing tumult of storm rescue ebbed low. The woodsmen took to their pallets, the Ingnaf family to their beds. Ibbot claimed one fireside chair and I took the other next to the still unconscious driver.

The storm raged and roared against the outer walls. "You're a weather worker. Can't you do anything to influence the weather here?"

"This is beyond my skill. I deal with ocean currents and winds."

"Hmm." I remembered the freezing mist he'd created at the harbour. "Did they plan to leave him here by the fire? Or did you ask them to?"

"I told them you wanted him left on the benches here."

"Best you get some rest now. I'll watch him."

I banked the fire while he settled a blanket around his shoulders. The family certainly had plenty of blankets, woven of soft, long-strand wool. I wanted to see the sheep that gave it, for it was very fine. I wrapped my blanket around myself in my turn.

I would have liked to read my small folio of healing magic by the firelight, to refresh my mind before Hengel brought me ill folk on the morrow. Yet I misliked to pull it out. For some reason I could not name, beyond mistrust, I did not want Ibbot to see it. Certainly, I more so did not want him to see my mother's thick book of magic, still wrapped within my sea bag. I suspected he would have no trouble reading all of it. I had a sense it would give him power over me if he knew of my book and the lore within.

So instead, I brooded and picked mats out of Wieser's coat. She thumped her tail on the floor gratefully. I only barely heard a rapping at the window, over the moans and howls of the wind. When I rose to open it, for I knew who had come calling, no one else stirred beside the hearth.

A cascade of snow accompanied Gargle through the gap and I shut the window just as his tail feathers cleared the sill. He shook himself elaborately, gave a look as if to say, "Mean night, you see?" and flew to stand on the hearthstones as close to the red coals as he dared.

"Take care you don't singe your feathers, or the stink will be awful."

He paid no mind. Typical for him.

While I kept a close eye, Ibbot made no move against the driver that I could detect. In fact, he was soon snoring. I could rather the muleteer had not turned up where we were sheltering, but for my part, I had not wanted him dead on the road and did not want him dead now, either. He was only a threat to us if he woke. And if he remembered. He might linger the rest of his days in his insensible state, which could be a kindness if he was destined to lose his feet and hands. Who would care for him, in such dire condition? How would he eat?

I was lost in such thoughts when the driver moaned softly and shuddered. I stood over him to find his eyes still closed, but he stretched his arms and shifted his legs while I watched.

Ibbot appeared at my side. "Unwelcome change in your charge?"

"He's likely beginning to get the feeling back, so the pain is starting."

"But you can do something to relieve him, yes? So he rests quietly." His voice, despite being soft, was heavy with suggestion.

"If he wakes and sees us and says we caused his troubles, we claim he is addled. That is as far as I will go. If I relieve his pain it will not be out of self interest." I did not look at Ibbot as I spoke, but made my voice carry weight equal to his.

He looked at the surrounding tree cutters, who slept on. The coals hissed and a spark popped onto the hearth, to die on the flagstone. He scuffed it away with his boot.

"Have it your way, if you feel you must. But realize, there is nowhere to run if you have misread these people, who you know so little."

Yah, he knew them more, perhaps, speaking their language. But he valued them little. I suspected him of valuing all others well below himself.

In the wee hours, the driver roused enough to cry out from the pain. I brewed the ameliorating herbs I carried in my waist pouch and had Ibbot help me hold him up so I could press the mug to his lips. He was not really aware, with eyes closed and wits elsewhere, so he choked and dribbled most of it out. I had to resort to a twisted cloth to dribble the potion into his mouth while Ibbot, with a long-suffering expression, held the jaws apart. I then tipped the muleteer's head back and stroked his throat to get a few mouthfuls down him, and he rested again, whimpering now and then.

"Seems a great deal more trouble than what I had in mind," Ibbot said when we were through. I did not comment.

It was still dark when Yuli and Kunitka came in to stoke the fire and start the day's work in the kitchen. Yuli nodded approvingly after sniffing the pot of herbs and looking over my charge.

After the miners had all been fed and catapulted out into the blinding white morning, accompanied by Gargle, the night workers dragged in and had their meal before climbing the stairs to sleep. We ate with the other refugees in the kitchen, once the boarders were finished. Cilliyon had also slept in snatches, for the baby was fretting with teeth, the mother told us through Ibbot. I resolved to work all the harder on learning to speak and understand for myself.

I begged to rest my eyes for a bit before Hengel rounded up the folk he wanted me to heal. Cilliyon sat by the drowsing muleteer with Ibbot hunched on the arm of a chair nearby. *He puts me in mind of a vulture*, I thought as I fell into hard sleep.

I woke to see a dozen folk of disparate ages sitting on the benches in the common room. All stared at me as if I were some rare sort of plant that had sprung up in amongst the beans and cabbages in the garden. I shook my head to clear it and asked Ibbot to tell them I would go up and wash my face before starting to see to them.

"What d'you mean? I'm no part of this scheme."

"How am I going to ask them what the trouble is? And understand the answers?"

"You can tell by looking, surely. They live in a horrid place and so feel wretched. Give them pain potion and send them on their way."

"Do what I tell you. You need their goodwill too, depending on how things play out."

That gave him pause. "I suppose I've nothing else demanding my attention at present."

"I thought not."

At the outset, I saw four old miners. They no longer worked below ground, but the years in the dust and the lamp soot had made their chests stiff and clogged with stale air. The worst one had blue fingertips and labored as hard to breathe as he said he had once labored with a shovel and pick. I gave them what I had of lungwort for their use at home and advised all of them to make sure their flues drew well, since wood smoke would aggravate the coughing fits that afflicted them. It was only plain sense, but they acted as if I was wise indeed.

The mother with itchy chewed-up children needed to stuff all her mattresses with fleabane, anyone should know that. I didn't have enough of it for her needs, for her house must be fair crawling, but I had enough she could see what it was and find more come spring. In the meantime, I told her to throw out all the old straw and ticking and start over with fresh. I expected her to balk, but she kissed my hand instead. I swore I itched after that.

I had to give some more potion to the driver when he became restless. This time Kunitka came to help hold him. Ibbot hung back. The man still didn't open his eyes, though.

One young miner waited for his turn. The bone in his upper arm had been badly broken and badly set. It was healing awry and would be of no good use to him for the rest of his life unless tended. "I have no skill with bones, tell him he will have to go to a city where it will be put to rights."

"What will they do there?"

"Break it again and line it out better. Keep it strapped straight while it knits together."

Ibbot grimaced. "Perhaps I won't tell him that part."

The man accepted that I couldn't fix it, without showing too much distress. He had to use his good arm to pull his cloak over the damaged side and it clearly pained him to move it. His clothes drooped on him, as if he had been going hungry. I bade Ibbot ask him how long ago he had been injured.

"In summer. He can no longer work in the mine, so has no money for food. Charity runs thinner in the winter months, he says."

"Take him through to Kunitka. Ask her to find him something to do one-armed—sweep or carry a water bucket. So he can earn some meals."

Ibbot seemed about to complain, then shrugged and led him away to the kitchen. When he returned, I waved the next one forward.

She was an old woman, not as vigorous as Yuli, who had a sore jaw. I peered in her mouth to find a boil on her upper gum, above a fragment of broken tooth. I asked for something to make her a bit drunk, which Hengel fetched with a mystified grin. After I packed numbing nettle into the socket I settled the old dear by the fire with her cup. "Tell her to drink it up. Ask Hengel for a tool from the smithy. They surely have one here? I need the tool they use to pull horseshoes."

Ibbot winced. "I believe I will be needed somewhere else for that interlude."

"Think again. You'll have to help hold her."

I put salve on the burned arm of a very pretty girl. She had unusual eyes, the color of violets. I told her I should check her arm again the following day, as I wrapped a bandage around it.

Ibbot snorted a bit and translated my instructions to return.

"What?" I said. "It's a deep burn."

Next, I cleaned a festered sore on a genial fellow's ankle. He'd been trod on by one of the mine ponies. "He says he has not been a swift healer in the past few years," Ibbot reported. I had the man open his mouth and smelled his breath, asked him if he was thirsty a great deal and needed to make water often.

"Yes to both. What are you suspecting?" Ibbot asked, interested in spite of himself, it seemed.

I sighed. "It is some sort of whole body sickness, I don't know the cause. But a poisoned wound usually takes them, their bodies forget how to mend. The piss smells of cider and they thirst all the time. Nothing to be done but keep the wound clean and hope. Take the foot off if it goes rotten in the end." At the look on Ibbot's face, I quickly said, "Don't tell him all that! Tell him he must keep it clean, wrap it in a freshly boiled cloth every day."

"Where did you learn all this?" Ibbot asked as the man shuffled away, leaning on his crutch.

"A great deal of it on the farm, animals and people are not so very different. And my brother's wife was known for her skills. She taught me." I was not old enough yet, when my mother passed, to have learned all her knowledge of healing. But I had pored over the book she left me and memorized much of the practical lore it contained.

We had tended the last rash, boil and wheeze when Hengel came back with my tool. We helped the tipsy giggling lady from the fireside over to the chair where I had Ibbot explain I would take out the bit of broken tooth that was causing her problems. She obediently opened her mouth wide. As Ibbot held her shoulders against the chair back, I grasped the fragment and pulled it out before she could change her mind and close her jaw.

She did yelp, but let me repack the socket with some drawing herbs in milkweed fluff and more numbing nettle. She thanked me, mumbling around the packing.

I turned toward the fireplace to find the muleteer sitting upright on his benches and watching us with a furrowed brow.

I dropped the fragment of tooth into the fire. "Ask him how he feels, Ibbot, and call Yuli or Kunitka in. In case we need witnesses."

Ibbot spoke to him. The driver squinted and grunted something back, translated to me as "Where is this place and how did I come here?" while the man looked at me groggily.

Would he recall I could not speak Yeganil, from our encounter on the road? I could not remember under the pressure of the moment if Ibbot had spoken to him by the wagon ... or in what tongue. No, I had tried to see to it Ibbot stayed quiet, he had stunned the driver without speaking in the native language. That was the way of it.

Though both of us looked the same as we had then.

The driver's ears and nose had lost their waxen appearance and were merely reddened now. Those parts might not slough off. The hands and feet were another matter. "Ask him if his feet and fingers are paining him much."

Ibbot put this to him while on his way to call into the kitchen for the women. I had to wait for him to return to translate the answer, which was delivered while Yuli, Kunitka and Hengel, too, were ranged in front of him expectantly.

"He says they are burning him, and why is that when they are hurt by cold." Ibbot's eyes shone bright in the firelight.

Keeping my voice even, I told Ibbot what to say.

The muleteer nodded once, twice, asked again where he was and this time, I heard Hengel answer him and was able to catch 'Lunenhelm' in the response. The driver seemed to know where that was, which made sense as he had been traveling the road that led here.

He acted dazed and somewhat vague, which could only be to our advantage in concealing our earlier encounter with him.

In fact, I was beginning to unwind my guts a bit and take a deeper breath when he suddenly pointed at me and barked out a short declaration.

Ibbot told me what he said. "I've seen your healer before."

CHAPTER THIRTEEN

This was the sort of time when telling yourself to stay calm doesn't work a lick. My mind seemed to fill with impenetrable dark mist that seeped into all its workings and mired fast every logical and rational thought. I was lucky to remain standing upright.

Hengel laughed and said something that sounded light-hearted in tone, despite being unintelligible to me. The muleteer developed a stubborn set to his mouth in response. Kunitka came forward and dimpled her apple cheeks at him prettily, while she held out a mug of something steaming. He took it with a curt nod, gripping it awkwardly with his bandaged hands.

I now felt as if I had fleas in earnest, from the mother and her itchy children, and my eyes watered with the effort of not scratching. It could only be my nerves, after all; it was too soon for it to really be vermin crawling.

The driver said something sharp again and I nudged Ibbot to get him to tell what he heard. Out of the side of his mouth, he said, "Hengel assured him he remembered you tending him through the night. He does not think that is it at all, though he cannot place you. He has not visited a healer in a long while and you are too young to be anyone he saw in the past."

I decided we would continue to hang our tale on my being at his bedside while he was in and out of awareness. It was good he had seen me treating others when he awoke, for it made evidence shoring up our story.

Cilliyon came into the hearth room toting the baby in her arms. The driver barely gave her a glance. Nor did he look on Ibbot with any curiosity.

He did persist in staring at me, however.

While I most wanted to turn and bolt from the room, I said instead, "Ibbot, tell him it is time to soak his feet and hands and replace his bandages. Ask him if he wants some more of the pain drink first."

Yuli went to gather the bowl of warmed water and new wrappings. I decanted some of the brew for him, a generous amount to make him sleepy, and added it to the drink Kunitka had brought him. He had difficulty guiding the cup to his mouth with his thickly swathed hands. I steadied it for him. I bade Ibbot tell him we had to drip the potion into him during the night, which he did, to an ungracious "Huh!" from the man in answer. Kunitka looked disapproving at this display of ingratitude. I blessed her for it, silently.

Cilliyon jiggled the baby on her knees, sitting only just close enough to hear what Ibbot and I were saying to each other. She was managing to look merely interested and I tried to do the same, though my heart still galloped.

We tended his growing blisters on toes and fingers, this being a bad sign in frostbite, and I wrapped them as gently as I could after the soaking. He kept his gaze fixed on me throughout. Despite the dose of herbs I had given him, he only developed heavy eyelids after I was finished. He drifted off to sleep with a piece of buttered bread in his belly. Kunitka had found she must hold it for him to bite, he was too clumsy to manage it without buttering his bandages. I did not hear him thank her.

I invited Ibbot to venture outside with me and have a look at the snow depth. Wieser must need to get out a bit, I suggested, when he appeared to be on the verge of declining. With a heavy sigh, he told Yuli that we were going for a while to get some air. We put on our woolens and walked outdoors.

It was no longer actively snowing, as far as I could tell, but flakes continued to swirl on the gusts and pile upon fences and drift against walls. Smoke rose from every chimney, every roof was heavily burdened, and few folk had pushed the mounds away from their doors as yet. Only a couple of men were out working on shifting the snow out of the way of travel, but no wagons rolled by at all. The miners must walk to work and back, I decided.

I turned to Ibbot as Wieser sniffed and poked her nose into varmint runs beneath the snow. "He is not convinced, but everyone else is. I say it's as good as we can expect."

He hunched his shoulders against the cold. "If he remembers us truly, the only thing to do is stun him again."

"Because that won't attract any attention at all! Have sense." I blew out a cloud of frosty breath. "It's me he seems most fixed upon and our hosts believe he half-remembers me from the first night. I say everything we speak and do must support that. He is a grizzly old creature and not making friends with his ways. I don't like being at risk of discovery either, but since we cannot leave, that is our best path."

"It would be easy enough for me to take care of him—I can be subtle."

"No. He has enough trouble and so do we. What we need to do is make sure we are gone before Piet can get word on us as fugitives from the port authority's justice. Get me the map I need, that is what I want from you."

"I'm not sure I meant to have you boss me about on this journey when I decided to take you along. I could have gotten this far on my own—"

"You'd have died in the mountains before you ever got here," I said flatly.

We locked eyes for just a moment, before he shrugged his shoulders and said, "I find I am quite full of fresh air now. Can we go back in?"

And so we continued on for weeks into months. Storms came and went, though the pass never cleared. The muleteer suffered his dead flesh sloughing and insisted he had seen me before the boarding house hearthside. He could remember his name and his journey with the wagonload of turnips but was unsure how he had been injured or why he waited in his wagon for the storm to overtake him. He agreed he would be dead but for the lumbermen, though he showed them no gratitude either. He attracted no followers to his theory of previous acquaintance with me, for I watched closely. Ibbot did not figure in his ramblings, nor Cilliyon. Only me.

I continued to see the sick and injured, making friends among the families who lived and worked in Lunenhelm. I grew better with Yeganil by the day. Cilliyon, too, began to pick up the language, though more household talk than men's conversation. She took to wearing the requisite scarf over her hair as it lengthened, since a covered head was considered proper for a woman. Ibbot grew restless and bored and began to ask how long until spring. He paid only enough attention to Cilliyon that our hosts might think them sweethearts, largely because she would tolerate not a whit more.

He reported Hengel took him aside one day and asked him if he was still set on reaching the uncle. When he said he was, Hengel offered him a map of the country so he could plan the route. For of course, he must be growing impatient to claim his marriage rights, with such a lovely intended?

I was jubilant when he showed me the parchment, scribbled in faded ink. Naturally, it was in Yeganil, but I was gaining enough facility with the terms that I could mostly make sense of it. I longed to try my hand with the passages in my magic book, but still dared not take it out and risk it being seen.

I got quite used to everyone calling me Fenn.

However, as time passed, I began to grow lax about pushing to depart for Lohr Island. Though pleased we now had a map, it seemed as if I was safe from the mages of Scythera here in Lunenhelm. For if Ibbot was one, he did not seem to have my demise on his mind, or urgently delivering me to his fellows in Scythera, either. For Cilliyon's part, she was as safe here as she would have been in Lohr Island's temple and her safety was her father's goal in sending her abroad.

However, Ibbot chafed at staying ever longer and pestered me to plan a route away from the town he saw as dreary and dull. I picked a place on the map to say Cilliyon's and my uncle lived and plotted a journey I estimated to take us two weeks to cover on foot. The route would take us by a good spot to turn south and head for the coast again. I planned to avoid the harbour where we had arrived in Yega, I spotted it on the map labeled Port Freyzik. We would make for Port Anlia instead.

"On foot!" Ibbot exclaimed, aghast. He wanted a horse. I told him the journey would cover terrain better suited to mules, which cost too dear in the mountains where their sure-footedness was prized. He wanted to leave at first thaw; I told him no, the mud season was even more treacherous than the snow season for travel. He pouted and was snappish, which Hengel took for an impetuous groom's frustration at being kept from his bride.

I found I avoided spending time with Piet, who was inclined to question me as my ability to speak the language increased. If he had been probing for information with Ibbot, I had not heard of it. Hengel took us as what we said we were, especially since I began working as a healer. Piet had a more inquisitive bent than his brother and always craved more facts than he had. Which fitted a constable, I supposed.

As the season went by, I found out the people of Lunenhelm also marked the winter solstice with feasting and song, as we did at home. Though the miners had to work the day around, Yuli and Kunitka prepared the festival foods, music, mead and ale for them, too, on the night of solstice.

When the festivities were in full sway, several of the boarding house miners, being single men, asked Cilliyon to dance. After asking my permission, as her brother. She seemed to want to, so I allowed it. Ibbot complained they ought to ask him instead and I laughed at him, for he knew that was not the way here. So he asked me if he might dance with her.

"See if she'll have you," I said, but in Mercedish.

The girl with the violet eyes had been coming round to my healing sessions quite often; her burn healed with only a little scarring and that pleased her. She attended the party with her family, so I asked her father if I might dance with her. He gave his consent with a twinkling eye.

I had watched the evening's dancing enough that I thought I could manage the steps. It was really not as complicated as what we did at home. When I watched my brother Wils learn our way of dancing from some of the village girls, I fell down laughing at his tripping feet. I had never tried it myself, though.

I did not trip or step on her. Able at this point to ask her name, I learned she was called Sefina. It suited her. She was quite light on her feet and rosy-cheeked when we finished our turn around the floor. I offered to fetch her a drink but she came with me to the table where they were laid out.

When I handed Sefina a cup, I found Cilliyon glaring at me as if I had slapped her. She flushed red and turned back to a miner who was plying her likewise. *What could be the matter?*

Ibbot, watching from across the floor, swaggered up to Sefina and me. "Maybe you should dance with your sister. She seems out of sorts."

"I thought you were dancing with her?'

"I, it seems, must wait my turn. But I do appreciate fire in a woman. At least with a spark in them, they are not boring."

I looked for Cilliyon, but as she was out on the dance floor again, I invited Sefina to take another turn. When we passed each other, Cilliyon acted as if I was invisible. Truth dawned; I realized it was just the sort of nonsense that Wils used to get into before he was married, with different girls from the village staking a claim on him and acting put out all the time. I used to tease him over it. Now that it was happening to me, I found I possessed far less tolerance than he had shown.

I delivered Sefina back to her father, who invited me to dance with her again. Anytime. I began to see that someone had planted the idea of keeping the healer in town. I saw a future that fenced me in like a fruiting tree, sending down roots in Lunenhelm according to other wishes than my own.

I said certainly, a little later perhaps, and went off in search of Cilliyon.

I found her backed up against the wall of the kitchen by her dancing miner, crying and struggling to push him away with both hands.

I had enough Yeganil to say, "Get off her."

The eyes he turned my way betrayed too much ale, as did his voice when he slurred, "She came along in here."

I stepped through the threshold and let the door swing shut. "Let her go."

If he heard he gave no sign, He easily trapped her wrists above her head in one great hand and pawed at her bodice with the other. She stifled a cry and tried to put a knee in his groin. He only laughed.

"Help me, Judian!"

When my hand shot out it seemed to happen without my deliberate intent. Fury and fear drove me but I spoke no spell word as Ibbot had done to the driver. The result was the same, with the miner flat on his back when the flash of blackness cleared. Cilliyon cowered against the wall, eyes wide in horror.

"Ah," Ibbot drawled from the doorway, "Now we see some true high magic from you, Judian Lebannen."

CHAPTER FOURTEEN

N ow I had done murder.

For the miner was dead, and if my stunning had not killed him outright, it must have been the knife that pierced his heart when my bolt of magic flung him backwards into the butcher's block.

I learned of the knife when Ibbot stepped past me, where I stood rigid as ice, and gathered his robes about his knees to crouch beside the man. He peered into the blank eyes and lifted the body to reveal the handle of the blade in his back. By that time, Hengel and Piet crowded through the door. Piet went to the body and Kunitka pushed past me to gather Cilliyon in her arms.

I made little sense of the Yeganil that rushed in a torrent around me, for I still had to concentrate to understand and I could not force my mind into any sort of focus.

Though I was able to form one thought: *Ibbot knows my true name.*

Wieser came to bump her head under my hand and lean against me. I lifted my eyes at a sharp *grock* to see Gargle perched on an upturned bucket on the drainboard. His regard was merciless harsh. *"What a Fool"* it seemed to say.

Cilliyon sobbed while she tried to pull together the torn edges of her blouse. Kunitka stroked her and wiped her eyes with a corner of apron, crooning softly.

I looked at the body again. Ibbot knelt and gestured, coolly explaining to Piet. He spoke slowly so I could follow his words as he told how I had found the miner accosting my sister and fought him, with the stabbing making an end of it. No mark was evident on me, such as would be expected if I had been fighting a man who made at least two of me. Sharp-witted Piet was bound to notice that; I could not hope otherwise.

Ibbot stood and went to Cilliyon's side. I thought he meant to comfort her, or to make a pretense of it, but he gently extracted her from Kunitka's embrace and led her over to me. I had some dim recognition that I should act protective and endorse Ibbot's version of what had happened. I could do nothing but stare at her wide eyes. She would not let him hand her off to me. She hung back looking at me with stark terror. As if she feared I might strike her down as well.

I had no idea why I had not killed her, in truth. I had never stunned anyone, never learned anything of it, let alone how to aim or direct it. And why had my blow been a burst of blackness rather than bright light like Ibbots?

When I fought the mages under the sea cliffs, blackness had welled out of my obsidian blade to blot out all light. Enemy soldiers died and both mages vanished. The obsidian being a gift from kavsprit, I believed its dark power came from those same spirits. What if it had all been my own doing? I was a murderer many times over, if so. Albeit an unwitting one.

Feeling compelled by all the eyes on me to do something for my erstwhile sister, I held out my hand to her. She shrank back against Ibbot. I shook my head, at a loss for what to say that might soothe her. Hengel patted my shoulder.

It took me a moment to understand what he was saying to me. He was apologizing. "I should have watched. I should have seen he was drunk. I am so sorry for what happened."

For the second time in my adventures beyond Merced, I lost the power of speech.

Not by some twist of magic, in this instance I was simply astounded.

Cilliyon, too, for her look of fear was gradually replaced by a sagging jaw and dazed eyes. Ibbot alone among our party appeared unruffled by Hengel's abject sorrow at not preventing what happened.

And it was not the killing of the miner Hengel was regretting. No, it was that he had not intervened before my sister had been sullied by a man I was then honor-bound to dispatch.

"Come, Fenn, come." Yuli pulled at my sleeve. "Sit by the fire."

The revelers had been sent to their quarters upstairs or out into the night to their homes. The woodsmen and the muleteer were in their customary places at the hearth and watched me somberly. Actually, the mule driver was not so much somber, now I looked closer, but puzzled. Putting together murder with me? I hoped not.

Piet followed me with his eyes, too. He supervised the miner's body being carried out on a board, where to I did not inquire. Yuli busied herself clearing away the food and drink. When Piet returned, he joined me by the fireside. Cilliyon had been spirited away by Kunitka and other women. Ibbot sat beside me as if he was my friend and soon-to-be relation, concerned for my circumstances. I had not spoken since I killed the man, now not because I could not, but because I did not know what to say.

I wished for Da to come and sort things out, which was something I had not wished since I became a man. He was across an ocean, far away. In his mind, I dwelt on Lohr Island learning spellcraft and magery.

There was no one to sort it out but myself, then.

"Fenn," Piet began, "I have heard from Ibbot and Hengel, but not from yourself. Say what occurred, in yourself's own time and words." He used the formal word to refer to me, which was typical in Yeganil for speaking to any outsiders. So, I felt no worse for that, at least.

I said to him, I did not like to say the miner was not to dance with my sister, since I was dancing as well. I told how I wanted to do what was usual for their celebration of solstice, as we were their guests. I also, like Hengel, did not realize the man was so much the worse for drink, but became concerned when I looked for my sister and did not see her. I went to the kitchen searching for her and found him alone with her. He had his hands on her. He was hurting her. He would not stop when I ordered him to, so I had no choice but to make him stop.

When I tried to pull him away, he was too strong. In the struggle, I reached for the knife.

All this challenged my command of the language and Ibbot had to fill in what I did not know how to say. He kept his detachment throughout, while I fought to keep my voice from shaking.

"How did it happen yourself stabbed him in the back?"

"I was behind him at the time. I could not pull him away."

"Why did yourself not call out for help?" Piet's voice was even, calm.

"I don't know. The music was loud, I had not heard Cilliyon cry out until I went in the kitchen."

Piet's gaze sharpened. "Did she only cry out when she saw yourself?"

"No. No, she was fighting him, trying to."

Ibbot said coldly, using the same formality with Piet, "I know yourself does not mean to imply my intended would encourage a man to maul her, and only protest if she was discovered." He had to repeat it for me in Mercedish.

Piet did not back down. "I am charged with investigating any untoward event. I must ask unsavory questions in my work, to ferret out the truth in such matters."

"And is Fenn not within his rights, *in such matters*, to use deadly force to defend his sister? As her only male relative present?"

"That is the law," Piet acknowledged. "I must determine if that is what occurred here tonight. A man might be stopped, short of being killed, as a preference. And have a trial for his crime, with punishment meted out as called for."

"That would have been my … preference, too, Piet. I regret I acted out of anger and my desire to protect her from hurt. I lost control in the fury of the moment."

"Justified, surely," Ibbot added.

"A circuit judge will review my report and make a ruling. I suppose it does not matter since yourself cannot leave anyway in this weather, but now yourself must stay until a determination is made."

I'd had better news. "Will I be held in a jail?"

"No, for I do not have one. Yourself will remain here as before.

The miner was well-liked among his fellows. I will wish to keep yourself under my eye to be sure none of them would seek to do any harm."

Better and better. "Thanks for that. Do you—er, does yourself think people will still come to me as a healer?"

He lifted a shoulder. "Hengel will encourage them, I am certain. Yourself wishes them to?"

"I prefer to have some use while I am unable to complete my journey. Our journey."

"Do not despair. If I have any insight, I think yourself can expect the women to propose an abandonment of the plan to reach an uncle for the wedding, and see the sister married at once to her betrothed." He smiled at Ibbot. "That will put the stamp of respectability on all, and aid yourself's cause."

Ah, the best news yet. I dared not look at Ibbot for fear I would kick him if he showed even a trace of smug eagerness.

Instead, he took me aback by saying, "Better not to rush, I am thinking. I will have to consider … all that has happened."

I wanted to conclude the interview as soon as I could, for I still had to find out what Ibbot knew aside from my name. He could have learned that aboard *Moon Road* and only humoured me thus far by calling me the false name I gave. While laughing up his sleeve at my attempt to disguise my identity.

And the other part of his remark, about finally seeing high magic done by me—What did that mean? He had said before he had heard about my involvement in liberating Bale Harbour. He seemed to accept that I had done little enough. Perhaps the tale was not something he had been told on *Moon Road* at all, perhaps he knew all about me before he ever arrived with the slavers. Plus, I had never yet pressed him about where he was from, exactly.

Scythera seemed more and more likely as his home country.

Piet sat looking at me expectantly. I had not the least idea what he had asked me. Ibbot prodded me with his foot.

"I'm sorry?" I said, leaning forward. "What did he say?"

"He wondered if we would like to have a better bed than our chairs by the fire."

"I thought there were no more rooms."

"No, but there is an empty bed that can be brought down."

The dead miner's? Please, no! "We get along well enough. The muleteer might welcome it over his benches lashed together, though."

Piet smiled briefly as he stood. "I'll see it done, young Fenn."

Even with the lawman gone from the fireside, I could not have a talk with Ibbot with all these other ears still open—even if none of these Yegans had ever given a sign of understanding Mercedish. It seemed forever and a day before snores and deeper breathing came from them all.

I did not wait further for Ibbot to broach the subject. He was drowsing, and I nudged his chair with my boot.

"Tell me what you saw and tell me what you know."

He yawned and rubbed his eyes with the knuckles of one hand. "I saw you stun a drunken miner. Which if I recall, I caught no end of chaff from you for doing to a different fellow. One who was set on killing you moments before." He yawned again. "Oh, and yours died and mine is over there in a bed by the fire. You have an unusual style of conjuring the black fire. Is it a cantrip you use?"

It seemed better not to admit I had no idea what a cantrip was, or how I summoned the "black fire" at all. "It was the kitchen knife that killed him."

He shook his head, hair highlighted in the yellow glow of the fire. "His heart had already stopped when he struck the block. Otherwise, the knife would have brought more blood. Did you not see me push it farther in when I lifted him? To make a fatal wound's depth?"

I had not seen him do so, staggered as I was at the time. "Do you think Piet realizes there is not enough blood?" I asked, not sure I could bear the answer.

"He is clever, is he not? Yet, I have to doubt he sees murder often in his small burg. Most likely drunken family spats and disputes over property. How many stabbings might he see in his career? Precious few, I'm guessing."

How blandly he speaks of murder, I thought.

"And you know my name. What else?"

"Judian Lebannen, the young man from Merced's mountains. A Sending came to Mage Balin, while I was there to see it, too.

Scythera's mages are hunting you. They are aggrieved by what you did at a western fort. Even more infuriated by some incident on the coast. They do not tolerate anyone who interferes with their aims."

"Yet why take so much trouble over me? With all their power and spellcraft, do they not have more to concern them than a farm boy with some bit of magic? And if they want me dead, why do they not just strike me down with magery and be done?"

"Oh, they would if they could. But they haven't been able to find you."

"What prevents them?"

"The Sending admitted, they do not understand how you have been eluding them. The cabal of mages has demanded you be brought before them so they may pick apart the reason your magic proved strong enough to obstruct them in Merced. Or, failing that, pick you apart. You were rumored to have fled on a ship. So, Mage Balin was one of those given the task of searching for you at sea.

"As a master weather worker, Mage Balin cleverly watched for your spellcasting to be provoked by the storm we sent—it was meant to snare you, trick you into revealing your nature. He realized we had to prevent you from crafting a way to escape our alteration of the current and winds, until *Chikoro* could reach the vessel he now knew bore you. Together, we took your voice for the intervening time. Kruthe, as always, proved willing to snatch a prize on the waves. But don't forget, I had also heard of and then seen your power. And once aboard *Moon Road*, I ensorcelled that old goat Balin to forget he sought a mute and tap the girl instead. Then the sleeping draught. All so I could escape and bring you with me."

"Why keep me from him? Do you want to be the one who delivers me to Scythera? Will you receive some reward for turning me over?"

"Bah! I do not want to turn you over to the cabal. *My home* is decimated because of their greed. Scythera is barren and starving because of their meddling with the weather and the land. Why did they bring the Keltanese army to over run your homeland? So they can expand their plunder to every other country since there is nothing left of ours but dust. And yet, still no end to their ambition and avarice."

I hoped none of the others were awake to hear him, for though they might not understand the language, the bitterness of his last words rang plain.

"Tell me what you think I can do, if you intend to stop them."

"Are you truly unaware how magic flows from you into everything you touch? It is hard to believe you could be that oblivious."

"I have only begun to learn the craft. My mother's folk on Lohr Island were to be my teachers."

"Ah, yes. You were going home, you said." He flashed his teeth. "Your formal course of study would take much too long. No apprenticeship for you, Judian Lebannen. We must fight them now, before it is too late and they tip the world into disaster. While there is still time."

CHAPTER FIFTEEN

F inally, it became clear to me there was no point in trying to convince Ibbot that I really possessed too little magical training to be of help in his quest. I told him we must consider things overnight, so as to get him to leave off about it. And I still didn't trust him.

If Cilliyon had not had the mother and baby in her room upstairs, I would have liked to go up and see she was calmed and no longer terrified of me. Instead, I pulled my blanket around me in my chair and allowed Wieser to lie on my feet to warm them.

Gargle hunched by the fire, looking daggers my way before he closed his eyes in sleep.

I closed my eyes as well. A poor idea, as for the longest time all I could see was the miner lying dead on his back. I had not meant to kill him. At least I didn't think I had. Did a mage have to set an intention when the black fire was summoned? My paltry low magic spells all required a purpose to be fixed in my mind for them to work properly.

All the high magic I had ever accomplished had ... just happened.

That could not be the way magic was supposed to work. Otherwise, why have schooling in it?

To learn how to wield it, wood wit, so you don't harm one and all, I told myself severely.

I could not help but think my destination should still be Lohr Island.

I thought of my obsidian knife, which I wore at all times in the sheath strapped to my leg. Ibbot had certainly been interested in it when I drew it out on discovering the body in the stable. The blade sometimes hummed with power during my fighting in Merced, especially when I was in the caves. It had been completely quiet while I sailed on the *Moon Road*. I had reckoned the earth to be so far below the waves that obsidian was too far out of its element. Could the knife be what shielded me from the mages' fury?

My blade had also been quiet in these mountains of Yega, though, despite the similarity to my home range. Were there kavsprit in Yega? Surely the miners made offerings to them, if so. Perhaps I would ask on the morrow.

My mind ran down at last and I fell asleep.

The following morning, I discovered just what Piet had meant about the fallen miner being well-regarded by his fellows. Hard stares and set jaws showed on all of them when they filed downstairs to be fed and sent off for their shift. Many muttered remarks to one another while looking my way, remarks quickly silenced as soon as Kunitka, Hengel or Yuli were in earshot.

Piet was not in evidence. Perhaps I would talk to him about whether there might not be somewhere else I should stay, where all the man's friends were not also in residence. Even Ibbot, not one to be attentive to others' discomfiture, commented that it seemed particularly chilly in the hearth room this morning, did it not?

It did indeed.

Cilliyon entered carrying the baby before the last of them had left. I was more distressed on her behalf than on my own. They glowered at her as if she was a bold and devious girl, who should hesitate to show herself at all. Some sneered, others pointedly turned their backs. She stood tall, though, and I was proud to see her defy their judgments of her. I swallowed hard when she sat at the table and I saw the bruises on her wrists, each of the miner's fingers plain.

Kunitka and Yuli were on her like hunting falcons as soon as the workers filed out. Kunitka dove in with, "If yourself wishes to be married at once, I have my bride dress still and yourself truly welcome to wear it. We will only need to alter it a little. Try it on now?"

"It is better to give the tongue-waggers less to labor over," Yuli advised.

Cilliyon looked at both Ibbot and me, questions in her eyes.

"Little enough has gone as we planned," Ibbot said smoothly. "I believe Cilliyon will want to have her uncle's blessing when we reach his home. I see no need to feel compelled to silence gossips."

I added, "Cilliyon did nothing wrong. She has been properly sheltered and so did not expect anything untoward from the man."

"He is—was—a nice enough fellow, always. I never expected him to act that way, or I would have warned yourself, Fenn." Kunitka's eyes were downcast. She was taking the entire thing hard, I saw. Feeling responsible like her husband.

Yuli spoke plainly, turned toward Ibbot. "If yourself does not marry her at once, there are those who will say it is because yourself thinks her ruined. That she is no longer worthy of a decent man."

"That's making it her fault, blaming her for what he did!" I felt my face grow hot as I clenched a fist on the table.

Yuli raised her shoulders. "People do often say it is the woman's fault, because men will always be men if given any temptation at all."

"I never heard such—" I started.

Ibbot cut me off. "I hope it is not too hard for yourselves to understand. We come from a place where each one is responsible for their own choice. A woman is not to blame if a man trespasses. It is for him to keep himself in check."

"Of course, there can be differences in how such matters are viewed," Yuli allowed. "But it would be better for all if he was not dead."

"I cannot argue with that," I said.

"Just have a look at my dress," Kunitka implored. She laid a hand on Cilliyon's arm.

"I'm happy to see it," Cilliyon said softly, "but I must defer to Ibbot. If he does not wish to let others drive the marriage forward, I will of course do as he says."

A breath might have tipped me out of my chair, I was that shocked. Ibbot smiled like a cat with cream on its whiskers.

Later on, I had a typical number of folk come in to see me with this and that. Scours, a fever, a cut to stitch up and such like. No one mentioned anything about the dead miner or my role in it. Although, it seemed to me they were somewhat less chatty than usual.

Ibbot said to me during a lull, "I had been thinking we should leave Cilliyon here when we go. I see that will not be possible now, if they think her a hoyden. She'll end up in the town brothel without us."

"We cannot abandon her here!"

"Not now, I just said as much."

"What brothel?" I might as well have said, 'what's a brothel?' but I did not like to admit I didn't know. He seemed to think it was something anyone would know.

"There is one in every town of any size, Fenn. Where do you think the unmarried miners go when they want a woman?"

"There wasn't one in my village."

"I'm sure there was one in Bale Harbour for the sailors."

I supposed it was possible. Lichan's mother Virda certainly would not have directed my attention to one when we were lodging at Guthy's there. Gevarr had talked to me about camp followers he knew as a soldier. I reckoned the women of a brothel were like that, only stayed in one place.

Cilliyon could not be left to such a fate.

Kunitka called me over to look at the muleteer when she changed his bandages. Half of each foot and most of his fingers were dead and black. If I had been a bone cutter, I would have taken them off for him. He would be crippled in any case, unless rot took him. I regretted he had ever discovered us departing his wagon. I told Kunitka to wrap him up again. At least the dead flesh no longer pained him.

The women had been caring for him; caring for invalids was women's work here despite the necessity of being over-familiar with an unrelated man in the process. His disposition had not improved over the months. If anything, he had grown more sour. To my relief, however, he had mostly given up trying to pin some earlier acquaintance on me.

Ibbot came to look as Kunitka wrapped and said in Mercedish, "He might have been better served by ending up like your miner."

"Do not call him my miner."

"Cilliyon's miner, then?" he suggested mildly.

"No." I paused. "I do not even know his name."

"Ask someone for it, if you think you want to know. I should think his anonymity would rest easier in your mind."

"I am not you."

"No, true enough. My target is not dead." He walked off and I did not trouble myself to note where he went.

When I had no more ill folk to devise a cure for, I put on heavy gear and went out the back of the house. The miner with the crooked arm was making himself useful by loading firewood on a sled and dragging it in to the kitchen and hearth room. I thought assisting him in the fresh air might suit me better than being cooped up inside.

He gave me a friendly wave when I walked toward him. He must not have heard of the events of last night. I assumed he would know the dead man. I wondered if they had been friends.

With our faces covered against the cold, we did not engage in much conversation. I began to add logs to the ones he was stacking. We continued side-by-side until the sled was full.

He pulled it one-armed with no difficulty. He may have suffered from not enough food before Kunitka's generosity, but he was still a strong man. I lifted the back of the sled when we came to the stairs, to keep the wood from spilling, but he muscled it through the kitchen doorway.

Kunitka objected to me doing work, still thinking of me as her guest. Piet had come in for something hot to drink and told her to leave me be. He seemed to understand my need to occupy my mind, especially now.

With his scarf away from his mouth, as we stacked logs by the stone hearth, the man told me his name was Dusek. "I thank yourself again for setting me to ask for work to do here. They have been very good to me, feeding me plenty. Perhaps I will grow fat!" He laughed, which he had been far away from doing at our earlier encounter.

"I am pleased to hear of yourself doing better. Come the pass opens, waste no time getting to a healer who can set that arm properly. Yourself may yet be able to return to the mines."

"I do not miss the dark below. When my arm is fixed, I may think of something else to do to make my way in the world. Is healing yourself's only work?"

"No, I come from farm life. Goats and crops. I liked that well enough."

He made a wry face. "A hard life, too, I'm thinking. All my family have toiled in the mines. Yet, my mother's mind would be eased if I found another way."

"Does yourself live with her here?"

"Aye, here in Lunenhelm. Yourself should come and meet her, yourself and the sister."

"We would like to do so, thanks for asking." Did his mother have enough to eat, I wondered, if Dusek brought in no money? I might ask Kunitka or Yuli for some bread and cheese to take along when we called on his mother.

Next, we scooped the ashes from the hearth and the kitchen into metal buckets and strapped these to the sled to be taken outdoors. The ash pit was much farther from the back door than the cords of stacked wood, so we were well out of sight of the kitchen windows once we reached it.

Dusek hefted one bucket with his good arm. I took up the other but needed both hands to lift it clear. We dumped the ash, raising a cloud of drifting soot, and put the buckets one in the other on the sled for the walk back.

As we turned to go, a voice came from behind us.

"What's the hurry, stranger?"

"It's cold," I said, peering through the cloud of ash. I could see the darker shape of a man beyond the heaped pile.

"No need to rush off. We would speak with yourself." Another voice, on the far side of the pit, to my left. I turned to the right as well and counted six men altogether. I could not see their faces in their hats and scarves.

"What is this?" Dusek said to them.

I thought I knew.

One of the men grunted. "Go back to the house. This is not your business."

"Alun?"

"No names," snapped the man he had addressed.

"What business is it you have with the healer?"

"Some healer," snorted another of the men.

There was nowhere to run, even if the snow had not been so deep as to prevent running. I thought I might be quicker on my feet than these men, because I certainly was not stronger. I'd have run if I could have, and no mistake.

I had my knife.

I reached out to the sled and slid one of the empty buckets free.

"What do you mean? What do you mean to do?" Dusek looked from one to another.

"Have you not heard? Last night your healer stuck a knife in Stas Royka. He's dead."

"No!"

"That's right."

"Say why I did it." I said, hefting my bucket. I edged away from the sled so I could move more easily when they came on.

"He *says* Stas was bothering his sister at the solstice dance. No one saw but him."

"I wouldn't have stabbed him for bothering her. He was hurting her. The bruises are plain this morning."

"He can't tell his side, can he? She may have asked for it."

"She didn't."

"So *yourself* says. He was a good man. And our friend."

"I wish he hadn't hurt her, and I wish I hadn't killed him but only stopped him. I did what I had to do at the time. I'm sorry he's dead but I can't change that."

"No, but yourself can and will pay for it. Go home, Dusek. And be more careful who you take up with."

Instead, Dusek picked up the other bucket.

"I told you to go home. This is not your fight."

"Beat me, too. Not much worse than six on one, six on two. One barely a man and one a cripple. I can stomach it if you can."

If a braver man, I would have told him to go on as they had said. Instead, I was glad to have him on my side, one arm or two.

"Have it your way, then," snarled the spokesman, and he signaled two of the others to rush us.

I crouched to pull my knife from its sheath and swung the bucket low across the legs of the closest man, knocking him into the ashes. The pit was still hot where he landed. He screamed and rolled away into the snow, beating at the flaming woolen trousers on his thigh and hip.

The other man aimed a kick at my bucket to try and send it flying away from me but missed his mark. He lurched backwards when I raised the black blade high.

Dusek caught him a ringing blow on the temple with the other bucket. He dropped like a stone. Dusek spun around to face another man coming up at his back.

The burned man crawled away from the fight but did not get up, nor did the one Dusek cold-cocked. That left four, but only one went for my friend, and only to drive him farther from the pit. Farther from me.

The other three came on fast. I cut one on the shoulder, the obsidian blade slicing through the dense leather and wool as if through warm tallow. He cried out. I backed up and slashed at a second man but he dodged away. Though I swung my bucket and jabbed with my knife, I could not hope to keep clear of all three men at once. The cut one came from behind and wrenched my arm back. He struck a blow to my wrist, trying to force the knife from my grip. I held it fast while I twisted to strike his head or cut shoulder with the bucket. He ducked low and hauled me sideways, off balance. Another of them shoved me to my knees and the first one pinned both my arms behind me before I could wrench out of his grasp.

Alun stood before me.

Dusek shouted at each blow I took, until the man chasing him seized his bad arm and clapped a hand over his mouth. Blood from my mouth spattered the snow in front of me. Alun's boot caught me in the ribs brutally hard, I heard them crack. Body blows did not seem to satisfy him as much as drawing blood, so he pulled my hat and scarf away to have better chance with my head and face.

I forced myself to cease all struggle against the two holding me, for there was no point. *They'll stop*, I thought, closing my eyes and going limp. *They'll stop soon.*

And finally, they did.

CHAPTER SIXTEEN

I had enough wits remaining that I heard their footsteps crunch off into the distance. I waited where they had dumped me onto my face in the snow, because the numbing cold was what I wanted for the moment. I spat blood and felt with my tongue for missing or broken teeth. All there, as best I could tell, though some of them wobbled in their sockets.

Dusek came into view of my one eye not swollen shut. Frozen tear tracks glinted on his cheeks. I did not know if he cried because I looked so bad, or if his sore arm had been re-injured. I would have asked, but my jaw hurt and I decided it did not really matter so much, at that.

"Can yourself move?" he asked, patting me gingerly on the back.

Maybe I could. If I did, then he might leave off patting me, because it was not gingerly enough. I shifted my head a bit, in sort of a nod.

He leaned back from where he had crouched over me and I slowly levered myself over onto my side. I could not gather the will to try to stand.

He pulled the sled alongside me and aided me to shift myself over onto it, on my back. "Hold on if yourself is able," he said, and pulled me over the snow toward the kitchen door. The distance seemed to have grown double and more from the ash pit.

Gargle landed on my boot at the halfway point. I couldn't think of anything worth the effort to say to the creature. Some warning before the attack wouldn't have gone amiss, I thought, but one thing I had learned was not to count on the mercy of crows.

Dusek shouted loud enough that he raised Yuli and Kunitka, who came running. Such a lot of fussing ensued that I just closed my eyes and let Dusek tell the sad story. They summoned Hengel, who came at a trot to carry me up the backstairs while I bit back a moan. He placed me before the fire in the hearth room. I had two benches lashed together for me as had been done for the mule driver. It felt about equal in comfort to the sled but was indoors.

Both Ibbot and Cilliyon turned up next. Cilliyon insisted she be allowed to help wash the blood off me. Ibbot paced at my side, fair spitting in fury. At first, I believed his anger to be sparked by the attack, but what he said to me in Mercedish made it clear: he was furious with me.

"Why in the name of any kind of sense did you not call forth the black fire?"

I managed a mumble. "… didn't want to kill anyone. Anyone else."

Piet loomed over me. "Who did it?"

"Didn't know … them."

He turned on Dusek. "You know."

With a spasm of agony, I shook my head. "Don't say," I told him.

Piet protested, but I forced more words past swollen lips. "He has to live here. I don't."

He didn't like it. I would not be swayed. He instructed Kunitka to oust the father and young sons from the room under the eaves, so I could be carried up there and put to bed with a guarded door.

I did not want to be stuck in there for days, I would go mad, but I could not say all that with the way my jaw ached. I only said, "No. Too far away."

"What is it yourself feels like doing that raises a need to be closer?"

Upon reflection, I did feel like lying in a bed just now, for a fact. "Only tonight," I said.

It was not until I was tucked up that I thought of my obsidian knife.

I sent for Ibbot and asked him please to go look for it in the snow by the ash pile.

"How will I know where to start?"

"Where the snow is bloody. Churned up. Two buckets nearby. I must have ... lost my grip when ... pinned my arms. Hope they didn't take it." That long a speech took every bit of strength I had. I rested on the bed breathing hard. Or as hard as I dared with my ribs creaking.

He went at once without further discussion and I was grateful. Perhaps I should not have taken it from its sheath when they came at me. I did not think they would have recognized its nature, but I could not be sure ... I wondered how the man I had cut was faring.

Ibbot returned with sorry news. "I saw no trace of it. You don't remember if one of them wrested it from you? Or picked it up?"

I shook my head. And regretted it. Much as I was loathe to be without it, I took a shred of comfort in what I knew to be true: "It will not serve them," I said.

"What do you mean?"

"Because ... a magical gift given to me. Only if I give or lend ... will it have power."

"How do you know this?"

"Annora said ... when Wils wanted to borrow. When better, I will seek it out. I must have it back ... important."

"I'll help you. When you are better."

"Thanks."

"They could have easily killed you. Six of them, for gods' sakes."

"They would have done so, if had wanted. Don't know why ... they didn't."

"Maybe the dead man wasn't quite the fine fellow they have claimed."

If true, I wished I might have known that when he asked to dance with Cilliyon, so I could have forbade it.

No taking any of it back now.

His name had been Stas Royka. I did recall that from earlier. Would I feel any better if I found out what sort of man he had been? Wils told me once what Da had said to him about taking life—that the shades of the dead rode by your shoulder, whispering when you were pleased or irritated, how they would give much to feel either way, if you had just not killed them. Did the ghost of Stas Royka hover by me now? The thought made me shiver under my warm blankets.

"Are you cold?" Ibbot asked. "I can fetch you a hot stone for your feet."

"You're kindly of a sudden."

He snorted. "I want you alive and hale for what I want to accomplish. You'd be wasted as a corpse."

"Not cold. Need rest now, though."

He went out the door, giving me his crooked smile as he closed it.

I was almost asleep when my eyes flew open at a thought that came unbidden: What if Ibbot had found my knife and was keeping it from me? He seemed quite curious about the way it worked, or rather, didn't work unless given properly. Did that mean anything?

Maybe not, the blade had captured his attention from the moment he saw it in the port city.

A knock on the door interrupted my thoughts. Cilliyon put her head in.

"Do you feel like a hot mead or some broth? Kunitka is desperate to do for you. She feels so awful for letting you help with the firewood and the ashes."

"Nothing now, thanks. They'd have found a way to me sooner or later. It's not her fault."

"I'll tell her." She started to withdraw.

"Cilliyon."

"Yes?"

"It's not your fault, either."

She nodded once, not meeting my eye. Then she was gone.

I turned over in bed, stifling a groan afterward, and resolved to ask for my bag to be brought to me when the next person came asking what they could do. There was no reason not to look in my book in this rare privacy, while it lasted, and I might find some potion or spell to speed healing of bruises and battered bones.

Hengel turned up next, so I tasked him with the errand. He quite a lot later carried my bag to me. First, he had to wait until both Cilliyon and the young mother left the room unoccupied. Then, he had a bit of trouble finding it within the room. I had enspelled the bag with a low magic charm. It was the same one Annora used to help garden beans escape a rabbit's notice. I didn't expect it was the sort of spell that would confound mages, such as Ibbot or his master, but it had been doing a fine job of guiding others' attention around the bag itself and diverting thoughts from what might be inside it.

After Hengel left it with me, still looking perplexed at why I had had to send him down the hall twice when it was really in plain sight after all, I set about unwrapping my book. I had to move slow, since I was mightily sore all over and not just where the brunt of the blows had fallen.

Because of my creeping pace, I had to shove partly undone oilskin wrappings and heavy book under the blankets when Piet came calling.

"I have heard," he said, after inquiring how I was feeling, "that a seamstress in town had a visit from a miner who has a cut shoulder that will not stop bleeding. She sewed it up, but it oozes continuous and brisk, she says. She cannot figure it. Does yourself know anything about that? Which yourself would like to say?"

I gave him my best wooden face.

"No, then." He sighed. "Would yourself care to take a look at it and see if something can be done—if I can get him here?"

"If he can be persuaded to come here, I will look. Did she say if she tried a poultice of spider silk?" It was subterfuge; I knew that spider silk would not staunch a wound from a magical weapon. I was not certain I could stop it bleeding, though I would try if he came. I did not wish him dead by my hand as well. Despite what he had done to me, I wanted no revenge. It tasted too bitter.

But I was not above planning to ask Cilliyon to be there to help me if he came, with her livid bruises on her wrists for him to see.

He did not come that day, or the next, or the next after that. I read my book, looking for what to do for a wound that would not cease bleeding. I found many healing spells to study, though none were specific to a magical wound. As I delved deeper into the pages, at last a possibility came to light ...

Next, I tested some charms and spellwork that strengthened me. Wieser came to sleep with me each night and I also drew strength from her sturdy presence. Gargle came to the tiny window, mostly I am sure because I would open it and give him crumbs from the trays of food carried up to me.

I drew my runes of protection on the floor and windowsill, but only where they would be out of Kunitka's sight when she came to clean. I enspelled them to escape her notice for good measure.

And on the following day, Piet and Hengel brought me a ginger-haired miner of surpassing pallor, who had a wad of bloody cloths bound to his shoulder.

He looked as though he might faint from his walk up the stairs. Indeed, Piet had an arm around his ribs keeping him upright. I rose from my bed and told Piet to lay him there.

All of them looked askance at me. "He'd fall out of a chair and I don't care to work on him on the floor," I said.

I sent Hengel to find Cilliyon and instruct her to bring a basin of hot water, fresh bandages, some brandy. And a sharp kitchen knife. The man tried to rise when I asked for the last item but proved too weak.

"Does yourself want my help?"

He nodded warily.

"Then lie still."

When Cilliyon came in, I had her remove his bandages. With her purplish green wrists in front of his face, he could not help but see his friend's hand marks on her. I could see it was not lost on him, what I was doing, but he only pushed out a sullen lip and said nothing.

The wound was only as long as a man's finger. I had not sliced him a lengthy gash at all. It looked as if the edges were fresh cut and though neatly stitched with dark thread, I had to wipe away the plum-red blood that welled from it in order to see even briefly before it was obscured again.

"Where is the blade that made this?" I said, with no emphasis to draw Piet's attention. I might not have bothered to be subtle. Piet at once hung over my shoulder to hear the answer.

The miner shifted his eyes from one to the other of us. "How do I know?" he muttered.

"It is not a metal blade, but a special one of black stone. I need it to staunch the flow." Necessary for the complicated magic my book had ultimately revealed. "If one of the friends has it, they can save yourself by bringing it."

He said nothing.

"Will they want yourself to die to protect them? Death is drawing closer. A man has only so much blood. The body cannot make enough fast enough to keep up with this." I wiped away the pooling in the hollow of his shoulder. "What if I can promise none of them will have punishment for what they did to me?"

Piet said at once, "Yourself cannot make that promise."

The fellow looked at me defiantly. I wiped the blood away again, slower this time, while I looked into his face.

He narrowed his eyes. "Yourself be a cold-hearted cur. Kill Stas, cut me with a cursed blade. Why should I believe yourself will help me at all?"

"Because he says he will," Cilliyon said. "And I have never heard him say false when his help is asked for."

"A sister must say that, about a brother. And yourselves all are strangers here."

"That's as may be," Piet said, "but I have seen him heal many of our town's folk and ask for nothing but shelter. From any of us here. If I say I will leave you and the others be, if that is what Fenn wants, will you say on about the blade then?"

He looked to his wound, fear in his eyes. Fear of death or of his fellow miners it would be hard to have guessed. I mopped it again.

After a long moment, he rolled his eyes and said, "I don't know if one of them picked up his knife. You will have to ask each of them, Piet, and they will think it is a way to trick them into admitting they were there. Or tell them plain I have played the rat."

"No," I said, "there are the two who held me, and you were one of them. And the man who beat me. The other man who held Dusek, perhaps, but not the one he knocked out with the bucket or the man I shoved into the ash pit. Yourself would have seen if they picked up the knife, yes? When the one came to and all left."

"What's the point?" he asked, glaring.

"Start with the ones it most likely could have been, not everyone at once. If yourself proves lucky and we send Piet to them one at a time instead of calling them here together, the one with the knife may be the first one asked, not the last. So the others need not know."

This appealed to him, made clear by the hope in his eyes. Piet arched an eyebrow, saying, "Has yourself thought of a career in the laws?"

"Never," I said.

Piet went off on his errand, given the names that meant nothing to me, but which caused him to press his lips flat and scowl. I busied myself mixing some of the man's blood with powdered herbs to bind it, while I silently mouthed the charm to mingle it deeply. I requested a brazier of some sort to be brought, for heating the obsidian blade. For I believed that Piet would return with it.

I asked Cilliyon to find Ibbot when she went below stairs and tell him I wished him to come up. I would let him see what I was about and give him a chance to offer up my knife if he did have it after all. I believed Piet would find it, but it does not do to carry the whole load of ale in one barrel.

Soon Ibbot himself tottered up the steps carrying an iron cauldron. He set it beside the bed with a *thunk*, where it squatted on three stubby legs while tendrils of smoke wafted from its mouth. I bent to peer inside. Bright orange coals from the fireplace smoldered within.

"Yuli asks that you avoid burning the place down upon their heads and says if you are cold, she will heat you any number of stones instead," he recited like a boy saying his lessons. He grinned at the end.

The miner on the bed cast his eyes to the heavens, as if he might as well die and have it over with. Ibbot had spoken Mercedish to me, and coupled with the grin, the man must have thought he had reached the end of his road for certain.

I told Ibbot to repeat it in Yeganil for the miner's benefit, which he did. He came close to watch my preparations with lively interest.

Cilliyon sat beside the wounded man and wiped away the accumulating blood. He took care not to look at her, which seemed to suit her well enough. She looked only at the wound.

At length, Piet returned. "Second house," he said shortly. He unwrapped a swath of fox pelt he took from inside his coat. On the skin side rested my obsidian knife.

"Ah," said Ibbot in Mercedish, "the lost is now found." He paused. "And you can see I didn't take it. No apology necessary."

I might have known my suspicion was no news to him.

I took up the blade and felt it vibrate ever so slightly at my touch. I shoved it into the coals to its hilt. While it heated, I picked up the ointment I had concocted using his blood and also the sharp carving knife. I went to the bedside.

"Here is what must be done now. Piet and my friend Ibbot will hold yourself down firmly, for any movement at all could result in death. Cilliyon will wipe away blood to help me see. I will cut the stitches and carve away the edges of the wound. It must be new flesh, untouched by my black knife, which I bring together. I will spread this poultice—" I held it up "—over all, then cauterize the fresh cut with the flat of my heated blade. The pain will be great. Yell all yourself pleases. Just do not move."

I expected him to raise a fuss and refuse now that we had come to it, but he only nodded, even if his eyes looked a bit wild.

I called on all five gods to aid me and set to work. The man hollered curses aplenty as I cut away his flesh but could not budge, for Piet was a powerful man and Ibbot was stronger than his lanky frame might suggest. Of course, the miner was weak from days of blood loss, too. I did my cutting as fast as I could and Cilliyon did not get in my way with her cloth. I smeared the ointment over quickly. I plucked the knife hilt from the coals and pressed the hot blade against his skin.

He screamed.

The smell was sick-making. Steam rose in a fine red mist. I said the spell I had learned by rote, but only in my head not aloud, and counted slowly as the miner whimpered. When I lifted the blade, no blood followed. The wound was sealed.

I said my thanks to the gods, and also to my lore book that seemed somehow to sense what knowledge I needed and yield it up for me. When I lifted my gaze, it was to see Ibbot looking at me with half-lidded eyes.

"I see why they fear you so," he said softly, and released his hold of the man on the bed.

CHAPTER SEVENTEEN

Ibbot made himself scarce for the next few days, so I could not ask him who he meant feared me. I reckoned he meant his fellow mages from Scythera. *What has Ibbot seen in me that made him say what he did?* I asked myself that dozens of times, since I could not ask him.

The miner I cut and then mended was carried away to recuperate elsewhere. He had managed to summon up the good grace to thank me as Piet and Hengel bore him from the room, though he did not apologize for his part in my beating. What he did say about it suprised me: "We intended yourself to die for killing Stas, a life for a life. I don't know why we stopped short of that end."

What had guarded me, or distracted them? My moonstone pendant? Some trick of Gargle's? When I drew my knife, had that exerted some protective force beyond the wounding of one attacker?

I learned Wieser had tried to come to my aid. Kunitka told to me later that the dog had gone wild shortly after Dusek and I left the house with the ashes, barking and charging at the back door. They thought she had scented a weasel or rat outside and dragged her back over and over, with a scolding for acting up so.

I asked that she be fed some extra eggs.

My bruises and aches faded. Thankfully, I showed no signs of hidden damage that might cause later crippling. After a fortnight, I begged to be allowed to return to the hearthside, to surrender my private room to the young father and his boys. I told my hosts I felt guilt at being waited upon, once I could do for myself again. In truth, I hoped by being closer, I could track where Ibbot might be hiding himself away.

Trouble brewed below. When I returned to the lower floor, I discovered the muleteer had redoubled his efforts to convince everyone that a man who would knife two miners, killing one, could not be trusted among decent folk. Even if I were not to blame for what befell him on the road, in some way he could not recall, surely the prudent thing would be to lock me away from the townfolk for everyone's safety.

This time he was gaining ground, at least with the miners who sat around the tables at mealtimes.

Ibbot had not seen fit to come to me upstairs bearing this bit of news. Instead, he had spent his days out in the town seeking the latest information about road conditions to the east and even the pass to the west.

"It could come to the necessity of a quick escape," he maintained, when at last I cornered him by the hearthside. Direction might not be as important as swift departure, in his view.

Cilliyon, sitting with me at the fire, took Ibbot seriously enough that she fretted aloud, though in Mercedish, whether I was recovered sufficiently to travel. I assured her I would of a certainty summon the will to flee rather than receive another beating. Or worse.

I decided to part with some of my money, reckoning that we would want heavier winter clothes for the journey, and also that folk are more kindly disposed toward someone who has put gold into their open palm.

"Can't we use this to buy a mule?" Ibbot raised wide eyes from the coins I placed in his hands.

"What do you propose to feed it and where do you want to stable it until we go? I can perhaps see the point of one mule. Maybe two,

Cilliyon can ride with me. But we only want them when we are ready to depart."

"You have that much more money?" he asked.

"I do not have enough more that it is worth your while to crack me on the head and steal it."

"This is already more than I've seen in one man's possession, with the exception of Kruthe the pirate. Perhaps I am more easily swayed by wealth than one inured to it, such as you."

"It's money my da gave me to live on, during my studies on Lohr Island."

"Never knew my father," Ibbot said, fingering the coins. "My mother told me he was a soldier. He never left me any money, to be sure."

"Did she give his name?" I could not imagine never knowing my da and what people I came from.

"You assume she knew his name," he said. He rose abruptly from the hearthside and walked away. Cilliyon looked after him, frowning.

Here I had thought he knew about brothels because he went to them. What if he had been born in one?

The world was a much wider and deeper place than I had known, coming up on the farm in Merced's mountains. Folk held beliefs I never heard tell of, and lived by customs which seemed so strange. Perhaps our ways in Merced appeared equally odd, when viewed from the outside looking in?

Of course, our hosts continued to take up for us despite the mule driver's campaigning. I had no appreciable decline in folk coming to me for healing. So for the most part, it seemed the muleteer was only finding support among the miners, who were not disposed favorably toward me anyway. Since I had made an end of Stas Royka.

I came upon Kunitka scolding the mule driver one afternoon. "Maybe yourself thinks to try and find some others to take yourself in for care. Ask around of these fellows yourself seeks to turn against Fenn Tedesch and just see if any of them will feed and wash and wipe as I do. I think I know what the answer will be!" She whirled away and saw me standing at the door. "Just so, it needed to be said." She went through to the kitchen with a swish of skirts. The driver closed his eyes and turned his face away from mine, huddled in his bed in the corner of the hearthroom.

Dusek became my perpetual shadow, whenever I left the lodging for any reason. My one-armed protector. He often came to sit with me at the fireside when he arrived for work, to share news of his mother or happenings in town.

All of us fell into the rhythm of the mine shifts, punctuated by the tolling of the bell. It became such a predictable routine that I sprang from my kitchen chair, as alarmed as everyone around me when the ringing came *at the wrong time*. The bell commenced and did not stop. Kunitka turned from her kettle with a hand over her mouth. Hengel threw down his forkful and began to pull on his outer gear, Yuli helping him while apparently praying.

Dusek dashed through the door from outside and said he must be able to do something to help, even with only one good arm.

"What's happened?" I said, looking one to another.

"They ring the signal for a mine disaster—collapsed tunnel or fire, some calamity. We must all go see which shaft and what we can do."

"I'll find Ibbot. Which of the mines is it? Can yourself know from the signal?"

Hengel paused to listen to the rhythm of the tolling. "The near ore. But I am not sure yourself should come. The miners who came to … they were all from that mine. Better yourself stay here with the women, I'm thinking."

"Can we ask Piet? I do not like to think of being left here if I can aid the injured." As I spoke, my obsidian blade, restored to its sheath on my leg, was suddenly thrumming.

Cilliyon turned imploring eyes my way. "I do not like to think of you being hurt like that again," she said in Mercedish.

"Everyone will be too busy with the catastrophe to worry about me, surely. And I'll have Ibbot with me."

"You don't know anything about mining!" she said in desperation.

"No," I admitted, "but I spent the greater share of last winter living in caves. I do have some proficiency below ground."

Hengel gripped the door handle, ready to go. "Find Ibbot and come on then. Dusek, bring them along to the mine with you."

When we arrived, we came upon a throng of milling men, gathered in deep snow by a black gash in the earth. A wooden tower rose, perched atop the rim of the hole, with a giant bellows poised above tubing that snaked into the opening. Dust and acrid smoke drifted from the mouth of the mine.

I looked for whoever might be in charge. One group of men lit lanterns, while others rushed up with pole picks and buckets. Another group tried frantically to repair the bellows where it had pulled away from its mooring lines along the tower. Men scrambled atop the thick timbers, yelling to each other and cursing when they could not reach the chains that dangled loose.

I asked Dusek the purpose of the tower and bellows.

"Fresh air," he said, distracted. "The bellows are pumped to send good air to the men working deep, otherwise they cannot breathe."

"So how are they breathing now?" Ibbot wanted to know.

He earned a withering look for that.

"Is the bellows what must be fixed first, before anything else can be done?" I asked.

"Yes, only then men will be sent below to see what has occurred, and exactly where."

I took Ibbot's elbow and led him closer to the tower through the crowd. "Can you help the efforts to restore this with your magic?" I kept my voice quiet to avoid being overheard, despite how busy everyone seemed around us.

"If I understood how it was supposed to work," he said uneasily.

"It's plain enough. Like a blacksmith's bellows, only many times larger."

"Living at sea, I have not spent a deal of time in a smithy's, as you might imagine."

I pushed his chin to the right and pointed with my other hand. "See where the mechanism to expand and compress the bellows is operated by men working those pump handles? The bellows must be bound tight to the tower with those chains in order to draw evenly. That is what they are trying to fix, where it has pulled away and bent. Can you aid that endeavor?"

He studied the men attempting to capture the loose chains. Gargle landed on my shoulder and looked around the ground by my feet with mocking care.

"Yes, I left Wieser to take care of the women. Can you do anything to help those men?" I pointed for Gargle, too.

This at least prompted Ibbot to mutter and place a hand to his brow. To the others he might have appeared to be praying. The stance he struck put me in mind of a man trying to recall where he had left something—as if seeing the misplaced item in his mind's eye and retracing his steps. He continued murmuring under his breath, swayed slightly on his feet from time to time, and gradually I became aware of a stiffening breeze coming down the snow-swept slope of the mountainside. It was not harsh enough to endanger the men clinging to the tower's timbers but it stirred and swung the chains sufficiently for them to be caught at last by the reaching men. A cheer went up around us at the sight.

Ibbot was sweating, I saw, and passed his arm over the moisture on his face to keep it from freezing there. He rolled his shoulders and cracked his neck, tipping his head to one side and then the other.

"What now?" he said. "Shall we make a run for it while they are all occupied here?"

To think it was on my tongue tip to congratulate him for helping. "No, now I am going into the mine to see what I can do to aid injured men. You could come along."

"You won't find me any help down there," he said.

"I suppose I am not astonished to hear that." I turned to go.

"Wait, wait. There is Piet, ask him to go with you, if he thinks you are not mad."

Piet did think I was mad to want to go into the mine, but he took me to the entrance with him anyway. My knife buzzed so against my skin that I felt numb where the sheath was strapped. Perhaps it was calling somehow to the below-ground spirits of this mountain?

Ibbot stayed above with Gargle, but Dusek accompanied me where

Piet led. We walked into the haze by the entrance. The breath sound of the now-drawing bellows faded as we penetrated the dark with our lanterns held aloft.

Other men walked ahead and behind us, grim and silent, trudging through the head-high tunnel hewn out of the rock. Timbers braced the roof and walls at regular intervals, and here and there a side passage gaped by the main, wider channel we paced. We arrived beside a pit in the floor, with a rickety rail around it. A windlass, such as might be used to draw up a bucket from a well, straddled the opening. The structure was many times larger than a water well's, the flat-sided bucket large enough to hold several men.

Dusek said this was the way to lower miners to the deepest workings, which was where he'd been told a tunnel roof had caved in, sealing men behind the rock. Piet spoke with the miner working the man-lift to learn more and came back to explain what they knew so far. How the miners had been testing the ceiling before the collapse by 'barring down', using a long iron bar to tap at the rock above. If a ringing sound was heard, the rock was solidly anchored; if it sounded like a drum, it threatened to come down on them. They had just heard the telltale hollow *thump* and begun to withdraw when the rocks gave way.

"There are men hurt below who need to be loaded onto the bucket platform and brought up. Able men need to go down and try to shift enough rock to free those miners trapped in the tunnel beyond the fall. Now that the bellows are pumping, rescue work begins."

"Send me down," I said. "I can get the injured men sent up as they are able to be moved. Bind up any that are bleeding, give them something for the pain if bones are broken."

Dusek said, "I'll go with him. I cannot shift rock, but I can help load men. I am still strong enough to do that."

"I'm not in charge here," Piet said.

"Tell whoever is in charge what we can do. I don't see any men being brought up, only going down with tools. We must be needed."

While Piet walked back to the lift worker, I looked about in the amber lantern glow. The tubes that brought the air from the bellows also snaked into the pit, presumably to the deeper shafts. They seemed to be made of oiled leather, from the way they glistened wherever they were shielded from a thick coat of dust. Particles wafting in the air clogged my throat and made me cough.

"Yourself does grow used to that, after a time," Dusek said knowingly. "There's always some drifting but after a collapse there's so much more." He waved a hand in the lantern's light and stirred the dust motes.

Piet returned to say we would be loaded into the bucket and sent down. "Much luck to both. May we all live to yet again see the light of day."

As the winch squeaked and the bucket dropped, I thought I also heard the whispery dry-leaf voices of the cave spirits.

Welcoming me, knowing me by the blade of power their brethren in Merced had given me.

Come down to us, the whispers seemed to say in my mind, tell us of our brothers and sisters far away. Come.

I looked for some source of the sounds, playing my light over the hewn walls of the shaft as we sank lower. The beam caught a sight that chilled me.

The air tube was crushed, split apart. The soft shush of air emptied into the shaft instead of being carried down to those below. "Look," I said to Dusek, pointing. He sucked in a breath and nodded.

"How do we signal to those above? It must be fixed, yes?"

"When we reach the bottom, I will send word back up with the injured to fix it before the air runs short."

We went deeper still, swaying slightly in the lift. The bucket landed with a solid *thud*.

Chaos loomed on all sides. Men stumbled against the walls or fell to their knees, gasping. Many lay sprawled about the passage. At once I, too, could feel the stale air drawing my lungs dry. And there was something else in the air as well, some scent that did not belong. The lanterns were dimming …

"Oh, we are too late. Too late," Dusek said, pulling at his tunic neck with his good arm, trying to gather more breath.

I looked up the shaft behind me, hoping to see a way to signal I wanted the bucket raised. How long would the man above wait for me to load the injured before lifting the bucket? How could he know when it was time? Or would he pull it up to unwittingly send more men down into this hazard?

I gripped Dusek by the shoulder. "How do you send word to those above? There must be a way. They are dying here from lack of air."

He shook his head, already growing slack-witted.

I put my knife between my teeth and hauled myself up to balance on the edge of the bucket. A pair of iron bars arched over the top like handles and I shinnied along one to grasp the rope secured where they crossed. I climbed the thick, twisted hemp as fast as I could. Hand over hand, gripping with legs and feet. My goal: to reach the break in the air hose, before I passed out and fell to my death. Once there, I would try to think what to do.

I rose into darkness, beyond the reach of the weakening lanterns, for I had no hand to carry one with me up the rope. I needed Ibbot's light stone, I thought, but I had no hand for that either, even if I could somehow obtain it from him on the mountain above. The moonstone pendant slipped from the neck of my tunic on its leather cord and swung side to side slapping my shoulders as I pulled myself higher. I let go of the rope to shove the moonstone back inside my shirt and felt a shock of cold course from my hand up my arm. I looked to the stone in my fist. Seeing iridescent gleam between my fingers, I opened my hand. The moonstone shone like a full moon in a clear night sky. I let it drop to my chest and looked about me to see the walls of the shaft softly illuminated. If I had accomplished the light by magic, I had again done it unawares. Could only my need make it so?

I began to climb again. What would I do when I reached the break?

We are watching, the voices sighed.

Will you help me? I thought.

No need, they whispered.

The sound of the hissing air reached me first, then my light shone on the sundered tube. I looped one arm through the rope and twisted it tight once I hung alongside the break. By rocking myself to and fro, I set the rope swinging toward the wall of the shaft. After two lunges that fell short, I managed to snag an arm around the tube. I found shallow toe holds in the rough stone wall and braced myself as best I could. Thank the gods the tube end had not come completely loose, it was attached by a slender bit of leather, or else it would have fallen to the bottom of the shaft.

In Merced, I had learned a spellcasting to halt a team of horses. I cast this now, but over the man who wound the windlass. The rope must remain where I hung. Hastily, I also cast every warding spell I knew to confound the thoughts of the other men at the top of the shaft so they would not haul the bucket up before I did what needed to be done. If Ibbot could read my thoughts, I implored him to likewise distract them from any urge resulting in me pulled up and away.

I gripped rope and tube and used my free hand to stretch the upper end wide open where it had been flattened. I tipped down as far as I dared and just barely reached the sagging lower end of the tube to draw it up closer to me. Next, I used my knife to cut a wedge in the leather and overlapped the lower end enough to jam it inside the upper. A couple of feet would do, *must do* because that was all the slack in the tube. Trying to ignore the burning, trembling muscles in my arm and shoulder, I slit the leg of my trousers and pulled away a long strip of fabric. That done, I put my knife back between my teeth. My palms were growing sweaty despite the chill air. Now with a coating of oil from the tube's leather, my slickened hand could scarcely hold fast. I could not afford to slip. Or worse, to drop my blade down the shaft. My toes cramped where I had jammed them into crevices in the hewn wall. Could I hold on long enough to finish? I stuffed the fabric strip in the waist of my trousers.

I took up my knife again, cutting slits easily through the double thickness of treated leather where I had pushed one tube end into the other. No other knife would have sliced it. Blessing the kavsprit of home for their gift, I slid the knife back in its sheath. I took one end of the fabric strip between my teeth and wove the length in and out of the slits in the tube, poking it through one hole and snagging it with my finger from the next to draw out again. The air rushing through the tube pushed the strip downward but I learned where to feel for it. At last, nearly faint from the wrenching strain in my shoulder and legs, I fumbled to tie a knot with the scant length left over. Barely enough, but it held.

Muttering the words to strengthen my spells, so the bucket would not be hauled up just yet, I hung and watched to make sure the graft had taken. Air no longer hissed and sighed away that I could hear or feel. I descended as slowly as I could, wanting to give the passage below time to receive sufficient good air that I did not climb down only to die. For how then could I help any others?

Good, seemed to hush through my mind.

Did you help me know what to do? I thought back.

The spirits made no answer.

CHAPTER EIGHTEEN

Dusek and I worked together readily once the air began to freshen. We dragged the unconscious men closer to the openings in the tube, where they could benefit from the restorative effects. The odd smell I had noted faded gradually. The men still on their feet when we two had come down must have been those who came below most recently. They recovered fastest. The lanterns' glow grew to proper brightness, so I tucked my pendant into my tunic. The jumble of rock blocking the passage could be seen through the swirling dust. Miners set to work with their picks and shovels.

Dusek showed me the cord to be pulled to signal those above to raise the bucket platform.

"I knew there had to be a way! But why did they keep sending men down when none were coming up? Did they not wonder why no one was calling to come above again?"

"In an emergency, perhaps not." He tugged on the rope and frowned. "It rings a bell above. But it should have more give than—"

The rope fell into coils on the stone at our feet. The end was frayed and unraveling.

I prodded it with my boot. "Caught up somewhere above and rubbed to the breaking point. Maybe by the same shifting that crushed the air tube. Let's move the worst injured into the bucket. We must get word to those above about the signal. Put the bell cord onto the platform, too."

We put two of the worst injuries, a man with both legs broken and another with a mangled hand and smashed shoulder, propped as comfortably as we could manage against the sides of the bucket. I chose a man who had an arm broken like Dusek's to carry the message up about the sundered signal rope, since he had his wits about him though in pain.

First, I straightened his arm as best I could. I cut off his shirt sleeves to tie to a broken pick handle, to splint the arm so he might avoid the ill healing that impeded Dusek.

"Wish yourself had been here when I came up hurt," Dusek said, helping the fellow to the bucket.

Once they were settled, I released all the spellwork I had placed. The bucket began to rise soon after, which drew moans from the men within. I hoped they would be taken down into the town without delay, for their wounds to be cleansed and seen to by the women waiting there. I bade Dusek stand at the descending shaft, ready to send the men who came down next into the collapsed tunnel where their strength was needed.

"Be sure to ask the men who come down how we will signal now to have the bucket raised, if the signal rope cannot be restored," I said as I turned to the other miners lying injured.

The wounds from falling stone, which shattered and crushed bones, marked the worst injuries I saw. Miners ignored scrapes and bleeding, so focused were they on reaching the others who were beyond the rubble-choked tunnel. Two men, uncovered beneath the rock, lay dead. When the bodies were freed from the wreckage, Dusek and I moved them away to a side passage. They could wait to go above.

Once I had seen to all the injured who needed to be treated and sent up, I stepped beside the toiling men. Picking up an abandoned shovel, I scooped rock dislodged and broken up by the picks and moved it away to the side. The man I worked beside turned to cast me a brief glance. I saw he was the one Dusek had called Alun, the leader of the miners who came to kill me.

He drew back sharply. I merely nodded. I had no wish to betray I knew him. I carried on working, and he resumed his swings of the pick. At least he swung at the rocks and not at me.

I concluded in no time at all that I did not aspire to be a miner.

When we had shifted enough rubble, the men called for the iron bar. Everyone stepped back to make way for the miner who came carrying it over his shoulder. He rapped and banged the rock above, directly over his head. A brave man, in my estimation. All listened in tense silence for the sounds from the rock brought by his blows, ringing out clear, no drumbeats this time.

Miners crowded back to the jumble and the rhythm of their metal clanging against the rock grew more urgent. Men could be running out of time, it seemed to say. If the spirit voices spoke, I could not hear them in the din.

Another body was uncovered. Dusek and I took him to lay beside his fellows in the side passage. Young men, all three.

We worked on, but progress seemed so slow. My shoulders and back ached. I coughed and my eyes streamed from the fine dirt that wafted in the air like lake mist. Grime coated me, especially my sweaty leg exposed by the strip cut from my trousers.

More fuel was sent for the lanterns. Also water flasks, one of which Dusek pressed on me. He too saw Alun but said nothing once he glanced my way and met my eyes. Though Dusek could not dig, he directed much of the rescue effort. He kept careful track of men who were flagging and replaced them with fresh arms.

However often such disasters occurred, someone like Dusek with a gift for overseeing the response would be invaluable. The mine should keep him on just for that role, I decided. I would ask Piet who among the miners might make use of the suggestion.

Unless Dusek truly did not want to come down here anymore. I could understand better now if that was the case, having broken my back on the rock for just one day.

Barring down was performed again. The roof still rang and we toiled on.

When I had stopped thinking any longer and only moved by rote with an empty mind, we broke through to the far side.

Of the half dozen within, only two remained alive. A pair had been crushed by the rock fall, two others had succumbed to blood loss from sundered limbs. One of the living was unconscious with a wide gash in his scalp, the other unmarked but sore in need of air, talking in gasps and making no sense.

Alun had held out a hand to aid me when I clambered through the opening to examine them all. He helped me carry the two living men out over the rubble to the bucket. And when we stood together watching the platform rise, under the wary eye of Dusek, Alun said to me, "Yourself does not belong here, outlander. Leave."

I dragged a weary arm across my face. "So, leave the mine, or leave Lunenhelm?'

He spat. "Hold a smart tongue behind the teeth yourself wants to keep. Get out of town."

At that, I decided it was time to go above in the next bucket. I asked Dusek to come with me, as I didn't like to leave him down there with the surly Alun. Some injury to my friend might not be questioned, what with all men focused on working.

Dusek might better consider becoming a healer, instead of managing disaster aid, I thought as we went up the shaft. I would copy some of my folio of Annora's teachings for him, if he showed willing.

Before I fled Lunenhelm at my earliest opportunity.

Above, I did what more I could for the men with broken bones. The man with both thighs broken was more likely to die than to heal, from lung fever due to being bedfast for so long as it would take to knit long bones. I splinted him and told his wife to have a frame placed over his bed with rope handles for him to grab and pull himself up, thus to keep him moving as much as he could while bed bound.

"If I was a pit pony, they would be merciful and slaughter me," he groaned.

"Maybe," I said. "But a pony has no wife who wants him around." I gestured toward the woman who hovered near his side, twisting her handkerchief. "I'll leave this potion with her. Use it for the pain. But do not ask her for so much of it that yourself sleeps the day and night around, or no one will have to make an end of it. When a chest fills up with phlegm, death will follow."

Not happy words, but I did not hold with anything but speaking plain.

Dusek evidently did not either. He wasted no time finding Piet to tell him about Alun's warning me to leave town. I suppose I could have told him not to mention it, but I was enough of a coward and eager enough to avoid another beating that I did not mind if the law realized I was still under threat.

Piet escorted me to the boarding house in the early dawn light, together with Ibbot and Gargle. He'd told Dusek to bring his mother and come stay there as well. "Those men will be unpredictable in the aftermath of the collapse. Miners have a need to blame the bad on some curse or ill luck they can eliminate—it gives them the illusion they can steer their fate."

"As superstitious as sailors, it seems," Ibbot mused as Piet walked away from the fireside.

"Perhaps it is true wherever men do hazardous work," I said. I ruefully examined my ruined trousers and made ready to go up to wash.

"What I mean is, I believe Piet, and I think it is high time we leave here. I do not much care which direction we go, either. While you were busy saving the men who want to do you further mischief—"

"Calling it mischief is a bit pale!"

He waved a hand impatiently. "While you were off in the ground doing that, I discovered that men here glide over the snow on slats of wood and make good time, too. I think we should learn to do this and depart."

"You mean like sled runners?"

"Not a sled, slats strapped to their feet."

In Merced's mountains we used snow frames. A pair of them, strapped to the feet, were broad enough to keep a man from sinking into deep snow. Travel was arduous and hardly fast, though. "Where did you see this?"

"Go and clean up. I'll tell you all about it after."

My trousers had disappeared when I came out of the washroom, leaving me to rummage in my bag for the only other pair I had. I found

Yuli and Cilliyon in the kitchen using the damaged pair as a pattern to carve some of Hengel's trousers down to my size.

Yuli pointed her shears at me. "Yourself needs warmer clothes. Winter is a long way from finished with us here."

I thanked her meekly and stole a biscuit from the pan cooling on the side table. I knew she saw me, but she looked the other way as if she hadn't. I slipped Wieser half of it.

I was that glad we had come upon her home in the woodland, and no one else's.

I took myself off to round up Ibbot and learn about travel by ... slats?

Dusek insisted on coming with me out of doors, and more or less dumped his mother at the hearth to do so. "Yourself must take Piet seriously. I'd like to think by having worked to save miners, it would temper the feelings against yourself, but I know how they are in their grudges. Just as Piet does. All yourselves will always be outsiders."

There being little use arguing with him, since he was right, I greeted his mother. She was another round, rosy-cheeked woman who looked to be the living future of Kunitka's appearance in years to come. I told Yuli about the new guest on our way out the back door, Wieser pushing alongside me with the same insistence as Dusek.

We discovered Ibbot in the back yard enclosure, holding two head-high, narrow, utterly straight planks of flat wood. "Oh," Dusek said with delight, "skis!"

There ensued an hour of profound hilarity for Gargle, who perched on the porch rail in the pallid daylight. One-handed, Dusek could not demonstrate how to strap the slats to our boots, so attempted to describe how it was done. He was a man more used to doing than telling. Once we each managed to get the things on, Ibbot and I took turns at tangling the tips or sliding on our backsides. Because I had tried to teach Keltanese soldier Gevarr how to walk on snow frames, I realized the challenge of such things. Gargle had been amused by that, too, as I remembered.

But still! How could these ever work?

"I do not see how a man can make good time traveling this way," I complained, pulling my face out of the snowbank I had stumbled into. Wieser licked my numb nose.

"By practicing," Ibbot said. "I saw men coming toward the mine from the west, gliding along the roadway. They could go uphill by setting the slats at an angle into the hillside. And placed them side-by-side to slide down a slope. They covered ground quite well."

"Let's see you do more than fall down, then."

"Let's go in, I need to see to mother," Dusek said. "Strap them onto me tomorrow and I will show how it is done."

We were thawing beside the kitchen fire with mugs of hot cider when Piet came in and waved a thick packet wrapped in oilcloth. "Some news has made it through the pass. Perhaps the decision regarding the miner's death at solstice, if my courier reached the council."

He sat at the kitchen table with us and welcomed the mug Yuli set before him. If he noticed Ibbot and I sat motionless and neglected our own mugs, he did not remark on it. He picked apart the knots and spread papers before him. Though good to hear if I was found blameless by the authorities, I did not think it would matter to Stas Royka's friends one way or another.

In my relief at Piet's smile when he lifted his eyes and said, "No penalty. Justifiable," I forgot to worry about what else might have made its way into a news packet.

I looked back at Piet after accepting happy sentiments from my friends to find the big man frowning at his remaining papers. "A killing in the port—the stable owner slain. Three male fugitives …"

We were a party of two men and one woman now, I told myself. I willed Cilliyon, who looked as white as a frosted windowpane, not to faint. Ibbot raised an eyebrow at me. I wondered if the muleteer's memory would be jogged anew if this news reached his ears.

"And here's a reward in the offing," Piet continued, reading down the sheet. "Escaped slaves, two men and a girl. A goodly amount, they must be valuable. Perhaps they escaped from the market?"

"Folk will be hunting them hard for that kind of money," Kunitka said, looking over his shoulder. "Wouldn't they run away to sea this time of year? Instead of over land?"

"I would think so, if they had sense." His voice was mild, his attention on the rest of the news sheets.

Even though he did not fix us with an icy official stare just at that moment, I could not but think he would add it all up eventually and come up with the sum of us.

There was nothing else for it. We must leave before first light and take our chances in the mountains to the east.

CHAPTER NINETEEN

As soon as our fellow hearthside sleepers settled for the night, Ibbot leaned close to me and hissed through clenched teeth. "Just how is it you propose we get supplies, obtain skis or mules, leave town without being noticed, and do anything but die in the cold, cold snow?"

"Do you want to stay now? And wait for someone to collect the reward by marching us back to Kruthe and Mage Balin? Because you were the one who has been pressing me to leave, as I recall."

"Yes, and no one would ever believe it is me who's showing some sense by saying we have to leave in an orderly fashion."

"Just how is that to be done?"

He was silent for a moment. "Cilliyon," he said. "I think Cilliyon was so distraught about whether you would be punished for murder, that now you are free and no longer required to linger here for the ruling to reach us, she is eager to travel on for our nuptials. That is why we will ask for help to ready ourselves to brave the elements and journey on to your uncle. Cilliyon has been through so much. We must show the maiden some compassion, you see?"

"They'll try to talk us out of it."

"I shall be resolute in support of my bride-to-be. I cannot bear to distress her further." His tone turned dark. "And neither can you, her only brother."

"Know that I expect you to do the convincing. You're the better liar."

"I am, at that. It isn't that I have not come to appreciate our hosts. I admit it has been pleasant enough here, for the most part. Though dull." He gave a mirthless chuckle. "They are plotting for you to stay on and be their healer, you know. Aimed that girl at you. Still, young Sefina is a pretty one. Did you cadge a kiss at least?"

"Gods, no. I'd surely have been strung up by my thumbs for it if I had. The way they feel about their women folk here."

"It seems they are of two altogether conflicting minds about women," Ibbot said. I could only agree, remembering the scene I had interrupted in the kitchen.

I got to my feet. "I'll go up and tell Cilliyon."

"Why you?"

"Because I'm the only man who can come knocking on her door in the night. I'll tell her to express her eagerness to depart to the young mother, to lend some ring of truth to your tale."

"Take care not to stir up the whole house." Ibbot shifted in his chair and closed his eyes.

So, it came to pass within days that we set out on the road, Cilliyon astride a decent mule, which also carried food and even a pair of cooking pots. We were well-outfitted against the weather and Ibbot and I were managing adequately on our skis. It seemed for novices, usually children in these parts, a pelt strapped to the bottom of the slat helped keep the wood from slipping backward on the snowy crust.

Our map had been helpfully marked for us by Hengel and Piet, identifying known way stations for those foolish enough to be out on the winter road. These stations were kept stocked with firewood and preserved food, as Yuli had done in her home when she came to the boarding house. It was a Yegan custom, Kunitka told me. Travelers were expected to leave a bit of money when using the places, for the owner to collect in the spring.

"But how would they know who you were if you didn't?" Ibbot had asked, when I told him of the practice as we organized our gear.

Cilliyon cast her eyes toward the rafters. "It's the honor system, Ibbot. I can see that it is unfamiliar to you."

Our departure had involved more lady tears than I cared for, and even some from Dusek, too. He was evidently of a tender-hearted bent. Not necessarily bad in a healer. I had given him the pages of herb lore copied from my folio and encouraged him to study up for the future.

Skiing proved heavy work in the soft snow, though not as hard as laboring in the mine. I was still sore from that toil. Ibbot and I would surely be very fit if we covered all the miles before us on skis. In fact, after only an hour he began asking me when it would be his turn to ride.

"Save the mule's back. You are not so feeble as all that, are you?"

"Save the mule and not me, I suppose. Cilliyon should learn how to ski, in case she needs to get about without being coddled."

Though winded, I spared enough breath to declare, "If all the folk I was charged with hauling around Merced evading soldiers had been like you, I'd have left them in a ditch."

He in turn found enough breath for a short laugh.

Whenever we paused to rest, the silence of the heaped snow and crystal-bright air made me homesick for the mountains of Merced. Casting my eyes up the slopes and crags, it was clear we traveled in avalanche country, though. The risk here appeared even greater than the valleys at home where snow slides sometimes came; these mountainsides funneled steeply to the roadbed along a narrow valley. There would be nowhere to flee if the snow came thundering down.

When Wieser barked at taunting Gargle, I shushed her sharply. Cilliyon looked at me with a question in her eyes, but I did not like to worry her about the danger. She knew no more mountain lore than Ibbot, since she had grown up in the plains of southern Merced's river basin.

I carried my knife for protection on the trail and had begged a crossbow and bolts on the pretense that I might need to hunt. I did not expect trouble from brigands. Piet said there was little thievery to worry us in the wintertime, but hungry snow cats might see us, or the mule, as a meal.

Fingering letters I carried in my tunic, I remembered the bad moment during our leave-taking when Piet pressed on me the copies he had done of the news packet. He directed us to carry the missives to communities east. The escaped trio of slaves and the fugitives from the port murder both figured prominently, so I planned to use those pages for tinder at some hearth along the way.

A time or two as we prepared to leave, I had come upon Ibbot murmuring in his conjuring stance and wondered if he was making the weather favorable, or clouding Piet's mind so he did not recognize in us the criminals he was supposed to apprehend. I resolved to ask Ibbot later, but not until we were well distant.

The first way station we stopped at come bluish dusk was more a shepherd's hut than a home like Yuli's. I wanted very much to believe it was far enough away that none of Stas Royka's friends would have followed us. While I did not like the idea of Alun claiming he had sent me scurrying like a kicked dog, better my pride should endure that than my body endure him bringing a gang of miners to make sure we all stayed gone for good.

I told Wieser I wanted to know at once if anyone approached the round stone building. Snow lay heavy on a timbered roof, and no tracks marred the snow on the walk to the door. I did not use a branch to sweep our tracks away, since our presence would be evident anyway from the smoke curling out of the chimney. We had to have a fire or freeze, this high in wintery peaks.

A lean-to served as shelter for the mule, and for a wonder there was ample hay inside. We carried some grain for him, so he could travel hard, not expecting we would find stored grain along the route. I had Cilliyon scoop a pan of snow to melt for the animal's water while I laid the fire.

Ibbot grew impatient with my flint and waved a hand with a few words to make the tinder catch. "You have a daily job for the duration of our journey," I told him.

"You could do it easily, if you would only let me teach you."

"I'll see, later. Let's get more distance between us and the coast before I look to anything else."

Food for us consisted of dried fruit, smoked sausage and hard bread too reminiscent of ship's biscuit for my taste. I spent a few moments in thought and prayer for my shipmates, Cuffer, Lichan, Tobal the cook, Shipmaster Alisdar, wondering where they were now and how they fared. Even if we were trekking through the frigid mountains, we were doing so of our own free will.

Blankets near the banked fire made our beds. "You're not going to make us take watch, are you? I'm tired to the bone," Ibbot said.

"I have never known anyone so useless!" Cilliyon burst out. "Judian half kills himself herding us about and all you can do is—"

"I really think you had better keep up the pretense of calling him Fenn," Ibbot said judiciously. "You might slip at an inopportune moment. Again."

"Leave her alone, Ibbot. You know you can be useless. And you already knew who I was, before she said. I'll take watch. I'll try to remember you're here if a snow cat comes prowling, so I don't forget to wake you as I'm running for the door."

"Yes, I see there is only one door, not two like you told us was required in the mountains."

I laughed and pointed. "See the window into the lean-to for the mule? That's the other way out. Do you think you can haul yourself through it?"

"Depends on what is chasing me ..." he mused.

The night passed without alarms, or nightmares for Ibbot such as he had shown the first night away from the ship. It was curious to me that he had shown no more Night Terrors during our stint in Lunen-helm. I wondered if it was distance from his old master or sleeping indoors that had spared us at the hearthside.

At dawn, we rose to begin our trek again and discovered clouds of icy mist outside the hut. I entreated Ibbot to blow the haar away, so we could see where we traveled and not ski off a precipice. He did so, grumbling about being of *some* use after all.

We continued on in this fashion, traveling to the next place thoughtfully marked for us on our map and finding differing but serviceable accommodations at each station. We saw no other folk on the road and often had to guess where the actual roadbed might lie since no one had passed that way to break a trail.

It was a good map we had, though, and I said several way-finding spells over it, learned from my book. I continued to chalk my runes wherever we stopped, for protection and to escape detection.

Cilliyon did not comment, but Ibbot was derisive. "You know that is only the lowest sort of magic."

"It has seemed to help me more than once."

"That cannot be what helps you," he said, but he turned away and would say no more.

Cilliyon came to me one evening as I picked out the mule's feet and asked to be taught how to do it. I showed her where to squeeze the fetlock so he would lift up his hoof and what to look for while cleaning away mud and ice packed in from the day's travels. She bent forward with her hood pushed back. I noticed how long her fair hair had grown in the months since we left *Moon Road*. Soft curls fell over her brow and I reached out to push them back so she could see. She started at my touch. Then she smiled and looked at me curiously.

I was saved from having to think of something to say to her by Ibbot poking his head around the shed door and reporting, "The fire's lit. Where is the pot to boil snow in?"

"Don't boil it for the mule, only melt it." I turned to look at him. "We boil what we drink for tisanes."

"I'm so happy there is you to correct me at every turn."

I went with him to locate the pot. Cilliyon looked back to the mule's hoof cradled in her hand.

"A tender moment between the siblings?" Ibbot said by the fire. "Take care, or we'll have to change the tale to make you the bridegroom and me the brother."

If it had been my brother Wils teasing me, I'm sure I could have thought of backchat to offer. I felt at a loss just then, so I walked out to fill the pot with snow.

The lights in the sky were just coming out to dance and I stood to watch. Whatever else I remembered of Yega, this feast for eye and spirit sweeping across the heavens, these shimmering curtains of color, would always abide with me.

I stood there lost in wonderment and only came to my senses as Gargle cawed in the distance, then closer, then cawed just before my face with a great flapping of black wings as well. I looked to see what had stirred him and saw torches on the road, carried by riders coming toward the cabin out of the east.

It was difficult to make out details due to their heavy outer gear, but there were three riders on mules and another mule towing some manner of sledge with a person seated on it.

I went in to tell Ibbot and Cilliyon to make ready for company.

We moved our blankets and other gear over to one side of the fireplace. I hoped there to be enough room on the floor for everyone to sleep. The shed would be crowded with their animals, too, but all would be the warmer for more bodies within.

They came in without knocking. Indeed, why would they do so, we did not knock either at these stations. All were men and the one from the sled of a great age and blind besides. The others propped him close by the fire, called him *father* in voices of respect. We introduced ourselves all around and two of them went out to see to their mules.

"The smoking chimney was a welcome sight. I feared we were arriving too late to make a good fire before hard dark," said the tallest. He gave his name as Bryar.

We spoke our tale of journeying to my uncle for a wedding, they told of taking their father to Lunenhelm as he wished to go home once more before he died. They believed the old man's time was near, so set out despite winter's grip on the mountains. They knew many of the people we had met. Since they would be sure to mention having met us on their trek, I was beyond glad we had given out the same story as we told in Lunenhelm instead of weaving another.

I recalled the next town was Alberi and asked if we would be able to reach it with one more day of travel.

"Best allow two. Stay at the river crossing tomorrow night. There's been an avalanche on the high road and all travelers must go over the river, then cross it again to resume the climb." I pulled out my map and had him show me where to avoid and where to return to the upper roadway.

"How will we cross the river?" Ibbot asked.

"Oh, it is frozen solidly enough for walking on, even for the mule. It is months before the ice will break up."

"And what is this avalanche that forces us to detour?" Ibbot asked me, frowning over my shoulder at the distance this would add to our supposed route.

Their curious looks forced me to add, "Ourselves are come here from some distance away, across the sea. This mountain region is unfamiliar."

Bryar tilted his head. "I can think of better times than deep winter to acquaint yourselves with the Yegan terrain."

"True words," I said, not sure how much I should say about fleeing in disobedience to our imaginary family when these sons would brave the mountain winter for their da's wishes. Just then Wieser rose from my chairside and crossed to the old man, who slumped in his chair, drowsing in the fire's warmth. Bryar turned from scrutinizing me to watch her approach his father, gathering himself to stand, evidently concerned she would disturb or molest him. She merely sniffed his gnarled hand where it lay curled in his lap.

The old one stirred and smiled. He lifted his hand to stroke her ears, and she curled next to his feet with a satisfied sigh. He closed his eyes again.

Eyes downcast, Cilliyon bade me offer them some of the tisane she had finished brewing. She spoke only to me and not any other menfolk, as a proper maiden should do in this country. I saw she had thought to cover her hair with a kerchief in the manner of Yegan women, as well. She kept her wits close about her and no mistake.

I filled their cups and mugs with mint brew. They asked us no more about why we were so foolish as to travel about now of all times. Particularly as we had no dying father's last request to fulfill. Wieser opened an eye and met my gaze. As I passed her, I silently blessed her wisdom.

And wished for it to be contagious.

CHAPTER TWENTY

S ometime close to midnight, it was not Ibbot who disturbed our rest with a Night Terror, but the old man. He shrieked and wailed and beat at his temples, shocking us all from deep slumber. He gibbered and moaned, flinging his head side-to-side, as Bryar bent over him in the red glow of the banked fire. Wieser lay alongside him and he clutched at her with bony fingers.

I went to his side and knelt, not sure what ailed him but hoping to help in some way. "Has he done this before?" I asked Bryar. He shook his head, as helpless as I was. He and his brothers ringed the trembling man. The thin legs kicked at his blanket and he struck at his own head again.

Before I could think what to look for in my book, the aged man cried out once more, and jerked in a fit. His old limbs shuddered like ship timbers in a gale, while froth flew from his lips. His face grew dark in the ruddy firelight, and he gasped as his body stilled.

And breathed no more.

"He's gone," Bryar choked out. I reached out to close the slack mouth. Cilliyon gave a little sob behind us. The brothers bowed their heads.

Only Ibbot, who had not risen from his bedroll, appeared unmoved by the event. "What felled him?" he asked, in the tone I might use to ask if there was a biscuit left from supper.

I clenched my jaw before replying, "A sort of fit. Some sudden attack of pain in his head, it seemed."

His sons gathered him up and tenderly wound his blanket around him. I helped them carry him to the opposite wall, as far away from the fire's heat as possible. To lay his body outdoors for the greater cold would be to invite some scavenger to defile it. He seemed to weigh hardly anything in death; my little sister Morie might weigh more by now.

I thought of my own da, a great bear of a man. Surely he would not waste down to such a wizened bundle as this when his time came? I ached for my family and my home, witnessing this family's grief. Cilliyon came to my side and slipped her hand into mine. I gripped hers hard without really meaning to, but she did not pull away. She pressed her cheek to my shoulder.

Gradually, the men went back to the fireside in silence. Bryar shook my hand, why I could not guess as I had done nothing to aid their father. I only wished I could have done something. Or eased his passing, freed him from pain.

Sleep came slowly, not least because Ibbot was soon snoring like a dull saw chewing wood.

When I rose early, I stoked the fire and shrugged into my heavy gear to go out with our kettle for snow to melt. Ibbot stopped me at the door. He looked to the others, all still asleep as far as was apparent, then whispered, "They will want to travel with us. We cannot allow it."

"Why will they?"

"The old one wanted to go to Lunenhelm, to visit the place one last time. Now that he's dead, they will take him back where they came from for the funeral rites."

I said I did not know how Ibbot could be sure of this, but when I came back from the drifts with my pot of snow, Bryar was rousting his brothers.

"Ah, Fenn. We will all go east together. It is good to have a larger company, yes?"

I caught Ibbot's dark look from under his lowered brow.

So. He was right.

"Does not a larger, louder party make greater risk of avalanche?" I said.

Ibbot lifted a lip, as if my first try at evading an expanded company did little to impress him.

"Perhaps true. We are safer from wild creatures, though, with more of a herd." Bryar continued pulling from their foodstuff ration and generously proffered packets of dried fruit and nuts for the oat gruel Cilliyon stirred at the hearth.

I sought to bring our map to my mind's eye and to recall if we had told them exactly where we were bound, beyond 'east to our uncle.' I thought the brothers would have said if we had named their very town as our destination, if only to call us out for claiming we had relation there. Everyone knew everyone else and all their family business at little mountain burgs, in my experience.

But how could we turn away to the south toward the sea and unravel our lie? My goal was still to get to the port on the coast and buy passage aboard a ship. One bound for Lohr Island in my plan, whatever I had to do to Ibbot to prevent him making for Scythera with me in tow.

I said I would see to the mules, to snatch a chance alone to look at my map. The other two brothers, Sencha and Leran by name, rose and stepped that way with me at once. Offers of chore help did not usually cause my stomach to sour.

Our gruel waited warm on the hearth when we returned from readying the mules for travel. Cilliyon packed away the cooking gear and Ibbot sat staring at nothing. I ate in silence.

Bryar and Sencha lifted their father's body onto the sledge and Leran secured it with care. They each held their caps in hand and stood with bowed heads beside the corpse. I did the same. I had to give Ibbot a good poke to make him likewise show respect. Cilliyon did not need prompting.

I left two coins at the hut, to compensate for the lodging and also the portion of hay I stuffed into the emptiest cloth sack we carried. Bryar nodded approval as he added his own.

Ibbot and I skiied while the others rode. Bryar led, since they had traveled that route on their way to us and knew recent conditions. By midday, we approached the junction that required us to take the lower road to the river, in order to avoid the avalanche on the high road.

I saw Ibbot looking at the empty back of the mule that pulled the sledge as we labored on our skis. By the gods, I swore I would box his ears if he asked to ride. I drew beside him to tell him as much, when Bryar held up a hand to signal a halt to our party.

The brothers passed around hard cheese and dry bread, which we chomped as best we could without choking. Could their brittle-toothed father have eaten such challenging fare, I wondered. Perhaps they had brought softer food for him. Cilliyon especially nibbled at hers like a mouse at a dried bean. Hard cider came out next, hard indeed to keep from freezing in the bitter cold. Although it burned a path to my guts, it did moisten the dry crumbs clogging my mouth and throat. All of it proved more filling than the fragments of dried venison and fish we had been eating as we traveled.

A snow squall swept us, spinning flakes so thickly the trees blurred around our huddled group. My cheeks stung.

Cilliyon barely sipped at her cider and I wondered if she was thinking of the miner worse for drink who pawed at her. Gods knew I thought of him then, dead by my hand. The miner haunted me. The muleteer rotting by the hearth in Lunenhelm haunted me. Even the stranger dead in the port stable seemed to lurk at my shoulder, slipping alongside the others, each a darker shape in echoing shadows. I disguised a shiver, one not due to cold, by lurching to my feet and gesturing toward the trees at the edge of our path. This signal that I was going off to relieve myself was acknowledged with nods from the others, who then returned to their cups.

Except for Ibbot, who rose to join me in leaving the clearing.

Gargle landed on a branch overlooking my chosen tree and croaked at me gustily while I pissed. So great was his agitation that I took a closer look at him. "And what sets your beak cross-wise today? Trouble on the way ahead?"

Ibbot finished as well and came to stand over my shoulder. "Most likely he sees the folly of our excessive numbers, even if you will not." He spoke quietly. We were not far from the rest of our party, but no mistaking the intensity in his voice. I did not turn to face him, but he had my attention. And Gargle's, too, it seemed.

"Listen to me close," Ibbot continued, "for I am done sailing along with the current. You and I, and Cilliyon as well if you must have it that way, are striking out on our own. *No more delay.* We will leave this group with no ability to send anyone after us or name us to any who seek us. It is their bad luck to have run onto us and this is the consequence. You can aid me or I will do it alone. But be certain: I do have means to keep you from interfering and, once it is settled, Cilliyon pays the cost if you did not stay out of my way."

"Kill them all?" I kept my gaze on Gargle's beady eyes.

"I can leave them insensible in the cold like the muleteer, death would follow soon enough. I will be more merciful to extinguish each soul and send the brothers to be greeted by their father. You could help me, to make the transition quick for them. Summon the black fire as you did in the boardinghouse kitchen."

"I'll confess to you now, I don't know how I did that." *And if I did know, I would use it on you in their stead.*

I felt a puff of air on my cheek from his laugh. As if he had heard my thought, he said, "Indeed? Still you love me so little, after all I have done for you?"

Now I felt him move, as Gargle leapt aloft, cawing. I whirled about. He backed a bare pace away, both palms aimed at me, the cold of the high mountains a match to the cold anger in his eyes.

He opened his mouth to speak the word that would summon his blow of bright fire—I dropped and rolled away to my left as Ibbot's voice began, his word choked off as Gargle struck him with wings and claws.

Wieser knocked his feet from under him, leaping from somewhere nearby. I had not seen or heard her slip close. Ibbot fell hard on his side, then flipped to his back as he flailed in the snow, kicking, shoving himself backwards, desperate to shield his throat from Weiser, his eyes from Gargle's beak. He was unable to speak spellword or any word, only grunt as he fended her teeth and his beak with elbow and forearm.

I gained my feet and drew my knife. "Stop," I said, but did not shout, for we played out this conflict so near the others. Weiser darted in and gained his throat in her jaws, a great shaggy paw on his chest, the other leg braced at his shoulder. She flicked her eyes to me, then away with a rumbling growl, the first sound she had made. Gargle stood balanced with wings spread, poised to stab at an eye. Blood welled from a gash on Ibbot's temple and ran down to stain the snow beside his face.

I leaned over him. "Listen now and be told: As far as Bryar and his brothers, Cilliyon, too—any harm you do I will visit an equal harm on you, *this I swear.*" I pressed the knife's obsidian tip into the fur over his heart, could feel it beating at a gallop through the haft. "I will devise a way to part from the brothers. You agree you will do exactly as I say." Weiser growled again.

Of one thing I grew certain. Everything he'd told me about wanting me to help him fight the mages was a tale built of ash, collapsed now in a breath of chill air. His true aim was something else altogether. I said not another word and do not know how long we passed, eyes locked, motionless in the bursts of wind-driven snow.

At length, he closed his eyes, and gave what nod he could with Weiser's jaws fastened about his neck. Gargle sprang forward, snatched a lock of hair at his forehead and ripped it free. Ibbot put his hand to that patch of bare scalp first when we let him rise and winced as he felt it tenderly.

"Gods have mercy," Ibbot said, looking at his bloody fingertips.

"Expect no mercy from crows, nor from me. The others will be wondering what's keeping us." I motioned for him to go first, with the knife I still held ready. I could believe we'd convinced him not to strike the brothers now but held no trust at all that Ibbot would abide by his agreement to do what I told him. Not if he thought he might get away with doing as he pleased instead.

Both of us ski-less, he foundered forward slowly enough to make me want to prod him, until a keening wail carried our way that could only be Cilliyon. Then we both fairly tripped over each other sliding and staggering out of the trees.

CHAPTER TWENTY-ONE

W hat did I expect to see? Wolves snapping fanged jaws, a mountain cat slashing? One of the brothers, snow-maddened, leaping off a cliff to his death? The sight that met my eyes was not one summoned by reason.

Cilliyon had thrown herself across the wrapped corpse of the old man and sobbed fit to break the heart. She buried her face in the snow crusting the blanket's folds, with both her gloved hands wound in the fabric. How she wept!

Bryar, Sencha and Leran stood at the head of the sledge, hands clasped to their chests, eyes downcast. Cilliyon rocked to and fro on her knees. She smoothed the blanket draped over the body's head, and raised brimming eyes to Ibbot and me, where we stood transfixed at the edge of the trees.

"Oh, Fenn!" she cried. "What if it was our father lying dead, and the last he knew of us was my willful disobedience? I cannot bear to think it!" She covered her eyes with frost-rimed gloves. Her shoulders heaved and shook. Weiser bounded over to lean against her and Cilliyon flung her arms round her ruff of fur.

I pocketed the lock of Ibbot's hair Gargle had given me and stumbled to where Cilliyon knelt in the drifts. "Sister," I said, perplexed, and patted her on the back.

She instantly released Weiser and seized my arm. "Please, Fenn. I know I have cost you so much, trying to see me safely delivered to my marriage. But I cannot face it now!" The fevered look of her eyes turned carefully away from the others and only toward me … Cilliyon had hatched a plan to set us on a path away from the brothers.

Clever girl.

"Cilliyon, I know we are all upset by their father's death," I began. *Take it slow but I'm with you*, I tried to show her in my remark and sober face.

She kept her grip on me and spoke on, still in Yeganil so the brothers might follow the story.

Twice a clever girl.

"You know what Father is like, better than any other knows. He may be a hard man but he is a just man, too. What if he should die before I can beg forgiveness for my defiance? It will be on my soul forevermore! He could forgive me, dare I believe, if I went to him? Do not you think I can make amends? Before it is too late …"

Ibbot cleared his throat. "Ourselves are far and away from home, though. Look at all that's been risked, so sure this uncle was the answer."

She shook her head, still staring up at me, clasping my hand in hers. The time was right, I could feel it.

"Sister, if you wish to turn back, I will take you home."

"Will you? Oh, brother, will you?"

The three brothers now shifted their gaze to Ibbot. He reached out his hands and opened his mouth. I braced myself to strike him, but he was not summoning magic after all. With a ponderous effort at sincerity, he asked, "My beloved, do you mean yourself has now a changed heart? No longer a wish to marry?"

Cilliyon wrung out fresh tears. "I do not know. I only know I must make things right with my father. He could be deathly sick and we have no way to ken. He could be lying dead this very minute, his dying thought that his children are ungrateful wretches he wished had never been b-born!"

We all stared at each other as she cried. After more moments of extravagant distress, she dragged upon my arm to aid in getting to her feet, nearly pitching me over onto the old man's sled. With appearance of great struggle gathering herself, she squared her shoulders and wiped her eyes.

"What if Ibbot could go on with Bryar and his brothers?"

Thrice a clever girl, she even devised a way for us to get shed of Ibbot.

She faced him. "When yourself reaches my uncle, explain and enlist his help. If he will appeal to Father, even come to the family in Merced, ourselves can start a life together without the shroud of shame I now bear."

This sentiment pleased the audience of brothers, whose expressions softened further. Yet I could never let them journey away from us accompanied by Ibbot—for I knew he would kill them at his first chance. He had stated his intention plainly enough and I would not be there to prevent him. Then I reckoned he would pursue me …

"Sister," I said, "if Ibbot does not come home with us to face Father, I fear there is no hope that you will ever manage to marry. Father will think him a coward, and worse, no matter what I say about how chaste our travel has been."

Cilliyon looked hard at me, a flicker of confusion in her eyes. She quavered, "Perhaps you know best."

Indeed I did, for Cilliyon had not heard Ibbot's heartless plan to eliminate our traveling companions. I pulled my arm out of her grasp and ordered Ibbot and Cilliyon to gather our supplies.

I turned to Bryar, as the eldest, and found him alight with pleasure at my sister's change of heart. He pumped my hand, saying, "This will restore both yourselves in the father's eyes. I hope yourself finds him well at reunion. There is always a chance for forgiveness while life is yet in all."

There was no chance of my ever bestowing any manner of forgiveness on Ibbot, whether he was alive or dead. I nevertheless smiled and made all the proper thanks for the brothers' help and kindnesses.

Sencha handed generous amounts of their foodstuff to Cilliyon, who packed it with our gear. He looked closer at Ibbot and asked, "What did yourself run into off the trail?"

164

Ibbot swiped a hand at his bloody scalp and temple. "Branch. Wasn't looking."

Cilliyon still sniffled and dabbed her cheeks with the back of her glove as she worked. She paused when all was put away, to let her hand rest a moment on the blanketed body just where the heart might have been. "Peace in timeless lumber," she whispered.

Bryar and his brothers set off with their burden and we trekked back the way we had come, Gargle circling overhead. If his cawing signified approval, he alone knew.

As soon as Ibbot thought their party beyond hearing us, he swung his ski tips around to face Cilliyon. "Are you pleased with yourself for sending us over already covered ground? Making us out to be fools?"

She leaned over him from her perch on the mule. "Some of us *are* fools," she said, low and hard. "How long before we meet a party from where our supposed uncle lives? Or one of us gives the wrong answer to an idle question and we are snarled in our web of lies? And what were *you* going to do to get us apart from them, so we can travel to the sea?"

Ibbot opened his mouth, but I said, "You do not want to know. Who remembers our map? How far from our road southwards are we now?"

"I think we are close," Cilliyon sniffed. "Go on a bit further and we can stop and figure our place."

I wanted a look at the map and also at my book of lore. I was certain there was a reason, other than spite, that Gargle had provided me with a lock of Ibbot's hair.

I aimed to rein him in so tightly that he could harm no one.

Or else be rid of him.

CHAPTER TWENTY-TWO

"You still haven't answered me. Will this kill him?" Cilliyon asked. She watched me brewing and muttering over the pot. Ibbot slept nearby, a humped shape in the grey, frosty light.

I considered whether I should tell her.

I had observed Ibbot's every glance all through the waning day. He looked to me to be plotting, wound tight as spooled thread, with eyes unfocused and little attention to the trail. His mind might have been anywhere—such as along the road with Bryar and the others. How far distant could Ibbot be, yet still harm them with his magic? Loose an avalanche to sweep them off the mountain or a blizzard to bury and freeze them in their tracks?

I had seen his spellcasting at the mine disaster and his attack on the muleteer. I observed none of those gestures or murmurs which would indicate he worked magic. Still the skin on my neck crawled.

As soon as I devised a moment alone in the ramshackle hut we claimed for the night, I hunched over my book. I sought a way to confound and obstruct him, so he could not visit his murderous sorcery on Bryar and his brothers or anyone else we might encounter. My thought was to keep him docile, as Annora had done with an enemy soldier at our farm in Merced. Ibbot must perforce accompany us so I could watch him … thus he had to be alert enough to at least sit on the mule, if not ski alongside me.

I found no spell or potion to serve that purpose. Nothing.

"Let me finish. Then I'll speak."

The draught that did come to my searching eyes required a mix of herbs, all of which I carried. The potion could render him insensible for several days, if carefully concocted with the spell from the stained page and combined with a token—the scrap of Ibbot's hair I possessed. He would lie on the floor of the hut unaware while Cilliyon and I fled for the coast.

There was no denying he would freeze before he woke. The fire would die and so would he, unless some random wayfarer chanced upon him. The shelter we found for the night lay off the more traveled route because we had turned south late in the day. Way stations were not marked on our map for this trail but the condition of the hut showed it was seldom used.

Did this make the answer to Cilliyon's question 'yes'? She waited, barely breathing, for me to respond. I did not wish to burden her with knowledge of my scheme. Especially as the plan was not fully formed … Or perhaps, I did not want to allow the inevitable result of my actions to settle in my own mind.

Ibbot's callous words about the brothers stirred in my memory. *'It is their bad luck to have run onto us, and this is the consequence.'* Here, then, was Ibbot's consequence for threatening murder of inno- cent souls.

I shifted the pot to the stone hearth to cool. With a deep breath, I took her hands in mine and told her what Ibbot had planned to do to Bryar and his brothers. I did not spare her the pledge he had made to exact revenge on her, should I interfere with his murderous act.

She shook her head. "How he could he be so foul?" Her eyes reddened but she spilled no tears.

"This draught will not poison him outright. He will fall deep into sleep," I told Cilliyon after a pause. "He must drink this in the morning and you and I will make our escape once he is asleep."

When I released her hands she turned away. I could not read her thoughts, only watch her stare into the glow of the coals for what seemed an age. She could work out as well as I that a man left alone in a windswept hut with no fire was destined to die. I stirred the amber liquid as I spoke the last spell words, sprinkled a portion of Ibbot's hair on the surface, and set his fate.

I told myself I felt nothing. In my mind I said what my brother Wils had said returning from the war, *I did what I must*. Despite this oft-repeated thought, sleep would not settle. Whether I dreamed of the pot steeping on the hearth or saw it in truth when my eyes refused to stay closed, the sight remained before me throughout the long dark hours.

Cilliyon took it on herself to cook Ibbot's gruel in the potion water come dawn. Her share and mine, she prepared with fresh-melted snow before Ibbot woke.

We ate in ill-tempered silence, Ibbot cracking his neck and rolling his shoulders. I watched to be sure he emptied his bowl before I went out to tend to the mule.

He was snoring, sprawled by the fire, when I returned. He looked quite young with his lips parted in sleep. Cilliyon would not meet my eye. She cleaned and packed the cookstuff before she wrapped herself in the furs we had been given in Lunenhelm. Her woolen cloak, stolen for her by Ibbot when we escaped the *Moon Road*, she tucked close around him as he lay.

"That will not stave off the cold," I said, and wished my voice rang less hollow.

She did not answer, but stood and said, "I am ready now."

I placed one more log on the fire without asking myself to what end. We loaded and departed. Wieser looked back at the shut door and whined but came when I called. Gargle hopped branch to branch over the hut roof. Yet he lost no more than a little time catching us up as we made our way southwards toward the sea.

Cilliyon and I spoke only to the barest need for our travel.

I dreamed of Ibbot that night. He lay as we had left him, but with lashes coated with frost, lips icy blue. I jerked awake and Wieser stretched her neck to nuzzle and lick me. I wrapped an arm about her and wound my fingers in her coat. Cilliyon slept on, a frown on her face.

At dawn, Cilliyon asked how much farther to the coast. I told her we would arrive roughly by full moon, so long as we pushed ourselves hard each day.

"Has he died by now?" she said when I brought her the morning kettle of snow to melt.

My throat tightened. "He must have done."

"The mule driver lasted longer. He lived until the woodcutters found him."

"It was not as high nor as cold where we left the driver. Not as deep into winter days."

Tears glittered in her lashes. When a drop ran down her cheek, I lifted my hand to brush it away. She shrank from my touch. Her breath caught as she pushed past me to leave the cottage we had shared for the night.

I wanted to say as Wils had taught me—I did what I had to do. Good or ill, necessary or no, the thing was done. 'No taking it back', as Ibbot himself had said about the muleteer. I wanted to run after her and tell her.

I set the kettle of snow over the coals instead.

When we finished our departure preparations and I aided her to mount the mule, she looked back the way we had come. The air seemed burdened with words neither of us could speak.

I took up my poles and pushed off with the skis. I heard her following by the mule's chuffs of breath. It raised clouds of steam at my back in the crisp, thin mountain air.

Gargle called overhead, as he wheeled in the shafts of sunlight angling through the boughs. Wieser trudged beside me. I tried not to think of what I had done.

Abruptly, I realized I could not hear the mule any longer. I turned to find the beast standing some ways behind. Cilliyon bent forward over its withers, her arms round the brown neck. I backtracked to her side.

"Are you ill?"

She lifted red-rimmed eyes to meet mine. "I cannot. I simply cannot leave him like that. I understand what he meant to do to the others, I believe what you told me, but ... it's just no use."

I didn't say anything.

"I'm going back. You can come or no. If he's dead, I'll—I'll bury him, I suppose. But I am going back to see."

"He can't be buried in frozen ground—" I began.

"I don't care! I'm going." She pulled the mule's head around and kicked him to a quick amble along the trail.

I watched her back, Wieser at my side.

"Do you think she'd ever believe me," I asked my dog, "if I said I was on the point of turning back myself?" As Wieser didn't answer, I pushed off with a grunt and followed the retreating mule.

Gargle cawed plaintively, but came along, as well.

I was not sufficiently ruthless, all in all, to be a mage.

I insisted Cilliyon allow me to enter the hut first. I even bade Wieser remain outside until I determined whether we had returned for a frozen corpse or a frostbitten man only half-dead.

As in my dream, Ibbot lay as I had left him, alongside the now ice-cold hearth. The hut had no windows, so the only light came from the door I left standing wide. In order to see in the waning daylight, I had to step close to him—and with amazement I saw he had pink cheeks and lips. He breathed as easily as if napping on a summer afternoon beneath a spreading shade tree.

I put out a hand to grip his shoulder and gave it a shake. He muttered and drew Kruthe's cloak closer under his chin. "A few more moments," he said drowsily.

I stifled a laugh.

"Are you crying?" Cilliyon asked from the doorway.

"No." I huffed out a breath. "Not a single tear."

I lit the fire anew, and Cilliyon cooked more gruel for our evening meal. I did not try further to wake Ibbot, since he slumbered so peacefully. I scoured pages in my magic-lore book, seeking an answer to what had gone amiss with my spell. If anything had—perhaps he was properly enspelled and protected from the cold by the self-same magic. Suspended in time during his long sleep.

Gargle glared at me from the slanted mantle of our derelict, tumble-down hut. "Just you leave off now," I told him. "I only wanted to be sure he didn't harm any others. It isn't as if I wanted to kill him." Although, despite that I could not go through with it, I *had* wanted to be rid of Ibbot.

"You may talk all you like," Cilliyon said, as though I had spoken to her rather than Gargle. "I know you didn't have to follow me back."

"Watch what you say to him when I wake him in the morning. He is too shrewd by half." I did not know what else to say. Was she forgiving me for my attempt at murder? She surely couldn't want Ibbot along any more than I did. Only just enough less that she could not face my having killed him. Such thoughts made my mind feel like some glass-smooth pond abruptly disturbed by a tossed stone: thoughts rippled out and back again, crossing over each other endlessly. My book gave up none of its secrets on the matter, so I shut the cover and packed it away.

Wieser and I went out for a last piss before sleep. The sky danced above us with the festival of lights and I again took time to watch, awestruck anew, despite mountain air that felt nearly iron-stiff with cold.

When we went inside, Cilliyon handed me a mug of hot mint brew. "Sleep well," she said, and settled near the glowing hearth.

Grock! complained Gargle. He glided down from his perch and bumped his shoulder against Wieser until she curled her body around him. He closed his eyes.

I checked that Ibbot continued in heavy sleep and stretched along Wieser's other side and shut my own eyes. Dawn would come soon enough.

At some hour after the fire had burned down to coals, Ibbot's cry rang out. I sprang up as Wieser jumped to her feet. It appeared to be the Night Terrors again, for Ibbot's eyes were still closed and he did not sit up. Rather, he stirred restlessly, winding up in the cloak to curl up small.

As before when his sleep had been ravaged by the Terrors, he spoke no intelligible words. He only made fearful moans as he tucked his head to his chest.

Cilliyon slipped beside me and pressed close. I put my arm around her.

Gargle showed no interest whatsoever, beyond fluffing his feathers as if indignant that his furry cushion and blanket had stood up, leaving him to the chill.

Ibbot lay still for the space of a few minutes. "It must have passed," I told Cilliyon. She nodded wordlessly. Then she hissed and pointed.

I looked along her extended finger, which trembled in the firelight. In the dimmest corner, a silvery shape wavered. By every sharpening detail, an apparition of the old weather-worker from aboard *Moon Road*, Mage Balin. The thing looked about over each shoulder. It leaned forward to peer at us where we stood before the fire. Took a step toward us to bend over the sleeping Ibbot and shake its head. Could a Sending see if the sender was blind? What manner of magic was this?

The creature never spoke, but it did pace about the hut and examine every cranny. To what end? Did the mage seek his apprentice and hope to learn where he was by viewing his surroundings in detail? Had Ibbot feared this occurrence throughout our journey?

After squatting to look at the skis and poles, the apparition straightened slowly, betraying the mage's creaky joints in image as in life. It reached around with a knobby hand to knead the fabric of its robe over the backbone.

I stood frozen, so stunned that I barely felt Cilliyon's nails digging into my arm. Wieser apparently was able to see the thing, too, since she followed its path about the hut with her eyes, every muscle taut. Gargle roused himself to look at it with first one eye and then the other. He made no sound and I was grateful, since he could make all too much noise at inconvenient times by history.

As we watched in rigid silence, the image began to fade. First the details of the features and the folds of its robe blurred, then the shape of the figure itself grew indistinct, less man-formed, and the silvery glow returned. My eyes ached, straining wide to watch it evaporate to a smudge, then to nothing.

I blew out a breath, and at the cloud this made, realized the image had created no similar evidence of living breath. Cilliyon's sigh beside me frosted the air, likewise.

Ibbot slept on.

"What was that thing?" Cilliyon asked. She still gripped my arm.

I put my hand over hers, hoping to reassure her enough that she would pull her nails out of my poor flesh. "Though I have never seen one before, I have heard of the mages causing a Sending—an image of themselves that can go abroad by magic. The mage is in two places at once, you see. They appear solid and can even converse with one another, despite that this one was silent." I tried to lift her fingers, but she held fast.

"But the old mage from the ship is blind. This thing looked around as if it could see."

I nodded. "If a mage rides an animal by sorcery, he sees through the animal's eyes. Perhaps Mage Balin can see when he is riding the ether currents as a Sending." I pried a couple of her fingers up. She snatched her hand away as if only just aware of the wicked deep hold she'd had.

Wieser walked across to sniff the corner where the Sending had recently stood. Gargle muttered and clicked his beak. He turned toward the glowing coals and away from the lot of us.

"What can it mean, that Ibbot cried out in his sleep before the thing came? Do you think the mage came before, that first night on the mountain when Ibbot cried out by the campfire?"

I wondered what it meant, also, but said, "I never saw any sign of it that time. No figure appeared. Unless you saw something?"

She shook her head. "Maybe the master couldn't find him that time. Maybe Ibbot was warding him off with magic, and since you cast your sleep spell on him, he is too deeply insensible and cannot ward the mage any longer."

Add that to my guilt. "I suppose that is possible, but we are beyond having any help for it now. We had best catch what sleep we can and talk to him about it when he wakes. If he can recall anything."

"Are you going to tell him you tried to kill him?"

"I will not put it just that way, if you please. And anyway, my goal was to render him senseless so he could not harm Bryar and his brothers. And you. That is more the way of it. I see no purpose served in telling him I tried to leave him to his fate, since that is not what happened." I drew my cloak closer about my shoulders. Wieser finished her sniffing and came to nudge under my hand and arm with her broad curly head.

"Does his master know where Ibbot is now, from what he saw? Does that mean he and Kruthe will come for him? And us as well, if we are still with him?"

"As there is no way to be sure ... How should we proceed, in either case? If Ibbot can be located, does that do the mage and Kruthe any good, if they are still out sailing the ocean? Far away from us, as we travel the mountains of Yega?"

"What if they are closer than that? What if they are nearby?"

"Yes, and if they are? Will we run blindly out into the night and fall off a cliff in hopes of avoiding them and whatever fate they plan for us?"

Cilliyon pushed out her lips, considering.

"I don't mean we should!" I said, loud enough to cause Gargle to hop toward me with a warning gurgle.

Ibbot stirred but did not open his eyes.

Cilliyon's look darkened. "I would just rather avoid being sold as a slave. If they can trace Ibbot's movements now, should we even be going to the coast?"

"We both still want to sail to Lohr Island, do we not? Or have you changed your mind?"

"No, I do want to go to the temple there as my father intended. How else will Da know where to find me? Yet I fear running up against Kruthe in the port city. He is ... he is not someone I care to see ever again."

It occurred to me I had never asked her about the time she spent behind closed doors with the pirate slaver on *Moon Road*. Before Ibbot brought her to me on deck for our escape, the intervening hours could have held worse events than I knew. She might have good reason to wish no further sight of the man.

"Sleep now, if you can. We will leave at first light, as we can leave no sooner. Where we should be bound for, I will do my best to choose with our safety in mind."

I would not say my words appeared to reassure her, but she did return to her place at the hearth and close her eyes. I curled around Wieser's back and Gargle stuffed himself between us with a sigh.

How is it I continually end up keeping care of everyone? I wondered, as sleep eluded me through what remained of the night.

CHAPTER TWENTY-THREE

"Get up, Ibbot. We'll never make the coast before spring thaw at this rate."

He grumped and grumbled as he rose and made ready to renew our trek, to all outward appearance unaware of the lost day and nights when he lay insensible by the hearth. Cilliyon pretended with me that he had merely slept through our morning meal as she handed him some dried, smoked fish and a few nutmeats.

Under smoldering glowers from Cilliyon and Gargle, to the point I expected my face to scorch from the heat, I surrendered and told Ibbot about the Sending we had witnessed while he slept.

He said nothing while I described the scene. At the end, I asked him, "Does this mean Mage Balin and Kruthe know where you are? Does it mean they are near?"

"He should not have been able to do that. Even when I am asleep … yet it cannot be anything else." He brooded as he swirled the herbs in his mug.

A fine opportunity for me to admit his sleep was enspelled, and that I had done it. Cilliyon looked on the point of speaking but turned aside to pack our kettle when I frowned at her.

"Is it no longer safe for us to make for the coast, to the other port?" I pressed him.

He snorted. "When was it ever safe? If we want to leave this blasted country, we must take to the sea. Our map suggests an entire continent lies to the east. Do you want to trek for years across the blighted place?"

"And if we come face-to-face with Kruthe and Mage Balin? Will you send out a bolt of magic to stun or kill them?"

"Kruthe I could possibly manage. Not Mage Balin. He is a master mage. Despite his lack of eyesight, he possesses senses beyond the norm." He rubbed the side of his mug with a fingertip.

"So we should not travel to the coast?" Cilliyon asked.

"No, we should make for the southern port as before. But now, Judian must allow me to instruct him in magical lore. Then we could coordinate our attack, if it comes to that. Or coordinate our defense, depending on how you wish to view the matter."

"What can you teach me as we travel? We will reach the port just past full moon. That is not long for a magical education."

"As I have told you before, you have shown yourself capable of high magic, abundantly capable. You recognize what you need to learn is how to wield it according to your will. This is what I can teach you. We have aided one another until now, however grudgingly. Let us put aside our differences and journey as partners along that path." He looked only at me and did not include Cilliyon in his words.

Like Cilliyon, I had no desire whatever to be sold into slavery. Unlike her, I might learn means to thwart the slaver captain. Possibly I could use that knowledge to evade the Scytheran mage seeking his fugitive apprentice. Complicating any encounter with Mage Balin, however, was the fact that the old weather worker had been tasked to turn me over to the cabal in his home country, so he was also after me. If, that is, I believed Ibbot's account of the matter.

Who would win, if Kruthe wanted to sell me and Mage Balin wanted to drag me to his fellows in Scythera? Kruthe seemed to be telling the old mage what to do aboard ship. But Ibbot feared the old man, despite how much he disdained serving him and called him an old goat. He had told me the blind mage could be formidable yet …

Which led me back to my essential distrust of Ibbot and his motives. What Ibbot told me he wanted me for, and what I suspected to be the truth, stood quite apart. I could believe he wanted to avoid a reunion with his former master. I did not believe he held any desire to save his homeland from devastation by Scythera's cabal of mages. What he had let slip about his early life did not sound like a pleasant idyll to wish restored.

I considered all this before I spoke. "If we must go to the coast to put Yega behind us, then teach me how to aid you in getting past Kruthe and Mage Balin."

Ibbot's teeth gleamed even in the pale morning light. He seemed like some wiry, dockside cur, waiting to snatch a scrap on the waterfront.

I would not have thought Ibbot could talk so much while laboring to ski at the same time. He talked my ears off my head. At one point I asked Wieser to go back and look for two worn-out ears on the trail but she did not get the jest. Neither did Ibbot, though Cilliyon laughed from her perch on the mule's back. Gargle circled too far above to express his amusement, if he had any.

Ibbot did bring to my mind Annora, who instructed me in the ways of healing and animal lore back in Merced. I seemed to have some natural gift with animals; in fact, I had summoned both Wieser and Gargle, though unaware of my ability at the time. Healing came readily enough, as well. I did not think I possessed any similar affinity for the lore Ibbot shared, working with wind currents and cloud portents to predict and alter the ways of the weather. He often pointed a pole-tip skyward to show me some feature I struggled to gather meaning from, as Gargle called overhead.

I hoped for Ibbot to teach me how to send a bolt of bright fire, which seemed to me the best use of magic if we were to attack foes or defend ourselves. He showed no inclination toward that topic as we skiied on. Perhaps no matter what I'd said he still thought I could call the black fire at will, since he had seen me strike down Stas Royka in Kunitka's kitchen.

I could have asked him for that lesson. Yet, I made a vow to myself when I accepted his teaching—I would never let my guard down and trust him completely. It was all too possible Ibbot chose to teach me only what would benefit himself alone.

He yattered on each day, calling a halt at times for me to practice freshening a breeze or sending snow-clouds scudding away. We eventually arrived at a place where rock thrust up at an angle from the surrounding mountainside. With the granite face blown clear of snow by gusting winds, we could see the layers all twisted aslant. He spoke then of ley lines. My somewhat wandering attention sharpened.

"The lines of power in the earth? Can you sense them, or do you need to use a staff to plot them and follow their path?"

He stopped and turned to me, face on. "You have seen this done?"

"The mages I saw in my home country, on my mountain. They paced across the land, holding their sticks in front of them. Virda said they were plotting the ley lines and used knowledge of the pathways to inform their spellcasting."

He nodded. "Did you feel anything, watching them?"

"Not then. Not from that pair. But at Fort Hasseron, when I slew a hawk. A mage rode the bird to drive a magic gale during the attack. I felt the power then."

"And in the cave, after the harbour battle?"

So. He did know details of that night. Could only know them from the mages I fought there or the Sending that had come to his master. I knew I had told him nothing. I stood straight though I staggered in my mind. I had never known if the two mages died that night in the darkness, or if they disappeared from the cave tunnel but still lived. And carried away their knowledge of me and exactly what I had done.

He waited, a deep frown creasing his features, before abruptly asking, "Was it your knife from the kavsprit? Did it allow you to feel and channel the power?"

Nor had I told him how I came by my blade, except that it was given to me. I *had* told the mages in the seacliff tunnel about the earth spirits' gift.

I had my answer.

I jabbed the tip of a pole into the heaped snow beside our track. "You have always shown a great interest in my knife."

"It may be of significant aid to us. If you wield it, of course. Since only you can."

"That is so. I alone can use its magic." I paused for him to contradict me, since I remembered telling him as I recovered from being beaten—how the knife would not work for someone if stolen. Another could use it, but only if I granted the boon of its loan, as I had done for my brother Wils. "Do your master and Kruthe know about my blade?"

"Only Mage Balin, and I'll thank you not to call him my master."

"How did he learn of it?"

"I have no patience with you playing a fool, when I know you for something altogether different. The mages you defeated in Merced have shared news of it. They want it."

"Why?"

"They believe the obsidian stone is the source of your magic. They have not seen, as I have, that the power resides within you."

Cilliyon stirred on the back of the drowsing mule. "Do the mages think taking Judian's knife will take his power?"

In the intensity of our words to each other, Ibbot appeared to have forgotten she listened as well. He snapped over his shoulder, "Mages covet any power they do not possess, or any object powerful in and of itself."

"And as you are a mage, do you also covet the knife?" She shaded her eyes as she peered down at him.

The look he sent her had a sharp edge. "Since your furs do not block your ears, you have heard him say he alone is the blade's master."

"Ibbot, do you want his knife? It is a powerful object, no doubt of that."

"It may be that a master mage could discover some way to wrest it from Judian and use it. I am, of course, only an apprentice weather worker, and do not have any such skill."

"You didn't answer what I asked. Do *you want* his knife?"

"No, for I cannot use it! You show a sudden lack of wit, girl. Keep your tongue still if you have nothing sensible to say."

"That's enough, Ibbot," I said. "She only asked what I wondered along with her."

"Asked and answered then, I hope to your satisfaction. Let's be on our way. The light is fading." He struck out, breaking trail for once. We fell in behind him.

~

Days passed. As we curved our way down the final slopes, I caught glimpses of the hazy sea, dotted with far away sails. This place looked different from the harbours I knew. At Bale Harbour in Merced, and our landfall harbour Freyzik in northern Yega, ships docked at the wharves. Here, the water must be too shallow near shore, so the ships anchored a fair distance away and shuttled goods and folk out and back on smaller craft. Rowing out and back must consume a great amount of time.

We approached a tall stone tower on a prominent headland. I noted flag after flag, this colour and that, strung on a tight line from tower top to ground stakes. Swatches snapped and rippled gaily in the ocean breeze. A way to ken which ships rode at anchor, and for what purpose, perhaps? We might discover which vessel was bound for Lohr Island and be able to buy Cilliyon's and my passage. I did not imagine I would be able to convince Ibbot to go with us and doubted I would want him along, in any case.

I did ask him, though, if what I thought about the purpose of the flags was correct. He nodded absently. His distraction had mounted the closer we drew to the ocean. The last day's travel he had spent no time on my lessons.

As we passed the tower, I could see spots of colour on the rigging of the ships, likely corresponding flags to the ones that now flapped beside us.

"Do you know Kruthe's ship by sight? What was its name?"

I had to ask him twice, but he said he knew the *Chikoro* and her colours, too. He scanned the outlying ships and said Kruthe's was not among them.

"Who do we ask, to find out what ship is bound for what port?" Cilliyon asked from above us on the mule. I poked him in the shoulder when he didn't appear to hear her and repeated the question.

"We ask someone who can read the flags," he said, with an irritable twitch of his head toward the tower. "Or we can give Judian a lesson in possessing a host animal and viewing through its eyes. Your crow is the better candidate between it and the hound."

Wieser swiveled her head to gaze at him impassively, or much akin to the looks she usually gave him. Gargle, I saw, had taken up a perch on the top of the tower.

"Come down," I said, though no louder than I would have spoken to Ibbot or Cilliyon beside me. Gargle would know I spoke to him. He would come down, if it suited him. I learned that not from Ibbot's lessons, but from living with the creature for long and long.

Gargle swooped low and alighted on the mule's rump, causing the animal to snort and shake its ears. Cilliyon patted its neck.

Gargle dipped his beak low and looked Ibbot in the eye. He cawed and stretched his wings wide preparing to fly, but I put out my hand to stay him. "Wait and see. I would like to learn this."

Cilliyon commenced shaking her head as Ibbot said, "Not here, we will need to find lodgings below and settle in before I can show you. It cannot be rushed."

"But what happens to Judian, while his mind is in the crow?" Cilliyon soothed the mule, now sidling at the worry in her voice. "And how does he get back to himself again?"

"Am I now teaching you as well? Keep to your place. Which is largely baggage, as far as I can see."

Wieser landed both paws on his chest, knocking him flat. He struggled to regain his breath as I grabbed the mule's bridle to steady it. "Never you mind, Cilliyon. Remember I told you—Ibbot agreed when we parted from the brothers, he will do as I say."

When I had spoken to her of Ibbot's pledge to leave the brothers unharmed, I had also cautioned her not to trust him any further than I did. He still served only his own aims, whatever they were. Nothing had happened in the meantime to cause me to doubt it.

Cilliyon couldn't let it go. "How do you have any idea if he is teaching you true, though? He could be fixing you in knots every which way. How do you tell?"

"I do have my suspicions," I allowed, rubbing the mule beneath his forelock.

Ibbot still labored to draw enough breath to speak. Weiser stood square on his chest while he shoved at her legs.

"He could steal your voice again, couldn't he? Then where would we be?"

I met Cilliyon's eyes. "If he has taught me anything, it is that I must be careful. And he may have learned, in his turn, I will be pushed only so far. Take care not to put yourself in the middle of it. You know I'll do whatever I must do."

I held her gaze long enough to be sure she took my meaning. I'd pledged she could trust me, I would not risk harm befalling her. Her cheeks coloured and she dropped her chin. I gestured for Wieser to release Ibbot and come to my side. Gargle shook out his feathers and lifted into the haze with a snap of glossy wings.

Ibbot stood and shook snow from his furs with a black look Wieser's way.

"And what is it," he said, biting off each word, "you wish our party to do now?"

I let him wait for my answer. "We will enter Anlia, below. I am Lichan Lebannen, traveling with my brother, Smyke, and our sister, Birgeet. We will find a room at a likely inn and suitable livery for our mule." I paused. "That is enough to be getting on with for the present. I will let you know what comes next."

He said nothing, beyond, "*Smyke*? Gods."

Cilliyon smothered a smile while we made our way down the trail toward the sea.

CHAPTER TWENTY-FOUR

Anlia proved to be more a fishing hamlet than a harbour town, though we could not have deduced its size from our map. The parchment Hengel gave us to seek our uncle in the eastern peaks showed mountain trails and passes in detail. It had served us well. However, the "X" representing Anlia on the coast was equal in size to the one denoting Port Freyzik. That both places sprang up on the seashore and bore the same indication on our chart marked their only similarities, in truth.

Once we walked down Anlia's market street, paved with rough, snow-covered stones that begged to twist an ankle, I could better see the ships at anchor in the bay. Single masts on all of them, no three-masted sailing ships such as at Bale Harbour in Merced, or indeed at Freyzik. Many smaller craft bobbed nearer to shore.

"This is not good," I murmured.

"It isn't much of a place, is it?" Cilliyon cast a glance about. "I thought you had been here before, *Smyke*?"

Ibbot grimaced. "I told you both when we arrived, I have been to Yega before, but not to *this part* of the blighted rock. I have been much farther south, nearer to—nearer to the southern border."

Something in his voice snagged my ear. "What borders Yega to the south?"

He hesitated, but then perhaps surmising I would find out anyway, he said, "Scythera lies there."

Splendid.

Lohr Island also lay south of this frozen land, but far south and east, if I recalled the ocean map on *Moon Road* correctly.

None of the small ships here could carry us such a great distance across the sea. Thoughts leapt and twisted through my head: we could return to Freyzik to seek an ocean-going vessel—and run into many complications we wished to avoid. Namely, greater risk of encountering Kruthe and Mage Balin since it held a slave market, with us thought to be escaped slaves. Furthermore, we were believed responsible for the stableman's murder there. Or we could buy passage on one of these smaller ships and travel down the coast to a port where Ibbot had been before. Which also took me closer to Scythera, where I dreaded to go. No choice rose free of complication.

"Ju-Lichan, you're so pale," Cilliyon leaned closer. "What is it?"

"Watch the folk going about. See if we can suss out an inn or tavern that might let a room. I'll look for a livery stable."

We found Anlia could not boast of an inn but offered two taverns. At the Jackadaw, a barkeep with a belly as round as his ale barrels wiped his nose on his sleeve and allowed that he might let the attic room. He gave a price surely mountain-high and waited, sucking his upper lip, to see if I would pay or protest.

I paid.

"Shouldn't we check at the other tavern?" Cillliyan asked, in hushed Mercedish. I shook my head. It stood at the opposite end of the shop row, much farther from the stall I rented for the mule. And I reckoned it gouged travelers just as much.

Though I nearly changed my mind when the barman refused to allow Wieser to join us in the room.

"Don't care what sort of a valuable animal it is. No dogs."

I entreated him every which way, even offered to pay half-again more, but he would not be swayed.

"I say no dog. It can sleep at the stable, and so you all can, too, if you don't leave off about it." I knew he was serious when he held out the coins I had just given him.

When I opened the door to take Wieser to join the mule, Gargle flapped in and perched on the bar.

"And no crow, neither."

I patted my shoulder and he settled on me instead. "We'll see if there might be a window to the attic room," I told him in a whisper, as we made our way back to the stable.

Weiser sniffed about the straw before curling in a corner of the mule's stall. She wagged her tail a bit when I apologized for leaving her. I caught the stable boy giving me a curious look and bade him keep special care of her. I promised him extra coin in his pocket in the morning if he made sure she stayed safe, and his eyes sparkled when he nodded. He knelt beside her, patting her head as I took my leave.

Scouting the eaves of the tavern, I could see no window that Gargle might slip into without the barman knowing. I took him back to the stable to lodge with Wieser and the mule. "More coins yet," I told the bedazzled boy.

At the Jackadaw, I found Ibbot staring at a mug of ale as black as night which smelt of bitter ashes. Cilliyon perched on a stool beside him, her skirts tucked close and away from the scum-crusted floor.

"D'yerselves want a meal, then?" The barkeep spit in a handy bucket and regarded us with ill-favour.

"Yes, for three," I answered.

"What is it to be?" Cilliyon asked.

"Fish, girl, what else?" He shook his head at her ignorance and pushed his bulk through a swinging door behind him.

A few more men entered and spoke to one another. Most eyed us boldly. Travelers must arrive seldom. I led us to a chilly corner table off to the side of the locals' seats by the hearth. Our host found us there and shoved across three shallow bowls of broth with scant chunks of pale fish flesh and onion. Half a loaf of crumbly dark bread and mugs of ale for Cilliyon and me completed our feast.

"Costs extra," he said, and waited with his hand outstretched while I counted more coins into his greasy palm.

When the man had returned to his place and commenced filling mugs for the other patrons, I turned to Ibbot.

He spoke before I could. "Aren't you displaying your purse a bit freely? Thieves can be found everywhere." He used Mercedish, and I observed no heads turn toward us at his words, nor ears leaned closer.

I shrugged and spooned up more soup. "I'm cautious. I do have to get the coins out of it to pay, after all. We have more urgent problems than a cut-purse."

"Will you say that if you wake from a crack on the head and find yourself poor?"

"I take precautions. I can cause many things to escape another's notice. My concern is, how will we get away from here, to a port large enough to serve ships that can cross an ocean." I gnawed at the dry bread.

Cilliyon tried sopping her crust in the broth. "Please tell me you are not thinking of a return to Freyzik. With the price we have—"

"Quiet, now. Just because no one has shown they understand our talk does not mean it's true. I do not propose to go back there. We also have no way of knowing if the other matter has been settled."

"Where, then?" Ibbot asked, scanning the men, most now smoking pipes before the fire.

I downed a swig of bitter brew. "South, instead. Tomorrow I will discover who can help us with passage arrangements and sell the mule. Or do you wish to resume our mountain trek?"

"Nay, not I."

"And is this where we part company? For I am taking Ci—Birgeet to the island. You may go where you will."

"*May* I?" he said but did not meet my eye.

I took another pull on my mug and could not help choking on the stuff. "Are we finished with our meal? We can discuss matters better upstairs."

We gathered our belongings and climbed the rough wood stair to a door fashioned of barrel slats. I peered at the rope handle by light of the candle stub our host had begrudged us. No lock.

"All will be well," I told Cilliyon, when she frowned at it over my shoulder. I pulled the make-shift door aside to reveal dangling cobwebs and dark corners piled with crates and boxes. Dust lay near as thick as the snow piled outdoors.

"Our huts in the mountains were better than this," Cilliyon said. "At least each had a fire grate."

"It's only one night." I began chalking my protection runes close-spaced by the doorway. I tasked Ibbot with shifting crates to open enough space for each of us to lie down.

"There are mouse droppings everywhere," he complained.

I snorted. "Are you surprised?"

Cilliyon shuddered and drew her hem higher above the floor. "Perhaps if we push some crates together? And lie on top of them? Some of these boxes are the same height."

"Indeed, just the right height for the mice to scramble about on top of, see?" He pointed to more dung pellets. "And these larger ones must be rat leavings."

She took a quick step backwards and tumbled over me where I crouched by the door. I gathered myself and stood, then lifted her onto her feet. She muttered darkly as she shook dirt from her skirts.

I reached into the neck of my tunic. "Here, wear this tonight," I said as I slipped my moonstone talisman over her head. "Brother Smyke, stop stirring up trouble along with the dust. Do the crate shifting for her. Furthermore, I'll enspell the vermin to stay clear for the night. Does that suit you?" She made a sketch of curtsy and I resumed placing my rune ring.

We ended reclining on crates padded with our furs, me with my sea bag for my head. Our candle stub began to gutter its last, stuck to a puddle of melted wax on a floorboard in the center of us.

"Where do you intend to go tomorrow, Ibbot?"

"And why does it matter, if you have set your mind not to aid me in my quest?"

"I've been wondering if you might not find some others among the young mages to join your cause. You cannot be the only one objecting to the ways of the cabal of elders."

The light had grown too dim for me to see how he considered my words. He answered after a short pause. "I would stand no chance of that, of gathering supporters. If I am discovered in Scythera or anywhere else, I will be returned to my master. I am indentured in his service unless ..."

Cilliyon stirred. "Unless what?"

"Unless I pay my debt."

"You owe money to Mage Balin?"

"If it was coin that would buy my freedom, do you think you would still have yours?" he said to me.

I smiled, though without humor. "No. What must you use for tender, then? Another apprentice for Mage Balin?"

"Balin is left out of it altogether if I bring the cabal the price of my freedom. I will be a master mage and indentured no more." He made it sound a dream beyond his grasp, from the depth of longing that seeped into his voice.

"What is the price?" I pushed up on one elbow.

"Is it Judian?" Cilliyon's words almost echoed as the candlelight shuddered and went out.

"If the price was delivering *Lichan*, why wouldn't I have kept him mute and dragged him to them by magic?"

"You have needed him to guide you safely back to the sea. You deceived your master about his nature and escaped with Judian so you can be the one to give him to the Scytheran cabal," Cilliyon accused.

"At one time, yes. Now I know what he is capable of, my aims have changed."

I believed the first, not the second of his answers. I wished Cilliyon could hear my thoughts, but she did not share Ibbot's apparently inconsistent ability to know what dwelt in my mind. I could imagine no opportunity to tell her privately, so she would let me carry out my plans without interfering.

"I offer you two choices. Accompany us to Lohr Island, where I will see Birgeet settled at temple." *And thus, you will continue to be under my eye.* "Or you can travel to Merced where you will offer your aid to my countrymen, if you want to fight the Scytheran cabal. I will give you letters of introduction to officers there who can use your skills."

"What do *you* intend to do after our sister is in place on the island?"

"Many months have passed since I started this journey. You and I are in agreement for one aspect—there is no more time for me to tarry for magical learning. Not so far from my home, when I feel home is where I am needed. Your instruction will have to suffice. I will return to Merced to fight, either sailing with you or following you."

"Or you said he could go off where-so-ever he wanted," Cilliyon reminded me. "Isn't that a third choice?"

This remark caused me to think of my little sister Morie, who could always be counted on to pipe up in the middle of any serious talk.

"Have it your way," I said to her. "Three choices. What say you, brother Smyke?"

Ibbot took long moments to answer, but finally said, "I have never been to Lohr Island. Perhaps that destination holds more promise for me than any other, at this point. And I can continue to teach you during our voyage there, and on to Merced."

"Let's call the matter settled, then. Catch what sleep we can."

My bag made a lumpy cushion with my book inside. I shoved the canvas into some sort of comfort and fell asleep with the smell of musty mouse in my nose and misgivings aplenty in my mind.

Ibbot woke me with our attic still in darkness. He held a light, his stone I had not seen him use since we entered the stable in Port Freyzik.

"Dawn is coming on. If I teach you now to ride your crow, you will have enough light outside to explore the waterfront from overhead and see how we should proceed."

"Too bad we don't have Gargle here to hand. I confess I am anxious to learn how to see through his eyes as he flies."

"His presence is not required. It is a kind of Sending, to place your mind in a creature."

"And you can teach me as quick as this morning?"

"You know the bird, are already bound to it in part. Much quicker in that way."

Cilliyon sat up, blinking. "Is there some new need to rush?"

"Do you want to risk another night as the Jackadaw's guest?"

"Not even a little." She drew her knees up and wrapped her arms around them with a shiver.

Ibbot bade me sit cross-legged on the floor, leaning against a crate. He sprinkled powder on his palm from a pouch he had tucked up his sleeve. As he dusted the back of my neck with it, I caught the scent of a ripe fruit I could not quite place. "What is it?" I asked.

"Mallowmeld. It grows wild in Scythera. Now, listen close and repeat the spell I chant."

"Wait, I want to write it in my folio."

"And the one to get back again," Cilliyon added, shifting uneasily on her crate.

"Aye," I said. "My brother's wife told me the mage must take care not to ride too long, or he risks losing himself in the mount's mind altogether."

Despite my desire to learn so useful a skill, I could not abandon all caution.

"This ride will be short, and to return he must only reverse the order of the words as he withdraws. Time for writing later when we sail. Commit the spell to memory now," he insisted.

I left off fishing in my tunic for the small folder of sheets and leaned back against the wood. I followed every rise and fall of Ibbot's voice, spoke the unfamiliar words that felt thick on my tongue. With each repetition I felt my mind loosening, drifting. My vision dimmed round the edges more and more, until I closed my eyes. I seemed to forget to draw breath, until faintness prodded a gasp.

"See the crow," Ibbot murmured. "Seek his mind and bid it open to you. Bind yourself over it, stretch your thoughts into the bird's, entwine yourself within. Feel him submit to your will."

Nearly I came back to myself then, for Gargle had never submitted to any will but his own since I'd known him. Not even to me, truth be told.

Ibbot perhaps sensed my wavering and bade me repeat the spell words three times again, on my own instead of following his voice.

After the third chanting, I opened my eyes. I saw the inside of the mule's stall, from my perch on the stable rafters.

CHAPTER TWENTY-FIVE

I n the straw below, Wieser barked in crazed frenzy. She twisted this way and that against a thick rope tied around her neck, the other end knotted through an iron ring on the wall. She leapt, only to fall to the straw again and again. I feared she would crush her windpipe. Or break her neck.

At the door of the stall, the stable boy cried out as she struggled, begging her to calm, calling on his dead da to help him keep her safe for me. The mule looked over the boy's shoulder from the breezeway, restive and shifting its hooves. The boy gripped its halter with white fingers.

Echoes of Gargle's caws faded as I surveyed the scene. I would have called Wieser's name to show her I was there—when I tried, it came out Gargle's croak. Wieser's barking drowned out any noise I tried to make.

The stableman strode up. "What doings here, boy? Is the dog gone mad?"

"I don't know what came over her, of a sudden she jumped up to run away! I only just got the rope off the mule and around her neck. She didn't bite me, she never tried to, just tried to bolt."

"I'll put it down if I have to."

"No, please! The man is coming for her. She's very valuable. He said so."

I nudged Gargle's mind, entreating him to fly down to Wieser. He glided to her side. The rope wrenched her off her feet again and, for an instant, she lay on her side panting. I prodded Gargle to lean over her head and looked her in the eye.

Wonder of wonders, she gazed back with the gentle regard that marked the looks we exchanged from the time she first came to me. She knew I stood on the straw beside her, I could feel it.

She made no more noise, nor desperate lunges. Her breath rasped in her throat, though. She had pulled the loop of rope so tight! How to persuade the boy to untie her?

Why had she gone mad of a sudden? Fear for me because of the spell I was attempting? Or was she somehow aware of an unspoken plan of Ibbot's?

I had no hands to loosen the rope. I hopped onto her shoulder and pecked at the thick hemp. Even with a beak that felt hard as a hoof, I could not see a way to work the knot apart. I needed fingers.

"If it's worn itself out and will lie there quiet, leave it be," the stableman told the boy. "Here, give me the mule, I'll put it in the next stall over."

With no hand to pat or stroke Wieser, I pressed Gargle's shiny black head against her muzzle. She tried a swipe with her tongue, but Gargle pulled away without aid of my will.

I felt tolerance but no welcome from his mind. I tried to entwine my thoughts in him as Ibbot instructed and plant a vision of flying over the half door and out of the stable. I wanted to see the coast and harbour, since that was the aim of undertaking the spellwork.

He hesitated a fraction, but then took wing. Wieser lifted her head and whined but did not resume her frenzy.

The boy called after us, "Wait, he said to keep you, too, bird!"

We sped away into the dawnlight.

I did not understand why Gargle wished to ride whenever he could, for I found flying a joy. The power of his wing-beats and the rush of fresh air exhilarated me. I wondered if my heart pounded in my body in the attic room as it seemed to hammer in this crow chest. My eyes were sharp as sharp, and from above I could see ... everything! Sleet streaked by. I could see each pellet. A woman with a rust-coloured blanket over her head and shoulders rushed out to gather an armload of chopped wood. Her door slapped shut behind her. The hiss of the sleet on the banked snow sang to me. I swept above the docks, where fishermen draped nets in careful piles within their bobbing craft. Tide would run soon, I knew somehow, or Gargle knew.

Swinging wide over the harbour, I flew toward the craft at anchor. Gulls cried astern of one ship. I felt a flicker of Gargle's disdain for their unruly scrabbling and snatching at offal pitched over the deck rail. I could see each fish head, nearly each entrail and scale. How wondrous to be able to see so clearly. I thought with a pang how I would miss Gargle's sight when I came back to myself.

Gargle rode the sea breeze around each ship. Each of them fishing vessels as far as I could discern, rather than merchant ships. The smaller fleet close to shore must seek small fish, while these vessels sailed farther and sought larger catch. Their nets appeared many times larger.

I counted a dozen men on the deck of several. Would I have to pass myself as a fisherman to board one? And what of Cilliyon and Ibbot? Cilliyon might serve in a galley, but what was Ibbot good for? Might these vessels have need of a weather worker? Or could Ibbot guide them to schools of fish beneath the waves?

Would the shipmaster of any of these vessels carry us south to another, larger port?

These questions could not be answered from my seat in Gargle's mind. I bade him turn toward the stable, wanting to see how Wieser fared, and to prepare to abandon my mount and return to myself.

As Gargle dipped lower by the slick dock, I saw Ibbot, hurrying along toward the waiting boats. He carried my seabag. And my sack of coins dangled from his belt.

His footing looked perilous on the icy wood. My first thought: have Gargle attack him with beak and claws. Make him slip into the cold black water and see if anyone would fish him out again. I'd wager not, with Gargle in a fury, flapping about their heads. Although, I could not carry this out because my bag held my precious book, not wrapped for sea travel but for our journey over the mountains. The water would ruin it.

I had tried every trick I knew to conceal my book from Ibbot. Had he known all along, each time I consulted it in what I believed to be secrecy? My only inheritance from my magical mother ... could *it* be the price of Ibbot's freedom?

He reached the nearest boat. Haggled briefly with the fisherman coiling a rope in its bow. He did slip when he stepped down to board, over-balanced by my bag slung over his shoulder, but landed in a heap in the bottom of the boat instead of in the water.

When he scrambled up to a bench seat, he met my eyes, where I hovered over the dock. He put a forefinger to his brow in farewell, then pointed it toward me with a quick upward jerk of his chin.

I pushed Gargle to strike him then; I wanted to see his blood running. Gargle would not. His mind felt every bit as cold as the pelting sleet while he held his place in the wind, watching Ibbot put coins in the boatman's hand.

And what of Cilliyon? Had he struck her down in order to flee?

Ibbot cradled my bag on his knees, as the boatman seated the oars and rowed away from the dock.

I bade, then begged, Gargle to carry me back to the tavern attic, or at least the stable. I must get back to my own body and eyes and see for myself how Ibbot had left Cilliyon. Then to set off after the devious thief.

Gargle rode the air, unmoved by my desperation. I felt near maddened by his circling. I vowed to wring the creature's neck as soon as I could get free of him.

What if I had no living body to return to? What if Ibbot had killed me? Would I sense that while melded with Gargle? *By the gods, I am every kind of fool ...*

Gargle seemed to agree, blast him. He swept his wings slowly, making wide passes above the boat where Ibbot rode. Ibbot never looked up to track him. He pointed to an anchored ship and the oarsman sculled close. When they drew alongside a dangling rope ladder, one of the crewmen above leaned over the railing in response to Ibbot's shouts.

I could not hear what they said, but Ibbot hefted my purse and the man above nodded. As Ibbot clambered up the swinging ladder, Gargle flew high and landed atop the single mast.

I cursed the bird yet again. We could not fly off chasing Ibbot and, at best, leave my insensible body and Cilliyon in this rat-trap village. Or at worst, let Ibbot escape having killed Cilliyon and me.

Was I at risk, by this time, of riding too long and losing myself in Gargle, if not already a corpse in the attic? He shook his beak irritably and tipped his head to focus an eye on the flag that hung coated with ice just below the mast tip.

Finally, Gargle's intent cut across the torrents of fear and fury in my mind. The ship's flag. Its colours. The design was impossible to discern, since the flag was plastered to the mast by the thick ice coating it bore. I could nevertheless make out the colours. Sky blue, yellow and white.

Apparently aware I had abandoned my furious struggle against his will, Gargle shook back his feathers and sprang into the air. Now he flew low around the bow and gave me a good look at the vessel's name. *Apella Bern.*

Still Gargle would not return to shore. He took up a perch on the rigging above the deck. *They cannot raise a sail in this weather, surely. There may yet be time to stop Ibbot. If we hurry!* Gargle bunched his shoulders against my urging.

Then I saw why Gargle made us tarry. Ibbot disappeared below, only to re-emerge shortly with a bandy-legged, bearded man at his heels. I recognized Ibbot's stance in the bow at once. He was clearing the inclement weather using magic, sending the sleet storm away inland.

The effect was gradual, but quick enough to impress the bearded man, evidently the shipmaster. He pumped Ibbot's hand and called out orders. Seamen swarmed, performing the myriad tasks needed to set sail.

As Ibbot turned, a glimmer on his chest caught my eye. He wore my moonstone talisman.

By the gods, if he had also stolen my knife, knowing it would serve only me, he deserved whatever havoc it visited on him. Had he left me anything? Or was I slumped in the attic, past the need for any possessions at all?

Now, Gargle? We know the name and the colours, and the ship's heading is south. Now back to shore? He leapt into the wind and beat landward.

I wrestled with memory as he flew. I must recall the spellwords in front order first, so I could reverse them to return.

Unless Ibbot had lied.

Gargle alighted on the half door of Wieser's stall. Within, the stableboy huddled on a bale, tearfully telling Wieser I would surely come for her. And if I never did, he would keep care of her for as long as he lived. She swept the straw with her tail where she sat at his feet. He had not untied her, so when she caught sight of us perched on the door, she stood in place but wagged all of herself from shoulders to tail tip.

"Oh, bird! You did come back! But where can your master be? He promised me coins."

Aye, a share of the very coins now hanging from blasted Ibbot's blasted belt as he traveled over the waves. Gargle had no teeth for me to grind.

I urged Gargle to return to the rafters, where he had been when I first joined his mind. He settled there with every appearance of a docile creature accustomed to doing my bidding. If I could have made a snort issue from his beak, I would have done.

Casting the spell in reverse devoured all my concentration. I studied over each word in my mind, tamping down a welling terror: I had spoken the words aloud to send myself to Gargle. The rise and fall of the chant was almost a song and, I feared, part of the magic. Gargle could make sounds but not words. Would chanting the spell in my mind work the magic?

When men fail the gods, is this the sort of demon existence the high ones create for our banishment? Bound to an obstinate mount, forevermore to ride as a human spirit lashed to a creature? I thrust these thoughts from my mind, told myself the thoughts were false. I knew Scytheran mages often possessed creatures and returned to themselves. I must be able to do so, too.

Bracing against a gust of icy wind that sought me on the rafter, I let surface my deeper fear—what if I loosed my mind from Gargle's and returned to the attic to find no living body? *Adrift forever—even worse than eternally bound. How to face such a fate?* I gripped the bird's mind all the tighter.

Gargle clicked his beak, glided out of the stall and stable, and flew toward the tavern. The stableboy's cries begging him to stay faded behind us.

We found the tavern door shut snug against the continuing storm. No windows ajar. Scant smoke issued from the chimney when Gargle flew over the roof and I screamed in my mind when he dived into the flue. All went choking black before he sailed over the banked coals, into the scant light of the empty hearth room and then up the stairs.

The attic door gaped and he tucked his wings to alight on the top step. He slipped within the dim room. Cilliyon sat on the floor, next to me where I sagged onto one side. She held my head on her lap and smoothed my hair back from my brow.

"You cannot die," she said, barely more than a whisper. "Not when I love you so." She bent low and pressed her lips to mine.

How queer to see instead of feel my first kiss. I nudged Gargle to make some sound so she would notice our presence. He did nothing, but she wrinkled her nose and looked up.

"What's burning?" She peered closer. "Are you in there, Judian?"

CHAPTER TWENTY-SIX

As I could not answer her question in words, I ransacked my mind for some way to show her I still rode my willful crow. Given a harsh shove by my thought, Gargle hopped onto my body's leg, and poked his beak into my boot top. When he tapped the hilt of my knife, still in its sheath, I'd have shouted for joy if I could have. Gargle croaked and shook himself, showering sooty droplets over all.

"It is you, isn't it? Not some further trick of Ibbot's?" Cilliyon shifted her eyes to look sidelong at Gargle. "How long were you standing there?"

I couldn't answer that either, in my present state. I aimed my crow eyes at my body's chest; with utmost relief I watched the shirtfront rise and fall evenly. Alive! Now to get back to myself.

Showing a sudden grasp of my intention, Cilliyon held out the small pouch of powdered mallowmeld. "I stole this from him. Will it help?"

I took back one of the curses I had laid on Gargle, when he bobbed his head for her in confirmation. She lifted my head and shoulders from her lap and laboured to prop my back against the crate. Despite the low light in the attic, with Gargle's sharp eyes I could see the spots of dusky colour that rose to her cheeks as she pushed and shoved me into place.

She copied Ibbot's dusting of powder over the back of my neck. She sat back on her heels and addressed my blank face instead of speaking to Gargle. "I hope you remember the words."

Devoutly to be hoped, indeed. And that the spell to return wasn't one of Ibbot's lies. Knowing I yet lived, as I chanted the spell widdershins in my mind I found I could allow my thoughts to loosen from the bird's, and set my will to withdraw. I sought reunion with my flesh and bone and beating heart. I felt a rush of breath escape my chest and drew air deep.

Steadying my mind, I opened my eyes to see Gargle standing before me on the planks, with Cilliyon kneeling alongside.

"Gods be praised," Cilliyon sighed.

"We have to get after him," I said, but when I tried to rise my head spun and I pitched onto hands and knees. I gulped air, and smelled Gargle's scorched feathers from our flight down the chimney. Wretched stink it was, too. No wonder it alerted Cilliyon.

"Sit for a moment." She pressed my shoulders back toward the crate. I could barely shift my legs aside to settle my rump on the floor. The effort snatched my breath away. I closed my eyes.

"Stay in yourself!" she cried, tapping my chest.

"I am," I said. "I didn't expect to feel so weak. I wonder if the mages always do when they come back?"

The only one who could answer that for me was sailing away. I shook my head to clear the lingering fog and pushed up onto my knees. I reached for Cilliyon's arm to steady myself.

"What did he say? When he took my bag and coin." I focused bleary eyes on her worried face.

"Nothing at first, when you ... left us. After a few moments, he pried up one of your eyelids, and your eye was rolled up into your head. That seemed to be what he was looking for. He stood up and put out his hand and told me to give him the moonstone. You gave it to me last night for the rats, remember?"

I nodded.

"I told him no, but he laughed at me. He said not to be a fool, he could take it and whatever else he wanted. 'Your champion is not here,' he said. He had such an awful look. I gave it to him, I'm sorry."

"No matter now." I squeezed her arm. I wondered if I could stand yet but decided to give a bit more time before trying.

She tossed her head. "I said I wished to gods I was a man so I could fight him. He said only another mage could fight him, and you were learning that lesson now. 'Let us hope he does not tarry too long in his crow, for all our sakes, or the lesson will be wasted.' Then he picked up your sea bag and turned toward the door. But he laughed again and came back to take your purse. 'I can't be left without means,' he said."

"And my folio?" I felt for it clumsily. Still safe within my tunic. "How did you steal his sack of mallowmeld?"

"He left it lie on the floor. I moved to stand so my skirts covered it."

"Did he seem to forget my knife?" I began to feel more myself, better anchored in my own mind.

"I don't know. He either forgot about it or figured your book of lore was more use to him."

She knew about my book, of course, had seen me seeking answers in its pages. She also was quick enough to reckon Ibbot hadn't wanted my bag so much as the book it contained.

Gargle jumped to the top of the crate beside me. He grumbled at me, seeming a bit unsteady himself. Perhaps fighting my will had drained him, much as trying to impose my mind on his had drained me.

I took a breath and levered to my feet. I only swayed a little and released Cilliyon's arm.

She reached out toward my hand, then dropped hers to her side. "What are we going to do?"

"I must go after Ibbot. I will have my book back."

"How can we, when he's taken what tender you had?"

"I have said what I must do, and you keep saying 'we.' Do you understand, Cilliyon? He is bound for the cabal in Scythera, my sworn enemies. I cannot ask you to accompany me into that danger."

She drew herself up. "Haven't I gone with you into whatever danger so far? Do you think to strand me in this backwater?"

"You could wait out Merced's war in relative safety. Who would look for you here? This is no slaver port. It's barely any sort of port at all."

"Indeed true. My family would never find me here. And I will live where and eat what? They have little enough in this place and naught to be generous with to a stranger." She crossed her arms.

I scrubbed a hand across the back of my neck, mixing the ripe scent of mallowmeld into burnt-feather smell. No use talking all around what plagued me. I fancied I felt a ghost of her lips' touch on mine.

"I will not bring you with me because I have come to care for you too much. I cannot bear harm to come to you."

She didn't speak at once, just stared at me. Thinking what? How to guess at the workings of a woman's mind? Gargle's was easier to fathom.

At last, she twisted her lips in a grimace and said, "I have some silver from my father. I have kept it secret."

"Wonderful!" I said, as Gargle cackled.

"I will give it to you only if you take me with you. I could use it to stay here, you see. But I will let you have it on the condition I go with you. I will not be moved on this."

I sat heavily on the crate behind me, jostling Gargle to one side. He gave me a stab in the elbow with his beak.

Our host set up a rapping on the floor, likely banging the ceiling below with a broom handle. "Get going yourselves, before I'm owed another night!"

Burdened with a stubborn crow, a willful girl and a thieving mage. The only tractable creatures in my present circumstances were Wieser and the mule in the stable next door. Besides which, a mule could be excused should it show a muleish nature. I cast my eyes to the rafters and appealed to the gods for some semblance of patience.

"Gather the rest of our belongings. If you cannot be persuaded to see sense, there's no point in lingering."

Cilliyon snatched up the cookstuff and our remaining gear. I told her to leave the skis. I scuffed out my chalked runes, stirring dust motes that stung my eyes and nose, and hoisted the heavier of the saddlebags. We clumped down the rickety stair with Gargle flying before us.

Our host pointed to the bird at once. "I said no crow. That'll be more!"

"He came down the chimney at dawn. Smell the singed feathers? Yourself's flue could use cleaning and the common room a good airing."

He squinted, clearly suspicious. "How would yourself know about the flue?"

"The crow told me."

The barman backed away, bullish look fading. "Keep yourself's black wickedness out of my place. Where's that other one? He can't stay here!"

I felt a surge of eagerness to see Anlia and the Jackadaw fade into the distance. "He's already fled this poor hospitality. Look for ourselves again—never!"

I held the door to urge Cilliyon through into the sleet and followed her out. Gargle circled the barman's head cawing raucously before he flapped out the door with us.

Cilliyon had to take two steps to each one of mine and plucked at my cloak. "Why do you hurry so? Are you certain you know where Ibbot is off to?"

"I saw the ship he boarded. It sailed south. I aim to follow."

"What will you do if you catch up to him on the ocean? He'll be on one ship with us on another."

"I am thinking no further than pursuit just now. Once we are headed after him, I'll make plans. Here is the stable. We need your coin, I promised some to the boy caring for Wieser."

Frowning, she reached to pat her hip. "I'll need a moment alone to get them out. Are you sure you are clear-headed after your turn with the crow this morning?"

"No," I said. "I'm not sure."

This did not please her, judging from a quick shake of her head. She slipped to one side when we entered the stable. I stood with my back to her so she could pull out her purse. I hoped her father had given her a generous amount for her keep on Lohr Island.

After a moment, she tapped my shoulder. When I turned, she placed a long muslin strip in my hands. Stitching divided it into sections all along its length, and I could feel coins sewn into each pouch. It made for a heavy handful. I reckoned she had worn it bound about her all this time, with the coins kept quiet by the muslin wrappings.

"I'm giving you all I have," she said softly.

"Cilliyon." I cast about for something to say. "Can I not leave you half to stay here, while I take the other half to follow Ibbot? I would pledge on my honor to return for you."

"And if you did not return, if the mages caught you, I would never in my lifetime know what had befallen you. No." She stepped past me to walk toward our mule's creamy muzzle, poking over the half-door of a stall down the way.

I plucked apart the stitching on one of the pouches and drew out three silver coins. More than enough for my promise to the stableboy. Perhaps enough to have us ferried to a masted ship at anchor, as well. From the length of the strip, it must have reached more than twice around Cilliyon. Her da had been generous with his girl.

Silently I blessed her da's heavy purse and at the same time chided him for raising a daughter so headstrong. Her presence at my side made me vulnerable in ways I would have rather avoided.

Gargle sailed into Wieser's boxstall, greeted by yips and the boy's thin voice crying out in relief, "Back at last! Oh, bird, you gave me a turn. I've earned my coin many times over with the two of you!"

The stableboy popped his head over the stall door and called to me. "This dog will be so glad to see yourself has come for her. She has been worried, I think."

Catching sight of Cilliyon, he bobbed his head awkwardly. "Good mornin' miss. Does yourself need a service? My master is about the place ..."

"She's come here with me." I pressed two coins into his hand as I entered the stall. "We'll set off by sea soon and I'll need to sell our mule. Would the stableman buy it?"

He raised his face, cheeks glowing. "So much! I hope no one thinks I stole it. But if I show my master, he'll want it."

"I'm sorry, I've nothing but silver. If yourself gives it to maman, can she reckon a way to use it?"

"I've no maman, now. Or father. But my sister, she might figure a way. She's a smart one. She's a fish-gutter."

"And the mule?" I heard the stablemaster greet Cilliyon in the passage. The boy hurried to tuck his wealth away.

It seemed the man did have an interest in our mule, at a trifling portion of its worth. After all, he mused with a shrewd lift of his brow, he would have to feed and board it while he sought a buyer. I accepted his offer and took his coins in haste since every moment allowed Ibbot to put greater distance between us.

Cilliyon gave the mule a last pat before the man led it away. She asked the stableboy about his sister who worked to gut fish. I did not chivvy her out the door, as I felt a small leap of hope that she might be considering a stay in Anlia, perhaps taking up fish-gutting herself. As the boy yattered on helpfully about how the catch was gutted, smoked and salted in boxes to be sent away on big ships, I saw a new purpose to her questions.

"Where do they ship the fish?" I interrupted.

"Mostly farther south from here. To Scythera, where there is a larger port."

Cilliyon asked, "Is there such a shipment leaving today? South-bound on one of the larger vessels?"

"They've been working the girls hard, getting the catch ready. I think my sister said a lot leaves today and then they can breathe a bit."

"Does yourself know the name of the ship?" I pressed.

He shook his head. "No, and she wouldn't know neither."

"Can't we ask on the waterfront? Someone there must know." Cilliyon pulled my arm.

At the docks, we bargained our way onto a flat craft stacked with wooden boxes, though I did have to count out a good bit of our precious coin for the privilege. "There is none ever asked to ride with the fish before," the boatman said. "And a dog and crow? The moon must be full."

The shipmaster of the cargo vessel *Traubent* likewise thought us lunatics but granted we might ride along in his hold for a price. I paid our passage, then paced the deck after I learned we would not sail until the next morning, when the tide ran more favorable and the loading had been completed.

I had forgotten, as well, all the dreaded particulars of travel on water. Rocking at anchor brought my seasickness on me before our ferry boatman had time to steer back to his slip for another load.

Cilliyon appeared untroubled by the shifting deck but looked at me with worried eyes. "Do you want to spend the night ashore?"

"No. That wouldn't make sense. We'd have to pay to be returned to the dock and then pay again to come back out. There's less motion below deck and no water all around to look at. Stay up here if you like. I'll scout us a place amongst the cargo. Wieser, come."

Gargle flapped away to the mast tip. He could find me below if he wanted me. I reflected that I had felt no sickness from swooping through the wind or perched on a mast while in Gargle's mind and decided crows must not be bothered by the buffeting of ocean waves, either. Cilliyon accompanied me down to the hold, perhaps to avoid the bold looks she got from the seamen working the hoists.

This ship being perhaps a quarter the size of *Moon Road*, the size of her cargo hold could only be called modest. I found us a place among the ranks of wooden boxes, away from the men who labored by the open hatch. The reek of our cargo of smoked fish hung heavy in the close air, despite the chill. The smell did nothing to settle my stomach.

Wieser curled between us and heaved a sigh. I scratched her ears.

Cilliyon cleared her throat. "Why do you think Ibbot is taking your book to the mages?"

"I cannot claim to know why. It is surely valuable to me, but to master mages such as they are? How would the lore-book of a country healer-woman interest them? My mother may have been more than I know. But the cabal cannot think the book was responsible for my thwarting them in the cliff caves, because my da had not yet given it to me. I knew nothing of it."

"He took no care to conceal his departure from you. What to make of that? He knew you would be riding Gargle over the port when he chose to flee. He sent you out."

I nodded. "He certainly saw. He gave us a sort of salute but then paid us no more mind. But he also had to have seen Gargle on the rigging when he did his weather work to push away the storm. Why did he not push Gargle away, as well? Or knock him from the sky, and me with him?"

"I wonder."

"Unless ..." my voice trailed off as I thought more. "Unless, knowing I would pursue, he is bringing me to Scythera. Me and my knife."

CHAPTER TWENTY-SEVEN

I woke flailing with fear, crying out in the black dark of the ship's hold. Cilliyon and Wieser stirred beside me, one with a murmur and the other a whine. I struggled to slow my breath.

"What is it?" She laid her hand on my shoulder.

I shook my head to clear it. "Ibbot and I stood in the center of a circle of stones. All around us, mages chanted in the shadows. The moon rose red as blood. And I had never felt so ... hollow."

"Empty in your mind?"

"In my heart." I rested a hand on my chest. My heart still thudded. "Empty. As if I was a cast snakeskin, or the husk of an insect."

"Is that what mages can do to folk?"

"I do not know. Two of them tried to kill Wieser, and stun me. In Merced's cliff caves. I still don't even know what prevented them from doing so. If I thwarted them by using my knife's magic, or if the kavsprit came to me when I called for their aid. From what I've learned in fragments from Ibbot, I suspect the mages don't know what happened either. That's what infuriates them, maybe."

"Did you have your knife? In your dream?"

Much as I wanted to push the vision away deeper into my memory, I looked inward again. "I had nothing."

"Was I there? And Wieser and Gargle?"

"I see none—except Ibbot. The others are too much in shadow to see their features, but they wear the black robes of Scytheran mages."

Her hand on my tunic gripped the fabric in a spasm. "I should have let you kill him, on the mountain."

"You did not stop me, truly." I spread my hand over hers. "I found I could not carry it through, aside from your misgivings. And, he seemed not the least harmed, whatever it was that prevented him from freezing."

"But his master came, while he slept that unnatural sleep. What if Ibbot felt he must hurry to Scythera at once to avoid being captured and punished?"

That I could not argue against—Ibbot compelled by his fear of a return to servitude, rushing to Scythera with the magical prize that could buy his freedom. My book. Or my knife and me, owing to a certainty I would follow him.

"I think you believed you had gained the advantage over him," she said, a tinge of reproach creeping into her voice in the darkness.

"More fool me. But I told you, I never took him at his word when he pledged to do as I said. Still, I should not have yielded to my desire to ride Gargle by magery."

"Yours is the only word to be trusted." She pressed closer to me and I shifted to slide an arm about her shoulders.

"I do have a portion of his hair left ..." I huffed out a breath. "If only I had a book of magical lore to help devise a use for the token."

She gave a laugh that was more a sigh. "If only."

Morning dawned clear and fine, with a fair wind to fill *Traubent's* sails. Cilliyon coaxed me onto the deck and begged a mug of hot water from the cook for brewing my herbs to quell the sickness. When that stayed with me instead of going over the railing, she persuaded me to chew some of the dried apples Bryar had shared. I began to feel I might endure the voyage with her care.

We sailed a day behind my quarry. I sought out the shipmaster to learn more about the Scytheran port, but he had little enough to offer beyond the name: Ulfar. He showed me his sea chart. This detailed more than I wished to know about currents and coastline, and nothing at all about the inland of Scythera.

It seemed the man's world was as small as mine had used to be.

He did know most folk on the Ulfar docks understood Yeganil, though he had no knowledge himself of their Scytheran language. Not a surprise. At Bale Harbour in Merced, I'd heard a dozen tongues along the wharves. If Ulfar was likewise a port for deep-draft ocean-going ships, seamen from many countries would make landfall there, bringing their various languages and currencies.

I hoped we could hunt down Ibbot without drawing undue attention, since the place was accustomed to foreigners. Neither Cilliyon nor I sounded native Yegan in our speech, I knew. In a busy port city, who would be concerned with our origins? Likely no one.

Cilliyon fretted still, restless in the dark hold that night. "If we go about asking how to find mages, surely that is out of the ordinary for travelers? And is there one cabal, or many?"

"Agreed. We are not fortified with all the knowledge we might wish. But if I ask Wieser to find Ibbot, then we need not ask anyone."

"A use for the token?" she said doubtfully.

"She will know what I want her to do. It's true she cannot tell me how far, or how we might best travel. I could ride Gargle again to scout ahead on the road."

"I do not like the idea of that!"

"Shush, now. Try to rest. Once we reach Ulfar, I'll know better what to do. When I have seen the sort of place it is."

She grumbled, but soon I knew she slept by the gentle weight of her head on my chest. I brushed my fingertips along her cheek and wished for some sign from the gods telling me my best path. If her trust in me proved misplaced, how could I bear it?

For me, sleep perched as far away as Gargle, high atop the mast in the night sky.

I only felt as though I could sleep once the sun rose, making it too late to try. Cilliyon guided me to the deck. She repeated the ritual of stomach calming herbs and dried fruit. She stood at my shoulder watching the stony cliffs crawl past on the landward side. She even begged an egg for Wieser and mixed it with broken-up ship biscuit. Gargle joined us on deck, and she fed him a share of biscuit, too. So long as the girl made herself useful beyond measure, how could I regret her presence? Yet, I could not shake a sense of foreboding—that if I did not go into this fight alone I would lose all I carried with me and held dear.

Gargle jabbed my ankle with his beak and flew across the deck to the seaward rail. When I joined him there, I caught sight of *Apella Bern* making her way home to Anlia. Her colours danced from the top of her mast, no mistake. I sought the *Traubent's* master and asked him if he could signal the passing vessel.

To answer his look of 'here is another mad request from a fool,' I explained, "I am pursuing a mage who stole from me. I want to know if he left that ship at Ulfar."

The man's stony expression only hardened further. "Whatever he took, you're better off without it. No one in a clear mind chases a mage." He made a gesture of warding-off and spat over his shoulder. "I've no way to ask anything. But if we see the ship on her way north now, bound back to Anlia, Ulfar is most likely where she's been. Doesn't tell you if he's still aboard."

Perhaps not, but I reckoned, would he sail to Scythera only to turn about at once and head back to Anlia? I decided to assume he had disembarked at Ulfar.

The farther south we sailed, the more arid the landscape grew. The piled and drifted snow of the steep Yegan coastline gave way to lumpy crags the colour of beach sand merely dusted with white. What sparse trees I could see appeared stunted and bore no green needles, only bare, twisted branches. When the ship veered closer to the cliff face, I saw that some of the white streaks I had taken for snow were splattered seabird manure from nests in the crevices. Hundreds of black and white birds rode the rush of wind at the headlands, swooping and screeching. Their bodies looked no larger than Gargle's, but their wings spread at least twice the span of a man's arms. I feared them, though I could not say why.

"Is this Scythera?" I asked a passing seaman.

He shook his head. "Not yet. Coming to it soon, though. We sail past the Barrens."

Cilliyon shaded her eyes to look closer at the man's face. "When will we reach Ulfar?"

"Tomorrow with the evening tide, if all continues fair."

Another long night for me to examine my dread from every angle. I pulled my cloak closer about my neck and listened to Gargle cawing as he took up his perch on the mast. I suddenly heard it as his challenge to the gods, every one of them. His defiance of fate, borne away in the wind that drove us. We sailed onward.

"Why does everything look so ... bleak?" Cilliyon searched the coastline with brows drawn close. "Did Ibbot say Scythera was a desolate place?"

I shook my head. "He claimed it was a ruined country. I heard from Orlo, a friend in Bale Harbour, that Scythera suffered from famine and drought. Some seamen told him so, he hadn't traveled there himself. Ibbot said the mages fought among themselves and had wrung all the good from a once-rich land. Ambition and avarice, he said."

"It's not difficult to see ambition and avarice in Ibbot, despite how he points to it in the others." After a moment, she continued. "Please might you consider going from Ulfar to Lohr Island? Or Merced? Could you let go of your book after all?"

"I have considered. I do not know if I can let it go."

We spoke to one another in Mercedish on deck. I noted one of the sailors pausing to catch our words. He ducked his head when he caught my gaze on him and went on his way.

Moments later, he crouched at my feet, making as if to rewind a rope already coiled there. He spoke in Yeganil. "I have heard that tongue before. In Ulfar."

I opened my mouth to speak, to ask him if he knew the folk that used it, when he snapped his head up to meet my eyes. "It was slaves I heard. Penned up at the sales there, pleading for aid. Yourself must be careful, especially guard the woman."

Cilliyon sucked in a sharp breath and I glanced at her. In that instant, the seaman slipped away.

She seized the rail with shaking hands, but she said nothing. Wieser pressed against her, leaning into her with the rocking of the ship.

The retribution of Scytheran mages, what I feared most. Sold into slavery, what Cilliyon told me she feared beyond any other threat. Was I mad to propel us both into the very risks we wanted at all costs to avoid?

No turning back, now we rode the waves. No getting off. I must think well and hard what course to take once we arrived at Ulfar. I could hunt down Ibbot to try to recover what he stole from me. We could choose passage to Lohr Island, or a return to Merced. I could abandon my mother's book forever but perhaps save our lives. Choices lay before me. Each choice felt the like the worst in its own way.

Have I displeased you so much as this? I asked the gods. *Have you sent a sign which I missed, showing me what I should choose? Or have you forsaken me?*

CHAPTER TWENTY-EIGHT

My home country of Merced had built Bale Harbour, known to me as a lively port bristling with commerce. The contrast with Ulfar of Scythera could not have been more dismal unless Ulfar were deserted altogether. Though also in a sheltered, deep-water bay, the Scytheran port bore stretches of empty berths marked by sagging docks. The blocky stones of the wharves lay cracked and gaping as the *Traubent* sailed past.

Cilliyon and I held hands on the landward deck. "It is a larger port than Anlia by far, but there are so few ships." She licked her lips free of salt spray. "And so few are ocean-going—look, only two." She pointed at a pair of tri-masted vessels at anchor.

I nodded. After a hellish night of scrambled dreams, I still could not decide my course once we landed. I sent up another prayer for guidance to gods apparently occupied with other folk. No answers were forcoming.

The helmsman steered *Traubent* toward a section of the docks in better repair, where a half-dozen similar craft rocked. I chanced to look behind us and saw a third deep-draft vessel in our wake. Small vessels sped toward her, to tend her into her berth. I tried not to wonder if she was a slaver ship. At any rate, she was not *Chikoro*, Kruthe's vessel.

Gargle lit on my shoulder as we made our way onto the docks.

Cilliyon and Wieser both hung close by my side. At each footfall, I felt as though I had a belly full of snakes, coiling and writhing. It was surely too near dark to set Wieser tracking Ibbot ... unless I chose instead to sail for home? Or Lohr Island—but no large ship would sail until high tide on the morrow. Where could we lodge overnight?

As we topped the uneven stone steps to reach street level, the sight waiting there froze my every thought. I seized Cilliyon's arm when she turned to run.

A crowd of folk milled before us, but ringed with fence like a shipment of stock. Most were men, but women pressed against the boards as well. Even some children, bawling like calves separated from milk cows for the spring sales. Some of the men called out, but in a tongue I did not know. Thin arms reached through the barrier toward us. Beyond the closest pens, more fences filled with folk stretched away; I could not see the end of them.

"Keep walking, and slow," I said in Cilliyon's ear. I tightened my grip on her arm until she nodded. "We walk straight out of town on whatever road heads inland. Do not look back. Do not stop."

Indeed, I found I could not stop. My feet carried on, one in front of the other, as the sun sank behind us and the light faded. We passed some who must dwell in Ulfar, traveling on foot and on horseback along the street. They paid us no more mind than I spared for them. None looked at the horror of the pens alongside.

The moon rose as the sun died in the sea at our backs. I continued walking and Cilliyon and Wieser kept pace. Gargle held my shoulder and would not fly. Tendrils of snow sifted over the stony track, which climbed out of Ulfar and then dove deep between mounded hills of reddish rock. After a time, I cannot say how long, Cilliyon stumbled in the half-light, and fell to her knees. I bent to pull her up, intent on trudging until I walked off the end of the earth, perhaps.

She tugged my sleeve, avoiding my outstretched hand. "Ahead," she whispered. "Something in the road."

I peered into the faint silvery light, without straightening. Some darker shapes, indistinct. Growing no closer, unless my eyes deceived me. "Wieser, what is it?" I murmured to her.

She sniffed and whined. Gargle stepped to and fro along my shoulders, clicking his beak. "Go fly and see," I told him. He shook back his wings and folded them tighter against his sides.

I pulled my sleeve free of Cilliyon and swept my hand across my shoulder to dislodge Gargle as I stood upright. "Wait here," I said to them all, and gave no one a chance to refuse.

I walked on until I could make out the figures of men with arms stretched wide and legs apart, blocking the way ahead. What sort of guards could stand so? Their clothes seemed to be no more than rags flapping in the night wind. I knew no words of Scytheran to hail them. Were we too far already from Ulfar to expect them to understand Yeganil?

I could only try. I walked four paces more and the words turned to ash on my tongue. Now I could see clearer. Thick crosspieces of branch held up man-shapes formed of twigs and brambles. Scraps of cloth fluttered here and there on the limbs but did not seem to move in a way that made sense with the path of the wind funneled between the road banks.

The obsidian blade in my boot shuddered in its sheath. I found I had to force my eyes away from those shapes in the moonlight. I looked up along the rim of the steep banks and clenched my fists so hard my nails bit flesh. The enspelled stick-men had been placed side-by-side along each bank, arching away into the dark.

A boundary, but of what? I had no heart to trespass by the light of a waning moon. I stepped backwards slowly, loathe to turn my back to the man-things.

I sensed some grievous malice there.

"We'll find a place to rest," I said to the others, as I had no wish to explain further. If I had to guess whether we drew closer to a cabal of mages on our chosen path, my guess was yes.

I led us back the way we had come, to the last place the road traveled over higher ground. I wanted to be able to see all around us if anything approached. Though a bitter night, I would dare no fire even if we could scrounge some fuel for it. This portion of Scythera must be a continuation of the Barrens the seaman had spoken about; we seemed surrounded by a dead land. My best hope was to find a boulder where we might huddle in the lee to escape the biting wind. As I scanned the featureless earth beside the roadway, a flicker of light caught my eye.

Cilliyon must have seen it, too. "Could some other travelers have a camp there? A fire to share?"

The thought of some warmth drew me only a little more than the thought of a possible threat pulled me the opposite way. "We'll go a bit closer and see. We may be wiser to keep to ourselves. Or be unwelcome."

After my legs ached with walking, it became clear we had gained no ground. Either the light moved away from us at a pace equal to our own, or it was some magic to trick us—to lead us astray into the wilderness.

"Stop. We'll go back to the roadside. Something is not right with this."

"Which way is it?" She spun about, voice rising. "I can't remember! Can you?"

"So, we stop here. No place is worse than another as far as I can tell." *Except the barrier of wooden men. That is much worse ...*

She allowed me to soothe her and settle her beside Wieser on the bare ground. I sat cross-legged beside them. Gargle burrowed his way under Wieser's ruff, out of the wind.

"I reckon I'll take first watch, then, shall I?" I muttered to him. Distracted by this irritation, perhaps it is no wonder that, in spite of my fears, I neglected to chalk the runes of protection around us.

Some time later, I opened my eyes and cursed myself for giving in to sleep. The moon still swam overhead among thin, hurrying clouds. I had not slept long, it seemed. The surrounding landscape continued featureless save for our huddled shapes.

My mind refused to cease an endless spiral. It plagued me with the sight of so many captive folk in despair. I could no longer avoid thinking about Cuffer, Tobal the cook, all the men of *Moon Road*. Kruthe had said he might ransom the officers, but that left many to be herded to the auction block. My heart sank further when I recalled the seaman's words of hearing Mercedish before at the Ulfar slave pens. Just prior to my sailing away from Merced, enemy soldiers had been rounding up all who could do magic ... what if Annora, and Virda, too, had been captured and sold?

In the darkness, I answered my heart's nascent call—my life work would change. I must labor to aid the enslaved folk in the world.

I stripped off my gloves to breathe on numb fingers. As I pulled them back on, the air before me began to shimmer, just as when Mage Balin had appeared in our wayside hut as a Sending.

The others did not stir and I did not rouse them. Gradually the shape coalesced into Ibbot, though shadowed as if he crouched low somewhere dark and moonless.

"And here you are. Just as pig-headed as I supposed," his image said. "Sad to say, my scheme has not proved clever after all. You must get away from here just as quick as you can."

CHAPTER TWENTY-NINE

"No. I may have been fool enough to come after you. I do have more wits than to flee across a strange land in the dark. Where are you, anyway?"

The shifty look that crossed his features, I knew well. "Where doesn't matter. I am a prisoner. So will you be if you do not heed me and turn tail." The Sending peered over his shoulder as if he heard something that frightened him. After an instant's pause, he turned to me again. "Use what wisdom you have and run while you still can."

Though Ibbot spoke in a hoarse whisper, Wieser lifted her head, ears pricked. Gargle, dislodged from his furry nest, waggled his beak and fixed a baleful eye on Ibbot's image. Cilliyon slept on.

"Are you a prisoner of the mages or the slavers?"

"What difference does that make? Your book impressed no one. It may be destroyed now for all I know. Despite my efforts to explain it as bait for a greater prize." He shook his head. "If I tell you I am sorry for its loss, will you do as I tell you and go?"

"I reckon I can believe slavers seeing no value in my book. Mages? Perhaps. My mother may have been more than a hedge-witch, but not on peer with the masters. At least, not in their view. Did you tell them I would exchange my knife for the book? Or did you plan to give them me—and let them wrest my blade away if they could?"

"I tell you it doesn't matter now. Why won't you leave?"

"Because I think I will come for you, if you will tell me where you are."

His expression would have made me burst out laughing, if the night had been any less dire.

He leaned toward me and had to put a hand down to steady himself. "There's no need to come for me to exact your vengeance. I am very likely to be dead in a matter of days, if that's any comfort to you."

"Be sure, I do not dispute your capacity to aggravate anyone to the point of murder. But your death would be a waste, as you once said about mine. No. I have other plans for you, plans which require a living mage."

His eyes narrowed. "It is said men go mad in the Barrens."

"I have only been out here a matter of hours." Then the barrier of bramble-men rose in my mind's eye and I huddled deeper in my furs. "Tell me where to find you."

He did not answer at once. Whatever had concerned him before seemed to come again, for he froze and then slowly glanced behind him. I heard nothing on the steppes except the hollow moaning of the wind.

Finally, he spoke. "There is a pit, a deep place carved out of the bedrock. A portion of the cabal resides there."

"A cave?" I had much familiarity with caves, so dared hope for kavsprit aid.

He shook his head. "They created it with magery. It is almost a palace, many levels, countless rooms. More like a canyon than a cavern, but it's filled from the depths to the brim with their stone Stronghold."

"Is it beyond the fence made of wooden men?" I asked, although somehow I already knew.

"You've seen that? Each figure imprisons a doomed soul, bound there with a curse beyond time. Do you still want to come?"

I swallowed. "How do I pass through?"

He told me the spell to obscure my free soul from the watchful evil there, a way to disguise the breath of the gods within me. "Cilliyon will not be able to do this," I said. "Can I cover her as well?"

"You must not bring her. If they discover you are fond of the girl they will find a way to use it against you. As I tried to. Find somewhere for her to hide and wait."

"I will come alone." Gargle leapt onto my shoulder and butted his head against my jaw. "With just my crow, then. Wieser, you have to stay and guard Cilliyon."

Ibbot nodded. And told me how to find the last place on this earth I thought I would have chosen to go.

In the morning, creating a refuge for Cilliyon proved less an ordeal than persuading her to stay there. I resorted to building a sort of hut by piling rocks in front of a narrow crevice between two boulders. A larger flat stone provided a roof, and a strained gut for me from shifting it. A trickling freshet at the back would give enough water for her and for Wieser. I gave her all the provisions we still possessed, save a bit of dried fish for Gargle and me to share on the journey. When I pressed my crossbow and quiver of bolts into her hands, she cast her eyes about as though expecting a fierce creature close at hand.

"Only as a precaution," I said, but I felt, too, a sense of something watching. "I won't be gone long."

She likely realized my words were empty. How did I know how long this errand would take? Ibbot had told me a day's hard walking would reach the Pit. I had not asked if the place had a name, but any term would be in the Scytheran tongue, which I did not know. And how long would it take to find him within and rescue him?

If there had been need for more water, Cilliyon's tears might have been caught and saved. I felt my patience fraying as I recalled Annora, my brother's bride, who shed not one tear the entire time Wils spent waylaid in the borderlands under siege, nor when he returned home, either.

Wieser, of course, did not weep. She laid her head on her outstretched paws and watched my every move, unblinking. I chalked all the runes I knew around the rocks above and below, while chanting the spells which would divert eyes and thoughts from the crevice.

Cilliyon's tears continued as she stood, holding the quarrels like a handful of dry grass. I tried to reason with the girl, truly. I reminded her she could have chosen to stay behind in Anlia, despite that being a bleak choice.

When I could bear no more, I pulled her to me, perhaps more roughly than I intended, and held her close. I whispered to her, stroked her hair and told her she held my heart as no other could. She calmed and stood in blessed silence while I then took my leave, pressing her lips with a trembling hand.

Though she did look a bit as if she would like to poke me in the eye with one of the crossbow bolts. Wieser came to lean against her.

Gargle rode my shoulder in preference to taking wing. I wanted him near to hand, as we approached the road that carried us east to the wooden men. I would need to help him pass the barrier with me.

The dreadful intricacy of the magic Ibbot had taught me in the moonlight seemed to weight my boots as I walked. I was to use the mallowmeld powder on both Gargle and myself. I might have known Ibbot saw Cilliyon take the pouch; he probably wanted her to do so.

I tried to convince myself his devious nature would serve me well for what I intended.

First, I had to free him.

When we reached the edge of the roadway, I dragged or rolled a half dozen stones into a shape I would recognize, so I would know where to turn south and make my way back to Cilliyon and Wieser. Gods knew how I would find them else, for the landscape had so little to distinguish one place from another. I made certain the tumble of stones seemed natural and would not draw other eyes, then enspelled it for good measure.

All too soon I came in view of the boundary. I stepped aside, off the road behind a boulder. There I dusted Gargle's head and wings, and my neck, forehead and arms with the mallowmeld powder, reciting the incantation to bind us together. Last, each of his clawed toes received a sprinkling, and I slipped out of my boots to spread more over my feet. On impulse, I rubbed a small amount over the blade of my knife, to bind it as well, since the obsidian seemed to carry a spirit of its own. Or perhaps it carried the will of its makers, the kavsprit of Merced.

I focused so entirely on the deep magic I performed that I did not see or hear a herd approach. When I raised my eyes, animals I had never seen before roamed only yards away. They looked somewhat like deer, but with wide flat fleshy hooves. They appeared to graze on bare rock. I looked closer to see the rocks bore a crust of greyish green which they nibbled and rasped with black tongues. Their coats were dun-coloured and shaggy. I could smell the oily musk of the bucks on the wind. Oddly, the heady scent of the mallowmeld seemed muted, now I thought to notice. Could the stuff lose potency? I had no way of knowing, out on the rugged hills. Doubt must not sap my resolve, not now.

I wondered if the animals were wild, or if folk tended the herd. I looked but saw no one near them. None of the creatures paid me any mind, displayed no skittishness or fear of man scent. Surely if prey animals traveled these steppes, predators followed after. Wolves or suchlike. Something like a wolf, or a pack of them, which could take down an animal as large as these wandering before me, could also prey on a girl or a dog. Time to make haste, I chided myself. I must set my fear aside and get done what I had to do, so I could get back to keep care of Cilliyon and Wieser.

I stood, with Gargle riding on my shoulder, and walked toward the stick-men barring my way.

The figures stood in silhouette with a wan winter sun low on the horizon at their backs. The scraps of cloth wound around the limbs or snagged between the brambles moved as though tugged by the current of an unseen river. The rhythm looked disquieting, somehow, as if the things struggled feebly.

The spellwork Ibbot had shared should cause the doomed souls to see—if it could be termed sight—me as bound, also. My spirit and Gargle's entwined and shackled, appearing to the guardians as another one like themselves. Doomed.

Gargle, usually with an opinion in all matters, dug claws into my shoulder and made no sound at all. I set out, walking on the edge of the stony track. The deer-like creatures ambled out of my path, headed generally south. A couple of them bleated and chuffed as they lumbered away.

When I drew close, mere steps from the boundary, I heard the voices. Or not voices, not really speaking, but low, low groans of despair beyond bearing. It reached my mind in faint echoes, the sound of utter emptiness where hope should dwell. Tears flowed down my face and froze to my cheeks, but I walked on. Each time I lifted my boot, it felt as if my leg was formed of sand instead of flesh and bone, and as if sand ran out on the ground before I could set my foot back down. My spirit leached away. I diminished with each footfall.

Gargle half-spread his wings and hunkered down on my shoulder. I could not feel his mind in the way I had when I rode him at Anlia, but his distress seemed to mirror my own. I tried not to think beyond forcing myself forward.

I set my eyes on the space between two of the figures, a gap where sticks like skeletal fingers stretched to touch and bundled bramble legs straddled wide but did not quite reach the man-thing alongside. I fell to my knees, my strength failing, but dredged enough will to crawl through the opening.

Nothing should be in my thoughts, Ibbot had said, nothing that reflected the gift of the gods' breath of life within me. That was what the tethered souls lacked, what left them bereft, endlessly grieving. And what they sought in any others passing by, so the mages would be warned of trespass by the bound ones' awakened hunger.

Moving a fisted hand, then a knee, then the other hand, my mind must be filled only with each separate motion. Gargle clung to me, as oppressed as I had ever felt him. Another knee forward. Banish from my thought even the sensation of the rough stone scraping my flesh.

It seemed as though I might have passed through all the seasons of my life, and thus would emerge as an old man on the other side, so garbled did my grasp of time become while I crept.

I felt myself exist both everywhere and nowhere with each beat of my heart.

As long as I keep moving ... moving through the sucking, questing misery surrounding me. Awareness seeped into my mind at last: the gnawing rumble of almost-voices quieted. I had passed, reached the far side of the boundary. A scum of fog obscuring my vision lifted; I had not noticed when it appeared.

I crawled on, craving more distance from the doomed. Blotting out the thought of a second time through the barrier. Did I have enough mallowmeld left? *Do not think of that yet, only keep moving.*

When Gargle shook back his wings and stretched his neck, I gathered myself to stand. Though weak beyond memory, everyone was still in danger if I claimed any time to rest. Instead, I walked.

Gargle's and my spirit spiraled about one another, with my blade a solid presence within our melded minds. Though I set one foot after another on the track before us, I did not feel fully present in my body. It appeared as if a shroud blurred the air surrounding us, while I viewed myself from a vantage just above the crown of my own head.

I prayed the distortion was the magic's protection, then shied away from bringing the gods to mind even in gratitude. My steps made scant sound and I could only barely hear the wind or feel its needle teeth. If I was as obscured from others' senses as I seemed to be from my own, I might hope to find Ibbot and bring him out of the Stronghold without being caught.

Yet, I did not drift across the Barrens as a wraith. Step after plodding step, I made my way. My heart still beat, Gargle still clung to my shoulder and I could still feel the weight of my knife in its sheath.

At last, our goal appeared before us.

The rim of the Pit, with a dark maw yawning across the canyon, its opposite wall lost in drifts of grey mist.

CHAPTER THIRTY

I bbot had instructed me to wait for his guide before attempting to descend. He assured me I would recognize the emissary. I settled in the leeward defile of a rockface and scanned the skies above. Brethren of the cliff-dwelling birds from the coast wheeled overhead and dived into the Pit, barely skimming past the carved walls. Some passed close enough to show their raw-looking featherless heads and necks. I looked away.

Ibbot would surely not choose to possess one of these vile gargantuans? Gargle could fly, but I could not, so how would I follow over the edge?

Next, I scanned the ground before me for a snake, which would be a fitting creature to share Ibbot's mind. None slithered into view, however. What if Ibbot could not find a suitable host? Or if his captors prevented him from possessing the animal? I despaired of finding him in the immense labyrinth that stretched below me without some sort of magical aid.

My chosen wait-spot overlooked the edge of the Pit, and I passed some time lying on my belly, my eye tracing the steep steps that wound around the periphery of the stone well. Columns and arches along the stairs seemed to suggest side passages penetrating deeper into the canyon walls. Perhaps leading to the countless rooms Ibbot had mentioned. The place did appear to be a warren, riddled with ways to become hopelessly lost. Gargle looked over the edge as well, then fixed me with a glittery stare.

"You wanted to come along," I reminded him as I again settled my back against the rock. "Now we are here for good or ill. No way out but through." He appeared unconvinced, and in fact looked back the way we had come.

I was spared further opinion on the subject by the scrabbling of tiny claws at my trouser leg. A sleek fawn-coloured mouse paused on my knee to wriggle its whiskers and regard me with glass-bright black eyes.

I knew at once the creature bore Ibbot within it. "Keep in mind the difference in our sizes," I said to the mouse. "I cannot squeeze through where this tiny one might."

It showed me a tail twice the length of its body as it turned and scampered down my leg and off to the edge of the abyss. The tail had a curious large tuft of longer fur at its end, snow white.

"Let us hope the tail tip can be seen when the light fades," I said to Gargle. "I may have to depend on your sharp eyes below."

I would have given much to have my moonstone talisman, remembering the light it provided me in the Lunenhelm mine. I had last seen the pendant around the neck of Ibbot the thief as he fled. I wondered if he had it yet, or if the mages who imprisoned him had taken it. Or if they had tossed it aside as something useless, like my mother's book.

Pointless musing. I would still go in and down. I clung to hope of encountering kavsprit deep in the earth, for they had aided me before within their realm.

I followed the mouse to the notch of rock rim where he waited. Rough-hewn stairs curved into the Pit. Whiskers twitching, the mouse leapt off the edge and onto the first stair, then turned to look at me. Gargle held tight to my shoulder as I stepped after the tiny creature.

At times my mouse-guide paused, and Gargle looked about sharply. I saw no mages, or indeed any folk, but could sometimes hear footfalls echo in a side passage or creaking that sounded like the wheels of a laden cart.

The stairs were so narrow and steep that if I had encountered anyone, we could not have passed one another whether or not I was visible to them. There was scarcely room for one of my boots on each chiseled step, never both together. Ibbot had chosen a little-used and more rustic path for me, it seemed. I clung to the wall and did my best not to look into the center chasm. I have never been troubled by the fear of high places some are plagued with, but as I crept into this abyss my guts quivered with dizzying terror. It seemed as if a portion of my mind could already see my body toppling into the depths. Not least of my difficulty was the queer way I seemed to view the place, as though from the top of my head rather than through my eyes. *Let that be the power of the magic holding strong ...*

I smelled no kitchens or midden heaps. No manure to suggest fowl or swine. Such places might be farther beyond any of the multitude of carved archways, with the spell working to hide my scent as well as that of the surroundings.

The mouse led us lower, into the shadows, beyond the tentative reach of weak wintry light from above. *Gargle can still see*, I told myself. I fixed my gaze on the flick of the white-tipped tail at my feet, and on each narrow stair tread. I prayed to the earth goddess, more afraid now of continuing into the darkness without her intercession than of calling the wrath of mages upon my soul. Ice pounded through my veins, making me tremble and threatening to pitch me headlong off the stairway.

After a dozen more steps in the ashen light, a curious greenish glow emanated from the side tunnels. I peered into one as I passed. The rock walls shone as though smeared with the entrails of summer lightning flies. Magic, certainly. And what had I expected in a mage Stronghold, simple torches lining the walls?

Always before whenever I brought my knife below ground to its birthplace, it had thrummed with the rhythm of the oldest of earth spirits, the kavsprit. I had heard their whispery voices in Merced's deep places. The spirits that spoke to me in the Yegan mineshaft had also been kavsprit, or their close kin, I believed. Here, in this palace of desolation carved out by the Scytheran mages, I felt nothing from the obsidian blade. Due to my labour of obscuring magic, or to the absence of the natural spirits in the earth? Could this place be made so foul as to cause even kavsprit to forsake it?

Only the goddess of all the earth could tell me, and she speaks in rustling waves of grasses and trees stretching limbs to the sky. Men hear her laughter in fields of flowers—I shook my head to clear it. What manner of mindlessness had overtaken me? Gargle gave me his most ferocious glare when I glanced his way. Our mouse-guide spun in frenzied circles on the stair below, squeaking pitifully.

Ibbot's spellwork had been discovered.

Gargle sprang from my shoulder and flapped through an archway three stairs below us. The mouse collapsed onto its side, tiny limbs wracked by spasms. I scooped it up before it could plummet off the edge and stuffed it into my pocket as I fled down the passage after Gargle. That I did not stumble off the stairs was miracle or magic.

The silent crow led me by twists and turns through eerie green light. If I lost sight of him, I would be lost forever, given the maze we traveled. I heard a shout ahead, then behind, and followed Gargle as he darted into yet another side tunnel. *Let him know where he is going. And remember the way back!*

Finally, as I sucked air into burning lungs, Gargle slowed and circled. He lit on the floor of the passage and hopped through a doorway into a room. More of an alcove, I found when I joined him. A trio of oozing ale casks rested on stones within. We tucked ourselves as best we could between the tuns and the far wall.

I drew the mouse from my pocket. Its limp body still fluttered with heartbeats, and shallow gasps. Whether Ibbot had abandoned it when discovered, or been torn away by the mages instead, I had no way to know. He could even possess it still but have been knocked senseless, thus causing the mouse to be likewise. I clawed about in my mind for some method to learn whether Ibbot yet lived. If the mages had killed him, we must flee the Pit and Scythera, for there was no more to be gained by remaining.

Voices drew nearer, two men talking as they walked. They spoke low, in the guttural, grating tones I recalled from my last encounter with mages, in the sea cliff tunnels of Merced.

I pressed a sweaty palm on the wall stones beside me. I strove for some sense of the kavsprit, even any sign of their presence if not their aid. Nothing. My obsidian blade offered no quiver of recognition. As in my dream vision on the ship, I was alone to face my enemies.

Except for Gargle ... Intertwined by the spell, I felt him part of me rather than separate. I could not risk riding him and leave an insensible body to be discovered by the searchers. Could I send Gargle to seek Ibbot? Would the bird understand what I wanted to know—where was Ibbot and was he alive or dead?

I regarded him, staring at his glossy back sheened with the green glow. He crouched at the edge of the closest barrel, peering around it for a view of the doorway. He held the pose for a few moments, then slowly swiveled his head to look over his shoulder and meet my eye. He huffed a breath.

"I'd think of another way if I could," I whispered, as I slipped the poor mouse back into my tunic pocket.

I would have sworn Gargle rolled his eyes, but as both were solid black and beady, I could not be sure. The voices from the corridor faded as the two walked past, but abruptly grew louder again.

The mages had turned back our way.

At first, I thought I must be jumping out of my skin, but instead what I felt was the mouse erupting from my pocket in a scrambling fury. It dashed out the doorway, to be met in the corridor by shouts from the two men. I heard the slap of running feet, gradually fading. If the pursuers were mages, why didn't they stun the mouse to stop its flight? If only I could understand their tongue, how much the wiser I would be.

I decided to believe Ibbot still possessed the mouse and had run away to draw off the searchers from Gargle and me. But how to find either the guide-creature or Ibbot now? Gargle was my best hope.

"Can you find Ibbot?" I asked the bird.

I thought of feeding him a bit of the tuft of Ibbot's hair, but before I could draw it from my tunic, he hopped around the corner of the ale cask. He gave a gurgle that I took for assent. After peeking around the corner of the door's frame with exaggerated care, he took wing. I noted he flew away to the left. The same direction the mouse had run.

After drawing the runes of deflection in the dust at my feet and murmuring the accompanying charms, I settled myself to wait. Mages had derided my low magic spells in the past, but their disregard led them to overlook me before. I prayed it would again.

I leaned on the rough stones at my back and searched again for some sign of kavsprit touching my mind or a snatch of their whispery voices. Only rock, no life within that I could detect.

Footsteps approached, a lone man, shuffling a bit. As the steps grew closer, I heard another sound, a muffled clanking. Ibbot in chains?

I heard no caws or wingbeats. I dared not hazard a sound. I pressed the back of a furry glove to my face to muffle my breathing. Only a fraction of the doorway was in my line of sight, between the barrels.

A fat man clad in black robes entered. He blew out a breath and mumbled words that sounded tired and irritated. A metallic clink told me he placed a pitcher beneath the ale spigot. The handle squeaked as he turned it, followed by a tinny rush that rose in pitch as he filled his vessel. He plunked the full pitcher on the floor and shoved a second one under the tap. I could smell the tang of hoppy ale and realized just how dry my mouth had become.

My mind lurched about—Where had Gargle got to? What could be happening to Cilliyon and Wieser while I crouched here? Would it be a relief to just stand up and be taken? Was there any faint hope of escape?

The man shifted with a grunt and twisted the spigot. A crack, followed by gushing mingled with an angry torrent of what must be curses, filled the alcove. Dark ale splashed on the stones and lapped at my feet. He threw his pitchers against the wall as ale ran in rivulets into every corner and out into the passage. He bellowed like a bull, likely for aid to stem the flow.

Over his shouts, I could hear many feet thundering toward us.

As the ale-fetcher leaned through the doorway and called out into the passage, I foundered through the ale river on hands and knees. I did my own share of swearing, but only in my head. The man looked to the left, so I slid to the right as I crossed the threshold. That he failed to see me scurry past his knees, I could only attribute to the spell.

I stood up when I rounded the first corner and fled with no sense of reason whatever. My brew-soaked trousers flapped against my legs. I turned right or left at random, before stumbling across a stairway leading down. I took it. Already lost, already going the wrong way from the ale room, eluding pursuit was my entire goal.

Alone. I could not feel Gargle. My knife might as well be a blade of hammered iron. I wove my way farther down the stairs, catching a scent of brackish water below. Lower still, where the eldritch light only gleamed in sparse patches on the rock walls.

I arrived at the end of my path. The stairs plunged beneath the surface of a vast pool of dark water, as though the mage palace had flooded from below as the earth reclaimed her stones.

Or perhaps this was their water well, by design. I looked up but saw nothing like a windlass in the ghostly green light. I peered across the pool and could just make out another stairway—no, three more flights of stairs spaced around the water's edge.

I did not have Gargle, who could fly over to discover whether I would be better off on the other side, climbing one of the other stairways. I bent to slip my fingers into the water—so cold it burned. I pulled my hand back and thrust the fingers under my arm.

What now? I flung my thoughts about, but all seemed as useless as the floppings of netted fish. Soon the blow of the fisherman's cudgel would fall ...

With a start, I thought of my brother's bride, Annora. As though she whispered in my ear, I heard the spell used to send bird-messengers carrying news of our plans as we fought the invaders in Merced. The magic demanded that the creature be fed a bit of something from the destination, in order to find the way.

I had a small amount of Ibbot's hair, could I use it with the spell to find him? I would have to swallow it, and the prospect made bitter gall rise up my throat, but the spell might work to guide me to him.

I fidgeted with the contents of my herb pouch, until I found the correct paper, folded around the remaining hairs Gargle had snatched from Ibbot's scalp. Thank the fates and fortune I had not used them all when I spellcast Ibbot's sleep in the hut. I plucked out a portion, not wishing to use them all or eat any more than I had to choke down. I placed the coarse black hairs, wrapped in a dried mint leaf, on my tongue and followed them with a palmful of the icy water. I only gagged a little when I swallowed. They felt caught in my throat, and I scooped another mouthful of water.

I spoke the words from memory, a spell Annora taught me when I first discovered I could work magic. I felt a part of my heart twist, the part I closed off when I fled my homeland to escape the mages' vengence. And here I stood in their Stronghold, working a simple spell.

I closed my eyes when I finished the chant. I did not know how the animal messengers felt when enspelled, but after only a moment, I felt an urge to be on the opposite side of the water, climbing one of those stairways. *That* one, in particular. The one most jagged and narrow.

I could not risk swimming across. The distance appeared great enough that the cold would sap my limbs of their strength before I traveled halfway. The weight of wet furs would sink me. If I bundled the pelts together and held them over my head, I couldn't swim nearly as fast and would surely drown even quicker. And if all the mallowmeld rinsed away, would the spell obscuring me continue?

Yet I felt a pull to the stairway on the opposite side I could not resist or deny.

Ibbot taught me weather-working on our journey through the mountains. Could I make the water just enough colder to ice the pool over, then crawl across? It was not salt water, by the taste, but not sweet water either. Fed by some mineral spring, perhaps. I began at once to try to conjure a crust of ice across the surface, without thinking further about the wisdom of the idea. One effect of the spell compelling me to seek Ibbot, perhaps.

For compelled I felt, and impatient, too. The water rippled as though a breeze moved over it, despite I felt no air stirring. No frost bloomed on the wet stair at my feet.

I nurtured my intention and called forth a vision of thickening ice in my mind's eye. I worked to manifest a strong layer, enough to support my weight. My eagerness to be away toward Ibbot both consumed my mind and scattered my wits.

As time passed, I grew colder but the water showed no change. My beer-sodden trousers stiffened, then cracked. I thought peevishly that I should just make-wish a fine boat of ice and float across. Maybe some frozen oars would speed my travel, too. In disgust, I spat into the black water.

With a creaking groan, the entire surface congealed into smooth milk-white ice.

With utmost care, since I was uncertain how I had accomplished the feat, I lowered myself onto my belly to spread my weight. By stretching as far as I could and jamming the tip of my blade into the ice, I was able to pull myself forward. Repeated over and over, in this fashion I neared the far shore. I dared not allow any thought into my mind about ice thickness. Or what duration to expect from the part of my spellwork which created the frozen surface, for I did not believe I could perform it again from underwater.

I dragged myself close by the stairway I felt drawn to, and on the bottom step rested a single black feather. Gargle's, I was certain of it. Still conscious of the need to consider the ice a fragile manifestation of magic, I gently pulled myself alongside and crawled up the first few stairs using my forearms and elbows.

Once able to stand, I somehow sensed even before I looked that the water's surface bore no ice at all.

The puzzle of the absent ice could confound me later. I set my foot on the tread above and returned to my spell-driven quest to find Ibbot.

CHAPTER THIRTY-ONE

I f all those messenger birds Annora and I enspelled in Merced had to endure the same gnawing compulsion to reach what we set them toward, I regretted any use of our magic not demanded by the war. I sped through corridors, at times breaking into a loping gait heedless of the risk I would round a corner and tumble into a cadre of mages.

I carried Gargle's shed feather in my hand. I fancied I saw, in the green glow from the rock walls, faint traces of the mallowmeld powder along its shaft. Mayhap this aided me, by keeping me concealed as I trotted along the passages. I encountered no one as I drove deeper into the Stronghold.

Though I felt as though I passed endless days seeking the man, after a time I began to sense that I drew near. I would not allow myself rest until I found him, for once begun the spell could not be set aside or undone. Low magic it might be, but the power of it thrummed along my limbs nonetheless, urging me onward.

At last, heart pounding with a surety of my goal within my grasp, I reached him. Ibbot lay curled on his side, face to the wall, in a low-ceilinged pigsty. All around him, sows and piglets grunted and snarfled through remnants of foodstuff. A low place indeed. I tucked the feather within my tunic. Next, I swung open the rickety gate and found I had to crouch nearly bent double to reach his side. Squealing pigs scattered, stirring up the stink of their piles.

"Ibbot?" I laid a hand on his shoulder and he lifted his head. When he turned toward me, I saw the dark bruises that swelled both his eyes near shut. "You're hurt. I'll help you."

"You came," he croaked, then coughed up a gobbet of blood.

I rummaged in my herb pouch. "Here, let this dissolve on your tongue." I pressed the lozenge between his cracked lips. "I might have thought mages could accomplish their ends without need to resort to a simple beating."

He sighed as the mint and yarrow in the dose soothed his sore mouth. "They have tempers, like anyone."

"Can you walk? We must be away." I heard a flutter behind me. Gargle lit on the gate and eyed our circumstances. With a faint *grock*, he turned his back and gazed the way he had come.

"I might walk, if you aid me. How do you plan to escape?"

"They do not seem aware of me or Gargle, thanks to your spell-craft. Can the guise cover you, as well?"

"Is there more …" his voice trailed away. I held out the cloth pouch of remaining mallowmeld. He nodded. "You'll have to do it. I am weak as a babe."

I performed the spell again. Ibbot's breathing, too shallow, caused worry which distracted my mind, but Gargle lit on my shoulder to prod me.

Ibbot had to crawl to the passage outside the pen but denied any broken bones. He insisted he would limber up by standing. When I helped him get his feet under him, he swayed like an hours-old foal.

I gripped the belt around his waist. After every half-dozen steps, he leaned on me heavily to catch his breath.

"Why do you smell as if you spent the night on a tavern floor?" he complained as he sagged against my arm.

"That's a tale for later. And you smell of pig."

"So I do, but that's no mystery. Do you know the way out?"

"Gargle is leading us," I said. The bird glided ahead, pausing to hop along the floor or wait above us on a stair when we stopped. "How soon would you guess before you'll be missed? Perhaps we should have stunned a pig to lie in the corner and glamoured it to look like you."

"Fancy magic," he wheezed. "I didn't know you had learned such a skill."

On the tip of my tongue to respond how short the reach to make a pig appear Ibbot-like, but instead I said, "My friend Virda Tedesch told me magical skill comes at need, in some folk. Mine does seem to."

"Is that why you are not scalding me scarlet about your stolen book?"

"I can if you like. But I'd rather put this place behind us first."

If not for Gargle, we would surely have wandered the labyrinth forever. Ibbot's steps grew stronger until I barely had to keep hold of his belt to steady him. At length, I saw a different light before us. Not the green glow of the passage walls, but a ruddy light.

"Is that sunset?" I wondered aloud. "We climbed this far? But it cannot be eventide so soon as this, can it? How long have I been below ground in this forsaken place?"

Ibbot rubbed his arms as though to warm them. "The river of time does not flow in this keep the same way as outside. Eddies and back-waters twist the channel within its banks. Master mages can even create new paths, though at a cost."

We emerged from the passage into a wide expanse of sand. A blood-red full moon rode the sky above. At least, it appeared to be sky. The rock walls all around told me we remained in the Pit, and not above on the plains. I looked for Gargle, but he was nowhere to be seen.

It was all too much akin to my dream aboard the *Traubent*. Mono-liths of stone encircled the sand, rather than mages in their black robes. Or I only thought the shapes to be made of stone …

"The moon should not be full," I said. "It was waning when I came here after you. And a blood moon is far and away out of the natural cycle."

"It will be the result of deep magic the cabal is casting forth," Ibbot said, with a sharp shake of his head. He yanked on my arm, for I had released his belt and dug my heels in, refusing to believe what I saw. "Come, let us be away before they chance to notice us."

Still I could not shift my feet. "I dreamt this—a red moon overhead, and only myself, alone against the mages' fury. I had nothing else, though you stood beside me. I had been drained of all my strength."

"Will you stand there yapping until your vision comes true?" He jerked at me again. "Move!"

I pulled free of him without knowing why and backed away out of his reach. A sudden wind whipped through the circle of stones, clawing past to rake my cheeks and bearing a mounting chant. Unintelligible sounds, at once sacred and utterly profane, seemed to issue from the standing rocks themselves. Stones without throats or mouths. Coursing faster and faster, the gust became a hiss then a moan, and finally a shriek, as sand whirled and spattered about me, tearing at my flesh. I feared I would be flayed bloody despite my clothes. The tones it carried dashed against my ears, teetering on the edge of cacophony, but still seeming to be words ... some kind of words ...

Gods alone could know how long I might have stood there slack-jawed and staring, as I tried to grasp meaning from a place so far beyond my understanding. Gargle saved me by returning to slap at my face with his wings. Ibbot snatched at what Gargle dangled from his beak—the leather thong of my moonstone talisman. He grabbed a handful of my tunic and pulled me around to loop the leather over my head. As soon as the stone struck my chest, I came to my senses.

I ran.

I was only dimly aware that I followed Gargle as I fled, giving even less notice to Ibbot's ragged panting as he labored to follow. I ran into another of the greenish passages, away from the noise and wind and awful bloody light. I trusted Gargle to lead me away from danger and out into the light of day—but gradually I became aware that I was not climbing. Wouldn't we need to go farther upwards to escape this cursed Pit?

More turns and corridors passed as I ran, keeping Gargle's gleaming wings in sight. Ibbot lunged toward me and caught my belt. I tried to wrest away, fearful of losing my guide and only half in my right mind. I snarled at him.

Ibbot cried, "Hold, hold! Where is it taking us?"

"Let me *run!*" I shoved him hard, his grip broke and he fell to his knees. I turned away to follow Gargle's flight, just as the bird sailed over my head, circled and flapped onward again, through an archway just ahead.

I lifted my foot to pelt after Gargle, then with a groan, reluctantly swung back and pulled Ibbot to his feet. "We have to keep up," I said.

"We need to get *out*," he said, but he came along with me.

Gargle had brought us to a chamber, not a further corridor. A long, low workbench stretched into shadows. Upon this cluttered bench the bird stood, every evidence of triumph in his pose.

Open at his scaly feet lay my book.

Ibbot whirled about with a sharp cry, perhaps fearing we had interrupted a mage at his work. We were the only occupants of the room, however. I leapt forward and gathered the book to my chest. "Now out," I said to Gargle. He sprang into the air and we streaked off at once in his wake.

CHAPTER THIRTY-TWO

L ittle of the climb out of the Pit and trek across the steppes wove
itself into my memory. Even breaching the barrier of doomed
souls for the second time remained a tangled blur just beyond the grasp
of true recall. I knew I must have done these things, because I stood on
the plain beside the pile of rocks I had left to guide me to Cilliyon.
Ibbot sat on one of the rocks, ruefully examining his blistered heels,
with Gargle preening himself on another stone beside him.

I had my crow, my book under my arm, moonstone talisman about
my neck and knife in my boot. I had rescued Ibbot from death, and yet
I felt as though I abandoned some part of myself in the sand of the
mages' Stronghold.

I felt ... sundered.

Or did I feel something accompanied me from under that unnatural
blood moon, and now lurked in a dark corner of my mind?

"We must reach Cilliyon and Wieser before dusk." I started
walking and both my companions grudgingly rose, one to his feet and
the other to the sky.

My steps quickened as we drew closer to the shelter. I knew
Cilliyon had spent a bad time worrying for my safety, as I had for hers.
Wieser was no doubt some comfort as well as protection, but nothing
would serve but to find them both as I had left them.

The scent on the wind gave the first clue of something amiss—a rank smoke drifted toward us. What could be burning? A fainter smell of roasted flesh came with a freshening breeze. I wanted to run to the crevice, but what if I was too late? I signaled Ibbot to stop, then to follow me up a rise so we would arrive just above the rudiment of hut I had built for them.

"Take care we keep downwind," I whispered to him. "Don't let our scent announce us."

I peered over the top of the roof stone I had heaved in place over the crevice, my heart hammering.

Cilliyon knelt, hacking the pelt from a wooly creature. Its wide jaw bore a great many curved yellow teeth. A smoky fire burned beside her, where Wieser sprawled to gnaw on a thick bone. More meat, cut in strips, lay draped on a rock close to the fire's glow.

She set aside the shard of stone she'd used for skinning and cracked bloodied knuckles while she murmured something to Weiser and rolled her shoulders wearily.

Wieser's head snapped up, ears pricked, and with a joyous bark she sprang away from her meal and bounded uphill to me. She bowled me over and covered me with slobber, as I hugged her ruff.

"Where did Cill—Watch out!" Ibbot cried. "Tell her it's us!"

Cilliyon herself clambered into view, with my cocked crossbow aimed our way, following Wieser.

"Can she see us? Are we still obscured by the spell?"

"It must be mostly worn away by now," Ibbot muttered, running a hand across the back of his neck and inspecting his palm.

"Cilliyon," I called. "We're here." Wieser barked and wagged her tangled tail.

"Oh!" She sprinted toward where I sat. Wieser whined and wound herself around me and over my out-stretched legs. I managed to hold the dog away and get to my feet in time for Cilliyon to fling herself into my arms. She kept the crossbow in her other hand, and it tilted aside to point at Ibbot, who nearly tumbled off the ridge in his haste to avoid a stray quarrel.

"I thought you must be dead, after all this time." She pressed her head to my chest, and I buried my face in her hair. She smelled of smoke and gamy meat—and I could recall no sweeter scent ever.

"All this time?" I murmured. "It's only been a couple of days, though it has seemed long to me, too."

She pushed away to look me closely in the eyes. "You've been gone a month, Judian."

I looked at Ibbot, who lifted a shoulder. "I told you, time in the Stronghold is not what it is in the wider world."

"But how can this be?"

"We must get down from here," Cilliyon interrupted. "Night is falling and the wolfen beasts come out."

We climbed down to the fire ring to join Gargle, who was gorging himself on a limb of the carcass Cilliyon had been skinning.

"Is that one of the beasts?" I asked, pointing.

"Not the wolfen. These are more like swine but with fleece like a sheep."

"What happened to it?" Ibbot prodded the flank with the toe of his boot.

"I killed it, what do you think happened to it? And what happened to you? You look to have crossed the wrong person."

Ibbot didn't look up from the animal, though he touched a fingertip to his purpled cheek. "What makes you sure it wasn't Judian who did this?"

Cilliyon snorted. "I can see why he might, but he did tell me he wanted to save you. And he has, it seems."

"A month," I said, my mind still spun about by her words. "How have you lived so long out here?" I gestured to the fire. "What have you found to burn? There's no wood in sight."

"Can't you smell it? It's dried dung from the herd animals. That's some of their meat, roasting by the edge. You'll find it easier to chew than what I've had of the swine flesh. Less stringy."

"I can't believe I've truly been away so long ..."

In answer, Cilliyon took my hand and led me to the mouth of the crevice. Just inside she showed me a pile of pebbles. "Count them. Thirty in all. I added one to the stack for each night I spent huddled here with Wieser. Each night we survived I added a pebble come dawn."

"If you decided I was not coming back, why did you stay?"

"Wieser wouldn't leave. I did try. I hoped she was stubborn because she knew better than I did that you would come …" Her voice broke, and she allowed the arm I slung around her shoulders. "So we had to work together, she and I, to hunt for food, to fight off the wolfen each night."

She rushed us through a meal of meat and water, saying the time was overdue to barricade ourselves in the crevice. While we tore at the strips with our teeth, she dragged the half-skinned carcass a fair distance away from the opening. She laughed when Ibbot and I offered to help.

Gathering the rest of the drying meat, she chivvied us into the opening, and set about pulling and pushing stones in place to block the crack. The last thing I glimpsed was the rising moon. The same silver crescent of waning moon I had seen when I left her to seek Ibbot. Or was that the moon of a month past?

Wieser stretched out at her side and Cilliyon braced against the rock wall with my crossbow across her knees. "The nights are long," she said with a grim smile. "Do not plan to sleep until dawn."

She had clearly learned the ways of the wolfen pack's nightly hunt. We heard them snuffling and whining outside at the pile of stones, digging at the base of the rocks and snapping at one another as their frustration grew.

"How many?" I whispered.

She held up four fingers, listened more and raised a fifth. I could hear others as well, howling in the distance. A few abandoned the crevice entrance and loped off snarling, presumably to the half-skinned carrion she had left out for them. I marveled at her.

"I can take watch. You are no doubt short of sleep in a month's time of this every night."

She hesitated, but passed me the crossbow in the end. "Only loose a bolt if they manage to shift the rock enough to poke a head *and* shoulders in. When it has wedged itself tight, shoot to kill and so block the opening with the body. In the throat," she said with a chilling jab at her own neck. She closed her eyes.

She knew whereof she spoke—the night crawled past. Ibbot snored through most of it. Gargle perched next to Wieser, who maintained vigil with me.

When Cilliyon relieved me, I made my best effort to close my eyes. I could not shake the unease I had dragged with me from the mages' Stronghold. I feared what dreams would come ... for I had some part of that wretched place with me, or it had some part of me still within its walls. Oddly, what I recalled was the cheese we made at home from goat milk, with tiny holes throughout—that was how my mind felt, as though bits of my memory and thought had become empty. Or as if my wits were skipped over as a stone skips across a pond.

My sleep, when it came, was dreamless. Somehow that seemed more ominous still.

As Cilliyon had told us, when dawn light seeped between the cracks of our stone hut the wolfen withdrew, yipping and slavering. When their noise faded away entirely, Ibbot and I shifted the stones and we crossed into the pallid sunrise.

There was little left of the pig-creature, but Cilliyon hacked free a shoulder joint for Wieser to gnaw. Gargle poked about the rest of the carcass gobbling bits here and there.

We settled ourselves for a repeat of the meat and water meal of the night before. Cilliyon invited Ibbot to light the fire with magic.

"How have you been doing it?" he asked, looking toward the horizon.

"With my flint, but it takes so long. I've tried every kind of tinder, scavenged threads from my skirt and bits of fur. Are you saying you won't?"

"No. But it seems I cannot, just now. I have not only been beaten, I have been shriven of much of my magic during their inquisition. When they discovered my attempt to use magic to escape."

Unwelcome news, for my plan to use him. "I'll light it," I said. "Is this permanent? Will you regain your skills?"

"I have no way of knowing. I heard the old tales while an apprentice, but I thought it was a false threat, only used to frighten us into obedience to our masters. Those tales are true, it seems. I do still have my knowledge, or I could not have taught you to renew the obscuring spell to pass the barrier on our flight." I could not pull this memory from my lump-of-cheese brain. He continued, "But now, I cannot cast or conjure on my own." I had never known him to admit anything so baldly.

I passed my hands over the fire ring with the proper words. Flames sprang to life. "Warm yourselves. We'll set off as soon as we gather our things."

Cilliyon watched Ibbot closely. "If one mage can strip the magic from another, why haven't they done so to Judian as they pursued him?"

Ibbot cracked his knuckles. "They'd have to catch him first. Why they can't accomplish that confounds the ones who've come to realize it. He is different, his magic is different. That is why I thought if I brought him to them ...none of that matters now."

"Have you told Ibbot your plans for us?" Cilliyon stretched her palms toward the heat. Our breath misted about us.

"No."

He shifted his gaze to me. "Please, I need to know."

I said, "We are going back to the port. I'm going to rescue the slaves there."

He rocked back on his heels. "Just as I feared. The Barrens have broken your mind."

I shook my head.

Cilliyon gave a short laugh. "If I haven't lost my mind in a month out here, he cannot have lost his in what you say is only a couple of days."

"*I* didn't say that, *he* did," Ibbot snapped. "I have no real idea of the time passed."

She pointed at him. "Which wouldn't be the first time you have no idea about something. If he thinks we can free those poor people, I, for one, will do whatever he asks of me."

"Indeed," Ibbot said. He turned to me. "How will we accomplish this?"

"I have no real idea," I said.

CHAPTER THIRTY-THREE

As we walked the desolate track to return to the sea, several of the sinister black and white birds swept by us, high above. Gargle cawed and croaked and puffed himself up, but the creatures never paused their soaring.

"What if we—or you, Judian—just use magic to knock down all the fences and pens? Then they can flee." Cilliyon proposed.

"Where can they go? Into this wasteland? They'll only feed the wolfen or be recaptured." I said.

"They are valuable to the traders. No slavers will let profits flee without pursuing." Ibbot appeared to find his bruises itchy and rubbed at his eyes in the sunlight.

"I believe our best course might be to join the crew of the ship that bears them away. We can foment a rebellion at sea. Then we will be able to set course for their homeland and turn the lot of them loose where they know the region and have a better chance."

I saw Cilliyon's face cloud, but she did not speak.

Ibbot turned to walk backwards in front of me. "What is it we will be hired to do as crew members? I'm no seaman."

"You have a weather-worker's knowledge and you still have your mage robes, tattered though they may be. I will pose as your apprentice and set about encouraging the slaves to revolt once we leave the port."

"Under the noses of their captors?"

"Slaves are treated like cargo, are they not? The crew will be sailing the ship. Maybe there will be a few guards, but as many as the pirates had for the crew from *Moon Road*?"

"My experience is on Kruthe's vessel, capturing other ships. I don't know how the slaves are shipped, what number of guards is customary or where we might expect this particular lot of captives to be bound for."

"We can discover this, surely? Do you fear you will be recognized at Ulfar as Mage Balin's former apprentice?"

"Unlikely, but possible."

Cilliyon interrupted. "What earthly reason is there for me to join the crew? Please don't say you are making me one of the slaves, slipping me into the pens."

This had occurred to me, but I did not like to ask it of her, knowing her terror of the slavers. "I fear we will have to cut off your hair and pass you as a galley boy again."

"What if they've no need of one? What if they already have mages for weather working? What then?" Her steps slowed and stopped. Wieser prodded Cilliyon's ankles with her nose and looked to me for some suggestion. The girl remained rooted to the spot.

"I can't know if my plans are possible until we return to the port and find out more. All I am certain about now is my intention to see those folk freed."

"What is their fate to you?" Ibbot asked, scanning the sky as more of the giant seabirds passed over.

I did not know how to answer. I studied my boots for a moment, and finally allowed, "I walked away from them once. I won't do it again."

"Blast you, Judian, you will make me feel a welch for not hiding among the slaves." Cilliyon squared her shoulders and strode away.

"I will not make you do that," I protested, trotting after her.

"Say whatever you like," she answered and kept walking. "Just *don't* remind me I said I would do whatever was needed."

We reached Ulfar by nightfall. The pens still teemed with folk, though different in appearance from the slaves Cilliyon and I had passed when we arrived at the port. This lot looked more like the slaves I had seen carted through my homeland of Merced last year, most with straight hair black as coal and bark-brown eyes tilted down at the corners. Fair Cilliyon could never pass unnoticed among them unless heavily glamoured.

I told her as much, as I pulled her aside into an alleyway in the deserted part of the waterfront. As Ibbot and Wieser stood guard, I used my knife to cut away all her fair curls. She said nothing as the ringlets fell around her. I lifted my talisman over my head and placed it over hers. Holding the leather, I leaned forward to kiss her cheek.

"Do you still have your bindings and trousers?" I asked. When she nodded, I turned my back so she could finish her transformation into a galley hand.

She cleared her throat and I turned to face her.

The months that had passed since her stint on *Moon Road* disguised as a boy had seen her change into a much more delicate, curved creature. As I well knew her to be female, I perhaps was not the best judge. Who else was there to ask, though? I called Ibbot over.

"Do you think she looks enough like a boy?"

He eyed her, crown to soles, with pursed lips. "Risky, at best. At least her shoulders are still quite thin. Give her your overtunic, it will be baggy on her. To disguise her contours."

The addition of another layer did not improve the costume enough. She persisted in looking female. I tried to herd my wits along to some better deception.

"Give her your robes," I said.

Both of them stared at me.

"Give her the black robes of a mage, you wear her trousers and my tunic, I wear what I'm wearing. Do it."

They scuffled about with their backs turned until they accomplished the exchange. Ibbot's shanks gleamed bare above his ankles in the too-short trousers, but the rest of his kit would do. He pulled on his boots and stuffed the frayed ends of pant-leg inside. Cilliyon's hands disappeared in the voluminous sleeves of Ibbot's robe and the hem trailed on the ground.

"Now," I said, "teach me how to make her appear extremely aged, as though she is an old, doddering mage who needs two attendants."

"You're after turning me into an old crone?" Cilliyon gasped.

"Appear, appear," I said impatiently. "It is only a glamour so when the sailors look at you they see an old weather mage. You can play mute and blind with your hood over your head, even stay below deck all the time, and we will say we are doing magic as you direct us."

"If he can tell you how to make me look like a hag, why didn't he change the appearance of all of us in Yega?" she stalled.

Ibbot spoke up. "At the outset, recall that I said I was fully occupied with the spells to get us away. I can—could—juggle only so much magic at once. Once in Lunenhelm, we were already known when the muleteer was brought in." He squinted as he looked her over. "Wouldn't it be less trouble to disguise her as one of the slaves?"

Cilliyon blanched before I said, "No. That has nothing to recommend it. As the aged mage, she can be kept out of sight of both slaves and crew."

Ibbot considered her further. "It could possibly work, but only if the shipmaster does not already have a weather mage."

"I'm going to find out. If there is one already, he might become ill or suffer an accident. Or forget to show up when they sail … I'm still reckoning that part."

"And just who will perform the shipboard magic, since I am not able just now?"

"You'll tell me what to do."

"I still think you've parted ways with your wits," he grumbled.

Which struck too close to the truth, perhaps.

Nevertheless, Cilliyon suffered in silence while Ibbot instructed me in sigils and chants to crook her back and grey her shorn hair. The sagging skin and knobby hands seemed to distress her the most, she kept rubbing her cheeks and stroking the backs of her hands to be sure they felt smooth despite the seeming wrinkles.

"Can we make her voice a little hoarse?"

He told me how to do that as well. She had a tremor and croak to rival Gargle's.

"Take care to hobble," I told her. "Let's find a room for the night and discover what slaver ship is slated to depart. Let Ibbot take your other arm. Come now."

With a cold glare from rheumy-looking eyes, Cilliyon allowed me to take her elbow. She eschewed Ibbot's outstretched hand with a sniff.

We found lodgings at a drab inn quayside, where all manner of sailors crowded the common room and the matron did not object to three men of magic with their dog and crow. She had a tired air of having seen everything at least once before and finding little to excite her imagination in any of it.

Once we got Cilliyon settled in our room with Gargle and Wieser, Ibbot and I went down to the hearth to see what we could learn.

We each nursed a tankard of sweetish brew before the fire. These seamen seemed nothing out of the ordinary. At least, those who spoke Yeganil, in which I could follow along with fair facility. I would have to rely on Ibbot to share what he overhead in Scythera's tongue.

The men drank and smoked pipes, played at games of chance and spun tales of great storms they had weathered, or ribald women they had known in this port or that. Some sang drunkenly with their arms about each other's shoulders, one played a mournful flute. The tune drifted over me so woeful it set up a fierce longing in my heart for home and family.

Ibbot grew impatient, as was his wont, for the knowledge we must have before any ships cast off with the morning tide. He bought a round for a pair of young Scytheran sailors, with some of Cilliyon's silver I had given him. I sought out the oldest of the salts and refilled his cup likewise. He hailed from Yega so I could talk with him.

He went by the name of Burack and claimed to have sailed away from home "when not even full-growed, see?" He told me the meaning of each tattoo he bore on his sinewy arms. He told me many stories before I worked around to the slave trade and what he knew of it. With another full cup, he knew plenty.

Near midnight, Ibbot and I returned to our room with the name of the slaver vessel, her destination, and the boarding house where the weather-worker who traveled with them might be found. That is, if the mage we sought was not too deep in his cups in some local tavern.

We told Cilliyon what we had learned, then I opened my book to review the spell for the self-same sleeping draught I had used on Ibbot. How we would connive to obtain some token from the mage and get the potion into him, I had not worked out yet. Rendering him senseless so we could supplant him aboard seemed a better course than confronting the mage and raising gods knew what amount of ruckus. Much more subtle. And less likely to get us killed, besides.

Handing over another silver coin, I dispatched Ibbot for a pint of spirits in a stoppered bottle. He returned with spare coin and watched in dismay as I poured out the drink and decanted my potion into the green glass.

When I tapped my shoulder to summon Gargle, Cilliyon spoke in her quavery old voice. "I don't see how this is going to come out well."

Striding with confidence I did not feel, I made for the door, gesturing for Ibbot to come along. "Be ready for us to bring you dockside at dawn," I told her.

We left to hunt our mage prey.

CHAPTER THIRTY-FOUR

I n one way the same as other ports, Ulfar buzzed both night and day despite that the place could be called half-derelict. Drunken seamen staggered through the alleys, lights shone from tavern windows and kitchens, and carts clattered over the cobblestones while dogs barked.

Old Burack had told me the place where our quarry lodged. I decided to seek him there first and next scour the ale-houses if we found he was still about town.

I brought Ibbot with me in case the innkeeper spoke only Scytheran. He answered my query after the weather mage readily enough in Yegan, but his words scuttled my heart.

"Aye, and which one of them does yourself seek?"

I had not expected there to be a pack of sorcerers in port at the same time. "The one for the slaver vessel *Megrite*," I said, grateful Burack had provided the ship's name, if not the mage's.

No help though. "How do I know which ship they each hail from? Don't I have enough to be getting on with here? What does yourself want with one of their sort, anyway?"

My sundered mind failed to keep pace with the demand for cleverness. Ibbot, the innkeeper and Gargle all stared at me in expectation. "A message," I said at last.

"Leave it," the man said, tapping his counter.

Ibbot shouldered me out of his way. "It is a spoken message from the master. It must be delivered in person before the mage sails in the morn."

"Ah. Yourself looks to have disappointed that master at least once before," he said, appraising Ibbot's black eyes. "Only one of them said he departs on the coming tide. Left at the top of the stair. See if yourselves can rouse him. He looked much the worse for spirits when he stumbled in." He turned away, and then back to glare at us. "Try not to wake the whole house, hear?"

Standing at the proper door, I did not have to press my ear to the wood to know what occupied the man within. Prodigious snoring akin to rumbling thunder, accompanied by an odd tin-flute whistling screech, filled the passageway.

"He may miss his ship without any mischief on our part," Ibbot said.

"We have to be sure. I need some bit of him—hair, nail paring, spittle." I tried the door. It bore no lock but would not budge. It might have been a picture, drawn on a solid wall.

Ibbot laid a hand against the boards. "He's propped his staff against it. The spell will keep anyone from coming inside to disturb him."

I pounded on the door, not knowing what else to do. No response from within the room. Nor from along the hall, for no one else could hear anything over the mage's racket of snarfling and wheezing. I gave the door a final thump along with a kick.

"What's come over you?" Ibbot pulled me away to the top of the stairs. "I don't understand what has set your mind to rail against slavery instead of getting home. Or seeing Cilliyon delivered to Lohr Island. You've recovered what I took. Yes, and recovered me as well, from my earned fate. What is this about?"

"If only I could say." I plastered a palm, still stinging from the last blow on the door, against my forehead and tried to think despite the fact my head felt brim-full with seafoam. "At first I just wanted my book back. Aye, and talisman and coin, and you could go hang for all I cared. I can't explain what happened when I saw those folk penned up, something shifted in my heart. The book didn't matter, nothing mattered but finding a way to stop this … this ravaging of souls. Why it is me who must see the injustice set to rights, and not someone else, I don't understand myself. But I must do it. And I will."

"Judian, you alone cannot stop slavers. They are all across the world. One man cannot set free all the captive people."

"It starts somewhere, so why not here with this shipload?"

He shook his head. "And another question is, why do I feel I must help you?"

"Not to put too fine a point on it, you do owe me your life." I jerked a thumb over my shoulder. "And what is it with weather mages? Are they considered lesser among their fellows, relegated to roaming the sea serving miscreant shipmasters?"

"There are all manner of rankings among mages, but this is something else. Those gifted with shifting ocean currents and storms at sea feel always … uneasy, out of place on land. Hence the solace of drink to induce sleep."

I recalled the look of rapture on Mage Balin's face as he turned his blind eyes to the wind and endless waves.

"Is it the same with you? Do you long for the sea?"

He looked away down the stairs. "I never longed to be aboard any ship. I told you, I was indentured to Mage Balin years ago. As much a slave as those waiting in the pens, in some ways."

"Perhaps that is why you feel compelled to help me now," I said. I jumped when Gargle gave me a poke in the ear. He was right. Time ran short until dawn. We needed our token.

If Gargle flew down the hearthroom chimney as he had in Anlia, he would still be on the wrong side of the mage's enspelled chamber door. "What if …" I paused and tried to recall the outside of the inn. "What if this room has a window? Do you remember?"

Ibbot glanced toward the mage's door and appeared to count on his fingers. "I believe so, but wouldn't it be closed against tonight's cold?"

"We've nothing to lose by checking. And nothing to gain by wasting more time inside."

The innkeeper was away from the counter, so we did not have to answer whether we had delivered our message or not. We rounded the corner of the building and ticked off windows under the eaves.

The mage's window stood open to the sea breeze. My hopes soared. I bade Gargle go up to the sill with instructions to snatch a lock of hair, since we could hear the mage's snoring continue from where we stood beneath.

Gargle leapt from my shoulder, mounted higher to the window, and just as he should have soared through, with a tumble of flapping wings he was flung out and away. He flew to the rough wood shingle above and scrabbled to cling there, shaking his feathers back into place.

Ibbot swore. "He's cast a spell to protect him from intrusion there, as well." He snorted. "He wanted to have the window open to smell the sea but kept enough of his wits about him to think of casting a barrier."

"Can't you tell me a way to counter his magic?"

Ibbot rubbed his palms on his trouser legs, considering. "Even so, we would still have to get the potion into him. Perhaps ... we might barricade him more thoroughly rather than try to break through. Keep him imprisoned until after the ship's departure."

"Won't he raise a hue and cry?"

"Not if I teach you how to steal his voice, as I did to you while Kruthe pursued your vessel."

"Have I told you of my confidence that your nature would prove useful?"

"I suppose you do not mean my better nature, eh? Perhaps then you are not sorry that I am not entirely reformed?" He arched an eyebrow over a swollen eye and taught me the cantrip to mute a mage.

Unsatisfied with only that, I also performed other magic. Guided by Ibbot, I sealed the chamber and suppressed other sounds from within—such as pounding on walls or bashing a stool against a window. Even the snoring faded as the final spell was cast. I vowed to remember that one if ever I chanced to lodge alongside a raucus traveler.

We set off to collect Cilliyon and Wieser. As we strode along over the cobbles, Ibbot proposed something I had not thought of with my mind in its current disarray.

"I noticed when we passed the slave pens that you could pass readily among them. With your dark coloring, it would take only the merest glamour to slant your eyes and straighten your hair. Do you not think you could stir the slaves better from among their number than if you rode above on the deck?"

"Leaving you above with Cilliyon? How will I perform the weather-working? I need to hear from you what to do. Unless you have suddenly recovered your ability?" How easy to fall into suspicion where Ibbot was concerned, regardless of the state of my wits.

"It's true I can feel a glimmer of power returning, but I cannot do much as yet. Light a fire, perhaps. I could pass messages to you below using your bird, couldn't I? He will have freedom of movement aboard. Once we learn where the *Megrite* is bound and where the slaves call home, then we will understand better what magic needs be done. In the meantime, you will learn some of their ways and gain their trust."

"Why do I fear that if your words make sense, it means my mind is addled?"

The glance he sent my way showed more concern than slyness. "You have not seemed yourself since we were ... reunited. It may be after effects of the spell to bind you to Gargle, or the weightier magic used to disguise your spirit. Even some glancing blow from the cabal's high magic as we passed through the arena. Do you have a guess?"

"No," I said after a moment. "Though I began to feel the most strange just as we escaped." I found I was unable to confess my feeling of something from the Pit clinging to me, or of abandoning some portion of myself there. "But you," I continued, "you don't seem your old self either, in some respects."

"I believe it could be the leavings of gratitude. I am, admittedly, unaccustomed to that feeling." He blew out a breath through his nose and lifted his chin to rub his throat. "Do you feel you can assume a place among the slaves as we sail? I will put my mind on recovering my abilities. As soon as I can figure a way."

There was truth in what he said, I could easily resemble the folk in the pens. Because my own plan carried little meat on its bones, I accepted Ibbot's idea and nodded as I shook his hand.

"I won't fail you," he said. "Just as you did not fail me."

If he did not speak from the heart, he gave every semblance of doing so.

On hearing our new plan, Cilliyon at once suggested Ibbot be placed among the slaves and she and I pose as mage and attendant.

"I cannot speak Scytheran and neither can you."

"You don't even know if that is what the shipmaster and crew speak."

"Nor will we find out standing here arguing. Come, I've been told the tide does not wait."

Grumbling, she hoisted the robes and remembered to totter as she made her way toward the door. She paused at the threshold and poked Ibbot in the chest with a bent finger. "Just you bear in mind who crossed the Barrens to save your sorry arse."

I tamped down a smile as Ibbot nodded gravely.

Our hasty magic to imprison the mage worked well enough, betimes, as we found no hurrying weather worker when we reached the ship. Signs that *Megrite's* crew made ready to load her cargo of folk could be seen. A gangplank led from the dock to her deck, with rails and ropes rigged to prevent anyone from leaping into the harbor to escape.

Ibbot carried my book and other gear, wrapped in my sundry furs, for the slaves did not appear to have more than thin, loose-woven clothing. Perhaps they came from somewhere warm, though if so, I wondered that none of them froze in Scythera's bitter nights. Within the book's pages, we had slipped blank papers and a stylus, so that Ibbot might write messages for Gargle to carry to me below deck. I carried several sheets rolled around another stylus in the sheath with my knife.

We paused on the walkway above the docks, out of the view of those below. I tapped Ibbot's shoulder to signal Gargle to perch there, which he did but with a restive air. Wieser whined and panted uneasily when I told her to stick close to Cilliyon.

I left Ibbot holding Cilliyon's elbow, with her querulous, "Gods keep you, I pray," still in my ears. She had insisted at the last instant on returning my moonstone talisman. I felt it, still warm from her body, lying against my chest.

Cocks crowed thrice as I made my way alone to the back of the ranks of pens. I chose the enclosure nearest the *Megrite*, so I could see

Ibbot and Cilliyon approach with their offer of service as weather worker, since one appeared to be needed this day. If the offer was refused, I would slip out the way I came in, and we would have to come up with another plan altogether. I must know if Cilliyon and Ibbot did not manage to get aboard, so I did not depart without them.

A nearby barrel provided a place for me to crouch out of sight. I quickly performed the dab of magic to cause my appearance to mirror that of the slave-folk. I wished for a puddle of water to confirm the glamour, but any pool would be frozen and not reflect in the dawn light. Ibbot had not given me wrong magic yet, I reckoned, so I made my way along the fencing.

As I searched for the best way in, I noted no interest on the part of those imprisoned within the barrier. Most sat cross-legged, back-to-back with another, staring vacantly. A few paced along within, aimless so far as I could tell. By far, the majority were men, and young to old. Some women, but few children, no babes-in-arms as had been in the group penned on the quay the night Cilliyon and I arrived in Ulfar.

And all of them utterly silent.

I had not noticed this when we arrived the eve before, but now I realized I had heard none of them speak then, either. No pleading, no reaching through the barricade to implore passers-by for aid. Were they so resigned? Or could they be an entire people who lived their lives as mutes?

A sudden gust of chill air made me shiver. I pulled my knife from my boot and slit the twisted wire in a corner of the pen before me. Only just enough room for me to press through and join the captives. I wound the wire ends together before I stood and slowly made my way to the opposite side of the enclosure, stepping around those sitting or standing. If any noticed me they gave no sign, either by lifting their heads or following me with their eyes. I might have been as invisible as I had been in the mage Stronghold.

I sidled up to a sliver of empty space at the fence line, shouldering between two other men who stood there, staring off into the harbour. I sought the *Megrite* and found her rocking peacefully at her mooring. Two other ships flanked her. Tall Ibbot and bent, old Cilliyon made slow progress up the gangplank, with Gargle riding Wieser's shoulders alongside them. I stood too far away to hear if Ibbot hailed the vessel, but a man appeared to wait on the deck watching their approach. The ship's rigging teemed with clambering sailors, preparing her for departure.

With a lurch of my guts, I saw the ships to either side of *Megrite* boasted crewmen likewise occupied with preparations. I cursed the weather mage's innkeeper, then recalled he had told us only one mage had *said* he sailed on the morrow. What if the other mages in port had not mentioned their plans to depart with the tide? Did each ship bear a mage to calm heavy seas and direct the vessel safely to its destination? I did not know. Could there be so many mages that every ship had one as a matter of course? *Moon Road* had none. What if Ibbot and I had waylaid the wrong mage and one was already ensconced aboard the *Megrite*?

I half-turned away, torn between a desire to run back to my corner and escape through the fence, but also desperate to see what took place when Ibbot and Cilliyon finally reached the top of the gangplank.

Another fear crashed over my heart like a drenching wave. What if I ended up herded onto a different ship, going somewhere else altogether? This pen stood closest to *Megrite's* gangplank, but now I looked, the other two vessels had planks extended as well.

Dark-clad men carrying coiled whips strode down all three planks. Ibbot and Cilliyon had to shuffle to the side and wait to let the men pass. At last, the pair of them reached the deck. I trembled as I watched, set to flee if need be as soon as I saw what occurred. If Ibbot could not talk his way aboard …

Cilliyon kept her head down so her hood shadowed her wizened features while Ibbot extended a hand to the man before him. The seaman did not clasp it. I balled my fists and called on every god I knew as the seemingly endless talk dragged on. Ibbot gestured back toward the port behind him, patted Wieser's head and snatched his hand back from a lunge by Gargle.

At length, the seaman nodded, though he kept his arms crossed over his chest. The men with the whips walked closer to the fences. The slaves about me began to draw back, bunching together. I had to shove against those next to me to keep the deck in view.

Finally, the seaman pointed aft and shook Ibbot's hand. In sudden fear as the men and their whips approached, I whirled to sprint away and escape the pen. I would come around to the *Megrite* and go for a berth as a sailor, or a galley boy, anything. By the gods I would not risk her sailing without me aboard, even if I had to cling to her rudder all day and climb up in the dark of night.

I pushed my way through the slaves, all on their feet and crowding close. Their silence now seemed a more ominous thing than simple resignation. What was the matter with them? Fighting panic, I elbowed men and women aside, for now I could hear shouts that seemed to be orders from the men outside. They cracked whips over our heads and bellowed words in a tongue I could not ken.

The slaves pressed hard about me, pinning my arms and legs and so ensnared me in their midst. I opened my mouth to scream at them, to say I must pass, to get out of my way—and a hand slid over my lips. Gently, so gently, the palm pressed, then tapped thrice against my mouth and slipped away. My eye tracked the hand to see the man who had touched my face. Wordlessly, he tapped his own lips three times. His deep-set eyes showed nothing, no emotion of any sort I could fathom.

Shaking with fear and now anger, I struggled to push free from the cage of bodies barring my escape. A score of hands reached out to stroke my shoulders, my arms and back, just as a rider might stroke a frantic horse to soothe it. Twist as I might, I could not throw their hands off me, they only patiently stretched over to pat and smooth me again.

Motion at the harbour side of the fence told me the slaves had commenced to leave the pen, herded by the men from the ship. Any remaining chance to choose where I ended up dwindled with each passing breath. I forced myself to let my limbs fall slack, ceased all struggle. I hung my head as though defeated. Or as though I surrendered to the press of the crowd.

The instant the hands drew back and the bodies eased a hair's breadth apart, I dropped my hand to my boot top, seeking my knife. Even as I bent to reach it, the face of the first man appeared before me. Again, he patted me three times, but on the knife resting in its sheath, as though he knew exactly where and what it was. I froze in astonishment, and he cupped his strong hands around my elbows and lifted me steadily until I stood upright. He moved his hands to briefly grip my shoulders, then turned to face the folk moving toward the waterfront.

Helpless, I felt myself borne along by the press of those around me. With so many of us, a river of folk flowing forward, I could not go any other way. I was put in mind of a herd of oxen funneled into a corral. I could see nothing but the backs of the people who walked ahead of me, hear nothing but footfalls and the crack of whips.

In the breadth of the streaming crowd, I could not tell which ship we were being driven to board. Distance was distorted beyond my ability to judge. Had I been able to tell, I might have at least tried to hang back or surge forward to be sure I found the gangway for *Megrite.* With folk so closely packed about me, I could not even hop up to try for a look over their bobbing dark heads.

The boards of the gangway met my boot soles and I still did not know which vessel I was being loaded onto. A woman slipped and fell against the ropes, but before I could call out and extend a hand to aid her, all the folk surrounding her pulled her back on her feet. Not a sound from any of them.

I looked up but could not distinguish the rigging above me from any other ship's masts and sheets. The plank leveled out into decking and still we were driven onward. Though forced to file only a few abreast into the passage to go below, I had no chance for a look about to tell where I was, for crewmen stood at the threshold. Each held a bucket full of rough-hewn spoons. One spoon was thrust into the hand of every slave as they passed. We all descended clutching our spoons, and at the foot of the stairs, crewmen pushed some folk to the right, others to the left. The end of my journey was a cramped hold where, packed among a dozen other slaves, we could neither stand fully upright nor all be seated at the same time. I wondered if we were meant to lie side by side, partly curled up or stacked like cord wood. Every animal in *Moon Road*'s hold had more room to move about, relative to size, than this hold provided. Even the geese in their crate could spread wings as wide as they wished.

A tiny slit of sunlight shone between two boards of the hull. Our hold rode above the waterline. To this scanty opening, I pressed my eye in the hope I might just possibly be on the right side of the ship and able to tell if Cilliyon and Ibbot stood over my head or floated along-side instead.

Indeed, as other slaves jostled me against the bulkhead, I could make out the name on the bow of the ship to our starboard side. *Megrite.*

I was trapped on the wrong ship.

CHAPTER THIRTY-FIVE

I f there are words to describe how I felt, as *Megrite* shrank and slipped from view, I did not know them. Words would have been wasted on my silent companions in any case. Whatever the name of the ill-begotten vessel that bore me away, I cursed her to the heavens and beyond. Aye, and cursed myself for an addle-brained goat. I had ploughed forward with a wood wit's plan to rescue slaves, sacrificing everything for a folk who showed every sign of contentment with their imprisonment. Indeed, they all stood around me calmly without even a glimmer of concern for their circumstances.

I had known I was not fully myself since the Stronghold escape. *Known* it. To be willful about a course of action was not necessarily stubborn, but I had gone beyond mere stubbornness—I was a pig-headed fool.

I sifted my thoughts for any comfort but discovered none at all.

The ship rode the waves and I endured the return of wretched sickness at the endless rolling and twisting. The men around me did not appear to suffer from it. When at my most miserable, some of them patted me on the shoulder or back. We had been provided a bucket for our compartment's collective muck. Someone would bring it to me when I got very ill, and the smell of it generally made matters worse. I reckoned if I sank any lower into despair, I would be dead.

Once each day, occurring for our compartment at eventide, all were herded to the deck with our spoons. We bore the bucket up with us to tip over the rail and saw other groups of a dozen slaves empty theirs as well. I surmised the crew brought the slaves up several compartments at a time, since an entire cargo of us would not fit topside all at once.

After the buckets had been dumped, each slave group gathered in their own circle amidships and a crewman delivered a tub of gruel to the center. The cargo of slaves appeared accustomed to this routine and continued to conduct themselves in silence. We ate the congealing mash with our spoons, each person careful to consume an equal share in turn. If I tried to spare my roiling belly, a hand would close over mine and guide my spoon into the glop and thence to my mouth. Not with force, but steady insistence. I yielded because I no longer cared what happened.

When spoons scraped the bottom of the tubs, crewmen stacked them to one side and herded us back to our separate compartments in the divided hold. Each group returned below with their bucket, as docile as flocks accustomed to daily turn out with pasture-mates, placidly returning to a snug barn.

I will confess: I soon grew to hate them all, and myself for good measure.

My companions pressed me to sit at times, at other times to lie on my side nose-to-shoulder with another, a man at my back likewise. I offered no resistance and gave over any attempt to speak to anyone. We all might have been sleep-walking, summoned once daily to the deck, relegated again to the portion of the hold reserved for our captivity.

When my seasickness waned, many days into our journey to only gods knew where, I could not help but notice more about how my hold-mates conducted our days and nights.

On a given day, one particular man seemed to direct our group of slaves, but leadership was taken in turns by each. By subtly shifting his hands, eyes or shoulders in gestures which had no evident meaning to me, he indicated who should sit and who should lie down and where. Those who resumed standing he directed to particular spaces on the plank floor.

So, they might not speak as other men did, but possessed a language of complex signs. I had evidently been recognized at once as not one of them, despite my use of magic to resemble their appearance. The seamen did not realize my otherness, but all the slaves treated me differently than I saw them treat each other. They noted my actions with a sort of kindly indifference, directing me only when I would have interfered with their routine, otherwise appearing to pay me little heed.

They watched me, albeit subtly. I watched them in return, days on end as we sailed. I began to think of them all as akin to a hive of bees, or a colony of ants. If I could learn their language of twitches and shrugs, perhaps a way out of my current dilemma could be devised in the dim, noisome hold.

Yet as time dragged on, I still could make no useful meaning out of the wordless 'talk' between them.

Determined to take some action or go mad, I planned to speak to the sailor who delivered our tub of hot mash on deck. Somehow, the slaves knew my unspoken plan. On the day I chose, they laid their hands on my arms as we sat in our waiting circle. I opened my mouth to speak, and the man next to me placed his spoon upon my tongue. I sputtered and spit it out again but took the message.

I gazed about the deck with wilting resolve. For want of anything else to think about, I noted that the air on deck had grown warmer of late, and the sun hung farther above the western horizon than it had when first we set sail. The days lengthened, then, with the passage of time. We also sailed into more temperate seas, with some southerly bent to our course.

What could our destination be? Listening to the crewmen, who mostly growled Yegan curses and grumbled about their burden of work, had not enlightened me. But the day of my thwarted attempt to speak to a sailor, later on a pair of seamen did at last pass some remarks of interest.

The two stood to the side of us, waiting to add empty tubs to the stack near the mast. It seemed they continued a conversation begun earlier.

"You have to feel a small bit sorry for them, I still say," the first said to a fellow behind him.

"Sorry for slaves? What about sorry for us, hauling the vermin-riddled lot of them around?"

There was truth to the vermin complaint. I scratched at my belly absently.

"Yah, but you and me, we can go home sometimes. Their home is sunk beneath the waves. Completely vanished, Eaker says."

"So why aren't they all drowned dead?"

"Eaker says when the slavers came to their island, they was all waiting on the beach and didn't even have to be captured. Loaded up nicely. And then when the ship reached open water, the top of the tallest mountain shot flames and smoke to the heavens and the sea came roaring and swallowed it all. All!"

"I suppose Eaker thinks they knew what was coming? You know he loves his drink. Did you buy him a portion for this tale?"

"What if I did?" the first sailor said stubbornly. "He seen it. They're stunned, like. That's why they don't none of them speak."

"They don't speak because they don't have as much wits as a moth." Their turn had come to add tubs to the stack, and I could not hear more of what was said as they walked away.

I had no idea who Eaker might be, and whether he truly was a witness or just a story-spinner. Sailors, I had learned, were known to make up wild tales on long voyages. The story might or might not have a kernel of truth.

An officer might know, but those men all kept well away from the slaves on deck. I had no chance there.

I mulled over the tale of the mountain's destruction all the ensuing days, for I had nothing better to occupy my time. I had never read of such a thing in my da's collection of books, but the world has so many strange places. And my fellow slaves did seem at times to *know* things in an odd way …

Our time on deck had been spent in waning dusk at the outset of the voyage, but since we now filed above during daylight as the days lengthened, I found I managed better if I looked at only the deck planks as we waited for our tub of gruel. Gazing out over the trackless glimmer of blue waves made me feel too dispirited. So I was caught by surprise when a sudden flutter over my head preceded Gargle dropping into my lap.

Though seized with astonishment, I jerked my shirt up and covered him at once. I crossed my arms over my middle, which must have squashed him nearly flat. He made no sound but did give me a good jab in the guts. I loosened my hold only a little.

My companions on deck betrayed no interest in what had just happened. I risked a glance at the sailors moving about us. Gargle appeared to have evaded their notice. The bird must have come from *Megrite*. Was she close by? Had Ibbot recovered enough to obscure the crow with magic? The bird surely could not have pursued this ship for the length of time we had been at sea, never alighting. Did he bear a message from Ibbot and Cilliyon? I dared not examine him until we returned below.

I ate my share of slop as my mind churned—so brimming with thoughts I feared all would spill onto the deck. The crew gathered and stacked the empty tubs, taking long enough I might have grown a beard and plaited it. Finally, our group stood to be herded back down to the hold. I tried to peer between my fellows to catch a glimpse of the water as we walked. I could see no masts to starboard and could not view the portside at all.

Once in the partitioned hold, shut up again for the rest of the day and night, I fished under my shirt and closed my hand around Gargle's stick-like legs. I drew him out, ruffled and squinty-eyed. I still could have kissed his beak, despite his angry demeanor. He hopped onto my forearm and stuck out a leg. A dirty paper wrapped the limb, bound with a leather thong. I prised apart the knots and pulled the paper free. He clambered to my shoulder.

I spared a glance at the slaves. I might have been staring into the fetid air with the rest of them, for none looked my way. Could my great black bird be obscured from them, as well?

The paper was covered with cramped writing which I could not see well enough to read in the dismal light. I pressed and shifted my way past the others to the sliver of daylight penetrating the hull, where I had viewed the *Megrite* alongside us on the day we set sail.

Still not enough light. Did I dare read it on deck the next day at feeding time? How could I bear to wait so long to know the message?

Gargle stretched and scraped his beak across my shirtfront, prodding the talisman moonstone that hung about my throat. I lifted it free of the cloth.

The stone had glowed in the mine at Lunenhelm. I did not know why or how that had happened, but if magical ability came at need, my need to know the contents of my message was great, no denying.

I turned the talisman over in my hands, looking at it from every angle. I enclosed it within my two palms and pressed my hands to my brow. I prayed to all the gods for inspiration of how to light its fire, but silently after all the weeks of not using my voice. *Please, help me now. I must have light!*

Visions spun through my mind, of the old Traveller crone who had handed me the talisman "for the strong magic" while she cackled and drooled. I saw my home, its rich fields and grazing herds and my da striding through the orchard wearing his tall boots, a brace of wild geese slung over his shoulder. Little sister Morie skipped toward him, followed by brother Wils and his bride Annora. This could not be a memory, for I had never seen this happen. And indeed, when Annora turned in profile, I saw she was heavy with child. She had not been carrying when I left my home, or if so, only just, and not filled out. Did I view events occurring now at my home, many months after my departure? If so, what magic brought the vision to me?

I hungered to see more of my family in Merced, but the scene shifted again. In the new vision, blackness streamed from my out-flung hands and Stas Royka fell dead. Next, I clung to a rope in a mineshaft, struggling to send the breath of life to those men dying below.

Another shift, and I found myself on the deck of a ship, watching aghast as a wall of grey water rose higher than the topmost mast and plummeted forward like an avalanche. I seemed to float into the air above the crashing water, to see behind the wave, where an immense cloud of black smoke billowed toward the heavens, bolts of lightning crackling within it. Was this the demise of the slaves' homeland? A flash of lightning arced toward me in the vision, and startled, I snatched my hands away from my brow in the hold of the slave ship.

The moonstone pulsed gentle light between my fingers.

I panted despite the stench as I tried to make sense of what I had seen. I looked about me for any common ordinary thing to fix my gaze on, to stop my head from spinning.

All of the slaves knelt before me, some bent atop others in the close quarters, each of them with both hands crossed over their mouths and eyes downcast. I lifted the gleaming stone higher, and they crouched lower.

I looked sidelong at Gargle on my shoulder. He met my eye and cocked his head to one side. I took this to mean he didn't know what had got into them either.

Something to consider later. I held the stone aloft to read the message.

Fleet of three ships. G & W are kept locked away in cabin with me by Ib. He is up all night reading your book. Terrors again—W seems to see something around him then, tho' I cannot.

He wrote msg but G would not allow him tie it on. I write in secret, sent G first chance. Where bound? Some of Ib's magic is back but not weather, says we are lucky so far but coming to bad seas. Send G back with msg but do not say about mine. I fear Ib.

Cilliyon's voice had seemed to whisper, close by my ear, each desperate word. I felt a rush of chill despite the heavy moist air of the hold.

I pulled stylus and paper from my boot, comforted slightly by my knife resting alongside in its sheath. Gargle waited while I held my moonstone in one hand and endeavored to write with the other, the paper pressed against my thigh.

What to write? I discarded a dozen foolish openings—such as: I am

Alive, Thank the gods Gargle found me, Forget about freeing these slaves as they've nowhere to go and seem suited by captivity—all as either obvious or pointless in current circumstances. Further, I could not let on that I had received Cilliyon's note.

Gargle shifted his feet, perhaps to suggest I get on with the task. I labored over the paper and secured it to his leg with the leather string. It read:

> *In hold with mute slaves. Escape must wait until landfall. Fair weather has helped thank you for that. Can you learn how long voyage and where to?*

When I slipped the talisman into the neck of my shirt, its light faded. My hold-mates uncovered their mouths and resumed characteristic positions, staring into nothingness. None of them looked my way when I edged to the gate of our partition and prodded Gargle to fly over the barrier and topside. He flapped out of sight, carrying my message and all my hopes with him.

CHAPTER THIRTY-SIX

H ad I nursed any expectation that my fellow slaves would view me with dawning respect after the revelation of my magic light, I would have been disappointed. As I held no such hope, their calm silence only seemed a return to our routine. Yet, at the same time, it meant there was nothing to distract me from spending hours reviewing Cilliyon's message word by word. I found I had committed it to memory instantly, as though an incantation of limitless power which required utmost clarity of intent.

What drove Ibbot to pore over my mother's book? Didn't he know far more magic than a country hedge-witch? What could he be seeking in its pages? I had read it through myself, many times, when I needed a course of magical action. From my study, I could call to mind all the lore recorded in those languages I understood. Some spellworks were inscrutable to me. Could he read those passages? For that matter, why might a mage have been studying my book in the Stronghold? That appeared to be the case, in the workroom where Gargle had led us. If only Wieser could tell me what she saw near Ibbot as he slept. A Sending? But Cilliyon had been as able as I to see the Sending of Mage Balin in the mountain hut on that long ago night. Might the mages be in pursuit of us despite our efforts to obscure the escape from Scythera? Could either Ibbot or I matter so much to them any longer?

I wrestled within my mind to reckon how long we had been at sea. So many days and nights ran together, with only the moments spent topside to mark them one from another. In my sickness and despair, keeping a tally of the time passed? Beyond my ken or caring. Given the darkness of the hold, nor could I track the phases of the moon or the angle of the sun's path through the sky.

When *Moon Road* set sail from Merced bound for Lohr Island, Lichan Tedesch—*where might he be by now?*—had told me to expect a voyage of two months duration. Roughly the same amount of time passed before the ship docked at Yega. A matter of two months to cross the vast ocean and we currently sailed west, or south and west, at a guess. Did that mean we could possibly make landfall on my home continent, if not at Bale Harbour itself? Perhaps too much to hope for. And Merced had no slave market in its port, despite I had once seen wagons of slaves depart from the port on the way west to Keltane. It could be the Keltanese invaders had retaken and made over Bale Harbour, turned it into a slaver port, since I sailed away.

But, Cilliyon's note said Ibbot feared some treacherous seas ahead. There were none such on the way to my homeland. Only when driven off course to the north had *Moon Road* encountered the gap winds blowing from the Tantec Mountains.

I knew too little of the wider world. I found myself again in great need of a map and with scant chance of obtaining one.

I spent a long night with my thoughts, pondering as well when Gargle might return with another message. I told myself not to expect him before feeding time on the main deck, but the bird surprised me yet again.

Throughout the voyage, I could hear little of what occurred topside while riding in the hold. Snatches of shouted orders and the occasional stumping of boots over my head. When I heard distant bellowing sometime in the morning, I paid little mind to it at first. Until the voice grew louder, more furious, and much closer. Many feet thudded by above me, then the angry sailor hollered at the top of the stair to our hold and I could make out his words.

"Thief! Rotten black-hearted—catch it, you fools! It's got my food sack!"

Gargle sailed into my pen, a grubby canvas bag dangling from his beak. He lit on the head of the slave nearest me and stuck out a leg. I wasted no time snatching the message tied there, but since I could hear the owner of the bag storm down the passageway, I knew the bird would not wait for me to read it and reply. I expected him to spring into the air at once, but he held his other leg toward me instead. A tiny leather pouch was bound there, and I tugged it free so he could fly before the sailor blocked his escape.

Relieved of those burdens, Gargle spread his wings and sprang toward the rage-purpled seaman at the gate to our pen. The man swung a stout club, but wide of the mark. He spat a bitter curse and lunged forward again. Gargle spun in the air and whapped the sack against the sailor's brow, scattering the contents. He sped away with a gleeful *grock*. I shoved my prizes under my shirt and adopted the same blank face my fellow slaves wore, though my heart clattered against my ribs.

As the sailor bent to retrieve his foodstuff, spilled across the passageway when the sack burst open, another pair of seamen joined him. I could see why he wanted his rations, for he gathered dried meat and a hunk of cheese, a half-dozen pieces of ship's biscuit. All looked better fare than I had been eating. Slavers fed their crew well.

He grumbled as he juggled an armload. "It was Eaker fed the misbegotten creature, showed it food came from sacks. Didn't steal his though, did it! I've some choice words for him, feeding the thieving, greedy—I'll wring its neck when I catch it. Feed it to the fishes!"

The other men nodded and groused along with him, while I waited for them to carry the split sack and its contents topside. None of the three so much as glanced at the slaves.

How long before our hold's turn to trudge topside for feeding? I felt the time to be midmorning, give or take. Our pen should still have some hours below. I decided to risk reading the note with my moonstone.

This time my appeal to the gods for light brought forth no accompanying visions. I would have liked to see my family again, but that was the only one of the missing sights I regretted. My hold-mates again bent before me when the stone glowed in my hands. I held it close to the slip of parchment and read a terse message from Ibbot:

RIDE CROW TO ME AT ONCE

In the small leather pouch Gargle had brought, I found a scant amount of mallowmeld. I feared no more remained than this few pinches of powder. With the spell seared in my memory from the first ride at Anlia, I had no doubt I could recall the magic. Gargle need not be present. So as long as I returned to myself before today's trek above for feeding time, my spirit's absence would not be apparent to any of my captors. I did not expect my fellow slaves to react to my lying insensible for a time. And I had no way to explain to them, in any case.

I slipped the moonstone into my shirt, the slaves rose from their genuflection. I watched for the man who seemed to be directing the actions of the others for the day, having finally gained a scant ability to tell as the leadership shifted man-to-man. When a couple of others prepared to take their short span of side-lying in the cramped space, I shifted in front of the next man designated for his turn. The leader flicked a glance and brow twitch, the other man turned away as I sank onto the deck planks.

I dipped a finger into the pouch and smeared the mallowmeld across the back of my neck, noting that it smelled better than anything else in the hold. Another of the slaves settled at my back, none of them betraying any interest in my actions. I worked the casting as Ibbot had taught me, though in silence. My vision faded as it had in the Jackadaw's attic … and I opened my eyes in a cabin aboard the *Megrite*.

My crow mount clung to Cilliyon's shoulder. I first spied Ibbot, who peered at me with bloodshot eyes and a grim set to his jaw. Next, I glanced down and saw Wieser's madly flagging tail. My heart soared to see her, how I wished I could stroke her. And put my arms around Cilliyon, who quivered beneath Gargle's gripping claws. Her crone visage seemed to flicker, replaced with smooth cheeks and dewy eyes for an instant—perhaps some effect of Gargle's sharper sight. Or fading strength in my spell to disguise her …

As I could not speak, I waited to hear what Ibbot had to say.

He spoke in a harsh whisper. "All three ships are bound for a remote land where Ironwood grows. To reach it, we must sail across the most perilous seas, around the cape through straits where storms are ferocious and constant. It is known to sailors as the Demon's Cauldron, as near as I can translate it. No shipmaster would attempt the crossing without a weather mage. That must be you, or we are all lost."

He held paper before Gargle's face. "I have written what I know, also what was in your book. The bird must deliver these sheets to you. I have also written how a mage accomplishes a Sending, for we must find a way to have you with me … is there no way to get you off the other ship and onto this one?" A twitch commenced by his left eye, and he licked cracked lips.

Would I be able to enact magic alongside Ibbot if I attended him as a Sending? Because all I could do from my perch in Gargle's mind was watch and listen. I bade Gargle to shake his head to show I had no way to get aboard, which he did, and then stuck his leg out for the papers to be tied to it.

Cilliyon twisted her neck to look at Gargle. "Can you jump in and swim to us?"

Gargle shook his head almost before I could ask him to do so again. Even if I could reach the rail and leap, I had no hope I could catch up to the other vessel, so many yards away and under sail as well. Or indeed any hope that anyone on the ship I abandoned would see fit to scoop me back out of the waves. They would let me drown, I felt sure, to become fish food as the aggrieved sailor had threatened for Gargle.

"Don't be a fool," Ibbot told Cilliyon. "The only chance of that might be—Listen, all three ships will take on fresh water in a few days. When we reach the western continent, there is a place where a great river flows into the sea. Fresh water floats atop the salty brine near shore, and the ships will pause there. They lower buckets and draw up the fresh water to replenish stores before sailing into the treacherous passage. If you can get on deck as this is done, you could have a chance. A faint one."

Would I know, down in the hold, when all three ships stopped? Did they stop all together, or each in their turn and then sail on before the next one drew near? And blast all, I could not ask! Gargle ruffled his feathers and squatted on Cilliyon's narrow shoulder, hindered somewhat by the folded sheets tied about his leg.

"Go back," Ibbot directed. "I will send the bird as soon as I may. Waiting for nightfall may be wise, I heard some fracas carried on the wind when last he flew to you. We cannot afford to lose him now." He pressed fingertips to his quivering eyelid and turned away.

"Oh, take every care, my love," Cilliyon whispered.

I closed my borrowed eyes on her tender face as I spun the cantrip in reverse—and opened them again in the dim hold to see the dark matted hair on my fellow slave's neck as he lay before me.

As I had been bound to Gargle only a short time, compared to my first ride at Anlia, I hoped I might not be so weak as before when I came back to myself. Good fortune still shied out of my grasp, however, because I could not rise when the other slaves lying with me completed their turn. Each stood and shuffled away, to be replaced by the next due their rest. Another man took position in front of me, then one behind. I closed my eyes and sank into a deep sleep.

I must have slept for several more turns, because when my neighbor jostled me, our hold was moving toward the gate. Time for the daily feed. I struggled to my feet, wondering if performance of a Sending left a mage so depleted as the spellwork to bind to an animal mount. I wobbled on jelly knees and felt a hand cup my elbow to lend support. I glanced to see which slave had aided me, but none of them met my eye. The hand had withdrawn. *By the gods, they are a queer folk*, I thought as I followed along onto the deck.

For the only time on this misbegotten voyage, I felt eager for the bland sustenance of our pasty gruel and held my spoon at the ready. A scan of the clear sky revealed no sign of Gargle. I hoped Ibbot would wait for darkness to dispatch the bird, as he had said. I might manage to restore some wit and vigor by then and be better able to apply myself to renewed study of magic lore.

Indeed, this proved true on both counts. Gargle arrived long after we had finished the pot and been returned to the hold. I began to feel more akin to myself, though I kept a hand on my sheathed knife whenever seated. I seemed to draw strength from it, or at least comfort.

Gargle's arrival during the night watch provoked no excitement above that I could hear. He glided into the hold, perched on the knee of the slave who squatted alongside me, and took wing again as soon as I relieved him of his packet.

My hold-mates bent low around me as I read the sheets by the moonstone's light. Ibbot's scrawl told me I had four days before the fleet took on fresh water. If able to join them on *Megrite*, I must be proficient enough to cast a wide swath of weather magic to see us through the hazardous passage. If unsuccessful at boarding their vessel, I must also become proficient at Sending, and so work the weather with Ibbot in that way. Much more complicated, he wrote, and I had to agree. The weather and current spell's intricacy daunted me, and where would I obtain an iron pin? A gull feather was more possible to come by. Or, I still had one of Gargle's feathers, saved when I plucked it from the stair in the mage's Stronghold. Which might do. Was a land bird's feather as effective as a sea bird's in this? A weather-worker would know, I thought in irritation. I was not one.

I read further, and discovered I also required a specific crystal stone to find the sun through thick clouds. Did Ibbot possess one—was that the crystal he had used in the stable in Yega to light the passageway? Now that I had learned to make light with my moonstone, perhaps it could be used in the spell. Or not, and I would learn the truth too late ...

I had no bowl to hold seawater for scrying, nor mirror either. I did not suppose our group slop bucket offered any surface fit for divination. Surely Ibbot carried what was required? Or the items were provided on the ship?

Since I could not unearth the answers to any of these questions within Ibbot's pages, it fell to me to glean every possible morsel of knowledge from the words themselves. No shade of meaning would avoid scrutiny. Every shape of every letter would be committed to memory, to be called forth to my inner vision in an instant. I bent my will to the task. If I failed, it would be fate and not from any lack of trying.

CHAPTER THIRTY-SEVEN

W hereas before, during my despair, I had ignored the passage of time, I now marked the bells that told the end of one watch and the start of another. I notched a beam in the hold with my knife to track them carefully. I would not be caught unawares when the four days passed and we stopped for fresh water.

I also used my knife to cut a sliver of wood from the beam. This I used as I practiced the weather working spells, as a substitute for a slender pin of iron. While I made no effect on the wind or current with my oak splinter, I became well-versed in casting the required spells.

Gargle's feather stood for a gull's in my practice, and my moonstone talisman for the needed sunstone. I worked my memory hard, as hard as ever I had before.

In the wee hours of the night, I practiced Sending. The spellwork for this was deceptively unadorned. I was initially fooled into thinking it a straightforward process but found performing it required all of my mind's reason and force brought to bear.

After the second night's work, I could send myself out of the pen, into the passageway. I could look about, even look in the gate and see myself seated there with eyes squeezed tight. I tried to open my eyes where I sat, to view myself as a Sending standing outside the pen, but the attempt promptly wafted the Sending's view into the currents of ether that surround us all. The magic drifted away, unraveled.

The next night I managed to trod the deck planks like a wraith, soundless and unseen by sailors passing beside me. I tried to send my spirit self across the water to *Megrite*, as I could see her pale moonlit sails off our starboard side. The third ship in our party followed like a shadow, in our wake and to port.

Though I tried mightily, some aspect of the silvered waves seemed to prevent me—I could not depart the ship, which I dubbed the *Despondent* in my mind. Whether the barrier existed in my mind or in the power of the spell, I did not know. A master mage had to be able to cross water, for Mage Balin surely must have the night he came to Ibbot in the mountain hut. Furthermore, something followed Ibbot over the sea now, Cilliyon believed.

And something watched me, too. My sense of a divided mind surfaced again as I practiced spellwork, as though whatever accompanied me from the mages' Pit stirred at the scent of magic. Some ... *awareness* ... held itself just out of my reach, noting my efforts as carefully as I noted the ship's bells.

Yet what could I do? I must prepare or all would be lost.

The Sending I managed to craft could neither speak nor understand speech—whatever spoken words entered my spirit ears as I roamed the ship seemed no more than the sibilant murmurings from a seashell pressed close. Both from my earlier encounters with mages and from what Ibbot had told me, I knew adept mages could converse with one another by means of Sending spells. For my part, I was able to move about the ship and use my eyes, but not touch anything, or feel anything touch me.

I began to wonder anew if Ibbot could ever be trusted. Had he delivered only part of the knowledge I needed, the better to keep me under his thumb? And yet, did he not bear the same risk as the rest of us, if I could not master the spellwork to save all three ships? I would have heaved a sigh in aggravation, but such was impossible for a spirit walking by magic.

If vision was to be my only sense, I resolved to explore every corner of the vessel. I would particularly seek a map in the shipmaster's cabin. Surely that would be some aid in knowing how much time remained before the reckoning at the strait must come.

As though the gods had not already strewn my path with enough obstacles to surmount, they cast another before me. While I made my way toward the shipmaster's aft quarters, I came upon crewmen tipping bundles into the sea. I thought at first they jettisoned refuse or rags, until an arm slipped free of one burlap wrapping, a bare foot from another.

The bundles were the corpses of slaves. Shocked, I watched sailors emerge from the hold with their burdens, stagger to the railing, and hoist the bodies over to tumble into the waves. In my own small hold partition, none had died. Clearly others had not been so fortunate. Many others, to judge from the line of seamen emerging into the moonlight from below.

If eyes of a Sending could shed tears, mine would have done. If a spirit throat could cry out, surely the gods would have heard my heart's sickness rend the air. But the slaves, as mute in death as in life, were swallowed by the ocean whether or not I could keen for them. I scraped my scattered wits together and sought some reason for the deaths and the discarded bodies.

Abandoning the path to the shipmaster's map, I made my way instead into the aft hold. Sickness from poor fare, or contagion spread by being packed cheek-by-jowl, either or both might exact a toll on the cargo of folk.

How did the seamen find the dead? No sailor had ever come checking our pen. Some slaves would presumably be asleep in each partition at any given time. It would be too dark, even with a torch or lantern, to determine if all those lying on the planks still drew breath.

I followed the passage deeper, to discover the sailors who bore a dead slave all emerged from farther aft. Their faces betrayed no distaste as they worked. They might have been carrying coils of rope or sacks of meal. At the back of the hold, a dwindling stack of corpses lay before me in the pool of lantern light. Perhaps a dozen remained. I did not know how many had already been cast overboard tonight. The crew must store the bodies here to await the nighttime. Did the crew dipose of bodies every night? From what I could see, the ship rats had not been at the dead as yet.

With growing horror, I surmised the method—and a danger. While each group of slaves in the hold traveled above for daily feeding at their set time, other crewmen not occupied with that duty must check the corresponding hold for any slaves who did not come up. They removed the left-behind dead, and likely those who were near death as well, placing them aside to be disposed of in the darkness. Slavers might pack the holds so tight with the expectation of this dead loss.

Much as the spoiled grain, the bruised fruit, or the sick animal is culled.

And the danger? I dare not lie insensible during a ride on Gargle or while wandering the ship as a Sending, and have my body be mistaken for a corpse. I must never overlook the timing and lie below when our gruel was meted out. Else I would wind up in the pile.

I could think of no other event aside from the feedings when all the occupants of a given pen would be doing the same thing at the same time. The slaves I shared my compartment with had never allowed me to remain behind at feeding time, I now realized. Not even when I was at my most ill after we set sail and wanted nothing to do with food. Perhaps the slaves had knowledge of life and death aboard from previous voyages. They had fallen easily enough into the rhythm our captors set.

And benignly protected me, while I hated them and thought them no more than a hive of strange, silent bees. I vowed to serve them better from now forward.

I set off again to the main deck, judged from the bell's toll that several more hours remained until dawn, and so returned to the task of viewing a map. I found the shipmaster's cabin.

Moonlight bathed the chart table, pale but enough to see by. More dimly, I could make out the humped shape of the shipmaster, abed and fast asleep in a narrow alcove alongside.

He was not alone.

A slave woman lay with him, her straight black hair spilled across the pillow like a swath of night sky. Her downward-slanted eyes were open and they tracked me as I moved nearer.

Though I did not know if she saw me or only sensed my presence with the slaves' curious way of knowing, I raised my hand and pressed my fingertips to my lips. I repeated the gesture three times, as one of the slaves had done to me in the pens at Ulfar. She did not stir, neither did she look away.

But most urgent for me, she did not awaken the shipmaster.

I turned my attention to the table. With little experience reading maps of the ocean rather than of land, I had no easy time of it. The writing on the largest was in Yeganil, which I had attained a passable fluency for speaking, but could only read a little. Other charts might have been written in Scytheran, the letters formed strangely, akin to thick runes I could not decipher. I recalled some similar lettering in my mother's book, though why she should have had passages and spells recorded in Scytheran, I could not guess.

Orienting by the compass rose, I scoured the western coastline on the Yegan map. I sought a wide river emptying into the sea. The ship's present position was not marked in any way. I felt I had a general idea of our course, which, coupled with Ibbot's estimate of when we would take on fresh water, allowed me to find a likely river's mouth.

Now, how far would we sail from there before we reached the dangerous passage? I searched the waves drawn in pale blue ink farther south, following the coastline as it curved into a scythe. Another land-mass beyond created a lengthy but narrow strait, and the blue ink had been laid on much darker there. Both coasts were marked with moun-tain peaks up to the water's edge. A Yegan word I recognized, 'storms,' had been printed across the strait, and bolts of lightning sketched throughout. 'Demon's Cauldron' might have been inscribed there, but I did not know the words.

My test would come all too soon, it seemed. Only a matter of days after we paused for fresh water.

I looked to the slave woman, who watched me still. She raised her fingers to her lips and copied the three-fold motion I had made. Then she closed her eyes.

I slipped away, withdrawing along the deck, and returned to myself in the cramped, stinking hold. I prayed the gods would see fit to aid me. The fates of so many had become inexorably bound with my own.

CHAPTER THIRTY-EIGHT

I thought Ibbot might send some further instruction, or any sort of word at all before the halt to take on water. Even a single word of encouragement would be welcome. Though I waited in sparse expectation, I saw no sign of Gargle even without a message tied to his leg. And so little mallowmeld remained, I could not risk a visit to the other ship by a magic flight with my crow.

I woke to the bell that harked sunrise on the day I would make my attempt to jump ship and swim to *Megrite*. If Ibbot's dates were correct, if I could get to the railing, if my fellow slaves did not prevent me from leaping, if I did not drown—if, if, if!

When might we take in the sails and drop anchor? I somewhat dourly did not suppose this would happen when our compartment was on deck anyway for feeding time. It would not serve me to assume such a fortunate turn of events.

I watched to note which man took charge of the subtle maneuvering within our pen. I met his eye briefly but did not go where he aimed me. Instead, I stood at the gate where I could look out into the passageway. This marked the start of my rudimentary plan.

From my post, I listened for shouted orders from above, knowing sometimes the cries could be faintly heard below decks. I silently unmade the spell I had cast before joining the slaves, which altered my appearance to match theirs. My hair returned to wavy brown, from straight and coarse black. Though I could not see or feel the change, I lost the downward slant of my eyes. My flesh, with much less of it owing to not enough food but more on display as my clothing frayed away, grew honey-coloured instead of ruddy.

None of my companions gave any sign of noticing the changes. Perhaps they always saw me as I truly was?

I held my moonstone talisman in my hand and waited for my cue to come from the deck above.

Hours passed. I began to wish I'd thought to take a piss before stationing myself at the gate. My back cramped from standing hunched over. I strained my ears while reviewing every bit of magic lore I knew. Although that ate up some time, I had no guarantee any of my knowledge would help me now. I practiced setting my intention for the outcome I wanted: reaching *Megrite*. I saw myself in my mind's eye, standing on her deck with Cilliyon and Wieser to one side and Ibbot on my other, while Gargle perched on my shoulder. I cracked my neck bones by twisting my head, so nearly missed the words from above that told me we had reached our watering place.

"Land to starboard!"

"Ready the barrels aft!"

The anchor chain rattled out.

Some more hollering, but I'd heard enough. I put my hand on the gate latch. Two men turned toward me, reaching out to stop me in their implacable way. Always, they *knew* somehow.

I raised the talisman high and wordlessly called forth its light. As before, all of the slaves crouched or knelt haphazardly, palms crossed over their lips.

I yanked open the gate and bolted into the passage, upwards into the daylight on deck.

Find Megrite, I thought as I spun around on the planks, shielding my eyes from the bright light. I spotted her just ahead off our port side. The instant I clamped my hands on the rail, lifting my feet to swing over, a heavy fist struck my chest and knocked me flat on my back. I opened and closed my mouth like a fish out of water, but every bit of breath had been driven from me. I could no more speak than if I had been a fish in truth.

"What d'you think you're about?" snarled a mountainous sailor. "Get back from there."

I rolled to hands and knees, still struggling to draw enough wind to speak.

"What have you got there?" Another crewman strode toward us.

"Must be a stowaway, sir. He's no slave. Caught him trying to jump ship."

The second man spat. "Drag him below. His lashing can come later, after we take on water."

The first sailor hauled me upright by my tunic, but not before I plucked my knife out of my boot. I held the black blade aloft and lifted my moonstone in my other hand.

"Fools!" I shouted, voice hoarse from disuse. "I am a master mage. Take me to the shipmaster at once, for there is coming greater peril than he knows."

The bearish man snatched his hand away from my tunic as though the cloth had burst into flame. He drew back a step and made a warding sign. My blade glinted in the sunlight. I turned to the second man, who seemed to have higher rank. And lesser fear.

He looked to port. "The weather worker is aboard our sister ship."

I sneered. "Know all about the ways of mages, do you? For a passage as trecherous as this, one of us must be aboard each vessel. I have news the shipmaster needs."

"What news?" He watched my knife, shifted his weight, gauging his strike.

Time slowed.

From that deep recess of my sundered mind, the awareness I carried since the Pit in the Barrens roused itself. *Now*, it urged.

A bolt of black fire sparked from the tip of my knife and splintered the deck by the toes of the doubter's boots.

He stumbled back, mouth agape. I drew myself up tall and strove to look contemptuous. The bolt had flown unbidden. I could not afford to let him see that in my face.

Gargle swooped over the rigging and settled on my shoulder with a jeering cackle. "Yes," I said, as though I conversed with the bird. "They are taking me to the shipmaster now."

The seaman shut his mouth and turned to lead me aft. I stepped behind him, past others who had been drawn by the raised voices and *crack* of magic fire. Only the slaves on deck for feeding time ignored me as I passed by.

Murmurs drifted after us as we mounted the steps to the shipmaster's cabin. The sailor knocked on the door and entered when summoned by a gravelly voice. We drew to a halt before the shipmaster's laden table. His meal, spread out on several platters, looked so glorious—roast meat and heady-scented cheeses, that I felt my mouth water like a spring. I sent a sideways glare at Gargle to discourage him from thieving a sample. The slave woman I had seen in the shipmaster's bed now sat crosslegged on the floor beside his chair. She stared ahead, giving no sign that she noted the presence of any of us.

I did not wait for the seaman to speak and started my tale at once. "Shipmaster, send me to *Megrite* with all haste, to attend the weather worker there."

"Who might you be, boy?"

"I am one of the cadre of mages. One of us is on each vessel, to assure safe passage through the strait."

"What? Where have you been keeping yourself? This is the first I have heard of more than one weather worker for a fleet."

The sailor cleared his throat. "Sir, I have seen him work magic. He about took my feet off."

The shipmaster frowned and tapped his finger on the rim of a battered pewter wine cup.

I needed more doing than pondering, or they would figure out I was spinning a story. "You are wasting time I don't have." I pointedly did not use the formal Yeganil 'yourself' for him. "My fellow mage on the third ship sickened and died. Her crew has pitched him into the sea. Now I must confer with the mage on *Megrite* to devise a way to protect all three ships."

The shipmaster fixed a baleful eye on the sailor. "Where did you find him?"

"He turned up at the rail, seemed to be trying to jump ship. I thought he was some sort of stowaway, sir."

"I have been in the hold with the slaves, using them to aid my magic. As was my fellow on the third vessel. I went to the rail to call my crow." Gargle bobbed his head.

"Yourself couldn't be mistaken for one of them." He laid a hand on the woman's sleek head, as though she were a hound at his feet. But he had used the formal word to address me. Good.

"I changed my looks, by spellcasting."

"How does yourself know the other one is dead?" The shipmaster challenged.

"I am a mage," I said coldly. "And that is how I know. I need to meet face-to-face with the others of my kind and cast new protections. Each of us must share the dead one's portion of the magic, lest all ships and cargo be lost."

Sweat had broken out on his forehead; I could see the sheen. *He's never sailed this route before,* I realized. *He's scared witless.*

The map I had viewed in the night lay off to the side of his meal tray. I still had my knife in my hand. I sprang forward and drove the tip into the strait of dark water and lightning bolts. The shipmaster heaved backwards in his chair.

"If you do not get me over to *Megrite*, this is where you will die." I twisted the blade in the parchment and the wood beneath and jerked it free. It left a rent in the map that looked like savage jaws.

"Put him in a longboat," the shipmaster said. He did not lift his eyes from the torn map. The slave woman shifted her gaze up through her lashes, to fix on me. And for the merest breath of time, she smiled.

CHAPTER THIRTY-NINE

The seamen readied the longboat. By clasping my hands in front of me, I could disguise the trembling of my arms. I managed to clamber down into the bucking craft without betraying stunned bewilderment, the cause of my shudders. My confusion about how the black fire had been called forth on deck.

When I killed Stas Royka, my desperate desire to protect Cilliyon had fueled my blow. While I did not know exactly how I had done it, I still knew beyond doubt it was I who sent the bolt.

This furious crack of lightning had seemed to burst from whatever I carried within my mind from the Barrens. Before, I had sensed a lurking watcher. Now I felt a coiled serpent with the capacity to strike, whether I willed it or not.

As though I did not have enough out in the world to fear, I now had to be on guard against something within, as well. I set my jaw and gripped my knees, sitting straight as a sapling on the bench seat. The men pulled smartly at the oars. Eager to be rid of me, I supposed. Muscle corded their arms and *Megrite* seemed to grow so much closer with each stroke. By the halfway point, I heard Wieser barking on her deck, soon saw her running to and fro at the rail. *Wait for me, girl, I am coming.* Gargle, still on my shoulder, clicked his beak at the rukus.

Once we drew alongside, the crewmen above cast a rope ladder down to us. I climbed to *Megrite's* deck, where Wieser bounced around my feet like a pup. However haughty I wished to appear, I could not resist kneeling briefly to scratch her wooly chest and ruffle her ears.

"The weather mage," I said, on standing. "Take me to him."

"If yourself please, sir," a man in the longboat called up, "do we wait, or return to *Galgen*?"

At last, the name of the ship where I endured my term as slave cargo. I would never forget it even if I lived as long as an old salt from Bale Harbour. "Go back. Tell her master to wait for further word before setting sail, but to take on water as planned."

No one questioned my authority to so direct the shipmaster of the other vessel. A pock-faced seaman about my own age led me to a shut door under the aft deck. He stood aside and I rapped on it.

Ibbot's voice answered, steeped in irritation. "Go away. Or if it's food, leave it and go away."

"Open the door, Ibbot. I've come to speak with yourselves."

Gargle cawed and Wieser growled low.

He flung the door open and sagged against the jamb. "By the gods, it *is* you," he said in Mercedish. He sounded fraught with despair, in truth. I could not see Cilliyon, or rather old crone Cilliyon, because he was blocking the doorway.

"I must confer with the weather worker." I swept past him and pulled the door shut on the curious sailor.

Cilliyon dashed from the bunk on the far side of the tiny cabin and caught me around the neck. She still looked the part of the ancient mage, but in my arms she felt as though made of every kind of softness and solace.

Gargle, knocked from his perch on my shoulder, grumbled from a chairback. Wieser leaned her head and shoulders against us both.

"Enough," Ibbot pronounced. "We have more work than time."

We sent word to *Megrite's* shipmaster, recounting my tale of a dead mage on the third ship and insisting on a pause at anchor while protection for the fleet could be portioned out. Ibbot hauled my book from under the bunk, and we set about our task.

≈

After a frenzied night of practice with Ibbot's iron pin, gull feather and sunstone, I threw up my hands when he asked me yet again if I could feel the forces woven throughout the spellwork.

"How does a weather spell feel? Until you can describe how it is supposed to feel, I have no way of telling if I am even casting it."

For Ibbot, despite regaining some portion of his magic, had never sailed these waters in his voyages aboard Kruthe's *Chikoro*. He confessed he had been instructed by Mage Balin on the weather working magic but had no experience performing it. His master guarded power jealously. As mere apprentice, Ibbot suffered through the old man's bragging about safe passages through the Cauldron achieved during his glory days, before his servitude with the pirate slaver.

Furthermore, I dared not press Ibbot too hard, despite my frustration. His wits seemed bound together with a hay whisp. He twitched and fidgeted constantly. Cilliyon sent me warning glances at my every attempt to pry more guidance from him.

I wiped my brow with the back of my hand and took a pull on a cup filled with sweet water the crew had brought. It tasted rich as mead. I thought of the sour murk my fellow slaves still endured. "Again," I said, and raised the sunstone and iron.

Some hours later, I took a turn around the deck to test my effect on the wind. Ibbot and Wieser walked beside me. The crew, we could see, wasted no time in idleness. Making ready for the hazards to come, Ibbot said. Some men worked securing iron straps about the masts, others tamping tarred shreds of rope into crevices between the planks. Ibbot pointed out the men in the rigging who hauled up smaller canvas to secure above. "Storm sails," he said.

A few seamen fished. The cargo of slaves continued to emerge onto the deck for feeding in groups as on *Galgen*. Once fed, they were relegated below each group in their turn.

How many more slaves would sicken and die, and be cast away in the dark of night, before I girded myself to brave the strait?

Aye, and how many folk would die, sunk and drowned, if I failed at guiding the ships through the treacherous passage?

Every last soul would be lost.

I squared my shoulders, sought a clear mind, and faced into the breeze on the bow. Methodically, I freshened and steadied the gusts, until ropes slapped the masts in rhythm and sailors leaned into the wind as they walked on the deck behind us. Ibbot worked his fists as he watched, clenching and releasing them in turns, with his trousers whipping about his legs.

"Now abate," he said.

Reversing the spell eluded me for some time. I had to dismantle it bit by bit, from the inside, so to speak, always in danger of losing my place in the strands of magical web I had woven. Because of the risk of loosing chaos, the power must be withdrawn with even greater care than that taken as it was cast forth.

By the time I managed to gentle the offshore breezes to their previous lightness, my head pounded. Whatever lurked deep in my mind stirred and writhed before settling. How could I hope to calm a tumult of waves, divert lightning strikes and focus my inner vision on the water channels between the cliffs, all at the same time? The vessels must not stray from the deeper path, for once in the shallows they would be dashed to shards on the rocks. I had seen the map that tortured Ibbot, now knew the hazards in full measure. I was afraid.

A glance at Ibbot spoke that he shared my fear. He signaled a return to the aft cabin.

Once inside, away from all the ears that craned toward us as we spoke Mercedish, he gnawed his knuckles and stared at me.

At length he said, "The shipmasters will refuse to linger here overlong."

I sank onto the bunk next to Cilliyon. Wieser laid her head in my lap.

"Did he not do well on deck?" Cillyon asked, looking at us each in turn.

He grimaced. "Not near well enough."

"I need time, Ibbot. How fast am I supposed to be able to learn skilled weather working of this sort? You said yourself you have never done such, and you were apprenticed for how long?"

"I see your efforts. You strive hard, but I see it will not be enough, or soon enough. You cannot do what must be done. The slavers will run out of patience before you achieve proficiency."

I blew out a breath. "What would you have me do? You cannot help me overmuch, so you say, because not enough of your own magic has returned to you. So what else is before us as a choice?"

"Have you considered making our escape to shore and seeking some other cargo of slaves to liberate? These are hardly the only ones. Another load may prove more feasible to rescue."

I was shaking my head before he even finished. "These slaves kept me alive. And more: safe from being cast overboard. Mute they may be, but they are wise. If you and I and Cilliyon flee, what will the ship-masters do? Attempt the passage without a weather mage at all?"

"They'd be fools to do so. And, if we do sail on and you die, along with all the rest of us, who is going to free any other slaves around the world?"

Cilliyon spoke in her quavery voice. "What *would* the shipmasters do, though? If we disappear. Would they sail back the way they've come? Choose another destination?"

"How can we guess? Their cargo is bespoke, they bear conse-quences if they fail to deliver. There is risk in remaining at anchor, too. Ships which stop to replenish their water barrels here take pains to accomplish it as fast as possible. The folk along this shore despise outsiders. When ships overstay the span of time they will tolerate, some of the tribes have been known to send warriors out to attack."

Cilliyon took my hand. Hers might have looked gnarled, but it felt as smooth and soft in mine as ever. "Then why would you suggest sneaking to shore to face them, if they are bent on killing strangers?"

"We would send the crow over for a look-see, ridden by your hero," Ibbot snapped. "That way we can avoid their villages ashore."

"And how would we take that look? I thought there was no more mallowmeld?"

Ibbot jerked up his chin in the tense silence that followed. After a moment, he drew a small pouch from inside his tunic.

"Ah, I see. I think instead, I will ride Gargle ahead to view the Demon's Cauldron. Or at any rate, that is what we will tell the ship-masters. I will report impossible conditions, owing to even more severe storms than usual, and require them to choose another course and destination."

"To stand any chance of being believed, our doddering master mage must be the one to tell the tale. Or rather, must accompany me to the shipmaster here, who speaks Scytheran."

"But Judian won't have to go to the other ships, will he?"

I cocked my head. "Yeganil was the common tongue on *Galgen*. And the *Megrite* crewmen understood me when I arrived aboard. I do not know anything about the third ship, even her name."

"*Labotel*," Ibbot answered. "She sails under a Yegan flag as well. But the crews use signals to communicate amongst the vessels. In whichever language fits the need."

His tone had grown vague, musing. He stroked a finger on his chin while Cilliyon and I exchanged a look.

"Come to think further on the matter, perhaps it would be best for Judian to go to each of the other shipmasters to convey our message. He can be dispatched in a longboat, as he came across to us."

Cilliyon growled low and squeezed my hand. "Why should he, if time is critical and the message can be sent by signaling ship-to-ship?"

"He can be so compelling. I'm sure you agree. Now that he is fluent in Yeganil, why shouldn't he go convince them in person? Harder to ignore."

"Easier to toss overboard, too, if deemed useless," I put in. Wieser flattened her ears. Although she did not growl as Cilliyon had, she lifted a lip.

"You must strive to be especially compelling, then, so they see they need you still. Let us look on the map and see where we will propose to sail instead."

Yes, let's do that, I thought. *While I try to suss out what you are up to now.*

It appeared we had sailed to the very end of the earth. No welcoming harbour opened her arms to us anywhere close to where we rode at anchor. Weeks away north up the coast, modest bays here and there boasted small ports of call. "Insufficient for three ships at once," Ibbot pronounced. "Too shallow, as well."

On beyond the hazards of the strait, which lay only days away now,

I saw an expansive deep water harbour that rivaled Bale Harbour at home, at least from its depiction on the map. If we could only pass through the strait, we might be able to liberate the entire cargo of slaves at such a place.

Staring at the scribbled waves and seaside cliffs, I began to nod off, eyes aching. When had I last slept? I could not recall.

Cilliyon drew me away from the map toward the bunk. "Let him rest, Ibbot. Tell the shipmaster he's off on Gargle looking over the passage."

Ibbot's face darkened and his twitching resumed. Cilliyon shot him an exasperated glance. "Just because you cannot sleep, doesn't mean he shouldn't either. And look at him, he's half-starved, besides. Maybe he can do the magic better after some rest. You've kept him up all last night and today as well."

He grunted and paced to the door. "Where is the cursed bird, anyway?"

"Probably atop the mast," I said. "That's his usual perch. Go with him, Cilliyon, and call him to come in. He can't very well be believed to be flying to the strait if he's in plain sight above."

"I have not been out of the cabin the whole voyage, Judian. He's told them I am too frail and do my magery from here."

Just as much a prisoner as I had been, it seemed. Better fed, perhaps. "Ibbot. Take Wieser. He'll come down for her." I dropped my head onto the ticking.

"But he won't for me, I suppose. Come, dog." She went, because I raised my arm and pointed to the door. As soon as they passed the threshold, I let my arm fall heavily to the mat.

What I wanted most was sleep, but this might be my only chance to speak to Cilliyon alone, if she could not leave the cabin and Ibbot slept so little. I forced my eyes open as the lids drifted downwards.

"Quickly. Do you think Ibbot is too unraveled to plan with us sensibly?"

Her lips twisted. "He is agitated all the time. Behaves very oddly but does make sense when he speaks."

"Oddly?"

"Pacing and quivering. Jumpy at the least thing."

I had seen his ceaseless fretting. "Does he talk in his sleep?"

"Mutters and moans, more like. The Terrors he showed before have lessened. To me, it's as though he is at a loss without his magic. And can't reconcile himself to depending on you."

Wieser came back in with Gargle riding on her withers. Ibbot closed the door behind him. He saw I was not asleep, and complained at once that if I needed rest I'd best get on with it.

"Look in my book while I do that very thing, would you?"

"Look for what?"

"The spell Lichan translated for me. The one I used on *Moon Road* to calm the storm that beset us. I lost his translation, but you could do it anew while I sleep. It was to raise a fair wind."

His brows drew down. "I have not seen such a one in its pages."

"It is written in Yeganil. The back half of the book. It could help me now since I know I can cast it. I looked for it in the sheets you sent me, but it wasn't there."

He pulled the book to him and opened it as he settled on the stool. I closed my eyes but could hear him rattling each page he turned and sucking his tongue. Though exhausted, I could not sleep through his noise.

"It's the spell I worked that enabled you to find me. You struck me dumb afterwards. You must recognize its sigil."

"Your book confounds me. I have read lore books and grimoire. This one is something uncanny—I can be certain I saw a given spell, then never be able to unearth it again. And why does it contain passages in Yeganil and Scytheran?"

I sat up.

Whatever lurked in my mind shifted a bit, as though leaning in to observe more closely. I tried to block it with my thoughts.

"You said my book impressed none of the mages at the Pit. Yet Gargle led us to a room where it appeared a mage had been studying its pages."

"I don't understand and perhaps the masters did not either, why your mother's low magic healing spells should be within a tome of higher magery. Writings from the Lohr Archipelago may be logical, since you say her people came from there. But why high magic spells in Yeganil and Scytheran? Nautical lore from around the world? It makes no sense."

"I don't know the reason. She died when I was young. My da said she told him I must be the one of her children to have the book once I came of age. To be honest, I have long wondered myself how the book seems to know what I seek and yield it up." In Lunenhelm, when it gave me what I needed to seal the cut miner's wound. Or, acting to prevent discovery of a spell to bind Ibbot to my will when the book judged I should not do so? Then show me a sleeping draught that kept him warm and alive in the mountains to thwart my ending of him? Could a book of magic be a mindful thing? But I only received the lore book after the encounter in the cliff caves of Merced, so the mages there would have known nothing of it as a reason to pursue me.

Did that confirm I had strong magic in me apart from the book's power? "You said once the other mages fear me."

He did not welcome the change of topic and sighed heavily. "The Sending which came to Mage Balin did not state it so baldly. But I could see between his words. For you to have obstructed them at the siege and then in Merced's harbour suggests unexpected magic in you. They fear your ability and crave to know your purpose."

Cilliyon placed her hands over mine. "And do they fear him all the more now, since he foiled them again by rescuing you?"

"Perhaps," Ibbot muttered.

"Is it really fear?" she persisted. "Or is it simply anger, at what he has done to frustrate their ambition?"

He fixed her with a flinty stare. "The cabal does not take a benign view of interference with their aims. That much is evident, is it not? Few have ever attempted to defy them in anything. Those who have tried have paid a price."

I said, "Tell me more about that price."

He balled his fists on the spread pages of my book. "You have seen some who paid. The doomed souls at the Boundary."

The line of tattered stick-men flashed in my memory and I gripped Cilliyon so hard she flinched.

"What?" she said. "What are they? You saw them in the Barrens?"

Unable to speak for shaking, I turned to Wieser and knelt beside her to sink my fingers into her ruff. Gargle lit on my arm, though he did not offer any comfort. He cocked his head and stared a challenge.

"There is something I must tell you, before we face the coming hazard." I said, to neither Ibbot nor Cilliyon directly. "Something I carry in my mind from the Pit. Can it be that some mage has attached himself to me—is watching me and able to act through me?"

Ibbot rose and took hold of my jaw. He tilted my face up and looked keenly into my eyes. "When did you begin to feel this?"

"When we fled through the arena with the blood moon. You said the mages were casting fierce magic there." I wanted to turn away, evade Ibbot's searching gaze. Or what was inside me wanted to, because I no longer felt certain that my urges were my own.

"What action has it taken? Or caused you to take?"

"When I demanded to be taken to *Megrite*, I let fly a bolt of black fire. But I didn't cast it forth intentionally. It seemed to be from—*whatever* is in my mind, crouching there." I shook my head out of Ibbot's grip. "But I cannot be sure." I paused and swallowed. "Can you? You have seemed to know my thoughts at times. What can you sense of this … presence?"

"I cannot sense it. If you say you can, I believe it is true. Something could have attached to you, followed you from that place. Not a mage, though." He rubbed his lips a moment. "This could be to our advantage. Or it could make matters worse."

"How?"

"How could things be worse?" He barked a laugh.

"No. How could some ether or spirit attach to me, if it's not the mind of one of the mages." I reached back in my memory. "Mages have sought me since I fled Fort Hasseron. I have felt them questing, but it is a subtle touch on my thoughts. This is different. It is coiled within me, watching. Waiting. Magic stirs it."

He closed his eyes before he spoke. "There are more worlds than the one we see about us. The realm of the dead, of course, but many others as well. When master mages work the most potent of their spells, they call forth … aids from these other worlds. Servants, in a way, who are bound to do their bidding. But it is dangerous, because if not bound precisely, the servant may slip the bindings and escape. Loosed in our world, they can do great harm."

My heart seemed to pump ice water for a few beats. "What are these servants? Demons? Shades of the dead?"

"I do not know. Only a few of the cabal dare to cast the dark magic that calls them from the other realms. That craft is rarely used and is feared by many of us."

"Feared because—?"

His voice came hollow and bleak, his eyes still closed. "So difficult to bind. So ravenous if they break free …"

"Ravenous." I did not like the sound of that. "What do they consume?"

"The summoning mage, from what I have heard. And then other souls, encountered as they roam free in the world."

"How could such a thing be carried within me, and yet not have consumed my soul?"

He shook his head. "I do not know."

With a sudden prodding from the presence in my mind, I blurted, "You know more than you are saying. When we hid in the turnip wagon, you threatened me, said you could call forth dark and terrible things, nameless horrors."

Ibbot's eyes flew open, but he did not speak.

Cilliyon gasped. "Is Judian possessed, is it like when he rides Gargle? Is some spirit riding him?"

I waved her silent. Continued staring at Ibbot.

Reluctantly, he said, "I have learned to call forth only the least of these servants. Petty things. The powers of the beings summoned by masters in the Stronghold are far beyond my ability to call or control. Yet you, little better than a novice, bear such a one without any consequence? This baffles me."

"I am not sure there is no consequence."

"You are yet alive."

Yes. I cast my mind back to the arena, the blood moon overhead and the whisperings and chants issuing from mouthless stones … and pressed my forehead to the top of Wieser's head, drawing strength from her. Then I stood and faced Ibbot.

"Teach me how to use its power."

"Believe me when I tell you, I do not know how! This is nothing that will be in your book—despite its pages' strange shifting magery This is the Dark Lore. Only a few down the ages have ever been versed in it."

"There is power in my squatter, I can feel that. If I can control it, we might use it to help us survive the strait. That is what you meant, I think, by suggesting this could be to our advantage."

"Recall, also, that I said this could make matters worse? I do not know how to teach you to quell its will, and subourn it to your own ends. You have not come by it in any usual way, with it constrained through spellwork. This was a calamity which seized upon you as we fled the Stronghold."

A rap on the cabin door broke the ensuing silence.

"If yourselves please, sirs—er, mages. The shipmaster sees bonfires on shore. The tribes there are telling us we have tarried too long. How soon are we leaving?"

CHAPTER FORTY

All eyes in the tiny cabin gazed on me, Gargle's and Wieser's, too. *By the gods, why did I ever wish to travel the wider world?* For, yes, I had set out from Merced to avoid the retribution of mages, but I'd also left my home eager to explore beyond the confines of what I thought to be a small life. No more than a foolish child's longing for adventure, that desire seemed to me now.

Since no one else chose to speak, I answered the boy at the door. "Tell the shipmaster to make ready. Signal the other vessels to do likewise. When the tide favors departure, we will sail on."

Retreating footsteps told me the messenger was on his way. I faced Ibbot. "How long before the tide turns?"

His eyelid resumed quivering. "Evening, moonrise."

"Then I must concentrate on discovering more about my squatter." I rummaged in the pouch of herbs at my waist, seeking the black leaves I could chew to forgo sleep.

"How?" Cilliyon bleated. "How can you hope to control such a thing?"

"It seems I am controlling it now, in some fashion. My soul feels right enough. Still mine, at any rate." I found the packet I wanted and plucked a few leaves from the folded paper. They tasted tart indeed.

"You do not understand the dangers," Ibbot insisted.

I cut across his words. "I understand I have not come by this presence in the usual way. But to some degree I have sequestered it within my mind and it has crouched there quietly for months now. I must be exerting a kind of suppression of it, if it has not yet devoured my soul during an unguarded moment."

"Your soul ..." Cilliyon sat heavily on the stool Ibbot had vacated.

I tugged at an earlobe. "I must spend some time looking within, I think. Trying to feel where I leave off and it begins."

Glancing at Cilliyon's face, drawn tight with worry, and Ibbot's incessant twitches, I decided to seek solitude outside the crowded quarters of the cabin. Short of clambering up to Gargle's favored perch atop the mast, where to find a quiet place on deck where I could consider things undisturbed?

The bow would serve as well as anywhere, I decided. Out of the way, for the most part, of scurrying seamen making ready to sail. I strode there, with Wieser at my side. Gargle stayed in the cabin to lend credence to the tale that he was away scouting ahead by magical flight. I would stand at the rail, pretending to watch through his eyes by magery.

For a man like myself, who prefers doing and going to time spent in reflection, little came to light from my solitary pondering. I tried mightily to look within and envision some sort of demon-creature curled up in a corner of my skull. I felt only my own thoughts, with the continuing sense of division. A shadow mind. It was as if I talked to myself, addressing some separate portion of my own thoughts. Rather than escort some demon into my head or spirit, what happened seemed to be the tempest of Stronghold spellwork severed a part of me from another part of me. Or awakened some part I had not known, but that was still me.

I could not know if any of this was correct, or even if I should be reassured by a divided mind as opposed to an occupied one. But if correct, then sadly I did not possess some untapped source of power I could use in our current predicament. The force I sensed would instead, most likely, be a reflection of my own magic gift.

Since the portioned-off part had shown it could strike out unexpectedly, I must be ever vigilant. The division could still be some queer contagion of the Dark Lore Ibbot mentioned. Which suggested I could only find a cure for my sundered mind by learning Dark Lore from a Scytheran Master Mage.

I wanted nothing to do with them, forevermore. I would sooner live on as I found myself now. For as long, or as short, a time as that might be.

I turned to go, supposing I might as well return to the cabin and study weather working with Ibbot, as the test of skill would come all too soon. I made my way aft, past the circles of squatting slaves on deck. As usual, they waited to be fed, some of the last groups of the waning day. For the first time since we sailed from Ulfar, slaves took note as I passed by, following me with their eyes, turning their heads and craning their necks. All of them. I had never shared the hold with these slavefolk on *Megrite*. A few even reached out to touch my feet as I passed, patting in the three-fold way common to them. Wieser wagged her tail as some petted her, too. Seamen distributing the tubs of gruel snarled at the slaves and kicked their hands back.

"Stop," I said. "Leave them be." These sailors did not appear to understand my words but ceased kicking when I scowled and shook my head sharply. To the slaves, I inclined my head and touched my lips three times.

One man, who I took to be his circle's leader for the day, rose to his feet. He touched his forehead with one fingertip, in the center just above his brows, repeating three times. Then, he spread two fingers wide, and tapped my forehead thrice, pressing a finger just above each of my eyes. He held the V of his fingers in front of my face, brought them together snug against each other, and repeated the three-fold gesture, this time pressing his fingers to my chest, over my heart. He looked at me expectantly, so I repeated the series of gestures. He nodded, flicked a glance landward, and sank into a squat with his spoon at the ready.

Now my mind truly reeled, and both portions of it, too. In all the months at sea with them, I had never experienced an exchange like this with the mute cargo of folk. Did the slaves have some sense of my inner dilemma? Of one another's inner workings as well? If so, how could I use it to warn them of the coming peril and my inadequacy?

Confess my original desire to find some way to free them, but all gone awry now?

The slaves on deck commenced eating, no longer paying me any mind. I continued to the aft cabin, Wieser alongside. On the way, I determined I would not tell Ibbot I had concluded my squatter was a shadowy part of my own mind. He seemed more awed by the possibility that I was controlling a creature summoned by Dark Lore, albeit my passenger by accident. That awe might serve me.

I did wish to know if the slaves in *Megrite's* cargo had ever taken any notice of Ibbot during the voyage. I asked him as soon as I shut the cabin door.

"No," he answered, "never. Why would they?"

I told him the group on deck had watched me walk past them and reached out to touch me. I did not describe the further details of the exchange, that which puzzled me most. Perhaps I would say on, once I had time to think more about what it could mean.

I gathered the sunstone, iron pin and gull feather. "Let's begin again. You can tell me if I've managed to hone the cantrip so it flows."

My intention was to practice until moonrise and the shift of tide, when the fleet would weigh anchor and set sail. The only interruption I allowed to our work was while we fell upon a heaped tray of food brought at dusk. Boiled eggs—still live hens aboard after all these months—cured meat and a strange sour fruit Ibbot insisted I eat. "It keeps your teeth from getting stuck in ship's biscuit and pulled out of your head," he said as he pressed it on me. It had better do something useful, I said, as I almost preferred the flavourless gruel I had grown accustomed to on *Galgen*. Almost.

Ibbot and I emerged onto the deck in the moonlight, Gargle riding on my shoulder to demonstrate he had returned from his magical flight. In truth, Cilliyon reported he had slept the afternoon away while I had been out of the cabin earlier, waking in time to gorge on some of our eggs. He did not disdain the sour fruit, and he would have eaten all of my meat if I hadn't caught him and snatched it away.

Wieser proved a good deal more mannerly in waiting for her share, so I made a point of giving her more. Gargle watched me sidelong, ominously silent. He seemed to still be sulking as we came out of the cabin.

Once out in the freshening breeze, we could see the glow of bonfires scattered across the high ground ashore. Ibbot gestured to the orange that rimmed the hills and said, "So many are gathering. I hope they see us preparing to depart. Clear enough we have pushed the tolerance of these tribes."

No chance of him slipping away to the land, with or without Cilliyon and me, with so many hostile eyes watching the ships? I did not ask if he felt regret now, that he had no escape of the treacherous strait yet left open to him.

Ibbot and I spent hours roaming the deck, once the sails filled and we were underway. We took up positions at the rail to starboard, then abandoned that post and crossed to port. Gargle fluffed his feathers and squawked irritably on my shoulder, in between poking my neck with his beak. My own ire rising, I pushed him off and sent him circling above to the top of the foremast. Abrasive cawing poured down from his high perch. I stalked to the bow, Ibbot trailing.

My task weighed on me. I must develop a sense of the currents that bore the ship along where a shipmaster could safely steer her. The wind which served to belly the sails was merely a portion of what carried a vessel from here to there, Ibbot told me. I had heard of these roadways or paths in the ocean before I ever boarded a ship, and seen tracery on maps while at sea that showed the route of each. Some were wide and placid, others narrow and frenzied, rather like broad rivers and rushing rapids on land, but within the immensity of the sea. Master Mages could alter the paths, as Mage Balin had done to bring *Moon Road* into Kruthe's clutches. What I needed to learn was how to send my mind into the depths to grasp the writhing current that passed through the Demon's Cauldron. Without a mage's steady guidance, the chaotic surface waves, driven by the endless storms, would carry a vessel onto the crags. The magery I struggled to learn would fix the ship's path to the deeper current where safety lay.

While, at the same time, I must labor to deflect the fury of lightning and gale that plagued the churning waters between the cliffs. I beseeched the gods to keep their eyes, and aid, turned my way.

"Tell me you begin to feel it," Ibbot begged.

"Saying doesn't make it so." I hunched my shoulders and leaned my elbows on the railing. "I can feel only the motion of the ship riding the waves. For a wonder, it is not making me puke this time. Perhaps I still have my sea legs, eh?"

"That is not enough to save us."

"Leave me be for a bit and stop your chatter. I want to try something." I waved him off until he paced a dozen steps away.

"What do you want to try?" he called into the wind.

"Be still. Something dark." Turning away from the alarm in his gaze, I straightened my back.

I drew my moonstone pendant from the neck of my tunic. Perhaps that, rather than my heart, had been what the slave meant to indicate by touching my chest earlier. Next, I felt about in my belt pouch for Gargle's feather, carried since the core of the mages' Stronghold. On an impulse, which I could trace to the separate part of my mind, I plucked my obsidian knife from my boot and held it with the feather.

As I had been taught by Annora long ago in Merced, I set my intention to focus the magic. My need: to sense the current that carried the ship, its depth and breadth and speed. My pendant gleamed faintly, reflecting the moon's light. Then, as I held it aloft to be bathed by the mist of seaspray, it began to glow from within. I had used my stone in the dim hold of *Galgen* to read the messages sent by Cilliyon and Ibbot. Now I used it to read the night-dark sea as it rose and fell beneath the bow.

I passed the knife blade and feather before my eyes, touched them to my brow as the slave had touched his fingertips there, and extended my arm to hold them just beyond the shimmer of the moonstone. I closed my eyes and chanted the words of a low-magic spell to meld a union of spirit. An old magic, to join a rider to his horse, a hunter to his hound.

I waited.

The hiss and splash of waves against the hull became a sensation instead of a sound. My flesh tingled with it, my breath rose and fell with the sea. I licked my lips and savoured the salt. Silently, Gargle alighted on my forearm, still held outstretched toward the ocean before us.

Gradually, my divided mind began to unfurl and intertwine, sharing the motion of the waves as though it was my beating heart. Tentative at first, then with a rush, I reached out with my reunited awareness, eyes still shut, and found I could—at last—feel the water road. The current ran broad and strong. Eagerly, I searched for the depth of it, casting my mind below the moon-silvered surface. The blackness there was as ink dark as the caves where kavsprit dwelt in the mountains of home. Were there suchlike creatures who lived below and breathed water? Could I find them and entreat them to aid me as their land-dwelling brethren had helped me before, when they gifted me with my obsidian blade? But I could not sense the end of the dark beneath, for it was too vast and featureless. Perhaps there was no bottom at all? Black pressed in on me from every side, from above and below … which way was up, to the ship, to the moon? Panic beset me; I might become lost here forever …

I blew out a deep breath as I fled back to the restless wave crests, it seemed I had forgotten to breathe while I plumbed the depths. My heart thundered like storm breakers. I gathered my wits and cast my mind's eye out beyond our tiny ship, out toward the horizon.

The current stretched away from us, the water within its confines somehow different than the expanse of sea to either side. Not different in color, or scent, or sound or any other sense I could name, but the feel of it in my mind utterly distinctive. I could also sense the other two ships following the path, sailing behind us in the night. I had succeeded in joining my sundered mind and sensing the current we rode. I drew a ragged breath. I knew I did not have it in me to do more now.

Spent, I lowered my arms and sagged against the rail, my forehead resting on the damp wood. Gargle clambered to my shoulder, gently for a wonder, and did not administer the customary jab in the neck to make his presence known. Ibbott rushed to my side.

"What have you done? You look only half here." He tugged on my elbow when I did not look at him. Gargle flapped and lunged at his hand.

I lifted my head, to find him sucking his knuckle where Gargle's beak had scored it. "I have done what I was trying to do. I feel the current. I still feel it, carrying us on."

"You used the servant within, didn't you! Fool. Do you not believe me about the dangers? See how it has sapped your spirit, you can hardly keep your feet—I should have prevented you. You cannot know the nature of what you are harbouring."

"Stop your fussing, you sound like an old scold. I did what I had to do." I bent to restore my knife to its sheath, head spinning enough that it took a couple of attempts. I stowed the feather and my moonstone. How could I do the rest of my tasks through the strait if just this much left me so enfeebled?

"Cilliyon will be worried," I said as I turned aft. "Back to the cabin."

One of the slaves stood on the deck by the nearest mast. He inclined his head, so I did the same. Ibbot appeared to think I had started to fall over and grasped me round the waist.

"Leave go." I looked into Ibbot's eyes. "You don't see him, do you?"

"See who? Are you addled?"

"A slave stands before the mast, just there." I pointed.

"No one is on deck with us."

The slave lifted his hand to touch his chest three times, raised it farther to press fingertips to his forehead. I did the same but spread my fingers to touch myself above each eye, as I had been shown earlier. Again, he slowly nodded. He sank into the crouched position with his hands crossed over his mouth, the same position adopted by the slaves in *Galgen's* hold whenever I used my moonstone's light. And he vanished, as though he was a candle flame blown out by a puff of breath.

"A Sending. He was a Sending. That's why the slave woman in the shipmaster's cabin understood what I was when I appeared there as a Sending, don't you ken?"

"Is he still there?" Ibbott said carefully.

"No. Stop looking at me as though I've taken leave of my wits. I don't know why you couldn't see him, too."

"I'm still somewhat wan as far as magical perception goes. But how is it we never suspected the slaves were capable of having such skills?"

"I lived cheek by jowl with them for months, gaining only the barest understanding. The Sending stood upright before me though, and below in the holds there is not enough room for any of them to stand fully upright, so that is puzzling. But he was some manner of Sending. I'm sure of it. How else could he vanish?"

"Has it occurred to you that your squatter, emboldened by your addressing it and entreating its aid tonight, could appear to you now in familiar form, as one of the slaves?"

I decided to keep close my conclusion that I bore no squatter. "Why? To trick me in some way to set it loose? Why take the form of a slave and not some ferocious and horrifying beast?"

He raised his shoulders. "If I knew more, I could tell more. Let's get you a chance to lie down and rest. We still have much to accomplish before sailing into the mouth of the strait."

I allowed him to lead me aft, with Gargle hopping along behind. I turned my head as we passed the place where I had seen, clear as clear, the slave standing on the deck planks. Only empty air remained in the shaft of moonlight there.

CHAPTER FORTY-ONE

The shipmaster pestered us with messages from his chart room as days passed. I consumed my every waking moment with practice and left it to Ibbot to placate him. When he returned from answering yet another summons, he cracked his knuckles and paced until I could ignore him no longer.

"What?" I slammed my book shut.

"He demands a heading, a *precise* heading for entering the strait. He fears for his fleet, and evidently you and I do not inspire confidence."

"You cannot provide this?"

"He insists the master mage come before him and point out the exact safest path on his map."

I turned to Cilliyon, in time to see the last vestige of color drain from her face. Her skin already bore little enough tint due to her months of confinement in the cabin. She looked like sun-bleached bone.

I scrubbed at my chin with the back of a hand. "Bring me his map and I'll make a mark on it. You can carry it back to him and say the master must not be interrupted further, as he is making urgent preparations."

"What do you think I've been telling him? It's gone beyond that now."

"Come, Cilliyon, I'll show you on this map, and you go and mark the shipmaster's in the same place." I pulled our copy of the map from between the pages of my lore book.

"I cannot go. I do not speak Scytheran. He's bound to ask me something about it, to explain the choice or reassure him."

"Ibbot did the talking when you came aboard, didn't he? He can give any answer required."

"Judian, you must come, too. Please. I can only keep heart if you are with me. Say it takes you both to bring me, due to my frailty. Carry me up in a chair."

"Very well. Ask them to send a straight-backed chair, Ibbot. I'll refresh her glamour so she is absolutely ancient in appearance. You might contrive to develop a raspy cough, Cilliyon. Your eyes look quite rheumy already. Come here and see, I'll show you where to point."

"Do you know what the heading needs to be?" she asked, leaning over my shoulder.

A few days before, my answer would have been that anyone's guess equaled mine. But after my spellwork, melding with the sea in the moonlight, I *felt* where the channel entered the strait, how she angled between the cliffs, the path to keep only deepest water under *Megrite*'s hull.

Now that I had thus joined myself to the vastness of the ocean, was I destined to an everlasting hunger for her, never to be at peace on land again? I remembered Mage Balin transfixed on *Moon Road*'s deck, and the snoring mage in the port inn ...

"It is here." I placed a fingertip on the drawn waves. "See how this spot is closer to the northside cliffs? But not any nearer than I show you, there are reefs beneath."

Ibbot stood still at last, staring, face unreadable.

I said, "Send for the chair. This stool won't do to carry her. Jump to, go on."

Cilliyon looked as though she wanted to say something more to me, brows drawn tight together. I waited to hear her speak doubts that I could truly know the safest course and what lay beneath the waves. She turned away instead.

In short order, Ibbot and I navigated the narrow passages, bearing our wizened master on an oak chair. Once admitted to the shipmaster's presence, we settled the chair alongside the chart table. Ibbot straightened and spoke in guttural Scytheran, gesturing the man close.

Cilliyon coughed and held out her arms so Ibbot and I could grasp her elbows and lift her to her feet. She trembled, probably in terror but giving the impression of aged palsy. Her second rattling cough caused the shipmaster to draw back and turn his face aside with a look of disgust. She wiped her mouth with a scrap of stained cloth she fished out of the voluminous sleeve of her borrowed mage robes. Stuffing it away again, she lifted glaring eyes to meet his expression of distaste.

She extended a wavering finger over the map, and her nail scratched briefly at the parchment before settling on the precise spot I had shown her in the cabin. The shipmaster spoke again, extending an ink-dipped stylus to her.

Setting her jaw, she grasped the stylus with a twitching hand. Ibbot put out his hand and took it from her, saying, I imagined, words to the effect that with such shaking as the master suffered, better he should mark the place.

Ibbot made a neat X, under the watchful eye of the shipmaster. The crossed lines lay just a shade too far from the northside headland.

Cold sweat broke on my brow. I felt as though he had drawn the mark on my flesh with a blade. Only a little off but catastrophically wrong. I forced myself to take a breath, and not vent an exasperated sigh. Careless wood wit, was he not watching when I showed Cilliyon? Had he not just seen her indicate the *right* place? More to the point, how now to correct Ibbot's error? For it could not stand. If the ship could be steered on so precise a course as claimed, entry into the strait's waters at the spot he marked would allow the crosscurrent to bear her into hazard at once.

Desperate, I shook my head. I opened my mouth to speak, determined to risk Mercedish even though the shipmaster might know the tongue. Before I could get a word out, Cilliyon gripped the table's edge and lashed out with the flat of her hand to box Ibbot's ear. The stylus flew from his grasp, spattering ink across the shipmaster's face.

The man barked in anger, wiping his eyes clear. Ibbot rubbed the side of his head and did a credible job of cowering. Cilliyon fell back onto her chair, wheezing as though from the effort of her blow. She gestured at me, and when I did not stir myself instantly, pointed her bony finger to the stylus lying on the table, and shoved at my hand.

I took up the implement, hunched away from my irate master, and made a strike through the wrongly-placed X. Next, I made the proper mark, and circled it for good measure. Cilliyon leaned forward to squint at the map and gave a wobbly nod. Without waiting for any response from the shipmaster, she swept her arm to point at the doorway and slumped back in her chair.

The shipmaster, still smearing ink across his cheeks with a kercheif, called out some rough demand. Cilliyon swiveled her head to look at him. She lifted her hand with an effort. She drew breath to speak, grimaced as though she would let fly a curse, but collapsed back with a wracking cough instead. Ibbot urgently shook his head at the shipmaster as we lifted the chair and sped from the cabin.

The pace we kept through the passages winded us both. Ibbot and I set the chair inside our cabin, then helped Cilliyon to rise. I shoved the chair out our door before I shut it tight. Let whoever was told to fetch it do so without disturbing us.

Ibbot rounded on Cilliyon, showing her the swollen ear she had cuffed. "You enjoyed that."

"I did."

I bit back a smile. "So did I, come to that. But what possessed you to think of doing it?"

She shot me a glance with a bloom of amusement. "I saw Mage Balin treat Apprentice Ibbot just so back on *Moon Road*. While I was questioned by Kruthe. I thought an irascible mage must be more common than not."

"I had better luck dodging that old goat, though. Being as he was sightless. And I wasn't expecting your blow!"

"Your map mark was off," I said.

He sniffed. "Not by much, from the correction you made."

"Be your age. It counted enough to place the ship in greater danger. I think Cilliyon's fix of the matter was brilliant. I wonder if he will tell the crew what happened, or let them draw their own conclusions about the ink stripes on his face? And black-ringed eyes?"

That won a grudging smile from Ibbot, and a sunnier one from Cilliyon. I returned to my lore book, with Wieser curled at my feet.

For with my new-forged bond with the sea, I sensed by looking at the map how near we sailed to the treacherous waters. We would reach the maw of the Demon's Cauldron by noon on the morrow.

CHAPTER FORTY-TWO

When night fell, I lit the lamp so I could spend more time studying my book and the spells for weather working. Cilliyon curled on the bed's thin straw mat and made a valiant and finally fruitful effort to sleep. Wieser and Gargle kept vigil with me, each to one side as I bent to my task at the table.

Ibbot sat on the floor, legs outstretched and back to the wall. From time to time, I asked him questions. If I conjured the favorable wind to keep the three ships in the channel, could he maintain it? Fairly certain. Which of these two spells is best for diverting lightning before it strikes? The second, but neither is reliable. Can the path of the current be widened? No. Can he feel the currents again yet, and help me track them? No.

I could feel them. The waves beseeched me, pressing round the hull, making me long to go out on deck to be nearer to their song ...

Finally, he did not respond to a query, and I looked over to see his chin sunk to his chest.

Better he got some rest, I decided, and let him be.

Not long after two bells, my own eyes scratchy and dry with fatigue, I saw the Sending take shape.

The form of a mage, robes of black, but not Mage Balin. Some other then, one from the Pit Stronghold following us across the sea?

He leaned over to observe Ibbot for a moment, as Wieser rose and quietly placed herself between the image and where I sat at the small table.

It—he—turned to face me. The features were quite clear, not filmy or blurred like the image of Ibbot's master in the mountain hut. His expression was, nonetheless, hard to read.

He took a step toward me and spoke. "Who are you? Why do you brave the strait?" He addressed me in Yeganil, but used no formal speech.

When I did not reply, he advanced another step. Wieser stiffened and bared her teeth.

He gestured to Ibbot. "Alone, this one will fail to see you through the danger ahead."

"He will not be alone in the attempt."

The Sending leaned forward. His eyes swept the book open before me, the gull feather, sunstone and iron pin lying on the tabletop. He looked closer at me.

"Where do you hail from?"

"Merced."

"Merced has no mages. You are lying."

I shrugged. "Have it however you like. But I am from Merced, a mage of Merced. Believe that or no, as you will."

He extended a hand toward me, palm out, but so slowly I did not fear he summoned the bright fire. Gargle, Wieser and I held fast, though the tension made my limbs feel rigid as stone. After a short time, he said, "You have been to the Stronghold. You carry the echo of it within you, as does that one."

He was not asking, so I did not answer.

"Something happened to you there …" He trailed off and closed his eyes seeming to sink into contemplation. A moment later, his eyes flew open. "Ah, your magic has ascended. This is a dangerous time for you. Why do you risk the strait?"

"Our course is set."

"No," he said impatiently. "*Why?*"

The better question: Why did I feel compelled to answer him? The urge to respond was terrible strong. Was this some magic he cast my way? I squeezed my eyes shut. "I will free the cargo of slaves when we reach our destination."

"For slaves? You do this to free the bound, who should be nothing to you?"

"These folk may be nothing to you. I do not feel the same."

As I spoke, another Sending appeared at my shoulder. The same slave I had seen on deck after I melded my spirit with the sea. Scant moments later, four other slaves had joined him. All standing, silent as ever, close around me.

The Mage Sending regarded them haughtily. "How do you call these servants to you? They have no speech, I've heard."

"They have a will of their own. And their own magic. Do you not feel it?" While I didn't feel it exactly, I had observed it to be true. And the Sending had claimed he could feel my magic.

He crossed his arms. "It is of no consequence. In order that you might survive a voyage through the strait, we will aid you. But you must first give your pledge to return to the cabal in Scythera."

Could such a bargain be worth the cost? The slaves and my friends, all the ships and seamen, safely through the treacherous waters? All I had to do was trust a Scytheran mage's word and surrender myself to my enemies afterward. I could have asked him then what they wanted with me. Instead, I asked, "Who are you? What is your name?"

"I am Mage Ocelli. I am curious about your book," he pointed, "and I want to know more about how you obtained it and practice the lore within. How you wield the forces."

"Tell me exactly what you offer. Will all three ships pass through unharmed? Will you give me help in freeing the slaves? Keep my companions safe as well?"

"The passage is too hazardous for guarantees. You have undertaken a foolish risk."

"Then why didn't you come earlier, before it was too late to turn back?"

"That one," he indicated the sleeping Ibbot, "impeded us. He escaped, has been elusive. He is not of great importance, so pursuing him has not been a priority. But you, it seems to me, are more interesting."

I wished I wasn't. But he did not suggest, despite my having tipped my hand by claiming Merced as my home, that he knew of my history with mages at the fort and the harbour there. Or knowledge of my part in rescuing Ibbot from the Pit.

"You will help us pass, though? Can you do this, only present here as a Sending?" Now I thought of waking Ibbot, who would have an answer to that question. At that moment, the slave Sendings, still clustered by me, extended their ethereal arms to clasp hands with each other. So doing, they cast a circle enclosing me with my animal guides. The air in the cabin rippled with a warm breeze.

Mage Ocelli frowned. "What is meant by this?"

Since I could not claim certainty, I went with a guess. "We will not require your aid. There is magic enough among us that I need not agree to the requirement you propose."

"Decline our help and invite our wrath. We can as equally interfere with your safety as we could preserve it."

"I will confess, such a threat is more what I would expect from Scytheran mages."

"Remember your choice when you are struck down. Or worse for you, I think, when those who look to you to save them, die as you watch." He commenced to waver in the lamplight and wafted away. The slaves beside and before me did the same, never having looked at me directly even once. Wieser pressed her head on my thigh, and Gargle shook out his plumage and preened with particular care. I stared at my hands, which trembled more than I would want anyone to see.

Ibbot snorted and startled himself awake. "What did you ask? I may have dropped off for a moment."

"You missed a Sending visit from a Scytheran mage. Our situation is more complicated now. What does it mean to say someone's 'magic has ascended' do you know?"

He snapped his head back and it cracked hard against the wall. I feared the sound would wake Cilliyon, but she slumbered on.

"Who was he referring to, you? Ascension of magical ability is an awakening, a release of great prowess. Some never attain it, even the masters."

"He said it happened to me at the Stronghold. How do I know if that is true?"

He shook his head slowly, drummed his fingers on his knees. "It could explain a sense of carrying something with you from the Pit. I feel more ease of mind at the idea of Ascension than the thought of you bearing a Dark Lore servant. It has not happened for me, so I don't know if you yourself can tell. Or if the Sending could tell, either."

"Does the name Mage Ocelli mean anything to you?"

"He gave his name? Willingly? Unusual. There are many mages abroad in the world, none of us would know all the others. I have not heard of him."

"He seemed to be charged with finding you and watching what you were doing. Cilliyon said she believes something has visited while you slept. But this Sending told me you were unimportant. Why follow you then?"

"Retreiving me may not have been urgent, or even desired. Particularly if a Sending could confirm I was destined to die in the strait, since my magical ability is unrestored. The cabal would want to be sure I did not avoid some sort of tragic fate. Vindictive, always."

"He did not seem to know who I was. He did not expect to find me here, I would wager."

Ibbot's lips drew back in a faint grin. "Your role in my escape might be unknown to them. Thus, you may also be thought unimportant. I recommend it, overall. My attempt to gain influence by going to the cabal did not result in success, as you remember."

"Do you think we can surmise he is a low-ranking mage, to be sent on this errand of little consequence? Because I must tell you, I angered him by refusing his aid. He wanted a promise, once saw my book and what I was doing, that I would return to Scythera, to the Stronghold. He said I was interesting."

"For pity's sake, why didn't you wake me? Antagonizing any master mage is reckless."

"I was just about to. Do you think he will return to interfere with us? All I did was refuse his offer of help, since it required a pledge I wanted to avoid. Some of the slaves appeared as Sendings while he and I spoke. They semed to be protecting me. So I declined to make the commitment to return to the Pit. Well, I might have done it in a way that angered him more."

Ibbot shot me a look from beneath furrowed brows. "What do they want of you at the Stronghold?"

"I never got to the point of asking him. It didn't matter once the slaves encircled me. I would have wakened you, but I thought their appearance already made clear I did not have to agree to return to Scythera. Besides, he offered no guarantee that his help would save us. He placed the blame on us for even attempting the strait."

"And if he had pledged to see us through alive? Would you have agreed to go back to the Stronghold then?"

"Ah, I don't know … Could I have any faith in his word? I have come to feel certain in your word, though. And I have a promise I want you to make."

"I thought we might come to this," he said softly.

I ploughed on. "If I die, and you live, will you swear to see Cilliyon delivered either to Lohr Island's temple or returned to her father in Merced?"

He swallowed. "If she and I survive, I will see it done, according to her choice."

"She absolutely cannot fall into the hands of slavers. Wieser must go with her. Gargle will see to himself."

"Help me understand. How is it you believe the slaves can aid us? If their Sendings mean they serve you."

"I wish I knew. My sense is they will aid me more than I aid them, even if I free them. I realize that sounds mad."

"It all sounds mad, Judian." His lips twisted. "We will see who lives."

CHAPTER FORTY-THREE

The restive shipmaster sent a messenger boy to the cabin, demanding the master weather-worker and his two fellow mages stand on the deck by the helm as *Megrite* led the way into the roughening seas. I said I'd sooner Cilliyon remain in the cabin, but she refused to stay below and wonder what was happening.

"If I am going to die, I'd rather see it coming."

A fair request, so we asked for the straight-backed chair again and bore her above to where we would all watch our fate unfold. Wieser settled herself between us, with Ibbot at Cilliyon's other side.

The seamen reported a flurry of inquiries from *Galgen* and *Labotel*, asking how they could keep sight of our sails when the clouds ahead loomed so dark. Shouldn't each ship have a mage aboard, as the one hiding among the slaves on *Galgen* had said? Ibbot translated these overheard missives out of the corner of his mouth as we stood on deck.

I leaned over to say in his ear, "Evidently ship-to-ship messaging has spread my ruse. I think you must use your ability to speak Scytheran to prevent them splitting us up now."

With a deep scowl, he drew the shipmaster aside and spoke to him for a lengthy time. As Ibbot walked back to Cilliyon's side, a sailor was summoned and dismissed. He sped away from the bridge toward the signalman stationed at the aft rail.

"Did you fix it?" I asked.

"For now, because the ship can light a lantern beacon, for the trailing ships to follow. But you must do your best to keep the three ships close together as we sail through."

"Yet more I must do, as if there wasn't already enough." I scanned the sea ahead, noted the foam blowing off the whitecaps. Clouds like clenched fists rose before us toward the heavens. "I'm going to begin by raising the fair wind. Then you will maintain it while I turn to the currents."

His haunted look told me he held some doubt he could support the wind without me. Once I had found the spell in my book, he had practiced it with me so rigorously we breathed in unison while speaking the words. Furthermore, we had no alternative to consider, since I must move on to spellwork with the safest water path. I could not manage both at once. I clasped his shoulder and nodded encouragement.

Cilliyon stirred. "What should I do? Or strive to look as though I'm doing?"

I looked about for Gargle. Atop the mast, as usual. "Hold your arm out, I'll call my crow down. When he alights, act as though you are enspelling him—whisper in his ear. Then we'll send him back on high."

"Where are his ears?"

"The sides of his head, I expect. I've never poked about in his feathers looking, but I know he can hear from my time riding him."

She accepted this, and imperiously extended her arm. Gargle made a point of staring the other way. I crooked a finger at him out of the helm's line of sight; I knew the bird could see us. Calling out a scream like an eagle, he launched himself aloft and circled down to settle on Cilliyon's forearm. She put her lips close to his sleek head and gave a good impression of secretive murmuring.

I saw the shipmaster watching them. His face still bore traces of inkstain.

Leaning over behind her chairback, thus blocking the man's view of Cilliyon and Gargle, I said to Ibbot, "Something occurs to me. You said the slaves are being taken through the strait to work in the Iron-wood forests beyond. Can we obtain a bit of Ironwood to feed Gargle and enspell him to find the place? He can add his magical seeking to ours."

Ibbot turned away to ask the shipmaster, and the order was relayed down the ranks until a young sailor left the bridge at a trot. He returned with an inlaid box the size of my palm, of exquisite craftsmanship. The Ironwood, nearly as black as the night sky between the stars, had been worked into an intricate pattern with pale strips of birchwood, and formed a carved knot on the lid in the shape of a soaring bird. I regretted the need to damage it but could hardly feed my crow the entire box.

Ironwood earned its name by defying most attempts to chop or saw it, which made the box even more remarkable. Yet I possessed a blade equal to the wood's strength. I slid my obsidian knife from my boot and shaved a bit off the bird's outstretched wing. The shipmaster lurched toward me, to object it seemed, but I finished before he could stop me. Such a fine thing must belong to him, I realized. He likely wished more with each passing moment that he had never accepted substitute mages on the voyage.

I handed the box back to the seaman who had fetched it. His wide eyes as he looked from me to his master spoke his amazement that the shipmaster had not clouted me for harming this item of obvious value. He clutched the treasure with both hands and fled.

The shipmaster grumbled a remark to Ibbot, who replied something sharp, all in Scytheran. Since we balanced on the edge of disaster, perhaps a display of ill-humour could be overlooked for now. As long as it did not interfere.

"Now Cilliyon," I said, "act as though you are telling me to get something out of my herb pouch."

Accompanied by a sharp smack of my wrist, she pointed to my waist. I meekly withdrew the mint leaves to wrap around the slender wood sliver and prepared the packet for Gargle with the proper spell. He glanced sidelong at first, as though he would refuse it. I looked at him severely, taking care to do so out of the shipmaster's gaze. The bird relented, snatched it from my fingers and gulped it down.

I jerked my chin toward the mast and he flapped up and away.

Next, I faced the fair wind spellwork. I began by handing a scrap of parchment to Cilliyon with instructions to press it to her forehead and close her eyes.

Her wrinkled face assumed a suitable expression of deep concentration and I prepared to call wind to fill the storm-rigged sails. The spell being the same one I used aboard *Moon Road* during the gale, it felt as though I relived those harrowing moments. Yet at present, no storm beset us, only heavy seas.

As we had practiced, Ibbot was to recite the spellwords along with me, the better to sustain the wind when I turned my attention to the flowing current path. Our rising, falling unified voices at least stopped the shipmaster's pacing to and fro, as he listened to the chant. It still did not seem that he spoke Mercedish, a relief to my mind, as I needed one less thing to worry about.

I set my intention on expanding the fair wind to encompass all three vessels, so none would lag behind. The fresh breeze followed on, obeying the call of the spell. I prayed Ibbot would be able to sustain the wind, for he looked to be striving hard. I signaled I would drop out, in the way we had arranged. He nodded and spoke on. Sweat glinted on his forehead. Cilliyon continued her pose with the parchment.

I took a step to the railing that stretched across in front of the helm. From my vantage point, I could see more and more whitecaps forming as the chop grew. We sailed close to the mouth of the strait, near enough to catch a glimpse of the jagged cliffs ahead. They rose to either side of the channel, peaks lost in the clouds as we approached. I cast my mind deep over the bow, and at once found the current, still wide and placid in pace, despite the wind-whipped turbulence at the surface.

I began to allow myself to believe we could sail through. The shipmaster barked orders to the helmsman, and seamen clambered above in the rigging, adjusting here and there to keep her true to the course we had marked. My united, or Ascended, mind traveled comfortably along the water's path, guiding the vessels. All exactly as it should be. As I had hoped and prayed.

Yes, the dark clouds ahead roiled amid winds buffeting off the cliff face on either side of the strait. Indeed, as depicted on the map, lightning flashed and cracked. Bolts split the sky with alarming frequency, it was true. But the fair wind carried all three ships onward, while the current flowed steadily ahead. I felt the current's power to draw us past the hazards lying in wait should we stray from the path. Everything seemed to be going well.

So, of course, this was the precise moment everything fell apart.

Sudden shouts in Yeganil erupted from the topmost rigging.

"Rogue!"

"Rogue wave to port!"

"Hold fast! Rogue! Rogue!" And more clamour in Scytheran, other men sounding the same alarm.

Frenzy burst forth all around the deck, barely an instant before a wall of water rose to catch the front quarter, smashing over the rail and scouring the planks of men and tackle. Screams rang as seamen were swept away, torn from the rigging. *Megrite* heeled far over. The helmsman fought desperately to right her. The wave struck and soaked us even though the bridge stood so much higher than the main deck. As the wave broke and receded, the ship seemed to wallow upright. I could see snapped spars dangling, ruined despite their iron bands. Injured men sprawled where they had been dashed against the railing. Other men lay unmoving on the deck, bent and twisted, flung from the high rigging by the savage water.

Cilliyon had been cast from her chair, and lay gasping and coughing on the deck, drenched. Ibbot bent over her, with Wieser nosing at her hands anxiously. More shouts—"Men overboard!"— accompanied sailors scrambling to throw rope-bound empty barrels over the side.

The shipmaster barked an order to the signalman, though I could not understand his words. To warn those behind, lest the following ships ram us before the men in the sea could be rescued? Some might have survived, clinging to the floating barrels. Or perhaps he directed that the other vessels try to save the men in the sea, since *Megrite* perforce sailed on. Such a ship cannot be brought to a halt like a wagon and team. Now crippled by the broken spars, *Megrite* faced a greater challenge in keeping true to course. She had more desperate need of my magic to guide her.

Instead, I leant over Cilliyon with Ibbot, and bade him abate the

324

wind we had just raised. He stood and assumed his conjuring stance while I looked her over quickly. A wide gash above Cilliyon's eye ran with blood. As fast as I could tug it from my pouch, I pressed a square of linen stuffed with spider silk over the wound. She seemed out of her head, mumbling about a mule.

"What mule?" I said, trying to look into her dazed eyes, still rheumy from the spell to make her appear aged.

"Needs its feet picked out. Too dark to see ... I can't see ..."

The shipmaster stood over the three of us, bellowing. I had to shout in order for Ibbot to hear me when I told him to take Cilliyon below. When he gathered her up, I signaled Wieser to go with them. The shipmaster seized my arm in fury and sprayed my face with spittle while he railed at me in a tongue I could not understand. Though knowing the words wasn't necessary, his rage at what had befallen us was all too plain.

I heaved my arm out of his grasp and turned back toward the bow. With my mind, I sought the current's path again, not knowing what else to do. We must keep to the channel or snag the hull on the hidden reefs. Time seemed to slow, the shipmaster's shouts became more thunder than speech, akin to rumbling blows against my ears. I plumbed the waters under the ship with my thoughts, seeking the flow ... feeling the serene oblivion of the sea.

"Shall we send another rogue?" a cold voice asked from behind me.

My eyes snapped open as I whirled about. Three black-robed mages ranged before me, Sendings all. One I recognized as Mage Ocelli, the other two I had never seen before.

The shipmaster still spluttered and flapped his jaws. He did not appear to see the mages, nor did any of the other men rushing here and there on the bridge. The shipmaster reached out to take me by the throat. I knocked his arms away and spat out the spell to take his voice. He staggered back, his hands at his own throat now, and stared at me, round-eyed.

"I warned you, Mage of Merced," mocked Ocelli. "Do you regret your refusal yet?"

A taller, darker mage lifted a hand. "Where should the sea strike next? This ship again, or one of the others?" He gazed at me with iron-grey eyes.

It would accomplish nothing for me to attack them, even if I could summon the burst of dark fire at will. They were only Sendings, and not really standing on *Megrite's* deck planks. But the trio had shown me they could still call forth a rogue wave to smite us, from wherever they stood in truth.

All might be lost now.

Ibbot appeared at the top of the starboard stair, eyes fear-wide and face stark white when he saw who I faced. The third mage pointed at him, and then to a place next to me at the rail. Ibbot stumbled, as though compelled by the mage's gesture, to my side.

"There's far more damage below," Ibbot gasped. "Water coming in. The pumps can barely keep pace, and those men are needed to help restore the rigging, besides."

"Tell the deck officer to bring up the slaves and set them to work the pumps. They will understand what to do, once shown." Ibbot hesitated—or perhaps could not move because of the mage who continued to point at his chest.

Ocelli's lips peeled back from his teeth. "It will not be enough to save you."

The mage who had paused with his hand raised now swept it across in front of me. "The *Galgen*," he said.

Deep within my mind, where my newly forged meld with the sea dwelt, I sensed the spell he cast forth. Felt it seek the waves and gather them like sheaves of grain. He intended to drive the swells over the Galgen and swamp her—I shoved Ibbot toward the signalman. "Quick, he must warn them! Rogue wave!"

Ibbot ran across the deck, the mage's hold on him broken. I sprinted to the aft rail, where I struggled to see *Galgen* on seas turned dark by lowering clouds. Lightning flashed and I picked her out among the waves, as her sails shone for an instant in the bolt's light. I could still sense the rogue wave building, drawing in the surrounding water, climbing.

I tried everything I knew to deflect the burgeoning rogue, to block it, drain it away, spin it up into the clouds. With soul-shattering effort born of desperation, I summoned a bolt of dark fire and flung it across the galloping crests. As far as I could tell, this only joined with the force of the roaring water. The spell he was casting seemed to be snatching my magic from me, dragging my mind into the cold depths. I shouted undoing cantrips, fragments of warding spells, anything to avert the coming destruction and death. My moonstone glowed as I held it aloft, but how could its magic protect the souls aboard *Galgen* from this catastrophe? I'd have flung myself into the waves if I thought that had any chance to help save them. I heard Gargle scream overhead, circling as the mountain of water gained speed and breadth.

Helpless. Helpless to stop this mage-driven magic. I had no understanding of this spell, no knowledge of a way to thwart it, nothing left to try.

I stood gripping the rail and watched the immense rogue he'd created mount higher and race toward *Galgen*. It struck her amidship and rolled her asunder. The pale sails vanished beneath blackness. The force of the wave's blow was so strong, the ship burst out of the current's channel. When lightning split the clouds again, I saw her hull thrust up and then dash in two on crags at the foot of the cliff. Each surge that followed smashed the timbers until no part of the ship hung together. The wreckage was too far away to hear any shouts, to see if any heads broke the surface, if any survivors struggled in the surf. The crew, the slaves who had protected me, all lost. *Labotel* could never sail close enough to the cliffs to retrieve any of them from the rocks or the sea. Straying from the current's safe path, she would meet the same fate on the crags if she even tried.

"Why?" I cried, spinning away from the rail. I stalked back to the bridge.

Ibbot came to stand beside me. The three mage Sendings ranged themselves before us, silent as stones.

"Why," I demanded again. "If you want me so badly, why do you not just *take* me back to the Pit. Why mete out this murder and destruction?"

Mage Ocelli spoke but made no answer. "Do you relent? Are you ready to pledge you will return to us in Scythera?"

Ibbot panted, "They cannot take you. Now you are an Ascended Mage, you must agree to the pact."

I felt an utterly useless mage, Ascended or no. Gargle lit on my shoulder. He ruffled his feathers and made a deep, growling call I had never heard before. He pressed his head against my cheek and I raised a hand to stroke his breast.

The mages had shown me, in as callous a way as I could conceive: I was no match for their power. I could not face the sacrifice of all the souls left on these two remaining ships. I could only believe the three of them would reap as many innocents as it took to accomplish their aim: my pledge or my death with the others.

If my magic came at need, here stood a need unanswered. Whatever talent or gift I posessed, I showed wanting in the face of this. Even the black bolt I ultimately summoned had done nothing but magnify the disaster.

Weary, chilled to my marrow, I said to the three, "See *Megrite* and *Labotel* safely through the strait, free the slaves once we arrive at port … and I give my word to return to Scythera." I closed my eyes and blew out a breath.

"Don't, Judian," Ibbot blurted. He laced his fingers together before his chest. "What do you want with him? The cabal saw no use for him but a few months ago. I tried to give him to them then and they did not care at all!"

Mage Ocelli replied, a smug pleasure in his voice. "The cabal is curious now, youngling. They wish to understand where his power springs from, since it seems it is a place apart. Nothing like for the rest of us."

The tall mage sent an icy look Ocelli's way. "He has interfered. That is not tolerated, no matter how he has done it."

"Nevermind, Ibbot," I said. "What would it serve to cost all these remaining lives for mine?"

I turned away, intent on going below to see how Cilliyon fared, but Mage Ocelli put up a hand to stop me.

"You must do your part to guide the remaining ships through these waters. The risk I told you is true. We will aid you, but we cannot do it all, nor guarantee success."

328

"Your name?" I said, pointing at the taller of the two other mages.

He inclined his head. "Mage Lahar."

"And you?"

The third mage hesitated, but then said, "Mage Rueck."

"Come, then. The ships are still under sail. Let's be about our work, if that is how it must be. I would salvage something yet." I strode toward the bridge rail, nodding as I went to the slaves on deck, working the pumps rhythmically as though they had no doubts about what to do and how.

Turning back, I addressed Lahar and Ruek, who seemed to be of higher status than Ocelli. "Can you restore Ibbot's magic? He will certainly be more help if he is at his former capacity."

The glance that passed between them made me think they could but did not wish to do so.

"If we face dire hazards and cannot pass without the efforts of us all, it is not you Sendings who will suffer if we fail. I cannot keep my pledge to return to Scythera if I am lost to the strait. Give him back what was taken from him. Unless you fear him?"

Lahar scoffed at that idea and gestured to his fellows to draw nearer. They joined hands and chanted in unison, walking widdershins on the pitching deck. They were not troubled by the yaw of the planks, since they were only Sendings and not truly present in the flesh. The naked hope on Ibbot's face as they worked their spell struck at my heart. He wanted his magery returned to him so badly.

The chant grew faster and faster, and suddenly they broke apart and sparking flame shot from their outstretched hands. Ibbot stood rigid as this struck him, it appeared to fly into his body like an arrow shaft.

He held out shaking hands, flexed his fingers and touched his brow, wavering a little. The smile he turned my way was like the sun breaking through after a storm.

"Now, Ibbot, together we will raise the fair wind again." The ship-master scuttled back as I passed beside him, rage and fear in his eyes. I waved a hand and unwound the spell which had gagged him. He choked out what sounded like the worst of curses, but it was of no concern to me. I bade Ibbot set the man about his business, directing the efforts to sail on course and keep afloat.

I looked to the horizon. Lightning cracked and leapt from boiling clouds to smite the heavy seas. If I thought the lightning could harm the three mage Sendings, I would not have had an instant's hesitation about drawing it down on them. As lightning could not burn Sendings, I instead enlisted them to divert it from striking the masts or sails of either ship. "Take care it avoids the seamen as well," I told the mages, noting as I scanned the *Megrite's* rigging that only slaves clambered there, striving to repair the broken spars as though skilled at seacraft. Was the crew all lost or injured?

Ibbot and I called forth the fair following wind. I drew back from the spell to allow him to continue it, preparing to send my mind into the water path for my part. I pressed my palms on the wet bridge rail. Aching with grief for all the lives lost, my focus faltered. Try as I might, I could not bring the current into my awareness, or recognize where the sea path should lead. I shook my head and felt for the iron pin, sunstone and gull feather, to start the casting from scratch.

"Judian, look." Ibbot laid a hand on my shoulder.

I turned my head toward him and saw four slaves mounting the starboard steps. Four more climbed the port stair, one bearing Cilliyon like an offering, with Wieser bringing up the rear.

The slaves walked in front of the trio of mage Sendings, ignoring their fiery gaze. They encircled me, and Ibbot beside me, and stood in silence with eyes downcast. The man carrying Cilliyon continued to hold her gently in his outstretched arms, as though she weighed no more than a babe. The glamour which made her look aged had given way. She looked young and fragile, and terribly pale. Wieser sat at my feet.

Next the group linked arms and bowed their heads.

"What does this mean?" Ibbot asked.

"They wish to help." I touched my lips thrice and turned back to the horizon. I could hear murmurings from the Mages where they stood behind me, outside of the slaves' circle. "Quiet. Keep to your work," I told them.

I took a certain satisfaction from the indignant huff one of the mages vented.

The current nearly rose up to embrace me when I sent my mind toward the depths. No longer obscured, thank all five gods. Or thank the circle of slaves, more like. Despite the seething surface, the current below coursed steadily and this calmed me. I began momentarily to let go my anguish at the losses as well as the pointless fury at my own impotence. Reaching through the vastness of the sea to lead the ships along the safe path, I saw myself as something quite small.

Yet, I felt my use in the wider world. If I had been granted power, its purpose was service to others. I resolved to see my service through to the end. To my end, if that was what must be. I felt too, the hive-mind of the slaves, lending me their strength. They held power, too.

We sailed between the cliffs, lifted and buffeted by the turbulent seas but true to course and driven before the corridor of fair wind Ibbot sustained. Gradually, the sky before us brightened from black to grey to a pale yellow in the west, promising the end of the strait. Only a few more hours and we would reach open sea, the treacherous Demon's Cauldron in our wake at last.

I allowed my awareness to reach up from the depths once more, back to the bridge where I stood. I noted that the three mages did not seem particulary good at deflecting lightning bolts. Some struck the sea all too close to *Megrite*. Irritated, I wondered if this could be due, as Ibbot had said, to the fact that neither of the two spells used for lightning worked especially well. Still, they were supposedly masters of their craft. It was on the tip of my tongue to complain about their proficiency, when the slave holding Cilliyon sank low and placed her carefully on the deck.

Wieser and I were at her side in an instant. At first, I feared she had died from the blow to her head, or the blood loss. But instead, her eyelids fluttered open.

"Judian, there you are, love. They showed me. They took me home with them." She reached up to touch the slave who had carried her. He had risen to his feet and gave no sign he felt her touch or heard her speak.

"I don't understand." Indeed, I feared she was still out of her wits.

"When they came to me. I didn't know where I was or what had happened. I couldn't see. They healed me. And I saw their island. Then the fire on the mountaintop."

I believed she described the same vision I had seen in the hold of *Galgen*, when I first used my talisman for light there. The shipmaster, having suddenly recognized that Cilliyon was not a wizened mage any longer, strode toward us with his mouth open. I raised my hand to show I had no qualms left and would silence him again. He closed his jaw with a snap and turned aside.

I did not think he would make any objection to us leaving the ship as soon as we made port. Delighted to see the back of us, more like.

"How do you feel now?"

"Quite fine, except for a sore head. What's happening? Do I need to act my part?" She looked about. "Where is my chair?"

"Smashed to bits when the wave hit the ship. You remember none of that?"

"No—was anyone hurt?"

How I hated to tell her. "Yes, many. Some washed overboard. The *Galgen* was lost. But now we are nearly through the strait."

"But that's—horrible. The whole ship? All those people? I can't … it's too awful. Please, you are not hurt are you?"

Mage Ocelli interrupted. "We are not through yet. Keep us on course."

I'd had enough of the three of them to last my life through. "Keep the lightning deflected. Do you need Ibbot to help you?" I squeezed Cilliyon's hand and told her to rest easy. Wieser wagged her tail.

I prepared to return to the bridge rail. I had just pushed to my feet, still holding her hand. The hair rose along the back of my neck and I was flung against the ring of slaves by a sizzling crack of bright fire.

A lightning bolt had found me.

CHAPTER FORTY-FOUR

I t seemed I swam in an ocean of light. The solitude enfolded me as my mind drifted. Nothing hurt, there was nothing to fear or strive against. I wafted along the blinding white current, lazily paddling my feet … or what might have been my feet … did I float on my back? My position in the traveling water, indeed my body altogether, did not matter so much as it had used to … I could not guess how much time passed in this way, moving without thought or intention.

What had Ibbot said, about how time passed in the Stronghold? *The river of time does not flow in this keep the same way as outside.* There, under the influence of master mages, time could be distorted. Twisted back upon itself. Yes, he had called time a river. I swam in some river or sea of time where the current bore me along swirls and eddies, downstream and even back the way I had come. It was impossible, but happening to me despite that I believed it could not be.

I gave up any search for meaning. I floated, let the water road take me where it wished. I could not raise the effort to care. If time no longer made sense with its passing, what did? Why should I be concerned?

Abruptly, I felt sharp pain in my wrist. Wieser brought me back to my senses. She bit my wrist, clamped it in her jaws and sank her teeth deep. Tugging me along with each stroke of her legs against the current, she dragged me sidewise, into the shallows.

Oh, let me go, I thought. *You can go on. I'd rather stay here for now.*

My body came gradually awake to the feel of gritty surf, as I tumbled against sand and stones. My leg flared with pain from a heavy blow—but what had collided with me I could not tell. Wieser continued to jerk and wrench my arm. I could suddenly hear again—as evidenced by Gargle's frantic scolding caws beseiging my ears. I choked up what felt like a bucket of seawater.

I supposed I must open my eyes and see where I had cast ashore, if the ocean would not have me. I longed to return to her timeless embrace and sank back toward the waves. Wieser would have none of it, and growled and barked at me feverishly, shoving her snout against my cheek and licking my ear.

I felt more wretched with each breath. I crawled out of the lapping waves, farther up the sand and shingle. My leg felt split in two. After a few moments rest, I rolled over and sat, slumped against a jutting rock.

The breeze chilled me as the sand crust dried on my skin. All but my right shoulder. No chill there, but firery gnawing that grew more savage with each beat of my heart. I craned my neck to see—a charred patch ranged across my shoulder with blisters down my arm. Farther toward my wrist and hand, a scarlet tracery of jagged lines coursed to my palm. I stared, dumbstruck. The lines looked like bolts of lightning, etched in my flesh.

As though recalling a distant echo, I remembered: I had been struck by lightning as I stood on the deck. But that happened in the strait, where was I now?

I staggered as I got to my feet and found my left leg could bear no weight. The lower bones must be broken. I hung onto the rock with my left hand, for I could bear no pressure on my right palm. Wieser stood against me, so I didn't pitch onto my face. The wan sun stood directly overhead, offering no aid to tell east from west. Looking right, I saw breakers and stacks of rock along the beach, with open water glittering beyond. In the surf before me, immense logs tumbled in the waves, cracking into one another and pounding against the rocks. One of these must have struck my leg. Lucky it wasn't my head. Looking to my left, at the far limit of my vision, I could make out the dark cliffs bracketing the Demon's Cauldron. Lightning flashed in the fisted clouds above.

We had made it through, or it had spit me out. What had befallen the others?

Gargle strutted around me, giving me the eye as he grumbled and chuffed.

"I wish one or the other of you could talk," I told him hoarsely, and patted Wieser as I coughed up more water.

He croaked and leapt into the air, winging inland.

I wondered what he was going after, since I was hardly in any shape to follow him wherever he was bound. I sat again, or rather slid down the rock when my leg would no longer hold me. I thought I might soothe my burn. The charred flesh did not pain me, but the blisters surely did, while the red streaks buzzed and ached.

My pouch of herbs and remedies had parted ways with me somehow, either when the lightning hit or when I drifted in the ocean. I felt for my folio: also missing. No talisman moonstone about my neck. With rising fear, I felt for the sheath strapped to my leg. The leather sheath was there, but it was empty. My knife was gone. It seemed I had Wieser, and Gargle if he saw fit to return, but nothing else, not even boots.

I sat, listening to the surf, and the sun eventually showed me west lay to my right once it arched across the sky. North behind me then, south before me. The strait to the east meant I had surely come through between the cliffs. Had anyone else? How could I learn their fate?

The tide was running in. I hobbled up the beach beyond the high-tide mark, using a driftwood branch as a crutch. I dragged along some more driftwood as I went, which I would need for a fire come nightfall. Some of the wood appeared to be planks, not branches. And those planks bore burned edges and scorch marks. Some had been mostly eaten away by flames.

Was this some older shipwreck, or the demise of *Megrite* and *Labotel*?

And what of my Cilliyon, and Ibbot, and the slaves and sailors? My wits came into better use as I prepared a fire ring of stones and laid the kindling. I looked for signs the weather would hold fair, and took heart in a red sky as night crept closer.

The land at my back boasted thick forest, deeply shadowed now as the sun sank. I would need to explore more at daybreak. This might be the place where Ironwood grew, the destination for the slaves and Gargle as well, since I had enspelled him to find it. The logs rolling in the surf could be Ironwood, impervious to the sea's lashing. A few yards away, a fresh water creek gushed out of the woods. Wieser found a shallow pool to lap, while I caught some in my cupped hands. Cool, but not cold.

So, I rinsed the sand off my wrist, where Wieser's teeth had torn the skin. I clenched my jaw and sluiced water over my burned arm, while I wished anew for my pouch of herbs to make a salve. And how would I survive without my obsidian blade? I needed to cut a splint for my throbbing leg.

Gargle's distant caws announced his return, just before full dark. As he came into view I could see a figure following him down the beach. A man, scarecrow-thin, picked his way in the dim light. I recognized the lanky, loose-jointed gait.

"Ho, Ibbot. Over here," I called across the sand. I quickly said the spell to light my fire, so he could see where to tread.

He breathed heavily when he drew near. "Blast that bird, he kept flying too fast for me to keep up! He near poked my eye out, wanting me to get up and follow him. Now I see why. But how came you here? I thought you were surely drowned, if not dead when you hit the water."

"Not dead yet. What's happened? Is Cilliyon with you?" I looked the way he had come, but no one else could be seen.

He hesitated, and I knew. My chest went hollow.

"Cilliyon's dead, Judian. You were holding her hand when you were struck. The bolt passed through you and she bore the force of it. It killed her."

"No." I looked away, the pain of my broken bone and burn nothing now.

"I'm sorry. It must have stopped her heart. The slaves surrounded you on deck and left her outside the circle, as if they knew. Mage Lahar stepped up to look at her and told the others she was dead."

I didn't want to hear more, but he spoke on.

"You were burned and knocked senseless. The strike sparked fires on the deck and everyone was frantic trying to put them out, but flames were spreading fast." He swallowed back something he had been about to say, rubbed his knees in the firelight. "The mages tried to get at you, where you lay. I don't understand how, but the ring of slaves blocked them. Mage Sendings—any of them should have been able to appear within the ring, or pass through. Why couldn't they?"

"Slaves have their own powers," I said dully. I looked at the jagged, etched lines running to my palm. *You were holding her hand when you were struck ...*

He shook his head, looking baffled. "Master mages, though. Mage Sendings obstructed by mute slaves? The slaves all put their hands on you, lifted you up. Through the smoke I saw them carry you to the port rail and pitch you into the sea. Wieser leapt in after you. I thought you must be dead, like Cilliyon. Or were they saving you? The mages cursed us all then disappeared."

I roused myself to ask, "What were you doing while all this happened?"

"Fending off the shipmaster. I seemed to be the last one left he could vent his ferocity on. He had me by my neck at the rail, nearly passed out. I thought I was done for when one of the slaves came and soon a dozen of them swarmed all over him and pulled him away. No matter how he struggled, they held fast and never spoke a word. The ship was listing badly by that time, so I strove to put her right and keep her in the channel."

"And so you got through the rest of the strait?"

"Not alone. It was the slaves. They aided my fair wind and fought the fires. We guided her through the channel, though barely, with so much damage. *Labotel* was also struck by lightning, and she caught fire. We could see the flames in our wake. Finally we didn't see them any more. She must have sunk."

I gestured at the burned planks I had collected. He nodded.

"Then?" I managed, throat thick.

"We limped into port, slaves sailing her. When we docked, they tied her up and all walked off the ship and away into the forest. The shipmaster made no move to stop them. He acted as if his mind was splintered like the spars. Any of the regular crew left aboard were sore injured and past caring what happened to the cargo."

"Cilliyon's body?" I managed to ask.

"I didn't see—but all the dead were … surrendered to the sea as we made our way to port. But what happened to you? How did you get here?"

"Wieser pulled me out of the water. I don't know why I'm not drowned. Maybe I was …"

"You were flung into the ocean miles away. How could she swim so far? How could you stay afloat so long?"

"I don't think I was really floating on the surface. I think I was *in* the ocean, a part of the current. For a time. I can't really make sense of it."

He stared at me for a bit, then gazed into the flickering fire. I'd found I had to angle my burned arm away from its heat, or the pain surged anew. We sat together in silence.

Gargle flew close with a small silvery fish. He dropped it at Wieser's feet and flew away again. She sniffed it carefully, then downed it in one gulp.

Ibbot stirred and drew his robes closer. "I went to get your book when I left the ship. I tore the cabin apart but I couldn't find it anywhere. It was gone."

"Can Sendings take things away with them?"

He lifted his shoulders. "I wouldn't have thought so, but … there was so much damage, timbers broken and seawater running in the passageways. Even so, it should have been in there somewhere, even in sodden pieces. Who else would have known about it? Mage Ocelli saw it, you said."

"He did."

"Perhaps they found some means to conjure it away to them, wherever they actually were. In the Stronghold, most likely. I did find this wedged in the deck, after the struggle." He fished in his robe and held out my knife. The blade as black as the caves of home, magic thrumming in it still.

I took it from him, head bowed with gratitude. All was not lost. *But my Cilliyon ... how could she be dead ...*

"What will we do now?" he asked. "You have pledged to return to Scythera."

"They believe me to have perished, surely?"

"Perhaps for the present. But understand, in their view they have fulfilled their part of the bargain by providing aid."

"Sorry poor aid it was, be clear," I protested.

He forged ahead. "You made a mage's vow to return to the Stronghold and that is profoundly binding. Eventually, the cabal will become aware through magical means that you have not died. There is nowhere you can hope to hide. The mages will hold you to your pledge or hunt you down, devising all the while some horrific way to destroy you. There is no mercy in them."

"They'll find none in me, either." I hefted my knife in the firelight. "And I won't be trying to hide. First, I must travel to Merced and find Cilliyon's folk. They deserve to know what befell her." I could not say more for a space. I heard her voice in my memory. Calling my name. "Then I will find how the Keltanese invasion has come out—to learn whether I, and you, can be of use in settling it in our favor. Nor will I abandon the enslaved folk of the world. You have skills to offer in aid of that quest, as well. You are coming with me, are you not?"

"I owe you that."

I nodded. "We should stay here by the fire tonight. In the morning I'll make a better crutch and we'll walk back to the port. See what comes next. I expect we'll need a map."

"Don't we always." His grave expression sank further yet. "Do not misjudge this. You have given your vow as a mage to return to Scythera."

"Indeed true, I made the pledge to return and I will. I didn't say when."

Ibbot shook his head, as Gargle returned laden with another fish.

One big enough to cook, which would feed us all. The bird would expect his share, of course. I would give him more than the offal. I set about cleaning it with my knife.

The End

ABOUT THE AUTHOR

Aimee L. Gross loves to tell stories. When she was 9 years old, she noticed an advertisement for The Famous Writers School in the back of a magazine. She wrote a letter at once, since she planned to be a famous writer.

She received a kind reply from the school's director, telling her that students must be grown up before enrolling. He advised her to keep writing and she always has.

She lives in the Midwest with her husband. They share their home with an adopted Cairn Terrier named Kizmet, and Kugel, the bossy tabby cat who arrived one day to fill a vacant niche. Many crows live in the hedgerow. They started bringing her trinkets when she changed their rations from corn to peanuts in the shell. The box of collected crow gifts sits on her writing desk.

Readers are her favorite people. She welcomes followers on Facebook as Aimee L. Gross, author and artist. Or connect on Twitter @Aimee_SanG. Send a message anytime to agross9999author.com.

Judian, Wieser and Gargle will complete their journey in the final book of the trilogy, *As Crows Fly Home*.

www.ingramcontent.com/pod-product-compliance
Lightning Source LLC
Chambersburg PA
CBHW020357260626
47156CB00007B/2153